I0754860

JASPER SANCHEZ

MEET ME AT THE PICKET LINE

HARPER
An Imprint of HarperCollinsPublishers

Also by Jasper Sanchez

The (Un)Popular Vote

HarperCollins Children's Books,
a division of HarperCollins Publishers,
195 Broadway, New York, NY 10007

HarperCollins Publishers,
Macken House, 39/40 Mayor Street Upper,
Dublin 1, D01 C9W8, Ireland

Meet Me at the Picket Line

harpercollins.com

Library of Congress Control Number: 2026932635
ISBN 978-0-06-302582-0

Typography by David DeWitt
26 27 28 29 30 LBC 5 4 3 2 1
First Edition

To Molly and Neal,
for not letting me storm the castle alone

AUTHOR'S NOTE

WE WOULDN'T NEED SOLIDARITY IF THERE WASN'T A *STRUGGLE*.

As such, *Meet Me at the Picket Line* contains depictions of transphobia, homophobia, and other sensitive content. This book is about queer characters and details their struggles, their victories, and their joy. This is a book for queer readers, but please read with care.

One thing this book is *not*: a manual on how to unionize your workplace. While I hope it has some educational value, I've taken certain liberties with labor law for clarity and plot. If you're considering organizing your workplace, please consult nonfictional resources. Above all, please take care of yourself and your fellow workers.

In solidarity,

Jasper

PART I

AGITATE

ONE

I'M GOING TO GET FIRED—AND IT'S ONLY MY FIRST DAY.

I won't even get to punch into my one-cent-above-minimum-wage summer job. My first shift—okay, *training*—starts in thirteen minutes, and I'm miles away from the Nuclear Seasons Experience.

Right now, I'm pacing outside a Spanish Mission Revival mansion that could eat my moms' bungalow for tapas. Harsh morning light reflects off stucco and punches me right in the eyes, as if the simmering heat and acrid benzine burning off Lola's rumbling, Fanta-orange Dodge Challenger wasn't enough.

The thing is, I'm never late. I have a reputation for being compulsively early. Rewind thirty minutes and I was pacing on my stoop fifteen minutes before the scheduled carpool pickup. I alternated between poking my head back inside to ask my sister, Naomi, to hurry; blocking my cat, Sputnik, from bolting outside; and texting our ride, Lola, for status updates that I instructed her not to answer while driving.

She pulled up one minute early, and once I was in the passenger seat and Naomi was in the back, Lola informed me we had another stop.

If I, Elisha Goldstein, am as reliable as an atomic clock, Efraín Juarez Reyna's schedule exemplifies radioactive decay. His plans have a half-life proportional to his interest level, and he isn't remotely interested in *Nuclear Seasons.* He once described the '80s cult TV show as "neoliberal propaganda in provincial drag," which is absurd. It's like he's never even watched past the pilot.

Besides, no one who lives in a feudal manor like this needs a summer job. I don't know why Efraín would want to work at the NSX unless he *wants* to personally sabotage *my* summer.

If that's his plan, it's working.

When Efraín finally saunters down the steps, I trip over a cobblestone. It has nothing to do with his skinny khaki chinos or tight uniform polo, collar popped and two buttons undone. It's how casual he seems, taking his time.

I square my shoulders and force my hand into my pocket because the last thing I need is for Efraín to see me fidgeting. Eye contact's out of the question, but I pick a spot on his forehead and steady my voice. "Are you *trying* to get us fired?"

Efraín looks up. Half his face twists—an eyebrow quirked, a single dimple. Is that meant to signify a smirk? Have I annoyed him? *Amused* him? I'm not sure which is worse.

"It's our first day," Efraín observes.

I don't understand why he's stating something so obvious.

I also don't understand how someone's eyelashes can be so naturally dense, and this is why I didn't want to look at his eyes. They're aesthetically distracting enough before trying to decipher the emotion buried deep in his oil-slick irises.

I blink hard. Again. Then again. If he hasn't already noticed my excessive stimming, he will now. Today of all days, I need to appear as professional and high-functioning as possible—not as a malfunctioning cyborg who can't handle a basic conversation.

"That's the point," I say. "If we're late before we fill out our I-9s—"

"Eli," Lola hollers from the driver's seat. "*You* have to get out of the way if you want *Efraín* to get in."

That's when I realize I've been blocking the door this whole time, which may account for his maybe-smirk.

Our would-be getaway car is a two-door, and as I tilt the passenger seat forward, my insecurities are on full display.

This is a comorbid side effect of being short and chubby while transgender: textbook *child-bearing hips* and that stupid pelvic tilt puberty gave me without a gift receipt. The simple act of climbing over the seat is like steering an aircraft carrier through the Suez Canal. Even after a year on testosterone, my body is an unwieldy vessel I can't drive.

This is why I can't afford to be late. By the end of the summer, I need enough money to make a down payment on top surgery. Dr. Mburu is one of the best surgeons in the country and, unlike some doctors, doesn't have a problem working on a DD cup. But he doesn't take insurance, and his schedule fills up faster than Taylor Swift concerts sell out. If I want to secure a surgery date for next summer, I need to make that down payment soon. My moms said they could afford half, but the rest is up to me—and this job.

That's why I'm wearing a fuchsia polo two sizes too large over a binder half a size too small. These thrifted baggy khaki cargo shorts are supposed to straighten out my hips. None of it works. I look like a plus-size pin-up model dressed as a park ranger for Halloween.

Meanwhile, Efraín looks like a straight-up model. Well. Not *straight*, but—cisgender. Six feet tall, Tour de France–quality biker's build, golden skin, glossy black waves down to his shoulders, and those *eyelashes.* It's not a fair competition.

It's not like I want to be on the cover of *GQ.* I'd just like to go five minutes without being reminded I don't *fit.*

"Elisha."

"What?" I snap.

"Seat belt," he chides, high and mighty about vehicular safety when all this is clearly his fault.

The buckle slips through my sweaty fingers before it clicks, and *finally,* Lola rounds the horseshoe driveway.

"Punch it," Naomi says, finger guns and all.

Lola raises her heart-shaped sunglasses and grins at the rearview mirror. "You got it."

"Please don't," Efraín grumbles, going through the motions

of an argument I've heard him lose during every extracurricular field trip.

"Why not?" I ask. "You're the reason we're late. We have to make up the time somehow."

Efraín huffs. "It was only a minute."

Fact check: It was six minutes from the time we pulled into the driveway until he opened the front door.

"I was listening to this podcast about adjusting taxes for cost of living, and I couldn't find my black Docs." He looks at me over his shoulder, but I keep watching grapevines roll past the window. "If you were so concerned, you could've left without me."

Lola clucks her tongue. "You really think we'd leave you behind?"

"I could've ridden my bike."

"If only," I mutter.

Naomi swats my arm.

"We're ride or die, my dude," Lola says. "You're late, we're late. You get fired, we get fired." She glances, pointedly, from Efraín to the mirror. "Right?"

I nod stiffly, and so does he.

It's a blatant lie. Efraín and Lola may be real ride-or-dies, but the rest of us aren't. Sure, we go to the same school, and we're working the same summer job. Naomi's my kid sister, but we aren't the kind of siblings who stay up late braiding each other's hair and gabbing about our crushes.

I'm friends with Lola in the sense that she aggressively befriends everyone, right down to the town troubadour. I consider her one of my closest friends by default because my other option is my cat. If Lola and I aren't better friends—well. Turns out just being the only two trans kids in Egan's Creek isn't enough to form a platonic soulmate bond.

As for Efraín and me? Personally, I don't care that we've been passive-aggressively competing for valedictorian since the fourth-grade spelling bee. Efraín's hated me since—well, it wasn't any one thing. Maybe it was middle school, when he rallied a group of students to crash a town hall meeting and demand rent control. Or freshman year, when he coordinated volunteers to canvass for an abolitionist county supervisor candidate. Or that winter, when he recruited every warm body he could find for a sit-in to stop a sweep at an unhoused encampment.

He never bothered to ask *why* I said no every time. Then again, it took me six months after he stopped asking to realize that I'd failed some unspoken progressive purity test and he'd written me off entirely.

Because Efraín *cares.* Some might say his greatest character flaw is caring *too much.* He cares about everything from racial equity in the state water wars to corporate culpability for wildfires. He cares enough to argue with NIMBY folk about tearing down the defunct hospital to build affordable housing, and he doesn't mind when they slam their doors in his face.

Apparently, he cares enough to listen to a podcast about

the cost of living, but he *doesn't* care enough to realize that while he's digging through his walk-in closet to find the *right* pair of vegan Doc Martens, there might be people in his own carpool who *need* the criminally low minimum wage because their family is drowning under the bloated cost of living in California wine country.

But it's fine. I don't care if Efraín likes me; I only care that he doesn't cost me this job.

Lola turns onto Highway 12 and punches it.

"You do realize," Efraín says, "that no fresh coat of paint can change the fact that this gas-guzzling muscle car was built before the EPA was founded, and speeding burns—"

"None of that!" Lola tsks. She has this way of making herself heard without yelling, a byproduct of growing up in a Dominican family of seven. "You know I did a full retrofit. The chassis might be Gen X, but she's all Gen Z under the hood!"

"That math doesn't check out," Naomi whispers to me, twirling a stray lock of faded green highlights around her finger. "The Gen Z cutoff was 2012."

More math that doesn't work out: the numbers on the dashboard clock, ticking up.

"Don't worry," Lola calls, as if she can hear my anxious internal monologue. "Hawkeye will get us there on time."

Hawkeye gets us there seven minutes late. Well, seven minutes according to my opa's watch, which I keep set two minutes fast precisely so I *won't* be late. So, technically, we're only five minutes late, but technicalities don't count when "late" versus "not late" is an absolute binary. And we are *absolutely* late when Lola turns down a narrow dirt road marked:

THE NUCLEAR SEASONS EXPERIENCE

The sight of that rusty, corrugated aluminum sign should hit like a defibrillator jolt to my heart, short-circuiting every current of anxiety and dysphoria. I have loved this weird, kitschy roadside museum so long; knowing I get to work here for the next three months should be *exhilarating*.

It isn't. Never underestimate the visceral panic of an autistic kid thrown off schedule and in danger of losing exclusive, behind-the-scenes access to their special interest.

Lola finds a space in front of the farmhouse. Efraín jumps out of the car as soon as she parks, leaving me marooned in the back seat. Important life lesson: "Ride or die" stops at the parking lot.

By the time I stumble over the front seat, Efraín's halfway to the ramshackle red barn—the museum entrance—and the girls are jogging to catch up.

Time of arrival: nine minutes late Elisha Standard Time.

Unequivocally and inexcusably *late*.

Efraín's already deep in conversation with our supervisor.

At least, I assume the stranger is lower management, what with the telltale slumped shoulders of a world-weary millennial and the civvies. If you can call a Green Day T-shirt so old that it's practically sheer *civvies,* that is. As I skid to a stop, he says, "You must be—"

"Fired?" I blurt. I'm sure there are social pleasantries I'm meant to observe, but there's no time if security is already on their way to escort us off the premises.

"C'mon, Elisha," Efraín mutters. "We're not fired."

"Excuse me if I'd rather hear that from—" I didn't catch this aging emo-pop-punk fanboy's name, but I mask my irritation with a lopsided smile. This is what contrition looks like, right? "Sorry, can you please just tell me if I'm fired?"

Efraín intervenes, and if his suave, chummy tone is what passes for apologetic, then I definitely missed the mark. "We were working out some carpool kinks. Won't happen again, promise."

The guy looks between us. His shaggy dark hair obscures his eyes like an English sheepdog, but there's something bewildered in the slack line of his bearded jaw. He squares his shoulders, shrugging on authority like an ill-fitting suit. "Um," he stammers. "I'm only the guest services assistant supervisor, but no? No one's fired? Anya hates hiring. So, like I was telling your friend here, I'm Dan. You can call me Dan."

I can't clear my head fast enough to sift through Dan's

words; I can't decide whether to point out that Efraín is not my friend or question whether an assistant supervisor really has the authority to decide we're not fired.

Dan interprets my delayed processing as tacit acceptance. "Let's head inside."

That's it. No security walk of shame. No consequences for tardiness. Just Dan opening the barn doors.

For months, I've been looking forward to seeing the museum like this, after hours or before. Let's be real, I've dreamed about exploring this place alone for *years*. But I don't get to enjoy my magical *Night at the Museum* moment. All I can think is that the track lights dangling from the rafters seem abnormally bright as Dan leads us past the ticketing counter and gift shop, all the way to the STAFF ONLY door on the far side of the ground floor.

As promised, Anya Sobol, the guest services manager, is waiting for us in the upstairs break room with two other trainees.

"Dan, you're just in time. Come, sit." Anya gestures to the table where she's holding court. For a woman who might be shorter than I am, she's imposing, with a bottle-red pixie cut and cat-eye glasses. "All our new hires in one place. Well." Her chuckles come out as a cough, like she's retired from an Olympic career in chain-smoking. "Not so new in Blake's case. Dan, did you see what she did to her hair?"

Dan grunts noncommittally at a trainee whom I vaguely

recognize from school. Blake Xie. I think she graduated my sophomore year. Now she has a badass undercut—sleek black hair past her shoulder on one side, shaved on the other—that reads *alternative lifestyle* in the best way possible.

Anya clearly disagrees, but her voice is Marlboro-light when she says, "We're so pleased to have you back this summer."

Blake smiles, but it doesn't reach her eyes—or eyebrow piercings.

Anya nods, back to business. "Dan, Blake, have you met our true new hires? With a little training, they'll make good workers, don't you think?"

Dan opens his mouth, but Anya steamrolls right on through. "Here we have Gwen, who was just telling us that her accent is Welsh, not English, no?"

Amidst the residual stress of our near-firing, I didn't even register our final coworker, Gwen Pryce, best known as Naomi's ex-girlfriend. They must be ex-friends now, too, given that Naomi's grimacing the way she does when Mom mentions hunting season. "That's right," Gwen says. "It's a common mis—"

"And this is Dolores—"

"I go by Lola! Emo phase aside, I'm no lady of sorrows."

"—and Effren—"

"Actually," says Efraín, just like he does at the start of every year, when, inevitably, there's one teacher who is oblivious to the teacher's lounge gossip that compromises his reputation, "it's Eh-fra-EEN. Three syllables."

"Oh, right. Of course." Anya nods, unfazed. "Finally, over there with the matching freckles, we have the Goldstein sisters, Naomi and Elisha!"

Oh, right. Of course.

Please excuse this interruption of our regularly scheduled programming for a minor panic attack.

TWO

WHEN I INTERVIEWED FOR THIS JOB, I NAILED IT. I READ DOZENS of articles on how to come off as competent and employable but not obsequious or overeager.

I rehearsed in front of the mirror. I memorized the NSX Visitor's Guide and reread my dog-eared, cat-scratched copy of *The Making of Nuclear Seasons.* I wore an oxford shirt with a high, starched collar and a scratchy tag, along with a bow tie.

I went in so prepared that I preempted half the questions before they were asked. I touted my unpaid customer service experience helping out around my moms' diner, judiciously exaggerating my ability to calculate change in my head. I had my transcript with my fresh-off-the-press A+ in precalc to corroborate my mathematical aptitude.

Most importantly, I had an honest answer to the number one interview question that, according to *Forbes,* trips everyone up: Why did I want the job? I didn't need to fumble through a lie to hide the inconvenient truth that capitalism necessitated I find any old job.

I could honestly say that I loved this museum and might not *kill* to work here but would probably bury a body if they asked. I was glowing with my love for *Nuclear Seasons*, like Rebecca Spector glows in episode four, "Singin' in the Acid Rain," after she goes skinny-dipping in the radioactive creek. I was a shoo-in for this job.

Until Anya asked one question I hadn't rehearsed: Did I have any questions for her?

I didn't want to ruin my chances by coming off as a problem employee, but there was *one* thing. I asked, "Is this a trans-friendly work environment?"

Anya's eyebrows scrunched together. I couldn't tell if she was surprised I was trans or offended I'd ask.

"I'm transgender, and I know tourists come from all over the world to visit the museum. So I need to be sure . . ." I knew management couldn't make every MAGA-cap-wearing guest respect me—they couldn't promise me a *safe space*—but . . . I cleared my throat and rephrased, "Everyone here is trans-friendly?"

"Of course," Anya said. "Billy in HR is gay."

Now she's here, proclaiming that I am a sister. A girl. Even though I *asked* her, and she *promised* me.

Maybe it's my fault; maybe I wasn't clear. I said I was transgender, but I didn't specify. I don't look like the trans boys on TV, so maybe she read my stereotypically feminine features and assumed I was transfemme. A passing, stealth trans girl, like Lola. Maybe that was why Anya was confused that I asked about a trans-friendly work environment at all; it never occurred to her that I'd need it.

But now she's standing here, smiling, and Dan and Blake are inscribing our names, faces, and implicit *genders* into memory, and *this wasn't supposed to happen today.* I'd come out at the interview and been hired on the spot, and yet here I am, on the spot. Except the spot is actually a bull's-eye, and I've already been hit, point-blank.

Most queer people learn fast that coming out isn't a one-and-done, no matter how you identify. But it's different when you're trans and don't *fit* the binary. Cis people might accept you, but that doesn't mean they've put in the work to relearn how they *perceive* gender.

When you look like me, coming out is something you do a million times a day. Every time someone sees you on the street, every time a stranger starts a casual conversation, every time you try to order a coffee. It should be an autonomic reflex, simple as breathing, but it hurts like an asthma attack. Or, on dysphoric days, walking pneumonia.

I have to say something. Even as my chest constricts—I wish I had my inhaler right now—I have to *fix* this. Otherwise, I'm going to be surrounded by coworkers who misgender me every day and, more crucially, *see* me as a girl. I need to open my mouth *now*, right now, before it's too late, but I'm shaking. In spite of myself, I hazard a glance at everyone who knows better.

Gwen's studying her nails. Lola's clenching her fists. Naomi's retying her ponytail. And Efraín—

"Goldstein *siblings*," Efraín says, with his stiff jaw and arctic voice. "Elisha's pronouns are he/him."

Although everything about his manner is cold, I sweat under Efraín's scrutiny. My face is hot, flooded with blood, and the limit to my embarrassment does not exist. But everyone is staring at me like I'm something interesting. If I was already on the spot, now there's a spotlight shining right at me, and I'm the kid who forgot his bit-part, two-line rejoinder on opening night.

Efraín said something, so why can't I speak up for myself? Then again, it's not like he has anything to lose. His family owns a vineyard, he hates *Nuclear Seasons*, and his identity isn't the one up for debate.

I can speak for myself.

"Yeah, I'm . . . boy," I stammer. Fuck. Apparently, I *can't* speak for myself. "I'm transgender. A trans guy, to be exact. He/him/his. Elisha—or Eli's fine, too."

Blake acknowledges me with an up-nod, which I choose to interpret as "cool," as in "queer recognizes queer."

"Um," Dan says, with that wide-eyed, pop-quiz look that cis people get when asked what a pronoun is. "Okay. Thanks."

Anya comes over, ducks down, and claps her hands on my shoulders. "Oh, Eli. I'm so sorry. I remember now. I'll remember in the future." Her eyes are very bright and shiny, like she might burst into tears. "I can't tell you how sorry I am."

She's still touching me, and I'm caged in, halfway to feral. I'm not comfortable with people touching me under the best of circumstances. After Naomi read one of Ma's college anthropology books, she told me I have "proxemics issues," which I'm pretty sure is not a real thing, but the weight of Anya's hands on my shoulders is very real.

Anya has trapped me in the performance of her apology. All I want is to get out and make it *stop*. So I force my lips to move into a self-deprecating smile-shrug two-step. "It's okay."

It's not okay.

But she smiles and steps back, case closed, and I tell myself it *will* be okay. She just forgot. She promised it wouldn't happen again, so it won't. This is just a blip in my summer of *Nuclear Seasons* bliss. I did the hard thing—with prompting from Efraín, yes, but it's over. Cuban Missile Crisis averted.

From here on out, I'm just a boy working the job of my dreams.

THREE

WHEN I APPLIED FOR THIS JOB, I WAS UNDER NO ILLUSIONS THAT I'd have access to the vault. I knew customer service was a far cry from the paid junior curatorial assistant internship the museum offers to one golden-ticket-lucky high school student each school year. But I didn't anticipate that my clearance would be only one step above that of the average *guest.*

Apparently, floor staff get the same tour they give to day-trippers. That's my grand revelation when Dan leads us out of the farmhouse, the ground floor of which houses biographical galleries about the late showrunner Victor Kane and the show's production history.

The only new thing I've learned today is that the farmhouse's second story, home of the admin offices, is verboten—even with the badges Divya from security delivered to the barn break room as we noshed on free pizza during lunch. Except for Efraín, of course, who scavenged for not-actually-vegan Oreos from the vending machine.

I have a tendency to get ahead of myself, especially when it comes to my special interests, and when it comes to *Nuclear Seasons*, my interest is just a few steps behind that of the superfans Divya warned us about who try to hide in the bathrooms after closing. I'm not about to pull a move from Mrs. Basil E. Frankweiler's files, but I can't help feeling bamboozled.

"This is the original silo used for exterior shots," Dan says as we loop back toward the barn. Beside it towers a massive grain bin of gleaming corrugated steel. Twenty-two feet in diameter, three stories high, with a floor plan of approximately eleven hundred square feet, not that Dan tells us that. I'm tempted to volunteer the information, except I've learned the hard way that teachers don't like students who know more than they do. I've never been a teacher's pet so much as the yappy runt at an overcrowded animal shelter of questionable ethics.

"People actually believed this tin can was a real nuclear bunker that could shield the human body from radiation for twenty minutes, let alone twenty *years*?"

Then there's Efraín, who's never thought twice about saying exactly what's on his mind, no matter the audience, no matter whether there's anything to shield him from the fallout.

Dan has that same lost sheepdog look, but I'm way ahead

of him. "It's actually a grain bin, not a silo, and made of steel, not tin. Everyone calls it a silo, though. Kane took some creative and scientific liberties. On the show, the silo's insulated with lead and concrete, plus regular insulation for climate control, then finished off with an interior corrugated steel wall." I spare a glance at Dan as he swipes his badge at the silo door. "Am I missing anything?"

Yappy mutt. Kill shelter. I know better, except for the part where I really don't.

"That about covers it," Dan says as he shepherds us inside.

It doesn't matter how many times I've been to the museum. Each time feels like the first time—like I'm stepping through the veil of screen static into an Egan's Creek entirely alien from my own. Eerie, otherworldly lights cast the gallery in pale blue, simulating the cooling filter employed by the show.

Even though I know the low temperature and dim lighting are optimized to protect the artifacts, they don't *feel* like artifacts; nothing is roped off or behind glass. Instead, the grain bin interior is set up as it appears on the show.

A luxury nuclear bunker. Industrial farmhouse meets midcentury modern chic. Canonically designed in the Eisenhower era, hastily occupied in 1962, and peppered with traces of 1982 that the Spectors acquire over the course of the show, like the Commodore 64 home computer in the living room, which is also the kitchen and comprises the entire ground floor.

The world's narrowest staircase, coiled against the curved wall, leads to the so-called kids' room on the second floor and the primary suite on the third. Tucked under the staircase and concealed by a false panel, the single bathroom is only slightly larger than an airplane lavatory, thanks to the shower that's roughly the size of an upright coffin. Definitely not for claustrophobes. Here, the panel's permanently popped. I know from my countless visits that fans are inexplicably obsessed with posing for photo ops inside, palms planted on opposite walls.

At first glance, you might mistake this gallery for the actual bunker, but once you blink, the real world reasserts itself. This is still a museum with explanatory plaques and interactive screens. All closets and cupboards are open displays. The once-state-of-the-art color TV plays fan-favorite clips on repeat.

It doesn't quite break the fantasy, but—

"The main thing you need to know," Dan says as we huddle by the can-lined pantry, "is that this space was never used during production. The bunker interior sets were all soundstages on the property. Those came down after the network canceled *Nuclear Seasons* in 1984 at the end of its first and only season. Kane personally salvaged as much furniture and costumes as he could and stored everything here at Mondo Kane Ranch. He became obsessed with finding another network to pick up the show." Dan's expression darkens. "You, uh, you all know what happened to Victor Kane."

"He shot himself in the mouth on May 8, 1989," I answer reflexively.

"Pretty sure that was rhetorical," Efraín mutters.

"Um, yeah. Kane eventually realized there was never going to be another season. The show didn't have fans back then the way it does now. Between his PTSD and depression—" Dan clears his throat. "Anyway, when his daughter, Dagny, founded the museum in 2001, she re-created the Spectors' bunker inside the old silo—uh, *grain bin*—for authenticity, you know? Once you've been here for few weeks, Anya might ask a couple of you to lead tours. Stanley and Ford—you'll meet them tomorrow—handle tours in the offseason, but tourist season can get . . . rough."

I jam my hand into my pocket before I volunteer. Because I could tell guests everything that Dan isn't telling us—everything that makes *Nuclear Seasons* special. That's where I'll shine.

My customer service acumen will come out on the museum floor, not behind the ticketing counter. That's how I'll prove I'm worthy of that paid internship, which I need if I want to save up for top surgery beyond the down payment. And if I want to earn docent duties, I have to prove my passion for the show and all its quirky idiosyncrasies any chance I get.

Now Dan's shepherding everyone up the staircase and into the "kids' room," which is another misnomer. Yes, Arthur and Rebecca were children—nine and seven, respectively—when Wolf Spector locked his family in the bunker on October 23, 1962. Viewers, however, only know Art and Rebecca as the rebellious, clueless naïfs who emerge from the bunker twenty years later. The bedroom was designed with an adult sensibility, not as a luxury playroom to rear children in the wake of a nuclear attack.

There are two twin beds—Art's neatly made, Rebecca's sheets haphazardly rucked. A closet bursting with neon leg warmers and sequin dresses. A shadowbox of patterned bow ties. A chest brimming with Art's Golden Age sci-fi paperbacks and outdated science textbooks. A desk covered with synth-pop cassettes and Rebecca's most treasured acquisition: a Sony Walkman.

Cinematic stills from the show and production photos adorn the walls, along with plaques nobody reads. No, guests flock to the mannequins artfully posed around the room, wearing Art's and Rebecca's most iconic outfits.

"There's always a security rover in the silo," Dan says, "and cameras on every level. But guests still touch the costumes. They want to feel things Sam Schatz and Judy Medina touched."

Each mannequin has an impossible-to-miss DO NOT TOUCH sign. It's also part of the spiel given at ticketing:

no food or drink, no flash photography, and no touching the artifacts.

"Especially that one, with the tassels." Dan nods toward the Platonic ideal of the little black dress—slinky, sleeveless, and cut just below the knee—by the closet mirror, as if Rebecca were looking at herself, except the mannequin's facing the gallery. "All the costumes on display were really worn on the show. Mostly designer, early sixties—stuff the Spectors would've had in their closets. People always ask that. So, that black Chanel dress"—he cocks his head back at the fringe dress—"is the one Rebecca wears when they open the bunker hatch and—"

"No, it's not," I blurt, on autopilot. I am a self-driving car, running a red light. "Rebecca didn't wear this in the pilot. It was episode three, 'Guess Who's Coming to Barbecue,' when the Davises invite the Spectors to dinner, which the Spectors assume will be a formal dinner party but is actually a barbecue. Art, Rebecca, and Deborah show up dressed like they're going to a night at the opera. Carol Davis fake-compliments Rebecca's dress, but Deborah rambles about how it's a reproduction of a dress that Coco Chanel designed for the French film *Last Year at Marienbad*—"

I finally hear *myself* talking. Rambling, just like Deborah about the dress. Dan's slack-jawed, not angry but baffled. I'm terrible at reading facial expressions, but even I can tell that not one person looks *interested.*

This silo has never felt as large as it does now, with this great, gaping chasm of *awkward* between my coworkers and me.

"Um," Dan says. "Okay, Eli. Thanks."

With that ringing endorsement, I'm sure to win Employee of the Month.

FOUR

"HOW DOES IT FEEL TO BE CARD-CARRYING MEMBERS OF THE proletariat?"

I've taken two bites of my habitual Wednesday night Thunderdome Lightning Mac and Cheese when the ambush starts.

Of course, if this were a normal Wednesday night, Lola and Efraín wouldn't be sitting in my favorite booth at my family's diner. Alas, much to my silent consternation, Lola insisted on keeping the gang together to celebrate surviving our first day.

Instead of delivering our meals with a wink and a maternal platitude like she would any other night, Ma slides in next to Naomi. She nods amiably to Lola and Efraín, as if they're perfectly normal additions to this family debrief.

"Our time cards are virtual," Naomi says.

"It's actually an app," I say simultaneously.

"Bona fide, then," Mom decides, coming out of the kitchen and sitting next to Lola. The flour smeared on her forehead does a poor job concealing that she has just as many freckles as Naomi and I do. It also means she just put a batch of pies in the oven. "*Bona fide* members of the proletariat."

"It's not my first job," Lola points out between bites of her sandwich. "I've been working at the body shop since I was old enough to hold a socket wrench."

"Family businesses don't count," I mutter. "It's just unpaid 'helping out.'"

Lola frowns. "My dad pays me."

Naomi doesn't look up from her quinoa casserole. "Eli means when we help out here."

Here being Lou's Deluxe Diner, a family establishment and a cornerstone of Egan's Creek, figuratively and literally. Prime real estate at one corner of the town square, the diner is a cultural institution.

Lou's looks like a '50s diner because it was one, in a past life. When Ma's Grammy Louise first opened the diner, it was ready for the proverbial sock hop, and Ma's dad never changed so much as a light bulb without consulting the town historical society. When Ma took over her namesake, she rebranded. She saw the neon writing in the window long before the avocado toast boom. She kept the nostalgic '50s mise-en-scène—vinyl booths, checkerboard linoleum, and neon signs—but adopted a farm-to-table ethos. Ma has a knack for updating classic diner fare into Instagram-worthy food porn accessible to every palate and wallet.

A decade ago, Lou's became a modest tourist destination thanks to a feature on a certain travel food show hosted by an infamous homegrown celebrity chef, but that publicity doesn't pay much in dividends anymore.

Efraín starts to say something asinine about unpaid child labor, but Ma waves him off. "Free food is a currency."

"Room and board," Mom agrees.

"Not that you two are allowed to pay, either." Ma points to Lola and Efraín. "Friends and family don't pay."

Which is no way to run a business when Ma considers half the town friends, as evidenced by the pleasantries she exchanged earlier with Mr. Jennings, the doddering accountant who rents an office upstairs and comes downstairs for the lentil-walnut meatless loaf every night.

I still don't know how to explain that I'm not actually friends with—

"I want to pay," Efraín insists. "Max and Jesus—"

"The fact that you know the names of our waitstaff just goes to show." Ma clucks her tongue. "You kids spend so much time here, studying, working on the paper . . ."

It's not my fault that this census-designated place has only one high school, with AP classes so small the district keeps threatening to cut them. The handful of kids in those classes who actually want to study outside of school amounts to Efraín, Lola, two or three rotating background actors, and me. It's not my fault that Lou's is the most convenient meeting place for us—and for the school newsletter staff, with our negligible budget. It's certainly not my fault that Efraín writes op-eds on every issue facing the school while I'm just trying to write my film reviews in peace.

Needless to say, Efraín and Ma have debated the payment issue more times than I can count.

"Consider it compensation for the carpool," Mom interjects. She nods at Lola. "For gas."

That appeases Efraín. For now.

"Speaking of the carpool," Ma says. "I want to hear all about *your* youthful hijinks."

"It's a job," I mutter, "not a sitcom."

"All right, how was your first day at your very serious first grown-up job? Tell us everything."

Mom glances at her watch. "*Reader's Digest* version. I have plum tarts in the oven."

I open my mouth, then shut it again. Naomi's looking down at her barely touched plate. Efraín's staring, inexplicably, at me.

Thank God we have Lola to fill the dead air.

You know that thing where someone asks how you're doing, and no matter how you're actually feeling, you say you're "good"? For most people, the lie is intuitive, instinctual. But I've never been good with social scripts.

When I was a kid and people asked how I was doing, I told the truth. How was school that day? Bad because Shawn

Rossi made fun of the one-eyed, threadbare teddy bear I brought to show-and-tell. I learned the hard way that no one wants the *mess* of your real, ugly feelings.

When someone asks how you're doing, unless you're talking to a doctor, a therapist, or a TV bartender, you're supposed to tell them some prettier fiction. They get to pat themselves on the back for performing their I-see-you empathy lines, just so long as you swallow your lies until you make them true. *That's* the social script.

I may have learned it manually, but I do know it. I also know it's only a matter of time before Lola runs out of steam talking about how great it was to see Blake again or how Divya invited her to the informal staff bowling night.

But as the conspicuous *NS* superfan in the room, Moms want to know how today went for *me*. "C'mon, kid." Ma reaches past Naomi to ruffle my hair. "Was it everything you dreamed it would be?"

The truth is, I *begged* them to let me apply at the museum. I begged them to believe me when I said I could handle it.

Was it everything I dreamed it would be?

I remember the look in Anya's eyes when she apologized for misgendering me and promised it would never happen again. I gave her the prettier fiction: *I believe you, it's okay, let's just move on already*. Then I told it to myself.

I can't let my moms know what really happened—that I barely made it through my first day without a meltdown.

I don't know what will happen if they doubt my ability to keep this job, if I can't come up with my share of the top surgery down payment.

It's not that they won't cover it. They understand that it's necessary medical care but not its urgency. They don't see the harm in waiting a few extra months or another year, like Naomi had to wait for braces.

I catch a glimpse of my reflection rippling on the surface of my coffee.

The truth is? Everything that went wrong today was my fault. If I'd been clearer with Anya, she wouldn't have misgendered me.

Moms don't need to know about the mess, so I give them the prettier fiction, too: "It was great. Better than great. Everything I hoped and more."

"What about you, kiddo?" Ma asks.

Naomi swallows a petite bite of casserole, then says, "Fine."

Moms share a grown-up look, a conversation that happens entirely in eyebrow acrobatics.

Ma sighs theatrically. "Teenagers, amirite?"

Mom disappears to check on her plum tarts. Ma goes to check in on the booth next door and gets sucked into a cordial debate about the recent small-business tax hike with Mr. Loman, the proprietor of Loman & Sons Hardware, and Ms. Sinclair of Blue Plate Picture Palace.

Lola digs back into her jicama fries. Naomi keeps quiet,

spouting neither random facts nor avian trivia. The lull is hardly companionable. I can't settle into the silence because the diner isn't silent. Ambient chatter and scraping cutlery across the room provide an unsettling soundtrack.

"You know, Coco Chanel was a Nazi," Efraín says conversationally and apropos of absolutely nothing.

"Pardon?"

Across from me, Efraín takes a slow, lazy swig from his Mexican Coke. "As a self-proclaimed *Nuclear Seasons* fan, how are you okay with the museum promoting that brand? Chanel was a Nazi agent. How can you like a TV show that made deals with—"

The Marienbad dress dances in my mind's eye. "Have you been holding that in all afternoon?"

"Doesn't it bother you?"

"Why, because I'm Jewish?"

"No, because you're *human.*"

"Okay, well, I'm glad to know you don't think I'm a lizard person, but it wasn't product placement," I object. "Almost all the sixties designer clothing came from thrift stores and estate sales. Victor Kane didn't have the production budget for—"

"Kane made a *choice.*"

Is this the part where I'm supposed to point out that the anti-graffiti coating on the Holocaust Memorial in Berlin was manufactured by a subsidiary of the company that manufactured Zyklon B?

Maybe this is why I don't get invited to parties.

I don't know what Efraín wants me to say, so I try, "Kane was Jewish. There's a photo from his bar mitzvah in the farmhouse."

"*Boys,*" Lola interjects, "let's leave work at work, yeah? I can't believe I have to tell *you* to keep the TV drama on the clock, Ef. Why don't we talk about literally anything else?"

Efraín's frowning at Lola's light chiding, and I'm wondering why I'm still here. I could be home with Sputnik, watching *NS* from the comfort of my own bed—

"I'm going to get fired tomorrow," Naomi blurts.

Cue the laugh track.

FIVE

"EXPLAIN THIS TO ME LIKE I DON'T HAVE A 5.0 GPA," I DEMAND. "Explain this to me like I'm a fifth grader or a chimpanzee trained by Jane Goodall—"

"Jesus Christ, Elisha," Efraín mutters.

"Hey." Lola whistles, commanding the attention of half the diner, townspeople and tourists alike.

Two booths over, Mrs. Babbitt, my ninth-grade science teacher, tsks. She always had a fixation on what constituted an "inside voice." Lola, Efraín, and I all failed that character test.

"Naomi," Lola tries, quieter. "Tell us what's going on. Does this have something to do with Anya calling you into her office after we clocked out?"

"What did management do?" Efraín asks, only quiet because he may be preemptively plotting murder.

"Why are you going to get *fired*?" Hysteria pitches my voice higher until it breaks.

"Because of *this*." Naomi yanks her hair tie off, lets her ponytail down, and fluffs out her long blond hair.

There's nothing visibly amiss, just another ironic reminder that no one can tell that Naomi and I are siblings from looking. I'm the Ashkenazi stereotype, but the Nazis wouldn't have clocked Naomi. She's tall, thin, and wiry, with honey-blond waves, while I'm short, curvy, and chubby, with auburn-brown curls. Her button nose is pert and petite compared to my prominent, hooked proboscis. No one would remark on her eyebrows, but mine would make Eugene Levy proud. The most we have in common is our medley of freckles and moles—we look like walking PSAs for skin cancer prevention.

We both have "weird loner" vibes, but where I'm budget soft butch geek chic, Naomi's the granola-in-the-trail-mix lesbian. The only feature out of place in the cliché is the messy DIY dye job from a few weeks ago, when she emerged from our bathroom with kelly-green streaks in her hair. I didn't understand what prompted my notoriously chemical-averse sister, who can't swim in chlorinated water without getting overstimulated, to slather noxious chemicals on her head, but—

Oh, right. I stare at those now-faded green streaks, a minty hue barely distinguishable from her natural blond. "Your hair—"

"Violates the dress code," Naomi confirms.

"Your *hair*?" Lola asks, incredulous.

"My queer birding Discord server called them peekaboo highlights?"

"What the fuck do highlights have to do with the dress code?" Efraín asks, fully credulous but righteously indignant.

"The dress code prohibits 'nonnatural' hair colors," I explain.

"I never thought I'd hear anything about 'natural' hair in a dress code that wasn't about hair like mine," Lola mutters, tapping her corkscrew curls. "But, wait up. *Anya's* red hair is more artificial than Red Dye No. 3."

"Either she doesn't see it that way," Naomi says, "or the rules don't apply to bosses. She said this was my one warning. It didn't matter that today was *training* because they emailed us the handbook."

"Did you read it?" I snap, a tension headache coiling at the base of my spine. "Did it come up at your interview?"

"I hadn't dyed it yet, and I assumed it wouldn't be a problem. It's just faded highlights and the underlayer. The rest of my hair hides the underlayer really well."

"Clearly, Anya disagrees."

"Anya called it *unprofessional*," Naomi states, "and said I shouldn't bother coming back tomorrow if I'm not going to take the job seriously. She had the chutzpah to tell me to just dye my hair a 'normal' color tonight."

Lola and Efraín offer colorful expletives, but I just blink at Naomi as she stretches the hair tie over her fingers.

"I don't understand," I say.

"Which part of her ultimatum is unclear?" Naomi asks irritably. "Dye my hair or get fired."

"It doesn't make *sense.*"

"I agree. It's completely arbitrary. Museum guests wouldn't even notice—"

"No, I mean . . . *you.*"

"What about me?"

I glance at my watch. "Why didn't you say something earlier?"

"Eli," Lola chides.

I know I'm being unfair. Delayed processing's a bitch, and if I were in Naomi's shoes, I wouldn't be saying anything. I'd be on my way to the drugstore right now, but then again, I'd never be in Naomi's shoes in the first place because I understand the dress code.

When Naomi shakes her head, her waves whirl around her, obscuring her face and tickling my arm. "Because I'm trying to fix this. I just need a plan—"

"Okay, we'll walk over to Foxglove Apothecary and buy a box of hair dye." I lean close and lower my voice. "I can loan you the money if—"

Naomi shakes her head—again and again—a negation and a stim.

"Naomi?" Lola is a soft touch, the only person at this table with a dose of bedside manner.

Naomi doesn't answer right away, the words caught in her

throat. I'm well-acquainted with the way strong emotions like distress can sever your vocal cords. No matter how fervently you want to speak, you can't.

Naomi must not be quite over the event horizon of shutdown yet because she warbles, "It isn't *fair*." She says it like how I say things don't make sense—when the world fails to compute, and neither the equations nor the checkbooks balance.

Across the table, Lola's eyes are wide and shimmery, while Efraín's are narrowed and pitch-black. I can't check the feelings wheel key chain on my backpack, but I'd guess Lola is concerned and Efraín is angry.

Of course, Efraín is usually some flavor of angry. It's just a question of which microexpressions draw the worry line between irritated and irate—and at whom he's directing his ire.

Naomi buries her face in her hands. "I don't want to re-dye my hair. I shouldn't have to. It isn't fair."

"No, it isn't." See? I am not without empathy. However, if my one day as a member of the workforce has taught me anything, it's that working means compromising your personal comfort. Watering that sentiment down for my sister, I translate, "But you need this job. Moms can't afford to hire extra help here, and all the other summer jobs around town have already been scooped up. So if you want to keep saving up for a car—"

"This is fucking ridiculous," Efraín grumbles. Spoken like a guy who woke up on his sixteenth birthday to find a brand-new electric SUV with a bow on the hood. According to Lola, the Rivian's maiden voyage was to the dealership, where he tried and failed to return it.

But if there's one thing you learn growing up lower middle class, it's how to MacGyver your way through crises the other half solves with cash.

I can fix this.

"If we get the hair dye," I propose, turning to better face Naomi, "can you just dye the green parts, not everything?"

"That would still be erasing—" Naomi swallows whatever truth she was about to spill and washes it down with a gulp of ginger beer.

"You don't have to." Lola coos a promise she can't keep. "We'll think of something else."

Naomi squirms, understandably uncomfortable with the way we're studying her like a science experiment.

"When you wear your hair down, the peekaboo layer is totally hidden," Lola says thoughtfully, "and we can style your hair so the highlights up top are practically invisible. Just give me some barrettes and bobby pins, maybe a headband—"

"This is fucking bullshit, is what it is." Efraín scowls. "Naomi's not going to dye her hair. We should dye *ours.*"

What the actual *fuck*?

"I'm sorry, I must have misheard you. Auditory processing

issues. I thought I heard you suggest that we should all dye our hair, but that can't be right because we're discussing how to prevent my sister from getting fired, not how to get *all* of us fired."

"You heard me right."

"You've got a real dark sense of humor—"

"This entire *situation* is a joke," Efraín interrupts. "The dress code is a joke, so let's make management the punch line. They can't fire us."

He's wrong. This isn't a joke; it's a prank. This is some reality TV show designed to make me look like an absolute moron in front of morons who spend their time watching lowbrow TV and probably got fired from *their* summer jobs.

"That's exactly what Anya said would happen if Naomi broke the dress code again."

"If Naomi broke the dress code *alone*," Efraín corrects me. "But the four of us together?"

"What difference does that make?"

"*Tourist season.* The museum switches to summer hours on Saturday. You really think they can find four new grunts on two days' notice? Dan said Anya hates hiring."

"Gee, I wonder why she would hate hiring when, after less than twelve hours on the job, her new grunts are discussing *mutiny.*"

"It's not mutiny."

"*Enough.* Boys, compare your testosterone lab levels on

your own time, okay?" Lola cuts in. "Now, Ef, before I break out my brightest clip-in extensions, can you please explain your plan here?"

"There's power in numbers," Efraín replies. "If all four of us show up with 'unnatural' hair colors—extensions, temporary dye—the museum can't *afford* to fire all of us."

Maybe that's true, and maybe it's not; my ticket-seller account doesn't give me access to the NSX accounting books. "It doesn't matter whether the museum can afford it," I object. "*We* can't afford the risk."

"Don't you get it? The problem is bigger than hair dye." Efraín licks his lips. "We have to stand on principle."

Doesn't *he* get it? *I* can't *afford* principles in this economy. Not if I want to pay for my top surgery down payment. Not if I want to keep this job and land the paid internship to earn enough for the surgery itself. I can't deposit my pink slip in the bank.

"Not everything is some crusade in waiting. Most of us are living paycheck to paycheck—"

"You're living rent-free in your moms' house. *They're* the ones who want to fire a teenager for exercising her right to self-expression." Efraín smirks, as if that's checkmate.

I'm not even sure who "they" are. I don't think Efraín knows, either. This is just how he talks. It's always *us* against *them* or *institutions* pitting *them* against *us*, and never have I ever heard him use proper nouns. It's *the museum, the school, the town council*, always some generic Big Bad, nebulous and ill-defined. He's the boy railing against injustice when he, himself, has never experienced injustice.

And I hate how he gets under my skin and makes me argue against what I actually believe because I know he *has* experienced injustice. His class privilege only insulates him so much; he's also brown, bi, and neurodivergent.

Efraín's always angry at the world in abstract, as a concept, *on principle*, and I hate it because it's always about the white horse. Which is fine for people like Efraín, who have stables full of pedigreed Thoroughbreds, but for the rest of us, metaphorical white horses are just as unattainable as the real deal. We're the ones left mucking out the horse shit. Because you can't ride in on a white horse if you can't afford riding lessons; saving other people is a *privilege* that most of us—

And now I'm talking like him.

This is what Efraín does: He twists me up in these discursive knots that I'd need a machine saw to hack through, but all I have is a knockoff Swiss Army knife.

Because everything I own is a knockoff. Including my generic progressivism, which has the same active ingredients as the Big-Name Brand, but you can tell it's not as shiny, not quite real. If I were a better progressive—a true, too-cool-for-blue leftist—I could have my organic vegan fruitcake and eat it, too. I wouldn't hesitate. I'd sacrifice myself to save another.

But how can I be a mensch when I'm such a selfish schmuck?

Efraín's still talking. Did he ever stop? How long have I been tuned out? It's not like his one-man production of *Eat the Rich: The Musical* needs an audience.

Efraín's saying, "Capitalism—"

"Come on," I groan. "This is about—"

"Listen," Lola interrupts, "I'm always down to stick it to the man, but we're not the ones with the real stake in this. Naomi? What do you think? I'm down to riot, but only if this is what you want. We can walk over to Foxglove right now. If not, we can meet up before work to style your hair—"

Goose bumps collide with freckles on my arms. Waiting for my sister to decide whether she's willing to imperil my job and torpedo my top surgery fund is torture.

"Foxglove," Naomi whispers, eyes shut.

"So that means"—Lola hesitates, fruitlessly waiting for anyone else to take the conversational relay baton—"you want to go with Efraín's plan?"

"Yes. That."

It's not exactly enthusiastic consent.

I hear it for what it is, even if Efraín won't: Naomi's giving up. She's burned through her circuits, and peer pressure is the path of least resistance. She's agreeing with Efraín's batshit crazy plan because it's easier to agree with him than to disagree.

Easier to agree with him and disagree *with me.*

"Then let's go buy some temporary hair dye," Efraín says with that insufferably smug, cat-that-got-the-cream smirk.

Under the guttering fluorescent lights of Foxglove Apothecary's hair care aisle, I regret the series of unfortunate life decisions that has led me here.

I never should've agreed to the carpool.

I never should've let my carpool buddies peer-pressure me into coming here.

Across the square from Lou's, Foxglove Apothecary brands itself as a boutique general store but is really an old-fashioned five-and-dime/pharmacy duo that is always a heartbeat away from CVS or Walgreens swooping in like carrion birds.

A few aisles over, Lola's trying to cheer Naomi up. After all, Naomi isn't going to do anything except touch up her highlights with the dye she has at home, and Lola has an extensive clip-in extension collection. Naomi isn't talking much, but Lola's getting her to make a game of rating Squishmallows and knockoffs by huggability.

Meanwhile, I've been holding the same random box of hair dye I picked up five minutes ago, pretending to read it, but primarily brooding and thinking: *I did not consent to this.*

If Efraín could read my thoughts—or found himself living out the *NS* pseudo-telepathy episode "American

Psychedelic"—he'd tell me that capitalism doesn't give a damn about my consent.

"Didn't peg you as a blond," Efraín jests.

Thankfully, I don't need a steel helmet or a tinfoil hat. I do, however, need to pay attention to which boxes I pull off the shelf. "I'm not."

"Besides, blond's a natural color, and that's permanent dye."

I shove the box onto the shelf, then immediately regret my carelessness. I don't want to make Dr. Andersen's life harder. Straightening the boxes is therapeutic.

"Temporary dyes are over here." Efraín cocks his head to the end of the aisle. "Selection's pretty limited."

"I'm sure whatever's cheapest is fine," I reply, even though nothing about this is remotely fine.

Efraín flicks his eyes at me, frowning. "Clairol tests on animals."

"Okay, which brands don't?"

Shoulder to shoulder at the end of the aisle, I consider the three rows of temporary dyes that Efraín considers a "limited" selection.

"Help me read the labels," Efraín says. "Just because the company says they're 'cruelty-free' doesn't mean they are, so check for the Leaping Bunny certification. But that doesn't guarantee they're vegan, so check the ingredients, and—"

"Got it." I grab a box from the bottom shelf.

Strategically placed box fans whir around us, the store otherwise a stifling space. Price labels flutter in the artificial breeze.

We find two true vegan, cruelty-free brands, one half the price of the other.

Efraín, of course, immediately grabs a box of the more expensive brand in pink.

"You really want your hair to match our uniform shirts?" I ask.

He looks down, as if he'd completely forgotten about the fuchsia polos we're still wearing. He shrugs, sending the tight fabric rippling over his irritatingly well-defined pecs. "It won't look that bright in my hair. Now, your turn."

I look down at the lower shelf of cheaper dyes, half a dozen colors on offer. Except I'm not asking myself if I'm more of an Impulsive Indigo or Vivid Violet kind of guy. I'm trying to remember when I agreed to risk my job for . . . what, exactly?

Naomi's signature hiccup-giggle punctuates Lola's throaty laugh. Operation: Cheer-Up is working.

"Do you hate all the colors or something?" Efraín asks. "It's just one day."

"Maybe I don't want to spend money on a single-day riot that's liable to get me fired before my first paycheck!" I burst out.

He studies me, brows furrowed, and says, "If money's the issue, I'll cover you."

I want to laugh because, God, he has *no idea.* Of course

money is the issue, but I can afford to dip into my burgeoning top surgery fund, which primarily consists of birthday and Chrismukkah gift money and cat-sitting gratuities from Ms. Sinclair, to buy a box of hair dye—even the one that costs as much as we make in an hour.

But it's not about that. It's about the part where there will be no paychecks to funnel into said fund if I dye my hair Mango Mash, Bolder Blue, or any other color of the rainbow.

"It's not about the money," I lie.

I don't know what he's thinking when he leans back against the shelves, long and languid, as he considers me anew. "You know, I meant to check in. About earlier."

I rewind the past eleven hours and pinpoint five discrete incidents that might warrant discussion, starting with his tardiness and ending with . . . "What, when you accused me of being a Nazi sympathizer?"

He has the courtesy to wince. "That wasn't my intention."

"Impact over intent, right?" I force a sardonic smile. Echoing Efraín's own mantras is a Pyrrhic pleasure at best. If I were to document today's myriad disappointments, that argument would barely make the list. "Don't worry about it."

"That wasn't what I was talking about. I wanted to check in about this morning," Efraín says, "when I corrected Anya about your gender. It felt like the right thing to do, but I realize now that I might've overstepped."

I blink up at him, nonplussed.

He's not checking in about the light misgendering but rather how *he* reacted? Are his priorities so egotistically misaligned that he thinks *that* is what warrants an apology? Is he even apologizing? Is that what's happening right now?

Then he elaborates, "I outed you."

"I'm universally out. Besides, I told Anya at my interview."

"So you don't mind that I corrected her? I know some trans people feel patronized when other people step in."

You know what makes me feel patronized? This entire conversation.

Efraín says, "I shouldn't have assumed what you'd want other people to know."

"So, instead, you're assuming you know how I feel."

"No, I'm *checking in.* I'm *asking* how you feel."

Not apologizing. Noted.

The thing is, I don't know how I feel. In the moment, I couldn't make sense of anything except that the situation itself *didn't make sense.* It wasn't supposed to happen, and I had to fix it. Then Efraín swooped in before I got the chance.

Maybe I do know what he means.

"I can take care of myself," I say, because it is crucial that he know this. I don't need his check-ins or not-apologies.

"Can you, though? You were just standing there, not saying anything." His words come faster, unpracticed. He just can't help himself. "It wasn't fight or flight; you chose *freeze.*"

I chose *delayed processing*, actually, except for the part where I didn't *choose* it at all.

The same thing is happening right now. Seconds are passing, and my lips aren't moving, and Efraín's staring.

I glance up at the anti-theft mirror, watching Lola's and Naomi's distorted reflections.

"So you checked in because you thought it was the right thing to do, but you've already convinced yourself that you were right to correct Anya, no matter what I say." I can't bring myself to look at Efraín. "Because you saw me as a helpless, hapless baby seal that was going to be clubbed to death if you didn't save me." I tighten my grip on my backpack straps. "You don't think that's patronizing?"

"What would you prefer I do next time, Elisha?" Efraín demands. "Stay quiet while someone misgenders you?"

"Kind of you to assume there's going to be a *next time*."

This is what Efraín looks like caught off guard: lips parted, brows scrunched, and shoulders pulled back, roiling with tension.

This, too, is Pyrrhic.

"No, you're right," I admit. The quieter his voice gets, the louder mine rises. Higher, too, because my body never misses an opportunity to misgender itself. "There will be a next time; there's always a next time. Because no one is ever going to look at me and think *boy*."

I get it. I'm lucky to live in a liberal place like Northern

California, and because Egan's Creek has the population of a snow globe, everyone knows I'm trans. But the diner gets tourists, and the first day of school is a wild card. People forget.

I really wish *I* could forget, but if I showed up at work tomorrow with pink hair, would *anyone* gender me correctly?

Just like that, Efraín deflates. Drops his shoulders and ducks his head. "I'm sorry."

There. The rare Efraín Juarez Reyna apology spotted in the wild. I'd call it an endangered species, except I thought it was a cryptid until now. Ironically, he's apologizing for the one thing he can't control. "It's not your fault I don't pass."

"That's not what I—"

"Isn't it? Tell me you're not trying to offer your condolences that the world doesn't see me the way I want to be seen."

He clenches his jaw. "They should."

"Yeah. But I understand why they don't."

"You know that I do, right?" The question comes fast and fervent. He leans in closer, until I catch a whiff of coconut, sunshine, and God knows what other fair-trade, vegan, cruelty-free body care essentials he uses, which probably cost more than we make in a day. When I meet his eyes, they're bright enough to make me blink, shining with some emotion I can't name. "You have to know that I see you as a guy."

Do I really *know* that, though? That's what cis allies have to say. They use the right name and pronouns and agree in polite conversation that trans people should be allowed to play sports, access medical care, and use public restrooms. But there's always this itching fear beneath my skin that they're just indulging me, like they indulge a child's imaginary friend.

They'll set a place at the table for Mr. Grizz Lee Bear, your invisible bow-tie-wearing, ursine bestie, but they can't actually see him, because they don't understand that he's as real as they are. Most people haven't done the work to decouple the signs and signifiers of gender in their minds and see others through a gender-expansive lens.

Has Efraín done that work? I don't know; he's known me since kindergarten. Efraín spent a decade calling me by another name. That's deep programming, the base code underwriting every memory he has of me. Can that ever really be overwritten?

I believe that Efraín believes he sees the real me. I believe that he needs to believe that. I believe that he can convince himself to believe whatever he needs to believe. He'd ask Mr. Grizz Lee Bear to work a phone bank, if it served his cause. Is that kind of belief better or worse? Is it more or less real?

Efraín doesn't want my honest answer; the only acceptable response is the one that soothes his conscience. "Yeah. I know."

He nods, quick and curt, like we've settled something crucial. Found common ground, signed an armistice, and laid down our arms. "So you know I just want to help where I can."

"I do know that about you, yes."

After all, that's why we're here, debating the price of hair dye.

"Then you know I'm not trying to be patronizing."

Impact over intent, I don't say because I'm trying not to poke the imaginary bear.

"Yep," I say instead.

It doesn't matter what I tell Efraín. He corrected Anya because I froze. *I* gave him the opportunity. If I'd said something immediately, Efraín wouldn't have had time to saddle up his white horse, and I wouldn't be trapped in this tragicomedy of errors.

If I just take care of future misgendering incidents by myself, then I won't have to deal with the Efraín of it all.

So I think about times I'm most frequently misgendered. My solution at the diner has always been to avoid interacting with customers, but at school? I'm proactive. The first week of every school year, I wear a pronoun button. "He/him" in a bold font. Impossible to miss.

I've never needed the button after Labor Day.

Because I can take care of myself. Really. I can solve my own problems. Honestly? I'm the only one who can.

And Efraín just gave me an idea how to solve this one.

"Elisha?"

I glance up at him. "It's fine. You have my permission for next time. And the time after that."

I'm going to make sure there are as few *next times* as possible, but none of that matters if I don't have a job.

Efraín claims this hair dye rebellion is about self-expression—that they're fighting for Naomi's right to express herself in the workplace. I just want to *exist* in the workplace—except I can't exist in the workplace and fight it at the same time.

I need to keep this job.

Once more, I peek up at the mirror, where Lola and Naomi are now trying on sunglasses, and then put down the box of Vivid Violet I don't remember picking up.

I can't make myself look at Efraín when I tell him, "I can't do this," and walk away without explanation—ignoring him when he calls after me, as well as the treacherous pounding in my chest.

I can only fight one battle at once, and I have to do it myself.

SIX

I CAN'T EMPHASIZE ENOUGH HOW MUCH I WOULD LIKE TO BE excluded from this narrative.

My carpool comrades have made the commute from the parking lot to the barn their personal slow-motion action movie shot. You know the one: the ragtag band of heroes marching into battle side by side, accompanied by an epic Hans Zimmer ditty. This is just like that, except instead of formfitting body armor, we're drab in polos and khaki, and instead of phasers, swords, or katanas, our weapons are sartorial.

Naomi's hair towers high, styled in a topknot that emphasizes her refreshed green highlights and displays the green peekaboo layer. Lola has dozens of rainbow extensions artfully clipped among her curls. Efraín's tresses are deep cherry pink, his waves pulled back from his face in a little half bun. They're all so confident, straight out of central casting.

Then there's me, with my same-old safe brown undercut.

My curls may be perpetually unruly, but they're dress code compliant.

The only reason I might belong in this lineup of rabble-rousers? The pronoun button I pinned to my polo. I got this particular button at my preliminary consult with Dr. Mburu, whose waiting room had bowls of buttons at the front desk.

A good pronoun button is clean. Simple. Dr. Mburu gets it: 2.25-inch diameter with a bold black sans-serif font set against a plain white background. Legible, accessible, and almost impossible to misinterpret. Foolproof, though not bigot-proof.

But I've been assured this is a trans-friendly work environment. None of my coworkers are going to misgender me today, and unlike some people, I am *definitely* still going to have a job in twenty minutes.

The daily pre-shift meeting takes place in the barn lobby.

I don't have time to take in the rest of my new coworkers before Anya claps her hands together. "Gather round, troops. Some quick introductions for our new recruits." As the seasoned veterans lazily assemble, Anya names them. "There's Ford, who puts on his supervisor hat on days Dan or I have off. Stanley, who's been with us since the day the museum opened. Jaime, who started last summer; some of you might've crossed paths at school. And that's TJ."

Anya rattles off our names, and she doesn't say "Goldstein sisters." We're just "Naomi and Eli." It's the first time Anya has really looked in our direction while she's been ticking items off her to-do list, and then she spies our hair.

I mean, *their* hair.

Anya's eyes flick between Lola's and Efraín's polychromatic hair, and her lips smoosh together into a tight line. Her face is almost as red as her own hair. She stares at Naomi's updo, fuming that a trainee had the nerve to deny an ultimatum and drag two others into noncompliance.

Everyone else has tracked the source of Anya's distress. Blake's barely holding back a smile, and the built, baby-faced guy next to her is energetically waving at Lola with an arm sporting a half-finished sleeve tattoo.

Our new coworkers are watching us with naked interest, like some nature documentary. It doesn't matter that my hair is unadorned; I'm guilty by proximity.

Anya squares her shoulders. I'm expecting fast, brutal, bloody, but then she calls, "Ford?"

The low-level, substitute supervisor Anya pointed out earlier hurries over. She thrusts her clipboard at him. "Finish up. I have to make some phone calls." I can practically hear her stomping up the stairs in the silence that persists in the wake of her dramatic exit.

Ford squares his shoulders like he's overcompensating for something. "Where were we?" He scans Anya's clipboard. "Ah, summer hours."

I don't hear another word of the spiel. I'm too distracted

by Anya saying "phone calls" instead of "fired." By the ghost of too many vicious, dog-eat-dog words I exchanged with the boy who is obliviously chipping away at his black nail polish beside me.

I'm unsettled. Off-balance, as if I were walking a tight rope in Lola's summery wedges instead of standing on solid ground in my secondhand saddle shoes.

I'm the one who sought out solid ground. So why do I feel so damn unsteady?

"And *that* is how you sell a membership." Stanley Pham, grizzled, battle-hardened guest services veteran, flashes a grin as a family of five walks away from the ticketing counter, sticking special member stickers to their shirts.

I'm rerunning the steps in my head, logging every keystroke in my mental database.

"Did they really need a membership?" Efraín asks. "They're never coming back."

"You don't know that," I retort, all thoughts of procedure down the memory shredder. "One visit doesn't do the museum justice."

"A family from Gary, Indiana, is *not* coming back in the next year." He whirls on Stanley. "How can you justify price gouging that family?"

For the thousandth time today, I silently curse the damn dress code.

Anya's disappearing act this morning has irreparably screwed the schedule. To learn the retail ropes, we were split into two groups, "boys and girls," like some schoolyard dodgeball game, each group spending half the day at ticketing, the other at the gift shop.

Anya never came back downstairs. The gossip indicates that she spent all morning holed up in her office, like it was her own nuclear bunker. Divya from security said that Eden from curatorial said she saw Billy from HR go into Anya's office.

After lunch, Ford took the girls to the gift shop and parked Efraín and me at ticketing, in Stanley's "experienced hands."

This is what it's been like all day. Me, Efraín, and some poor schmuck trying to teach us the ropes. I'm trying to learn, but Efraín has made it his mission to tank my work performance.

"It wasn't price gouging," Stanley replies, drawing my attention back to the membership sale. Stanley is unflappable—if anything, he seems amused by Efraín's antics. "I gave them the best deal. Do the math. Two adult tickets, two youth tickets for the younger kids, but the nineteen-year-old? Too old for a youth ticket, which is why you always ask for student or military ID, but that kid would've been another full-price ticket."

"Highway robbery," Efraín mutters.

"Pop quiz. How much would three adult and two youth tickets come to?"

Can I request accommodations for this pop quiz? It's not like I'll ever need to do this in my head in real time. When I'm actually at the till, the computer will do the math for me.

Efraín doesn't produce a sum, either.

"One hundred and twenty-one dollars," Stanley says, not unkindly, as if we haven't just failed to perform basic arithmetic. "Meanwhile, a family membership, which includes two adults and five *dependents*, costs—"

"Oneohnine," I blurt because I've repeatedly tried and failed to hand-sell that membership to my moms. "One hundred and nine dollars."

"Exactly right." Stanley beams. "The membership is twelve dollars cheaper."

"You could've just counted the nineteen-year-old as a youth," Efraín says.

"Same price as the membership, but against the rules." Stanley shrugs. "Listen, kid, I've worked at NSX since Christine Holloway fought George Rhodes over the giant scissors to cut the ribbon on opening day. After twenty-five years, you learn to pick your battles."

Efraín's about to argue—I can feel it in the air, the way dogs sense earthquakes before they hit. He's working his jaw, ready to defend every battle he's ever picked.

Abruptly, Stanley straightens up. "Look alive, boys. That's—"

"Dagny Kane," I whisper.

Silhouetted in harsh sunlight, I'd recognize her anywhere: grieving daughter, former child actress, cult franchise heiress, small-town museum mogul. But her most important title of all? *Boss.*

And she's making a beeline for the ticketing counter.

"Stan!" she calls with a starlet smile. "It's so good to see you."

"I'm here five days a week," Stanley quips.

"You know how it is across the lawn."

"Well, only downstairs."

Of course, Dagny Kane's office is upstairs in the farmhouse.

"But you picked a good day to stop by our neck of the woods. Have you met our new GSAs? I've had the pleasure of training the boys this afternoon. Meet Eli and Efraín."

My eyes flash to Stanley, unsure if he realizes the magnitude of what he's just said. Did he do it consciously, to clarify my gender upfront? Or was it just instinct because that's what he sees: two boys, at work?

Dagny turns her smile on us, and I can't help gawking.

In person, in Technicolor, she looks less like Victor than in the grayscale photos in the family room gallery. She has her father's trademark strong brow line and sharp nose, but her eyes are lighter, her chin softer. She wears her straight, dark brown hair in a blunt I'd-like-to-speak-to-the-manager bob, except she *is* the manager.

Meanwhile, I'm sweating buckets, a shape-shifter who's tried to hold human form for too long and reverts to alien goo.

"Ms. Kane," I say, my quivering voice nervous but entirely earnest. "It's an honor to meet you."

"Please, call me Dagny. We're a family here at the Nuclear Seasons Experience."

"Dagny," I say, even though it feels more taboo than calling a teacher by their first name.

Are we supposed to shake hands? What's normal workplace etiquette for the CEO of a small nonprofit business who also happened to do a brief stint on Nickelodeon? *Forbes* didn't have articles on how to—

Dagny reaches out to shake my hand. "Eli and Efraín, was it?"

I nod, and Efraín grunts an affirmative. She shakes Efraín's reluctant hand with his too-firm grip, but she never meets his eyes. Trust me, as someone who has perfected the art of avoiding eye contact, her sight line dances around his face before settling on his pink hair.

Dagny doesn't say anything. I wait for her expression to change—for her halogen smile to shatter—but she keeps smiling, resting customer service face.

She turns back to me. Giddy pride pulses through me, like when I won the sixth-grade spelling bee on *insouciant* after

Efraín guessed *e* in place of the *a*. I want to puff out my chest like I did in the photo Naomi took of the principal handing me the blue ribbon. I was so proud of myself.

Then Dagny says, "Nice haircut, Eli."

Except her words don't feel *nice.*

The way her lip curled at Efraín's pop of pink reminds me of another curled lip. The reason I *didn't* puff out my chest at the spelling bee, when I looked past Efraín and his red second-place ribbon to where Mrs. Reyna stood, fuming.

I don't know what I feel anymore, but "proud" isn't it.

I made my choice, I didn't dye my hair, and now I have to live with it. So I say, "Thanks," because that's my line in this script, even if my heart isn't in it.

"Just one more thing," Dagny says.

This is it. Now she's going to address Efraín's pretty-in-pink rebellion.

I'm not proud, happy, or self-righteously smug. I didn't predict this would happen because I *wanted* to be right; I wanted to *prevent* it.

Except Dagny isn't looking at Efraín when she says, "You can't wear that."

"Excuse me?" She's looking at my chest, I think. I'm wearing my uniform polo, tucked in, all three buttons done up. I'm *compliant* to the point of *complicit.* I made sure of it.

"The pin. With the . . ." She gestures at my pronoun button, and apparently, I'm supposed to read some deeper meaning in her inchoate gesticulations.

She could mean something benign as *text*, but I doubt it. Does she think *pronoun* is a dirty word?

"There's nothing in the uniform policy about buttons." I triple-checked the employee handbook last night.

"It's political speech," Dagny explains.

I don't understand. "Political?"

"We can't allow anything that might interfere with institutional messaging."

I blink. And I blink. And I blink as the barn flickers, and I see this set in 1962, when the Spectors entered the bunker, when Victor Kane grew up here, before Stonewall or Compton's Cafeteria, in the days when you had to wear at least three items of clothing that corresponded to your assigned gender at birth in case the gay bar in which you sought refuge was raided; and I see the barn in 1983, when the Spectors stepped into a new world, when Victor Kane filmed a show that said things were different, sort of, but queer men were dying in droves, and Reagan wouldn't say "AIDS" publicly for another year. I blink the barn back into focus, back into the present, and the scene looks exactly the same.

My binder's too tight, or maybe I just need my inhaler. I'm sweating again, even though goose bumps threaten to outnumber freckles on my forearms. The Fruit of the Loom tag on my polo scrapes my neck, and the polo sags where the button weighs down the cotton poly blend.

"Institutional messaging?"

"The museum welcomes everyone," Dagny says. "Partisan messaging makes guests feel uncomfortable."

"I—"

I want to object. I want to turn down the lights and crank up the AC and cut the tag out of this shirt. I want to know: How can a 2.25-inch pronoun button threaten an institution? How can a pronoun constitute a partisan message? How can the museum welcome everyone if my pronouns are unwelcome?

What does that say about my welcome, let alone my comfort or safety?

What about the welcome, comfort, or safety of any trans guests who step up to this ticketing counter?

"You understand, right?" Dagny's smile is a fixed point even as my universe shifts beneath me. "NSX is about bringing people together, just like *Nuclear Seasons* itself. That's the messaging we need to convey."

The messaging we need to *embody.*

Because my body is political. My existence is partisan. My very presence triggers arguments.

I'm half expecting Efraín to say something, but apparently, he's taken the saddle off the white horse. Of course he has. Telling a trans person to take off a button is such a microscopic microaggression that it wouldn't register on the transphobia Richter scale for most people.

Because unless you've won the genetic lottery, misgendering is a condition of living while trans. Accepting it without undue fuss is just one condition of parole—of this tentative cultural plea agreement where trans people get to exist, and cis people only curtail some of our rights and only sometimes try to kill us.

Because this is nothing. I know this is nothing.

I'm overreacting, and worse, every second I delay reads as insolence, but I'm not trying to defy Dagny. I've already made sacrifices to keep this job.

I don't understand, but even if I wanted to fight this, the arithmetic hasn't changed since yesterday. My cost-benefit analysis is the same.

With shaky fingers, I unhook the button and hide it in my fist.

Dagny says, "Thank you, Eli."

I have no idea what she's thanking me for. But I've learned this script the hard way. Someone thanks you, and you say, "You're welcome."

"I'm off to the salt mines. Listen to Stanley; he's a pro. And welcome to the family!"

She crosses the barn and badges into the employee stairwell, while Efraín immediately pulls out his phone and starts typing. I don't have the energy to chastise him.

Instead, I turn to the rattling barn doors as they slide open. An elderly couple in matching Hawaiian shirts make their way up to the ticketing counter, stars in their eyes.

I shove my fist, pronoun button and all, into my pocket and plaster on a smile that would make Dagny proud.

"Hi," I say. "Welcome to the Nuclear Seasons Experience. What can we do for you today?"

SEVEN

SPUTNIK GREETS ME AT THE DOOR, BRUSHING AGAINST MY SHINS. For a twenty-three-pound shelter cat built like a brawler, she has the most innocent, crystalline meow.

I crouch down, combing my fingers through her silky tortoiseshell coat. "Honey, I'm home," I whisper against her fur, and immediately feel ridiculous.

Is it more ridiculous that I'm talking to my cat or that I'm using the stereotypical 1950s hardworking-family-man-greets-housewife line, and what business do I have calling myself a *hardworking family man*, anyway? It's not like it was hard work choosing work over my *family*.

Then *work* called itself my family and told me that my identity was a threat, all in one breath.

In my room, I try to kick off my shoes, but they're too tight. I pry them off while batting off Sputnik's "help," then peel off my sweat-steeped socks.

Sputnik drops and rolls on my discarded shoes, luxuriating as if they're lined with catnip.

I wake up my laptop, open my "Songs to Avert a (Nuclear) Meltdown" playlist, all chosen for their steady tempos rather than lyrics or genre, and pick one to play on repeat. Stimming by another name.

I tug the polo over my head and ball it between my fists.

The thing is, I can take off the shirt. I can rub aloe over irritated skin. I can slap a generic bandage on my nape. But I can't cut out the tag like I do for every other shirt I buy. It isn't mine to snip out because this shirt isn't mine. I signed it out and swore to return it in good condition, lest the museum garnish my last paycheck.

How many previous owners has this particular polo had before me? It smelled clean when I picked it up, no obvious stains or holes. Whoever wore it before me took good care of it.

Did they wear the uniform with pride? Did they treat museum guests like family? Did Dagny Kane ever lecture them about *institutional messaging*?

I toss the shirt on the floor. It isn't supposed to land on Sputnik; it isn't supposed to be on the floor at all. I'll wash it later, just as soon as I remember that I give a fuck.

I swap my binder for a high-compression sports bra. I don't bother with a shirt. I know it's improper to gallivant around in just a bra, especially if you're packing flab at your waist, but I don't care. I'm alone.

Everything itches, from my skin to my bones. I'm

standing in the middle of my bedroom in a sports bra and boxer briefs with an outlawed pronoun button on my palm.

I shove the button in a drawer and bring my laptop over to my bed. I click through the fifty-odd tabs in my browser, find the appropriate streaming service, scroll to "Continue Watching," and hit play on *Nuclear Seasons.*

Thunk. Thunk. Thunk.

There are pebbles pelting my window.

Outside, it's dark. I must have fallen asleep watching *NS* hours ago.

Thunk.

It's like something out of a rom-com. I've been thrust onto the set of a John Hughes movie and conscripted into a lead role when I only came to play an extra in a punchy screwball workplace comedy. I'm neither prepared nor willing to play the part of sheltered heroine in her bedroom, her anger unconvincing when her bad boy love sneaks over to her bedroom window.

Especially not if that bad boy love interest is *Efraín.*

Because *who else* besides Efraín would've ridden his bike here, wearing a headlamp on his helmet and a neon windbreaker with reflective stripes and, oh, okay, those are actual cyclist shorts—the skintight, clingy kind—and thanks to the headlamp, I can see *everything.*

My window squeaks when I push it open. Cool, not-quite-summer air slaps me in the face. "Why the fuck are you here?"

"Why the hell aren't you answering your texts?" Efraín whisper-shouts.

Because I didn't realize I had any. Sputnik is napping on my phone.

"Why aren't you knocking on the door like a normal person?"

"It's the middle of the night."

Fact check: It's not even one. Hardly the *middle* of the night. "So?"

"I didn't want to wake Naomi or your moms."

"How thoughtful."

"Are you coming down or not?"

I'm sure as hell not inviting him up, but I know he won't leave until he gets his pound of gray matter.

Only when I go to grab a flannel do I realize I've had this entire window exchange in my sports bra. Fuck.

After I throw on actual clothes, Efraín's waiting at the bottom of the stoop, the light from his headlamp hitting me in the face.

I wince. "Can you take that thing off? You're going to burn my eyes out."

Efraín conscientiously clicks off the lamp before clipping his helmet to his handlebars. Now, illuminated only by motion-activated porch lights, I'm seeing Efraín with pink helmet hair. He really must keep a comb in his backpack pocket because I've never seen his voluminous tresses matted to his scalp.

Back in our PE days, he put his hair up in that signature half bun that always looked downright sculptural in its artful dishevelment, too intentional for sweat to do anything other than cast a sheen on a bronze statue, rendering him as untouchable as ever.

Tonight, sweaty and rumpled, he looks almost . . . mortal? Though those shorts would put Michelangelo's sculpting skills to shame, and I am resolutely *not* looking down.

I'm tired and frustrated, and I'm not going to let him distract me.

"How did you know which window is mine?"

I don't have to ask how he knows where I live. Efraín and I always end up paired for school projects. It's less to do with our alphabetically adjacent names and more to do with the fact that no one else wants to work with either of us.

Usually, we meet at Lou's or the library. For projects that require space, however, we end up in my living room, like that time we constructed a French Revolution diorama featuring a semi-functional guillotine built from an X-Acto knife cartridge and Popsicle sticks, with one of my long-abandoned Ken dolls under the blade.

"We used your window for the egg drop experiment."

That would be the physical science experiment where

Efraín told me he'd gotten permission from Mrs. Babbitt to use light bulbs instead of eggs. Spoiler: He did not get permission.

"Hard to forget the spot where we spent an hour digging glass shards out of your moms' herb garden."

"So you can remember my window based on one experiment in ninth grade, but you can't remember the pickup time for the carpool?"

"Are you serious right now? How are you still—that's what you're pissed about right now?"

"I contain multitudes of irritation."

"And contradict yourself."

I open my mouth and shut it again. No one ever seems to remember that half of the Whitman quote; they like the poetics of multiplicity but don't want to grapple with the politics of doublethink. Yes, maybe I'm contradicting myself by the second because as much as I want to tell Efraín to go mindfuck himself, I'm already screwing myself by asking, "Why are you really here?"

Efraín wrings the strap of his crossbody sling bag between his fists. "You know why," he says, in an ominous undertone. "Lola and Naomi spent happy hour downing milk-alternative milkshakes after work, celebrating like we won the war, even though I *told* them it was premature."

"Because of Dagny's visit." I understand now that Efraín texted their group-chat-of-three after Dagny's drop-in.

Efraín sees the same warning signs I do. What's worse, I can put two and two together and make five; Efraín's here to *convince* me.

Something clenches in my stomach, irritation and guilt laced with something ugly I have yet to digest.

I look away, to the hanging birdhouse Naomi built in woodshop two years. A chartreuse A-line cabin with whittled shutters over faux windows, it's basically the Barbie Sonoma Dream Birdhouse.

Efraín asks, "Can we walk?"

I acquiesce because it's the least of all evils.

We set out past the same collection of pastel rainbow houses featured in "Guess Who's Coming to Barbecue." Egan's Creek hasn't really changed; the town has only been lightly gentrified and spruced up for the benefit of roving wine tourists.

Two blocks away, the square is empty and dark. Shops closed, second-story apartments shuttered, and the red neon CLOSED sign flickering in the diner window. There is no clean, well-lighted place for nighthawks to seek refuge.

I was expecting a walk-and-talk—or a walk-and-excoriate—but Efraín has yet to say anything. He has definitely forgotten that I can't match his stride length. I veer off the sidewalk and make my way toward the gazebo at the center of the square.

The steps creak under me. I lean against one of the

columns and bounce on my toes, imperceptible to the uneducated observer.

Efraín makes a valiant attempt at standing still, but I'm not an uneducated observer. I know his stims if not his tells. He's clenching and unclenching his fists, telegraphing impatience and anger—that's what my emotion-sensation wheel key chain would say.

This is the standoff in every spaghetti Western. Like the high noon duel in the *NS* episode "The Good, the Bad, and the Uncanny."

I flick my fingers against my thigh, twitching for the trigger. Sick of watching tumbleweeds roll by, I shoot first. "Are you actually going to ask me anything, or have you already composed the lecture about what a terrible person I am for not dyeing my hair? Because you can save me the holier-than-thou spiel."

"I'm not—"

"Yeah, you are. Because this is what you always do." Efraín sees everything in black and white, but anyone who's watched a black-and-white movie knows the image has fifty thousand shades of gray. "You decide what's right, and anyone who doesn't automatically fall in line is in the wrong."

"You *are* in the wrong, Elisha." Efraín's still in motion, circling like a shark, and I'm the one bleeding out in the water.

"I don't understand why you care so much what I do. Is this some supermassive savior complex talking? Are you trying to save me from myself? Because, news flash: I don't need you to save my soul. That's what Yom Kippur is for."

"Because your soul is the only one that matters," he scoffs. "What does it matter if you throw one plastic bottle in the trash, right? Drink one bottle of almond milk? Buy one book from Amazon? In a culture where *everyone* is taught to think their individual moral trespasses don't matter, they *all* matter that much more. You showed up today with your regular hair knowing damn well that the rest of us were risking *everything*. That makes you just as complicit as management."

I don't need Efraín to tell me things I already know. I know complicity. I know this lecture is pissing me off.

This gazebo isn't big enough for two people to pace, but anger propels me like a wind-up toy. "Don't make this out to be something it's not. You're not risking *anything* because you don't *need* this job. You're just taking advantage of Naomi's problem to stir up controversy. Like you always do. I'm sorry, but I don't want any part of your anarchist bad boy shenanigans."

I thought I'd seen every shade of anger that Efraín can express, but I don't think the English language has a word for this. Blood turning his cheeks from burnished gold to copper, reverse-Midas-like. The throbbing vein at his temple. His flared nostrils and parted lips, huffing and puffing.

His default righteous indignation would be downright comforting right about now.

"Do you have any idea how—" Efraín sucks his teeth, like it's the only way to stop himself from saying something he'll regret. "How you sound right now?"

I imagine every expletive he might have swallowed, but even my grade-A imagination can't conjure up what rhetorical volley Efraín thinks would be *going too far.* "No, please, enlighten me. Because I'm pretty sure I'm the only one thinking rationally about this."

"All we asked was for you to dye your hair for *one day.*" He takes a step closer. "Are you really this coldhearted? I thought I got you. Some people just don't show up for strangers. I know the score: You're cynical, and apathy's easy. But it's supposed to hit different when it's personal. When it's *family.* Do you even care about anything besides your stupid TV show?"

He's wrong. He's so wrong, about all of it.

Yes, I do care about *Nuclear Seasons,* pulpy science fiction, and what other people would call lowbrow *guilty pleasures.* But I also care about whether my coworkers see me as a guy. I care about saving enough for my top surgery down payment. I care about Sputnik. I care about Moms and *Naomi*—

It does hit different with Naomi, and I do care about strangers. I'm not unaffected by any of this. No matter what Efraín thinks, I'm not coldhearted. I care about a multitude of issues—my cares contradict themselves—but this is a question of survival.

I can't tell Efraín any of this. If I tell Efraín I need the money for top surgery, he won't understand because cis people *never* understand the true cost of dysphoria. His overactive social justice empathy Spidey sense might tingle, and he'd pretend to understand while silently begrudging my inability to prioritize.

But I'm pissed, and I don't know when to shut up. "I *need* this job. Maybe you don't, and Lola can fall back on her family's auto shop, but I need *this* job. That doesn't mean I don't care about things. And people. And places? Which is literally the definition of a noun. I care about a lot of nouns—and grammar, in general?"

"Well, Elisha, riddle me this: What's the difference between a common noun and a proper noun?"

I *know* it's a rhetorical question, but pedantry is an autonomic reflex. "Capitalization. Technically, specificity. Common nouns refer to a general person, place, or thing. Proper nouns refer to a specific, named—"

"So your sister, Naomi, is . . ."

"'Sister' is common, and 'Naomi' is proper. I get it, okay?"

"Do you?" He moves closer, gets in my face.

For every step he takes, I stumble two steps back. I'm not afraid of Efraín. I know his hot air bluster might hurt to breathe, but it won't blister my lungs. It's not even about Efraín so much as the physicality of the scene: his body, all chiseled muscle and masculine angles, looming over my body, just baby fat and irrepressibly feminine curves. It isn't fear roiling in my gut; it's—

Suddenly, my back hits the column. I have to tilt my head all the way back to look at him.

"Do you understand, Elisha?" he asks again, so close that I can feel his breath where his words scorch my skin.

I forgot the question. Grammar. Parts of speech. Syntax and diction and, fuck, I'd really rather be diagramming sentences right now.

I swallow hard, so aware of my lack of Adam's apple when his eclipses my field of view.

"Naomi matters," Efraín says. "She should matter to you. Not because she's your common-noun sister but because she's Naomi Goldstein. A person. A human being. A real—"

"Naomi is a proper noun. I *know*."

"Then you should give a fuck if your boss is bullying her."

"I do care about Naomi," I retort, "and her job. And, believe it or not, yours and Lola's, too."

"That's the thing, Elisha. You should care about the person more than their job."

"There are those pesky common nouns again. Don't you mean that I should care about *Naomi* more than *Naomi's job*?"

Efraín leans improbably, impossibly closer. He's heat and sweat and overpriced coconut bath products and the bitter aftertaste of yerba mate lingering on his breath. Sensory overwhelm. Heat and sweat and coconut and mate. An assemblage of common nouns that don't come close to translating the human sum to proper-noun *Efraín.*

Then, just as suddenly as he annexed my personal space, he steps back.

"Fine," he seethes. His eyes are so dark and glassy, I can almost see my reflection, and I don't like what I see. "Have it your way. If you think management is right—that Naomi, Lola, and I deserve to be fired over this and that everything Dagny said this afternoon was *fair*—then fine. But it's not too late to do the right thing."

Seriously, *fuck him* for bringing up this afternoon. If he heard everything Dagny said, where was his concern about doing *the right thing* then?

Then again, doesn't that cut both ways? What right do I have to lash out at Efraín for his selective silence when my own silence was deafening? However frustrated I am with Efraín's persistent recklessness, it's nothing compared to the silent fury that's been simmering all day for Dagny, for the museum, for goddamn *institutional messaging.* It's nothing compared to my anger at myself for just standing there and *taking it*—which is exactly what I told my sister to do.

Efraín tugs his crossbody bag around, unzips it, and pulls out a small box. I fumble when he tosses it to me. My hands shake around the slick cardboard.

"You can make this right," he says again, quieter, and all the more dangerous for it. "But if you know this is wrong, and you know you could do something to fix it but choose not to? Well, then, Elisha, I don't even want to know you."

It isn't until he leaves and I've run through my panic breathing exercises that I finally look at the box he gave me.

Vivid Violet one-wash temporary hair dye.

EIGHT

I'M *DEFINITELY* GOING TO GET FIRED.

Forty-eight hours ago, that assumption was premature. I didn't have all the facts. Today, I'm drawing an informed conclusion based on observations. I've met the powers that be; I know the risks. I can say with clear-eyed certainty that I will be fired.

"Holy fuck, you actually did it."

I'm barely down the porch steps when Efraín rudely interrupts my anxious internal monologue.

Not for the first time, I curse Lola's two-door car. If Efraín didn't have to get out—to perform this parody of chivalry—then he wouldn't be looking right at me.

"Is it really that surprising? You literally hand-delivered the dye to my doorstep."

Efraín rolls his eyes. "Yeah, but I didn't really expect you to use it, Mr. Goody Two-Shoes."

Well, that stings, but I probably deserve it. Last night, I

didn't give him any reason to believe I might see reason—or his definition of it. But Efraín didn't plumb the depths of my anger.

So, for one day only, I've dyed my curls electric violet. And probably a good chunk of my forehead and the back of my neck, too. No one warned me that hair dye was so *messy*.

Lola peeks over the roof and lets out a low whistle. "Looking good."

Naomi's already slipping in past Lola's seat. She hasn't commented yet, but she has ringside season tickets.

Efraín's still gawping. "It's so *purple*."

"Technically, it's Vivid Violet," I correct him. "Although, with the auburn undertones in my natural hair color, the result is more on the plum side of the spectrum—"

Efraín mutters something to the effect of *so fucking pedantic* as I push past him and into the back seat.

"What changed your mind?" Efraín demands as he reclaims his seat.

I really should've prepared an answer. I knew he'd ask, but from the moment I first lathered dye on my hair last night to when I combed my curls this morning, I couldn't find the words to translate my decision into a language he'd understand.

Because the messy truth—that this hair dye is as much an act of personal protest on my part as a selfless show of support—wouldn't make sense to him. Instead, an ambiguous truth: "I'm sending a *message*."

Efraín meets my gaze in the rearview mirror, a cipher scrawled between his brows. Let him puzzle over which message I'm sending the institution.

Lola laughs. "My name is Dolores Mercedes Fuentes, and I approve this message."

"That's supposed to be Eli's line," Naomi pipes up. "If this were a campaign. The candidate is legally required—"

I bump her shoulder before buckling my seat belt. "In that case, my name is Elisha Goldstein, and you better believe I approve this message."

Naomi looks at me. Eye contact's even harder for her than it is for me, so the gesture itself is worth more than whatever words may follow. I hold contact, uncomfortable as it is, studying her hickory eyes. Her sclera are tinged pink; she hasn't been sleeping well. I wonder if Naomi reads the same struggle in me.

She doesn't say she approves, but then again, my hair isn't an apology. But that's fine. Neither Naomi nor I put much stock in words because what are social niceties if not a pyramid scheme?

"They won't know what hit them." Lola revs the engine. "Just watch Anya try to fire us now."

I agree with one out of two of those statements. I agree that, after my borderline brownnosing behavior, my defiance will shock Anya, but she's definitely going to fire us.

I check the mirror again because if I'm remembering Dagny's visit, surely Efraín must be, too.

But Efraín isn't looking at the mirror, though I can see a sliver of his face, tilted up, eyes shut, the hint of a smile on his lips. If I didn't know him better, I'd think he was . . . pleased? Hopeful?

If Efraín's feeling bullish about our continued employment now, after yesterday's broodfest, then something's changed his mind—presumably my hair.

Efraín's *hopeful* because of a choice I made. Efraín's pleased because of . . . me.

He sure as hell wouldn't approve *that* message.

If I had any doubts about my fate, Dagny's presence at the pre-shift meeting mere nanoseconds from midnight would break the Doomsday Clock. Discomfort wafts off my coworkers like bad body odor.

Blake and Jaime are huddled close, whispering either gossip or sweet nothings. Stanley and Dan are debating the merits of some new fantasy show. Gwen's asking Ford how to get ahead, but Ford has counted the same bundle of twenties twice and keeps sneaking glances over Gwen's head.

At the far end of the ticketing counter, Dagny's fiddling with her phone, presumably doing something of great institutional import. Anya's talking to her, but I'm too far to eavesdrop.

The moment our carpool quartet walks in, all eyes lock on our hair.

I expect Dagny to lead this pro forma kangaroo court, but Anya calls us to order. With forced cheer, she gets everyone to gather round while Dagny stays in the shadows—literally, because the lights over the ticketing counter aren't on yet.

"It's officially the start of tourist season, with our VIP anniversary party in August to close it out," Anya declares, "so the senior management team has planned incentives to help this well-oiled machine run smoother than ever. First off, we're increasing the employee discount at the gift shop from ten to fifteen percent, so now's the time to stock up on merch."

If I expected to still be a discount-eligible employee by my lunch break, I'd be excited. I've never bought anything from the gift shop before because it's basically Highway 12 robbery. Now it's a moot point.

"Second, we're organizing a collegial competition for membership sales. Every month, the GSA with the highest tickets-to-memberships conversion rate will receive a small prize. At the end of the summer, there will be a top secret grand prize!"

No one looks too excited for the surprise doorbuster. It's the equivalent of a white elephant gift, except you're working harder for the mere chance of earning what might be a coin sorter from someone's basement.

"Next, an update on our seasonal donation drive. We've checked with legal, and you *can* solicit donations for 'the museum and its programming,' just not 'educational programs.' Ask every guest if they'd like to donate!"

There is a limit to how much more employee minutiae I can tolerate when I am never going to sell another ticket again.

"Finally." Anya exchanges another glance with Dagny. "A minor update to the dress code. On a trial basis, we're suspending the ban on nonnatural hair colors. In general, any work-appropriate hairstyle will be allowed. If you have any questions about what constitutes a 'work-appropriate hairstyle,' please ask any member of the leadership team or Billy in HR."

Stop the Doomsday Clock. Put down the cell phones.

"Think of it as a fun little way to express yourself going into tourist season."

I don't understand. Anya's words are rattling around in my head, and Dagny's cataloging every reaction and possibly typing notes on her phone. Lola's beaming at Naomi, Naomi's blinking less like stimming and more like holding-back-tears, and Efraín's looking at me. His hand is on my arm, hot as a brand. His voice is in my ear, warm breath against my skin, saying my name, asking if I'm okay.

I'm bouncing on my toes. I'm staring at my shoes, except they're flickering. I'm blinking, not against tears. I'm just trying to *understand.*

Efraín says my name again, louder, and I look up at him

because I don't want anyone else looking at me right now. There's that little crinkle between Efraín's brows, but I don't recognize the shape of his lips or the gloss over his eyes. Thrice, he asks me, "Elisha. Tell me you're okay."

So, maybe he's not *asking*, per se.

But *I* need to ask someone, and he's demanding the whole of my attention.

Softly, I whisper, "Does this mean we're *not* fired?"

And Efraín—

Efraín laughs.

NINE

"I PROPOSE A TOAST!" LOLA PROCLAIMS, LIFTING HER TOPO CHICO like it's the finest champagne in the land.

After a celebratory bowling game, our gang of four relocated to Punch Bowl's dining area, overlooking the recessed lanes. It's usually occupied by harried parents while their kids go wild. At this hour, the clientele favors nine-to-fivers taking advantage of the cheapest happy hour in town.

And even for us, the underaged and exploited, happy hour means cheap snacks. I'd prefer free, as in Lou's, but Efraín whipped out a shiny credit card before Lola ordered for the table.

"What are we toasting?" Naomi raises her ginger beer.

"You!" Lola says. "We got the dress code changed because of you, Naomi."

Naomi ducks her head. "It was Efraín's idea."

"It wasn't the *idea* that won." Efraín's fingers curl tightly around his Coke bottle. "We acted *together*. That's how we won."

"Then here's to all of us!" Lola wiggles her bottle. "Ride or die, babes!"

I clink my generic red plastic tumbler of complimentary tap water, but I don't echo the words like Naomi and Efraín do. I don't belong here.

They're all smiles and good cheer and fizzy drinks. Who am I to revise history now?

Except, I should've known Efraín doesn't care much for history he can't read in Howard Zinn or an @workingclasshistory Instagram post. Efraín only ever has an eye to the future, one foot in the hydroponic grass landscaping his solarpunk utopia.

So I really shouldn't be surprised by the smirk stretching across his face.

"Congratulations, comrades," Efraín says. "We're a union now."

That word sets off air raid sirens inside my skull. Not *comrades*—Efraín's been known to make comrade jokes when he's feeling punchy—but *union.*

"What do you mean?" I ask, careful not to give away a flicker of my fear. "I mean, I know what a union is."

We did a partner presentation on the Bread and Roses Strike last semester, and when we had free rein to pick our topics for papers on social movements in California in the '60s, I marked up his passionate essay about the Delano grape strike while he proofread mine on the Compton's Cafeteria riot.

So, yes, I know what a union is; I know that unionizing can be dangerous. Union busting has gotten whole Starbucks shops shut down and Amazon workers laid off; historically, people have died for labor rights.

"I just don't understand what unions have to do with us, here and now."

Efraín's lazy smile reminds me of Sputnik sprawling in the sun. "We became a union as soon as we decided to defy the dress code. That's all a union is, legally. Two or more workers working together to—"

"Wait." His words are coming too fast, and I can't keep up. This doesn't make sense. "That can't be right. Unions are . . . official, regulated. Big. Bureaucratic. Byzantine. Did I say official? Industry-wide, like agricultural workers, rail workers or . . ."

"Auto workers," Lola adds.

"Teachers," Naomi says.

"Nurses."

"Teamsters."

"Service employees."

"Firefighters and cops."

"And prison guards."

"Really?" Naomi scrunches up her nose.

"Yes," Efraín cuts in with a grimace. "The California Correctional Peace Officers Association is one of the strongest unions in the state. Unfortunately. But to restore your faith in humanity, strippers and sex workers have had a branch of the Communications Workers of America since the seventies.

And don't forget trades like steelworkers, carpenters, and electricians." Then he flicks his eyes at me and adds, "The Writers Guild of America, the Screen Actors Guild, and whatever the 'AFTRA' stands for."

He's making an emotional appeal. Basic persuasive rhetoric. I like TV; I like *knowing* things about TV. That includes knowing about unions composed of people I respect. He knows I have every artifact in NSX memorized, but has *he* seen the photo of Victor and Judy, who went into script doctoring after *NS* was canceled, at the front picket lines of the WGA strike in the summer of 1988—one of Kane's last public appearances?

"I still don't understand what this has to do with us," I object. "Those are adults working full-time jobs, and they don't run their unions out of bowling alley bars."

"We're working full-time for the next three months, and business unions aren't the only way to unionize," Efraín answers without explaining anything.

"Business unions?" asks Naomi.

"Isn't Big Business what unions are working against? Or did I miss an episode of *Succession*?" asks Lola. "Just kidding. I missed every episode of *Succession*."

"Business unions aren't Big Business. They're the big, official organizations Elisha mentioned—monster conglomerates in their own right who make *unionizing* their business model. They're nonprofit, sure, but still concerned about their organizational bottom line, not negotiating the best contract for their members. It's not always workers taking control of their own workplaces."

"In other words," I say, harsher than I actually feel, "those unions *aren't* a precursor to seizing the means of production."

"Neither are solidarity unions," Efraín snaps, and *there.* That obsidian-sharp edge limning his tone, barely a blip on the Mohs hardness scale, but even this flicker of flinty irritation is so much more familiar than the Efraín of the past twelve hours.

"What's a solidarity union?" Naomi asks, with the same innocence she'd ask it in a social studies classroom.

Efraín explains, "Solidarity unions operate on the principle that workers can improve the workplace as a collective, without the middlemen. They challenge bosses without red tape. There doesn't have to be an official bargaining unit because the end goal isn't always a contract."

"Then what *is* the end goal?"

"Little hits. Small, tactical collective actions add up to major improvements in working conditions."

I mutter, "I've never heard you advocate for incremental change before."

"Think of it as a covert hostile takeover. Solidarity unions can operate underground."

A "covert hostile takeover" still sounds businesslike. Workplace-appropriate skirmishes at the outskirts of corporate warfare, but this? Efraín's describing unionizing as guerrilla warfare.

"And you want us to organize a solidarity union at the Nuclear Seasons Experience," I summarize.

Efraín nods as he polishes off his Coke.

"But *why*? Today was our *third day* of work. We saved Naomi's job and got the dress code changed for *everyone.* It's over. We won."

"You said it—incremental change isn't *winning.*"

"That's definitely not what I—"

"Haven't you been paying attention to all the little shit? They didn't give us our second legally mandated break on Wednesday. I overheard Gwen getting into a debate with Dan about whether her polka-dot Mary Janes qualify as black shoes under the dress code. Anya misgendered you in front of everyone, and Dagny . . ."

Now Efraín tries to meet my eyes, but I look away.

"I bet if we poked around," he says, "we'd hear we aren't the only workers with grievances."

Part of me is grateful that he's not proposing we unionize without consulting employees who've been there long enough to earn Employee of the Month, but the rest of me is still in shock.

"Unionizing on the DL?" Lola laughs. "Love that for us."

Naomi asks, "But wouldn't official recognition be a prerequisite for legal protection?"

"Nope. This is legal," Efraín replies with a snort. "For all the ways that corporations, Congress, and the courts have found to screw workers over, concerted activity is protected.

That means two or more workers acting together—recognized by management or not—have rights. Specifically, the right not to be fired for concerted activity."

"Like all of us dyeing or bedazzling our hair," Lola says.

Naomi frowns. "When you said they couldn't fire *all* of us—"

"It would've been illegal." My mouth is dry, but my hand's shaking too much to lift my cup. I stare at Efraín. "That's what you're saying, right? You knew."

"Companies don't follow the law. They count on workers not knowing their rights, not feeling *empowered*—"

"Why didn't you just say—"

Would I have done anything differently if Efraín had told me from the beginning that the hair dye rebellion wasn't the riot I was imagining so much as the equivalent of a constitutionally protected peaceful assembly? Does that distinction change anything now?

I blink back to the table, where Lola's piling nacho fixings, Naomi's rearranging condiment bottles, and Efraín's wearing the smuggest smirk I've ever seen.

So, I ask the question we've all been tap-dancing around. "You called us a union. What is it you're proposing we *do*, exactly?"

"I thought you'd never ask."

PART II

EDUCATE

TEN

"ALL RIGHT, HERE'S YOUR RECEIPT, A MUSEUM MAP, AND AN admission sticker. Make sure you wear the sticker somewhere we can see it, like the stylish fashion statement it is. We have guided tours led by our highly knowledgeable, slightly geeky docents every hour. If you'd prefer to explore at your own pace, you're free to do so. Remember, no food or drink in the galleries. Pictures are not only welcome but highly encouraged, just no flash photography, please. And no touching the artifacts. Unless you have any questions, you're good to go. We hope you enjoy your time here at the Nuclear Seasons Experience."

The thirtysomething guest stares at me, wide-eyed. I'm not sure what's confusing. I've sold enough tickets in the past two weeks to get comfortable with the spiel and stop talking at that nervous, patter-song auctioneer pace.

The man sweeps his pile of tomorrow's ephemera off the counter. He smiles and says, "Thank you, miss."

My own smile doesn't falter. It's set with quake wax; it

would take more than one tremulous, likely unintentional microaggression to—

It's fine. I'm still smiling as he places the sticker on his button-down with a genteel nod.

My first few days at the register, every honorific that guests aimed at museum staff baffled me, until I realized they were often accompanied by a telltale twang—that southern hospitality mentality that we Californian heathens tend to assume was gone with *Gone with the Wind.* I guess they'd just call it *manners.*

Still, I've lost count of how many times I've been *miss'*d—and only miss'd. I've kept smiling, though I couldn't be further from meaning it.

Because it's not just occasional southerners doling out gendered honorifics.

Maybe five transactions back, I sold a membership to a family from Sebastopol. Before I closed the deal, the couple debated the fiscal merits amongst themselves, as if I weren't there. Except I *was* there, in their domestic spat, as an expert witness. *She says this will save us money,* the husband said. *She probably gets a commission,* the wife said.

I said I sold the membership. Do I really need to spell this out?

"Damn, Eli, you're getting good at that."

I startle at Lola's voice. I have no idea how she got behind the counter without me noticing. I clear my throat with a tight, asthmatic cough. "Pardon?"

"The 'rules and regulations' speech." Lola taps her acrylic nails on the counter. "You're doing jokes now."

"I'm a regular Mrs. Maisel." It's not like I practiced in the mirror every night that first week, no siree.

"I'd watch your comedy special."

I scoff on instinct, a not-so-witty retort on the tip of my tongue when I remember that humor is easy for Lola. Just like she can befriend someone with a single handshake, she laughs like it's her favorite thing to do. Despite her airy tone, however, she isn't laughing now.

"You okay?" she asks, quieter. If she heard my spiel, then she heard what came after it.

"Fine." It's not a lie. It may be a joke, but it's not a lie. "What are you doing here, anyway?"

"I'm covering your fifty-two."

"Already?" I squint at my watch. It doesn't feel like lunchtime, despite Lola's use of the museum's official walkie-talkie break code: 52 for lunch breaks, 51 for scheduled morning and afternoon breaks, and 55 for emergency bathroom breaks.

"Time flies when you're having fun?"

"Fun," I echo, remembering the kind, oblivious sincerity in that man's eyes. "Right."

"Save the chitchat for when you're off the clock, girls," interrupts Ford, my ticketing partner du jour. "We're already behind schedule, so make sure you're back on time."

I bite my tongue—for more reasons than one. Ford has yet to learn that I am literally the least likely person to come back late from a break, but this is my punishment for getting caught up in illicit concerted activities. No one takes me seriously as an employee.

Ford also doesn't take me seriously as a guy, but Ford's a dick to everyone.

I clock out as soon as I'm in the stairwell and set a timer for twenty-five minutes. That five-minute buffer should give me time to clean up and get back downstairs.

I open the refrigerator, hoping it will leech the heat from my cheeks in the time it takes for me to fish out my lunch box. Meanwhile, Efraín doesn't clock out until the microwave's halfway through defrosting his Amy's Pad Thai bowl.

"Planning on closing the door anytime soon?" Efraín asks.

I slam the door, but I don't dignify Efraín with a response. We sit at the same table—or he sits next to me. Neither of us has an appetite for conversation.

Stanley rounds the corner whistling the *NS* theme song, and soon the *glug-a-glug-glug* of the water cooler fills the silence.

But if I've learned one thing about Stanley, it's that he likes to talk. He'll strike up a conversation with anyone, though even he can't spin conversational gold from my laconic misadventures in water cooler talk.

Said water cooler groans to a halt, and I catch a flash of silver in Stanley's palm.

Even from halfway across the room, I know it isn't a water

bottle. I'm about to file the observation away in my mental archive, but once again, I've forgotten that I do not keep the universe alone.

Efraín leans halfway across the table. "Hey, is that a—"

Stanley darts another glance at the open space where the door would be, if management believed employees could be trusted with doors.

"Why did you fill a flask with water?" Efraín asks, surprisingly quiet for a boy whose "inside voice" rivals my "outside voice."

Stanley takes the chair next to mine. "Can you boys keep a secret?"

I'm not just a locked vault but a hermetically sealed doomsday bunker. I know Efraín can keep a secret because he wouldn't be able to pull off any of his pranks without covert tactical planning that would put four-star generals to shame.

"Why are you looking at me like you think I'm going to tattle?" I whisper to Efraín.

"Because you did."

"What? When?"

"Freshman year, you told the librarian—"

"Because you were making her job harder! Ms. Petri was already planning a display on banned books. You didn't need to raid the shelves and bring in half your personal library. If you'd just *asked*—"

"What if she'd said no?"

"Then you would've found another way." The rebuke has evaporated from my tone, leaving only raw, gritty sedimental sentiment, and Efraín's jaw slackens. I couldn't testify under oath which of us looks away first.

"We can keep a secret," Efraín confirms.

"I trust you." If Stanley's put off by our bickering, he hides it well. He surreptitiously pulls out a hip flask, burnished silver, etched with a familiar radiation warning symbol. It could pass as a novelty item from the gift shop, if we sold flasks.

"You know it's against museum policy to bring beverages into the galleries, right? But when I'm leading tours, it's nonstop talking-and-walking, between the galleries, where there's no shade, or inside them, where everything's humidity-controlled. My throat gets dry; I get dehydrated. I can't abandon my tour group to go to the drinking fountain, and the walkie's only for emergencies. Getting a little thirsty doesn't qualify."

"But you're not talking about 'getting a little thirsty,'" Efraín cuts in. "You said you get *dehydrated*."

Stanley shrugs.

"If you feel thirsty, you're already dehydrated," I point out. "It's a medical issue. Management has to make accommodations—"

"For real medical conditions," Stanley agrees. "TJ's diabetic, so he has special dispensation from HR to keep a water bottle on him at all times. But I don't have any relevant medical conditions."

"Just the condition of being human," Efraín says.

"And needing water to perform innumerable bodily functions," I add.

Stanley smiles faintly. "Management doesn't see it that way."

"So you took matters into your own hands," Efraín says, leaning forward, elbows braced on the table.

"So to speak."

The flask is small, not much larger than my phone.

Efraín actually asks the volume, his tone cool, speculative, and, God, I wish I didn't know where this was going.

"Eight ounces, if memory serves."

If *my* memory serves, eight ounces is a single "serving" of water. Ten percent, at best, of modern medical recommendations for daily water intake. Still, small as it is, the flask doesn't fit under Stanley's palm.

It begs the question: "Isn't a flask a bit conspicuous?"

"A French tuck hides a multitude of sins," Stanley says.

I'm deep down the "but a French tuck doesn't hide hips" dysphoria rabbit hole when Efraín says, "Hydration isn't a *sin*."

It's not the words so much as his tone that magnetizes my attention. He's just so unbearably *earnest*; it hurts to look at him, but I can't yank my gaze from his profile. I've never met anyone else who can flip from dry sarcasm about all that ails our society to such naked compassion from one sentence to the next.

Multitudes and contradictions. It shouldn't leave me

surprised, let alone breathless. If anything, I should be profoundly worried, because Efraín's brand of empathy never stops at righteous indignation; it always leads to action, usually in the form of activist hijinks, from hauling his personal library into the school library to dyeing his hair pink.

Efraín already said he wanted to start a union, poke around, listen to the year-round staff for grievances and hopefully recruit some of them to the Cause—once he settles on an actionable cause, that is. Now he's getting *ideas.*

"I know water's important," Stanley says, "but try telling that to the powers that be."

"You said TJ got HR approval with a doctor's note, so they *do* take medical concerns seriously," I say. "If you just went to HR and told them what you told us, showed them studies about dehydration—"

Efraín snorts.

"What?"

"You still think management can be reasoned with?"

"I didn't say that."

"But you believe it."

I think about Dagny and Anya and shake my head. I'm not convinced reason would work on either of them. But we're not talking about management; we're talking about HR.

Maybe human resources would understand that employees are humans who can't do their jobs when they're unwell.

Efraín's saying something to Stanley—and maybe I should be listening; maybe I should be concerned that he's got the same look on his face that he had in Foxglove Apothecary's hair care aisle—but I'm light-years away.

Because I have an idea of my own.

ELEVEN

LOLA KIDNAPS ME AFTER WORK.

Call it a crime of opportunity. Efraín takes his foldable bike and pedals off to some activist meeting in Sonoma, and Naomi asks Lola to drop her off at Sugarloaf for golden hour birding.

Then, instead of taking a left at the town square, Lola neatly parallel parks in front of the Starbucks, which always has open spaces because locals know better, and Mrs. Morse at the Plumcot Inn directs tourists to the Last Drip Café for their coffee needs.

There must be a spurious motive in play. Lola wouldn't think twice about taking a two-block detour to drop me off at home even if she had to loop back to run an errand.

"Bring your wallet," Lola instructs.

My wallet and I groan preemptively.

At least, this is a distraction from obsessing about the email I've been mentally composing to Billy in HR ever since lunch.

Lola stops to listen to the town troubadour, crooning some indie folk song that was probably popular when he was our age. I'm anxious and on edge, tapping my foot to the unfamiliar rhythm.

Perfectly charmed, Lola tucks literal cash in his splayed guitar case. If I didn't work behind a cash register, I wouldn't believe anyone carried physical money anymore.

When the song ends, Lola squeals and claps, bracelets jangling and rings clacking. She chats with the troubadour—Joel, maybe?—like they're old friends. He happily accommodates her song request, and half a dozen people gather to listen as he plays.

Lola's still gossiping with Vanessa from Blushing Blooms while I'm trying to walk away. I'm exhausted from work and overstimulated from live music under the summer sun.

Finally, Lola leads me a few storefronts down. Tucked between Blushing Blooms and Taqueria el Pueblecito, Nine Lives thrift store donates a significant percentage of their profits to the Sonoma County Humane Society—and to the care of the two elderly cats who make napping spots in the strangest places around the store.

The store smells equally of catnip and mothballs. Irene waves at us from the register and Lola politely asks after Pippin's recent feline herpes flare-up.

Impatiently, I tap the ill-fitting saddle shoe I bought at this very store. "What are we doing here?"

Lola smiles at me like this is something we do every day. "Why, just some light gender retail therapy."

"I don't understand." *Shopping* is a word I associate with panic attacks, not therapy.

Lola clucks her tongue. "That's the problem, babe." She leads me through labyrinthine racks, into the heart of retail misery. "Have you been wearing the same pair of shorts every day?"

I look down at my shabby khaki cargo shorts. "Maybe?"

Lola sighs. "Eli."

"I wash them every other workday. I know Efraín would say that's a criminal waste of water, except I'm honestly still unclear on whether he believes in *crime*, so—"

"*I'm* saying it's a crime against fashion." Lola's already sifting through a rack of men's shorts.

"Look, I can't afford a shopping spree, not even a thrift store edition."

"Have you spent a single cent you've earned this summer? Or has every paycheck made a one-way trip to your savings account?"

I'm guessing my weekly discount ticket to Blue Plate Picture Palace wouldn't meet Lola's definition of discretionary spending.

"Look, I need to save everything I earn this summer for—" I hesitate. One of the things I hate about living in a small town is that everyone knows my medical history. That's why I want top surgery in the rearview before I start college.

It's not even about passing or not. It's about feeling like I'm trapped in the emperor's new clothes, no matter how many people close to me insist everything is fine.

But this is Lola, who overheard a customer and a coworker misgender me this afternoon in the span of thirty seconds. Lola, who is trans and gave me a coming-out care package. Lola, who unironically implied we're ride-or-dies.

Telling her the truth is the least I can do. "I'm saving for top surgery. Summer wages will cover the down payment, and hopefully, I'll get the internship to pay for the surgery itself. Moms will contribute as much as they can, but they can't afford—"

"Eli, I know."

"You . . . what?"

Lola looks up from the rack. "I didn't hack your accounting spreadsheets, but I assumed that was the reason—I just knew."

"How?"

"Because, I don't know, it is a truth universally acknowledged that every trans boy in possession of—"

"An unfortunate chest?"

"—must be in want of a top surgeon. We don't have to talk about it." Lola thrusts a fistful of hangers at me. "Don't worry about the money. We're not going to burn a hole in your top surgery fund, promise."

"I always worry about money." I wring the hangers between my hands. "I worry about everything."

"Listen, I come from generations of professional coupon clippers. Trust me, okay? I'm just picking things for you to try on."

She passes me another hanger.

"I don't need to try these on to know they're definitely too small."

"Ah, the classic T-boy problem."

"I know. My hips are—"

Lola mutters something under her breath, though I can't hear over Irene's New Age playlist. "Oldest urban legend in the lookbook. Transmascs wearing baggy clothes to hide your curves when it only makes you look curvier. It's Fat Girl Fashion 101: Wear clothes that *fit.* That's the best way to minimize your chest and your hips. Not skintight, but your actual size."

"That's the problem," I retort. "*Nothing* fits. I'm too short, chubby, and curvy for men's clothes, but I can't even wear women's clothes anymore because testosterone redistributes fat. So the chub's in my stomach, rather than my hips or my butt, but my pelvis is still an evolutionary blight. Even my *bones*—"

"Eli. Breathe."

"No, thank you," I whisper, petulant.

Lola snorts, but she steers me into the dressing room. She parks me in the chair, six pairs of shorts piled over my lap, while she leans back against the mirror, blocking my view of myself.

Then she's just looking at me, and I'm looking at her, still in the NSX uniform. The women's fitted polo paired with her paper-bag-waisted shorts successfully creates the illusion of an hourglass figure.

"I'm not going to ask if this is about what happened earlier," Lola says, "because I know . . ."

She knows it happens every day.

"Wait," I interject, finally putting two and two together and making *for fuck's sake*, "is that what *this* is about? What happened before lunch?"

"I wanted to check in. Make sure you were okay."

I don't understand the point of these constant check-ins. Lola, Efraín, Ma—everyone in my life who doesn't have alexithymia, basically—and their pathological need to ask after someone's feelings whenever something *happens.* I don't understand, which is the entire definition of alexithymia: difficulty understanding one's own emotions and those of others. I also don't understand the point because asking doesn't *change anything.* It just means I have to do the cognitive labor of deciphering my emotions and then covering up the ugly bits.

Lola asking how I feel about something that happened five hours ago doesn't change what happened, or that it will happen again.

Unless that's the point. Lola called it "the classic T-boy problem." She's giving me fashion tips to make my silhouette more masculine. Maybe this isn't a run-of-the-mill check-in; maybe it's a misguided attempt to *help*.

"So, you brought me shopping for 'gender retail therapy' to teach me what style shorts to wear to pass better? So I get misgendered less often?"

Lola doesn't even have the courtesy to be offended by my misdirected outburst. She just sets one hand on her hip and lifts an eyebrow. "You done yet?"

I shut my eyes, just for a moment, just to breathe of my own free will. "Sorry. You didn't deserve—that wasn't about you."

"Oh, I know. Just making sure you know, too."

"I do," I admit quietly. I can't meet her eyes, so I study the glittering gold tinsel extensions interspersed among her curls. The dash of sparkle suits her. She's been experimenting with new hair accessories every week in continued solidarity with Naomi.

I should compliment her. That's what friends do, but we're not friends. She may have kidnapped me this afternoon, but we're not friends.

I know Lola's checking in out of compassion, from a place of genuine empathy—sympathy, in this case. Because Lola cares about proper nouns (read: real people). Lola cares that I, Eli Goldstein, was misgendered in our shared workplace.

On the other side of the dressing room curtain, a bell jingles. Loud voices and easy laughs. Grouchy yowls as the cats rouse.

"You want to know the real reason I brought you here, Eli?" Lola asks. "Finding a cute new outfit always gives me a sweet gender euphoria sugar rush, so I thought it might cheer you up, too.

"I don't *need* cheering up. I'm not—"

"Not upset?"

"I'm fine."

"Sure, Eli," she replies with a salty-sweet smile. "Just know that you can talk to me. About any of it."

We both know I won't. The last time we really talked about the Struggle was when we collaborated on a rec list of "actually good trans films" for the school newsletter. Spoiler: It was a short list.

But Lola's trying to be a good person, and I'm just trying to feel like a person at all.

Real people talk. I try, "So, what do I need to know about these shorts?"

Lola smiles, bright, toothy, and warmer than apple pie. "Start with the corduroy."

TWELVE

"THE COAST IS CLEAR," EFRAÍN ANNOUNCES TEN MINUTES INTO our Tuesday morning gift shop shift. "You can take out your phone."

The barn is a ghost town. Tuesdays are the museum's slowest day, and the gift shop's lucky to see a single sale in the first hour. Now that we're a few weeks into the summer, on a slow day with a skeleton crew, Anya trusts two newbies to run the gift shop alone.

I should've been suspicious when Efraín offered to fold the new shipment of T-shirts before I could reach for the folding board. He's using it to shield his phone from prying eyes.

I've been itching to check my phone ever since the workday began because I have been waiting *four days* for a reply from Billy in HR.

But Efraín doesn't know about my email. No one does. And while I'm waiting for official communiqués from HR,

Efraín's been blowing up my phone with texts to a new "Ride or Die" group chat, which Lola created a few nights ago.

It was a mash-up of gossip and memes from Lola, and the occasional scenic photo from Naomi, until this morning when Efraín suggested that we hold a union meeting this week.

Every notification I received from the back seat of Ma's Subaru set my blood boiling because they had me obsessing over all the less savory reasons Billy might email me. Because if this were truly safe, Efraín wouldn't have instructed everyone to switch to an end-to-end encrypted messaging app for future union communications.

An invitation to a coup—a conspiracy, at best—and no one bothered to ask for my RSVP. It's a foregone conclusion that no one lucky enough to receive an exclusive invite to join Efraín's merry band of troublemakers would ever turn him down.

Not that I've made up my mind to turn him down, but I have other things on my mind.

"You should check the chat," Efraín says after I've logged into my sales account. "Lola's worried you were abducted by aliens. Naomi thinks you locked yourself in 'the compartment,' whatever that is."

I bite my tongue to stop myself from reminding him that "The Compartment" is the fan-favorite, homoerotic bottle episode of *NS* filmed entirely in the silo lavatory.

Instead, I say, "The shirts need to be tagged, too."

"I can do it." Honestly, if anyone's been abducted by aliens, it's Efraín, who has been almost chipper and surprisingly agreeable, except for his aversion to assembly lines. "But do you really think it matters whether we're done in fifteen minutes or twenty?"

"Does your grand plan to improve working conditions start with sabotaging T-shirt sales?"

He huffs a laugh, as if I just cracked a joke. "There's no reason to break our backs when we're not going to see a customer before noon."

"Dan might come by."

"Dan doesn't care."

"Ford would."

"And you care what Ford thinks . . . why?"

I don't *care* what Ford thinks, but I'd prefer to stay off his radar. After a dozen misgendering incidents, Ford's never once apologized, not even the time Stanley corrected him. It's not that I want the apology so much as an acknowledgment that it was an accident.

"I care whether Ford tanks my chances at getting the internship or leading tours this summer instead of . . ."

"Instead of hawking useless consumer-bait clutter masquerading as commemorative memorabilia at an obscene markup?" Efraín holds a shirt that reads: "Half-Lives Matter."

I wince. "No, yeah, that's offensive."

"Congratulations, snowflake, for noticing."

"Thank you, Snowball, for that high praise."

Efraín's brows furrow.

"Snowball as in—"

"*Animal Farm*, I know," Efraín replies with a predictable eye roll. "Just seemed like a weird choice coming from you. Low-hanging fruit."

I don't know why I lowkey implied Efraín is a tankie, either; I know he's not.

"You really should text proof of life, though."

"They know I'm at work."

"Didn't stop me."

"Yeah, because Lola's your best friend."

"She's your friend, too." He doesn't look up from his folding.

I frown at him, the tag gun and sticker sheets still lying on the counter, and this whole bizarro conversation in which Efraín expresses an interest in my social life rather than just crashing every facet of my academic and professional lives without ever—well. Getting *personal.* "What makes you say that?"

He frowns at me like I've said something incredibly obtuse. "You guys have been hanging out, right?"

"Once," I say, instinctively running my sweaty palms over my new-to-me corduroy khaki shorts. I would've thought the texture would aggravate me, but it's just the opposite. The worn corduroy is soft, the ridges pleasantly smooth against my hands.

They were the first shorts Lola suggested I try on, a size smaller and three inches shorter than any pair I would've picked on my own. Lola practically squealed when she saw them on me, insisting that the slimmer fit worked while reassuring me that there was nothing scandalous about showing my kneecaps.

But one hour at Nine Lives doesn't make us besties, and even if Lola's and my friendship has leveled up, it doesn't explain why Efraín's taking an interest.

After all, his messages to the group chat aren't harmless memes, salacious gossip, or pretty pictures. Every notification I checked before I clocked in was just him steering the conversation back to organizing; it was the most single-minded I've ever seen him about scheduling.

But now, he's doing work and cracking jokes and giving me the benefit of the doubt despite my dour mood, which isn't about him so much as my anxiety about an impending email notification.

Maybe I'm not being fair to Efraín, but he's not being straight with me.

"You're awfully obsessed with the chat this morning," I observe. "Why don't you just ask me what you really want to ask me?"

Efraín glances at me askance, a sly smile tugging at his lips. "Knowing you, you've already done your research. I bet you've got all the organizing handbooks memorized," he says, which is presumptuous but also weirdly complimentary. "So, you know we're not supposed to talk about baby socialist fight club on the clock."

That's why he wants me to check the chat here and now. We can avoid talking about specifics on the floor if I use our snazzy, secure e2e messaging system.

Once I've cracked the math, Efraín's actual words catch up to me. "Sorry, 'baby socialist fight club'?"

"That's what Lola's calling it, and we do need a code name."

"How about literally anything else? Give me the day, and I'll give you ten alternatives," I blurt.

"I'll give you until the first meeting," Efraín says. "Just tell me which day works for you."

No surprise Efraín's willing to bend his own rules about security and best practices when he gets impatient—or hyperfocused.

I can see the shape of his obsession, just how fixated he is on organizing here. I still feel like I'm missing half the story—I don't know *why* this matters so much to him—though I can acknowledge that it does. He's proved that through his actions.

But I can't get past the fact that his biggest concern is organizing this covert union meeting, while I'm struggling to just be here, doing this job, not knowing how many times I will be misgendered today. How will HR respond to my concerns? Will my *complaint* affect my chances of getting the internship?

No matter how careful I am, this might all backfire catastrophically. I can't afford to be reckless—not now.

Efraín deserves to know that. He's waiting for me to tell him a day, and I just *can't.*

"Listen, when I dyed my hair—" I clear my throat and keep my eyes on my own work. "Maybe I gave you the wrong impression, but I'm not sure I can be part of your Three Musketeers operation."

"Four," Efraín says, clipped and rapier sharp.

"Pardon?" I ask, but I know what's coming.

The bickering is automatic because we've done this so many times before. Any and every time he gives me the benefit of the doubt, lets his guard down, and offers me a way in, I trip the wire; then Efraín flips the switch and shuts down.

Honestly? I probably deserve it.

"You said 'Three Musketeers.' There were four."

I haven't read Dumas since I was ten, but I know what he means. The "three" in Dumas's *Three Musketeers* is a misnomer. Athos, Porthos, and Aramis may be the titular trio, but d'Artagnan is the protagonist, the hero who *tells* the story.

"I'm no d'Artagnan."

"No, you're not."

"Thanks for that."

"Sorry, were you waiting for me to disagree and soothe your conscience?" Efraín is staring at me with such intensity that I worry he's trying to pull a Medusa act. "I don't get you. I thought you were relieved to hear we couldn't get fired for organizing. You should be on board with making your precious museum a better place when there's no real risk to you."

I cross my arms over my chest, suddenly unbearably self-conscious. "No real risk? You said bosses don't care what's legal."

"You really don't get it, do you?"

"I get that that's a rhetorical question," I mutter.

Efraín isn't folding anymore, just white-knuckling one of those borderline white supremacist T-shirts, which is, painfully ironically, black. Darker fabric's less likely to show wrinkles.

"Tell me," I insist, resigned rather than angry. "What don't I get, precisely?"

Efraín stares at me for a moment longer, fury pulling him taut, tense, poised to—

"You know what?" he snaps. "I can't. Because I don't know how to talk to you. I don't know how to *get through* to you. Because whenever I talk about what's right or fair or *just* . . . Your eyes don't glaze over like other people's; you just look like you want to give me some erudite lecture as cover for an ad hominem attack about what a hypocrite I am for talking about ideas in the abstract. You say you want me to use *proper nouns.*"

I haven't heard anyone talk about grammar with such derision since—well, the last time Efraín and I argued about nouns.

But Efraín runs on anger; it fuels him. Hell, if scientists figured out how to siphon Efraín's anger, they could probably power a small country and dramatically reduce global dependence on fossil fuels.

"When I get specific," Efraín says, because, well, he never actually stopped, "when I talk about people you *know,* the problems they're facing, and what we could do to *help* them—you don't care. That's when *you* go off about how *it doesn't make sense* that corporations, politicians, or bosses don't want to help people."

"Now who's resorting to ad hominem attacks?" Then I remember this is my workplace, not a playground. "Sorry," I say, which is a word I use even less often than Efraín does. "I'm not trying to treat this like some APUSH debate."

"You just can't help it," Efraín replies, wry as day-old rye. "Just pass me those shirts so I can actually *help.*"

It must be a minor miracle that Efraín pushes his stack across the counter without any grumbling.

I assume that's it—that we've successfully dropped the matter without breaking any eggs. I sort price tags and double-check shirt sizes, and he folds. It's a brittle silence, delicate as Mom's Vanillekipferl cookies.

I'm not expecting me to be the one to crumble until I'm halfway through the first sentence. "What I don't understand is why we need to have a union meeting. I still don't understand why we need a union. You talked about little hits, but what does that even mean, practically speaking?"

He surveys the still-empty lobby and says, "It's about fixing broken things."

"Like the anemic coffee machine in the break room?"

"No—I don't know, maybe, but didn't you hear what Stanley said about his hidden hip flask? That it's the least obvious way to carry water when he's giving tours—because water bottles are banned?"

"Yes," I say, remembering how Stanley mentioned that HR has the power to make medical exceptions, "but—"

"It shouldn't have to be that way," Efraín interjects, as if *how things should be* has anything to do with this. He slams the folding board down on the counter, as if casual force will best punctuate his point. "An injury to one is an injury to all."

"Is that Marx or Dumas?"

"The Industrial Workers of the World." Efraín frowns. "Why would you—"

"Just sounds a hell of a lot like 'all for one and—'"

"C'mon, Elisha. Don't you see? We can do *good* here."

A one-man work stoppage in our assembly line, Efraín's staring at me, and there's nothing to distract me from the shimmer in his eyes.

He believes his own swill, while I've never cared about being the hero when I'm just trying to get by in a world that is hostile to my very existence, where my government keeps trying to legally erase me, where I'm desperately trying to access health care that might become illegal before I can afford it. I can justify the chip on my shoulder until the cows come home.

However, I'm not oblivious. Just because I don't want to play the hero doesn't mean the rest of the world's on pause. We're all trapped in this horror movie together, and I can admit, in the privacy of my mind, that my conscience can't always process all these multitudes and contradictions.

I have a vintage *Star Wars* "bad feeling" about what I'm about to do, and then—my phone vibrates in my pocket.

The jolt skewers my coordination, almost piercing the tagging gun needle through my finger. Thankfully, Efraín doesn't notice. With a shuddery breath, I sneak a glance at my phone. My lock screen lights up with the new email notification.

> Billy Lo
> Re: Meeting
>
> Hello Eli,
> Sure, I'd be happy to meet with you. Let me just check my calendar and cross-reference with Anya re: the GSA schedule so we can find a good time to pull you off the fl . . .

I stuff my phone back in my pocket and pick up the tag gun. I keep my eyes on the label because I'd really rather not waste that HR meeting on a workers' comp claim.

"Friday," I say, despite the pit of anxiety still threatening to swallow my stomach whole.

"What?" Efraín asks, flat and flummoxed.

"I have something Thursday afternoon. So it has to be Friday. We could all go somewhere after work. Maybe the diner? That might be too public, but—"

"Too public *for what*?"

I look at him, still folded over his workstation, face half-hidden behind his perpetually, perfectly windswept hair that I didn't think anyone could achieve outside of a professional film studio. "For a union meeting, of course."

"So we can count on you to be there?" He's asking so fervently, like it means something, and the last time he looked at me with this set-it-all-on-fire intensity, he was hurling hair dye at me in the gazebo.

"Yes," I answer, hoping I'm not making a promise I can't afford to keep. "I'll be there. Unus pro omnibus, omnes pro uno. All for one—"

"And one for all."

"Got it in one, d'Artagnan."

He wrinkles his nose. "How am I—"

"You're the hotheaded, idealistic one, right?" I smile, though I doubt it reaches my eyes.

If Efraín hasn't figured it out yet, far be it from me to tell him that no matter what the rest of us do or say, he's always going to steal the story.

THIRTEEN

"THANK YOU FOR MEETING WITH ME," BILLY FROM HR SAYS ON Friday morning, as if getting this meeting wasn't a quest of high fantasy proportions.

Ten minutes before my scheduled break, a man came up to the gift shop counter empty-handed. He let me give a whole spiel about snow globes before asking if now was a good time for our chat, as if I had any control of my time. So much for my legally mandated break—not to mention the prepared talking points I printed out days ago and stuck in my cubby, upstairs in the barn.

"Given the sensitive nature of the situation," Billy's saying, "I thought you might appreciate some privacy."

True. I would've appreciated an invitation to his office or the pint-size conference room next to Anya's office. I would've settled for one of the picnic tables behind the barn, precariously close to the dumpsters.

Instead, the venue Billy has selected for our meeting is

the most remote corner of the museum campus. The air is thick with the aroma of wild roses and golden poppies. We're seated on a cool granite bench. It'd be idyllic, if it weren't for the tombstone.

This bucolic little courtyard, sheltered by tall trellises wound with grapevines, is Victor Kane's final resting place. That's his grave, five feet away. Forty-two years summed up in the tidy epitaph "Beloved Husband, Devoted Father" and his navy squadron, surrounded by perfunctory Hebrew inscriptions, topped with an intricate Star of David.

I've been here before, of course. I've placed creek pebbles on his headstone and clucked my tongue at the bouquets of flowers left by other people.

"I was hoping," Billy says, "that you could tell me more about how you've been settling in. Anya mentioned a few incidents. She said she felt terrible if she'd done anything that made you feel you needed to go to HR instead of speaking to her personally. Not that you did anything wrong," he adds quickly, "or that you're *obligated* to talk to anyone, but . . ."

Personally, I only trail off when I lose my train of thought—or when all my trains of thought go off the rails. But I've been around the track enough to know that other people trail off when they want you to fill the silence for them.

I need to play Billy's game if I want him to take me seriously. "Anya isn't the problem." She's *part* of the problem, but systemic, institutionalized transphobia's a hell of a thing. "I'd just prefer to keep this confidential."

"Of course," Billy assures me, a portrait of concern. "That's what I'm here for."

I look up and meet Billy's eyes.

"Anya's right. There have been incidents. Mostly microaggressions, most likely accidental, but transphobic incidents nonetheless."

The silence builds, barometric pressure increasing in the microbiome of this trellis enclosure-cum-grave-site.

"Can you tell me about those incidents?"

"Misgendering, mostly. Pronouns and honorifics. Getting grouped in with the girls. Some snide comments. It's not—" *that bad*, I don't say. It isn't that bad, objectively, but I don't want to explain how *not that bad* accumulates. Microaggressions accrue like interest on a subprime loan. You can ignore it at first, tell yourself it's a problem for the future, but sooner or later, the debt will destroy you.

"Do you mind if I ask . . ." Billy scoots closer and lowers his voice, which is unnecessary because we are utterly alone except for the bees and, perhaps, Kane's ghost. "Who is it that's misgendering you?"

"Depends on the day. I was told this was a trans-friendly work environment, but I don't *feel* particularly safe. I know these sound like small issues, but—"

"I understand," Billy says, "and that's why I need to understand the scope of what's happening. Who are you having issues with? Is there a pattern? Is anyone giving you trouble about which bathroom you're using or . . . ?"

"It's not an isolated issue."

"I can't help if you don't give me anything to work with here. I understand that accidents can happen with anyone, but is anyone intentionally disrespecting your gender?"

I understand what Billy's asking me. He wants a bad guy because it's easier to make someone take a corporate sensitivity training course than to consider the possibility that workplace culture is transphobic. It shifts responsibility away from the museum; if I cough up a name, then it's one bad egg as opposed to avian flu in the henhouse.

What Billy doesn't understand is that there's no such thing as a tidy crime scene or an easy verdict. How am I supposed to know in my heart of hearts if anyone commits a transphobic microaggression on purpose? No one's slinging slurs, not to my face, so what evidence does that leave?

What good would it do if I told Billy it was Anya in the break room with "Goldstein sisters" or Ford at ticketing with "she/her" or Zach from security outside the cash room with "good day, ladies"?

"I don't know if Anya told you," Billy whispers, conspiratorial. "I'm gay."

"Congratulations. I'm bi."

"Thank you, Eli, for trusting me with that."

Does he think this is some tearjerker coming out scene

in a gay movie? If my trans identity is public record, my bisexuality never needed a headline.

"What I'm trying to say," Billy says, "is that I understand what you're going through."

I sincerely doubt that. I can acknowledge his experience as a gay man of color who probably came of age in the shadow of the AIDS epidemic, while also knowing his and my experiences are radically different. If Efraín were here, he'd ad lib a lecture on intersectionality in the workplace, but why am I thinking about what Efraín would say?

I contacted HR because I want to solve this problem. If I had my talking points in front of me, I'd be doing a better job. Instead, I'm off message and frazzled, without having even presented my case. I've let myself get distracted by the mere whiff of managerial hearsay and the cloying floral fug to which I may be allergic.

"It's not just about these one-off, maybe-accidental exchanges with colleagues. When I'm on the clock, I'm out front, in public, selling tickets and souvenirs. We may be in NorCal, but our guests come from all over."

"Forty-seven states and thirty-nine countries just last month." Billy beams, regurgitating some quarterly sales report.

"In some of those places, it's illegal to be trans."

Billy frowns.

"A lot of people have never knowingly met a trans person,

or they look at me and they don't know *what* I am. They see me, listen to my voice, and draw their own conclusion. If they happen to read my name tag, they get confused."

"I haven't heard anything from security. Incidents with guests should be on file. Be honest. Are guests"—Billy drops his voice so low I can barely hear him over the buzzing in my ears—"*harassing you*?"

"That's the thing. It's *all* harassment."

Alarm outpaces his confusion. "What do you mean?"

"Legally. It's sexual harassment. I don't have the precise California legal code with me or the *Bostock v. Clayton* opinion"—if only I had the words of Neil fucking Gorsuch to bolster my point—"but transphobia in the workplace is sexual harassment. Discrimination on the basis of sex, by another name. It's illegal."

"Of course," Billy reassures me in a rush. "Your safety is our priority, always. If any guests have ever put you in danger . . ."

"Danger isn't something I can measure. One weekend, I tallied every time a guest misgendered me, but after ten in the first hour, I gave up. I *felt* each and every incident, and I had no way of knowing who was making an honest mistake or who, if I used the men's restroom on the floor, might use something other than words."

"NSX doesn't tolerate harassment."

Billy takes off his glasses and fogs the lenses with a hefty sigh. When he puts them back on, he's sitting straighter, no longer leaning in close, speaking *friend* to win my confidence. I recognize the mannequin set to his features as next-level customer service face.

"Listen, Eli," he says, low and conciliatory, preemptively soothing the bear he's about to poke. "I'm not sure what we can do about guests. We can ask staff members to be more mindful, but guests are another matter. Under special circumstances, it may be appropriate for management to step in. The rest of the time . . ."

I was expecting this. I came to Billy with a vague problem, and I didn't expect him to have answers. That's why I wrote up talking points. I am a problem-solver at heart.

I couldn't give Billy the specifics he wanted before, but now? I don't need Gorsuch quotes when I have this ace up my sleeve. "There was one incident. I wasn't sure if I should say anything, but . . ."

I'm not going to win an Emmy for my feigned ignorance performance, but I don't need to convince critics, just an audience of one.

From Billy's sharp intake of breath, I'm pretty sure it's working. "You can trust me."

So I confide in him. I tell him how I thought I could stop *incidents* before they started by wearing a pronoun button. Then I tell him how I met Dagny Kane: a kiss with a fist with "institutional messaging" tattooed on the knuckles.

"I triple-checked the employee handbook." For once, I

don't curse the high lilt in my voice. "There's nothing in the dress code about buttons."

"Buttons aren't part of the dress code."

"Exactly. Buttons *should* be part of the dress code. If I were *allowed* to wear a pronoun button, there would be fewer incidents with guests and fewer accidents with staff. It would decrease the transphobia I'm experiencing in the workplace without threatening customer experience. Unless the threat is the reminder that I'm a trans person, breathing the same air, existing in their space."

"Eli, no one is saying that."

"It's what I'm hearing."

"Eli, you're overestimating the power of HR. I'm not the right person to talk to about guest experience or branding or . . ."

"Buttons."

"Buttons, right. That's not my division."

"I thought safeguarding employees' safety was exactly your division."

Billy's customer service mask doesn't slip. "Eli, do you really believe guests are going to read a one-inch button on your shirt?"

"So you're not going to do anything?" My voice doesn't sound like an ingenue's now. It's low and rough, bitter like tea leaves at the bottom of an oversteeped cup.

"I just don't see that there's anything I *can* do."

Billy keeps talking, but I don't hear him over the rush of

fury in my blood. My jaw is ticking, temple throbbing, fingers drumming my thigh; my body is a cacophony of angry, discordant tics and tells.

What did I think would happen?

I overplayed my hand, getting emotional, bluffing litigious. I didn't have the cards, or maybe I did, but it doesn't matter. Isn't that what Efraín's been trying to tell me all along? There's no such thing as a winning hand in a rigged game. Management weights the dice, stacks the deck, and *wins*, laws be damned.

It's just so rich—the irony, that is.

I work in customer service, where the core operating principle is *the customer is always right.* The other side of that coin is that *the customer service worker must always be wrong.* On the floor, we laugh off minor customer complaints as soon as their backs are turned, but with senior management? When the customer service employee clashes with management, the customer service employee is always wrong.

"Well, Eli, please let me know if anything changes." Billy stands up. "It's been a pleasure."

Billy sticks out his hand, and I shake it. What else am I supposed to do?

FOURTEEN

IN THE SUMMER OF 1984, A FEW MONTHS AFTER THE NETWORK canceled *Nuclear Seasons* due to tepid ratings and a rumored threat from DARPA, a stubborn cub reporter cornered Victor Kane at his ranch. Or, more accurately, an entertainment tabloid columnist, hoping to score her ticket to the big leagues of legitimate journalism, blocked Kane's driveway with her rental car.

Kane abandoned his truck and walked along the highway shoulder. The reporter tailed him all the way to the town square, hurling questions like pebbles plucked from the side of the road. Just outside Lou's, Kane promised he'd answer one question if she got lost and told her friends to stay the hell away from him.

The reporter asked, "What was *Nuclear Seasons* really *about*?"

Never one to mince words, Kane said, "Alienation."

Then he walked into Lou's and slammed the glass door in the reporter's face.

For a show best described as "*X-Files* meets *Schitt's Creek* with a dash of *Twilight Zone*, gilded in borderline-neurotic Cold War anxiety," that cryptic interview and Kane's steadfast silence were as compelling a mystery as the Spectors' secrets.

That mystique attracted *Nuclear Seasons*'s modest but rabid cult following, composed mostly of neckbeard-sporting Kane acolytes. There was a resurgence with millennials and Zoomers when *NS* hit the streaming services. The haunting, dreamlike cinematography and nakedly veiled homoerotic subtext appealed to a certain sensibility.

I ship #hartie—the ship name for Art Spector and disaffected deputy sheriff Harry Davis—as much as any good queer, but that isn't why I love the show. I joke that *NS* made me trans, but it's true. Art Spector—or actor Sam Schatz—was my first early puberty confrontation with the singular "do you want to *do* them or *be* them?" conundrum that every young queer must inevitably face. My answer? Art—or Sam—was precisely the kind of not-so-nice Jewish boy I wanted to be.

But what does it say about me that my role model is the protagonist of a show about *alienation*?

It means that I'm in no mood for socializing after my meeting with Billy. Any motivation I had to go to Efraín's union meeting evaporated around the time Billy as good as told me HR's job is to ensure employees don't demand human rights.

So, I ask Lola to drop me off at home instead of the diner, and Efraín glowers at me in the rearview mirror, his eyes simmering like I've betrayed him personally, worse than when I refused to dye my hair.

But Lola's internal sensors go haywire, reading the increase in tension, and she suggests we table our meeting until tomorrow night, cool as you like. She bribes Efraín with the promise of her mama's tostones, which mollifies him just enough.

At home, Naomi immediately disappears into the backyard, and I retreat upstairs with Sputnik and every intention of burying my sorrows in old comfort hartie fics.

Moms have other plans. A little after eight, Ma's deep-bellied laughter and Mom's clinking industrial-size key ring reverberate through the entire house. It's not often they both come home before closing; most days, Mom opens, and Ma closes. But once or twice a month, Ma worries they've accidentally raised us as latchkey kids and Mom problem-solves by suggesting family "movie" night.

Except *Nuclear Seasons* is the only thing everyone's guaranteed to watch.

Tonight, upon Moms' arrival, Ma shouts that family movie night is starting in ten minutes, participation mandatory. I make a brief detour to the kitchen for sparkling water and two slabs of diner-baked challah Mom brought home.

In the family room, my seat is taken; Naomi is sitting in

the La-Z-Boy recliner. She makes a strange sight in the dim light, her back straight and her arms braced on the armrests. She doesn't look remotely comfortable.

I suppress the red flags, all the semaphore alerting my subconscious, and hold out one napkin-wrapped challah slice. "Trade you? Sustenance for a seat."

"I'm not hungry," Naomi replies. A bowl of trail mix sits on the end table beside her.

"Okay, can I have my chair anyway?" I don't understand why the chair is in contention at all. We're a neurodivergent family stuck in our ways. Moms always take the couch, and Naomi curls up on the left-most cushion. The chair is mine by the sacred law of older sibling first dibs.

But Naomi looks up at me and says, "It's not *your* chair."

For a moment, I think she's going to challenge me to a staring contest, which seems like the worst possible game for two eye-contact-averse autistic kids, but she chickens out right before engaging contact.

"Fine," she concedes, finally ceding my chair. Except she hooks the matching ottoman under one arm and makes camp with her granola in her lap on the opposite end of the room.

I don't have time to run down all the ways Naomi's behavior doesn't make sense because Ma's already scrolling through the *NS* episode list. "If we pick up where we left off, that would put us at 'Whatever Happened to Baby Cain?' but . . ."

"No," Mom says. She doesn't actually like *NS* and only

tolerates it for the rest of us, but she has limits. The wacka-doodle de-aging episode is one of them.

"What about 'Guess Who's Coming to Barbecue'?" Naomi asks innocently. I look at her in her loungewear onesie, her hair piled in a fluffy bun, the green peekaboo layer on full display.

"No," I say emphatically.

"No?" Ma is understandably confused because I never veto episodes.

But I don't think I can handle seeing Chanel's infamous Marienbad dress after a day like this. I grasp for something, anything else, trapped in the memory of this morning, sitting within spitting distance of Kane's grave, closed in on all sides by trellises wrapped in . . . "'Grapevines of Wrath'?" I suggest.

"The tentacle monster episode?" Ma perks up.

"It's not a tentacle monster," I insist futilely. For better or worse, that is how episode fourteen is affectionately and infamously remembered by casual viewers and die-hard fans alike.

Naomi shrugs.

Mom hits play, and by the time the dark, synth-studded theme song starts, Sputnik clambers onto my lap, purring before I even start petting her downy fur.

Then I turn my attention to the show, promising myself that I'll hold back the commentary always on the tip of my tongue. That won't stop Ma from pointing out every time Lou's exterior appears in an establishing shot or identifying everyone in the crowd scenes where casting conscripted locals as background actors.

The slew of mysteries-of-the-week has the denizens of Egan's Creek on edge, looking for someone to blame. The Spectors have just reopened their winery, drawing workers from across the state, but after a few agents provocateurs whip the crowd into a frenzy at a town meeting, the Thatcheresque mayor orders a fence built around Egan's Creek, the winery just out of bounds. Except every morning, the construction crew finds the site trashed.

When Harry and Art stake out the scene overnight on sheriff's orders, they see grapevines slithering out of nowhere, prying the fence apart plank by plank. The mayor fights nature with barbed wire and orders Harry to safeguard the delivery, despite his and Art's fervent protests. When they drive up to the build site, half the town has congregated to block the freight trucks. Citizens and migrant workers of Egan's Creek link arms, and the vines recede into the fog.

Ma lets out a low whistle. "Still a banger."

"You say that about all of them," Mom mutters.

"Because they still hold up! Well, maybe not 'Baby Cain' or 'Tinker Tailor Insert-Borderline-Slur-Here Spy.'"

I nibble on my second slice of challah—the one I tried to give Naomi, who's now plucking the remote from the coffee table. I'm about to object because I like watching the credits, reading the names of everyone who worked to make the show great, but instead of exiting out, Naomi rewinds to the climactic shot: grapevines and regular people joining arms. Protecting each other.

Naomi studies the screen with an intensity she usually reserves for birding in places known for rare species.

Ma, meanwhile, reclaims the remote as a pointer to indicate the background actors at the edges of the human chain. "There's Mr. Jennings back when he still had a full head of hair. Irene O'Connor in bell-bottoms, with Cheryl Morse, back when they were the only out lesbians in town. Then that group of teenagers on the left. That right there's a teenage Ben Loman when he was just the 'and Sons' in Loman & Sons, with both his future wife, Laura, and his then-girlfriend, Andrea Gallo—that's Vanessa's mom—and oh, next to Andrea . . . You kids probably don't remember Mr. Sinclair—he died before you started kindergarten, Naomi—but that's him with the sharp flattop, maybe a year before he married Frances. She was probably just offscreen, actually; she babysat Dagny when they were filming."

"You know," I say, "there's an ongoing debate about this episode. Once people get over the 'tentacle monster' gimmick, I mean. I overheard some guys arguing about it in the gift shop the other day when they were looking at wineglasses."

"'Grapevines of Wrath' wineglasses," Mom repeats, deadpan.

"Bestsellers," Naomi adds, drier than a sauvignon blanc.

You don't grow up in wine country without learning these things, even before you're old enough to drink.

"What's the argument?" Ma asks.

"In the episode," I say, "it's ambiguous whether the vines are sentient, acting of their own agency, or if they're animated by the collective consciousness of the workers, the town, or both. Collective *conscience*, really. The 'strange new people' around town—the mayor's words—don't *look* like—I mean, I think it's pretty obviously an allegory about immigration, xenophobia, and racism—"

"Not just that," Naomi says, and nothing else. She's still looking at the frozen screen. The image hasn't changed; I still don't understand what she sees.

Then Mom says, "It's just the vines."

And Ma says, "It's gotta be collective consciousness."

They look at each other with matching expressions of surprise.

Mom shrugs. "The mysteries on this show always have simple pseudoscientific explanations. Like the diseased orange grove in the scurvy zombie episode. You just think it's a mystical psychic link because you know the people in the picture."

"It's not about who I know," Ma protests. "*Nuclear Seasons* is about the space between the common good and the common defense."

Dagny told me the museum was about bringing people together, just like the show. But that's not the same thing, is it? Not when the price of admission to bring people together is leaving a fundamental piece of yourself behind at the museum door.

I tried to protect myself. I wore a button, I was ordered to take it off, and I did. I asked HR for accommodations, and I got laughed out of the meeting.

I'm not going to cry and wail about how the world isn't fair because that's old news. I don't expect *fair.* I won't debate the diversity, equity, and inclusion culture wars about what "fair" means in the world, let alone the workplace.

But what avenues of resistance exist when the fence is going up around you?

How can you, but tender flesh and vital blood, resist barbed wire?

Moms are tenderheartedly sniping with each other about their differing interpretations. Sputnik has deserted my lap in search of kibble.

But Naomi's still looking at the screen, the green in her hair staring me right in the face.

Maybe I've been fighting two battles where there's only one. Maybe I'll blink and suddenly see where the institution ends and the message begins. Maybe the message has been right in front of me all along, but I was too afraid to see it.

FIFTEEN

LOU'S IS HOPPING.

I was worried we'd picked the wrong venue for an underground union meeting, but Lola assured me everyone's too busy living their best lives to pay attention to us.

We're lucky to snag a table, even if it is the obnoxious U-shaped booth near the entrance rather than my preferred booth in the back. I've ended up pushed to the middle of the curved bench, Lola claiming the outer edge beside me, Naomi urging Efraín in before she takes the other end, as far from me as possible, which is strange, but nowhere near as strange as how Efraín unpacks his backpack before Max takes our order.

I watch him arrange enough loose binder paper to fill a dozen notebooks, not to mention three Decomposition Books, a stack of probably-actually decomposing manila file folders, and his iPad.

Lola nudges my arm. "Order?"

After a decade as de facto hostess, waitress, and sous chef,

Max knows my order—coffee, always, and the salmon melt on Saturdays—but I vocalize it anyway.

I worry my lip, wondering if I should prompt Efraín, but Lola's already not-quite-whispering in my ear that she took care of it.

Efraín looks so intense when he's hyperfocused, oblivious to the world around him except for the ways in which he's trying to change it. A portrait of the activist as a young man with raging ADHD. He has his hair up in another too-cool-for-art-school half bun, an art pencil tucked behind his ear, while he's marking up a pamphlet with another pencil. He's whispering under his breath—rehearsing in a way I've never seen him do for school. Maybe he does this before the rousing, inspirational speeches he must give at his rallies, but I wouldn't know, would I?

Guilt roils under my skin. I turned down invitation after invitation before he stopped asking. Except he asked me to join his union, and I'm here, aren't I?

I'm even the one who texted the group chat late last night and suggested everyone make a social map in advance of our meeting. Speaking of which . . .

"Does everyone have their social maps?"

Efraín looks up from his papers, surprised, like he forgot we were here at all. He's still for a moment, before directing his mild irritation at me.

"Sorry, did you want to give an inspirational speech first,

or can we just get to work?" I ask, already reaching for my tablet.

"Yeah, you know I love your speeches, Ef, but I can't be here all night," Lola says. "I've got a date."

"Fine," Efraín relents. "Let's get to work."

Naomi pulls out a pad of graph paper, while Lola digs through her jumbo tote. "You know, homework is a bit much for baby socialist fight club."

"It seemed like the most efficient plan," I say defensively.

To my surprise, Efraín backs me up. "We need to focus on recruitment before we organize another action. Social mapping is the first step."

Lola's eyes flick between us. "Did you two read some secret job description for unionizing that Naomi and I didn't get?"

"Not a job description, but a playbook," Efraín says, shuffling through his tornado-swept clutter, reaching for a crumpled packet with a familiar globe logo in the corner.

"He means the Industrial Workers of the World Handbook," I clarify, just as Max shows up with our drinks.

Efraín blinks at the rhubarb iced tea Lola ordered for him, then frowns at me.

"You were right before—I did my own research," I inform him before sipping my coffee.

Research felt like the least I could do. I sat out the first union action until management came for me, too, and yesterday's post-HR meltdown single-handedly delayed this meeting. I just wanted to prove I could do one thing right.

"Social mapping," I explain, "is about charting the interpersonal topography of the workplace. Who's friends with whom, who hates whose guts, and who's whose ride-or-die. It's very *Mean Girls* cafeteria montage, but we have to identify cliques and social leaders. If we can recruit those people, they'll bring their friends. If we alienate them, we'll ostracize ourselves. So—" I must sound ridiculous. What do I know about spheres of influence outside of Cold War history books?

"Catch the big fish to reel in the rest," Lola says.

"Without poisoning the water supply," Naomi adds.

"Or," Efraín says, "any metaphor that doesn't involve murdering wildlife for human consumption or—"

"Would you prefer the Cold War? Because I—"

"Okay, let's just defund the metaphor police already," Lola says. "Should I share my map first?"

After dinner, we decamp to the tiny attic-turned-studio-apartment upstairs for privacy. This studio is where Mom, Naomi, and I first lived when we moved to Egan's Creek, so I'm well-acquainted with its persistent moth problem. It's been cluttered with storage for years, boxes of Opa's family keepsakes, Ma's cassette collection, and other intimidating artifacts I dread sorting through. But nothing here has ever intimidated me as much as this.

An organizer's primary recruitment, a one-on-one is, theoretically, just a guided conversation. Based on social mapping, organizers select targets and persuade them to join the union. There are rules, best practices, and a paint-by-numbers instructional acronym. But knowing what AEIOU stands for will only get you so far unless you *practice.*

Now Efraín's got that let's-go-storm-the-castle-and-guillotine-everyone-in-it look in his eyes, and I'm a dead man.

Over on the orange corduroy couch, Lola and Naomi look like they want to make popcorn.

Efraín and I scoot two screeching chairs across from each other in an ominous parody of those gut-scraping performing art school exercises that always end with someone crying or stabbing their scene partner with a pencil.

Efraín sits down across from me, pencil still tucked behind his ear. I need an antacid just imagining who's going to end up crying or stabbing. I flick my thigh with my thumb and forefinger.

Efraín's *looking* at me. Really looking, with an intent I can't read. "Pretend I asked you to coffee," he says, low and insufferably calm. "I pulled you aside after working the same counter and said we should hang out sometime."

Although I am deeply skeptical of this roleplay's verisimilitude, I play along. "So, we're at Lou's after work. The booth in the back."

"We have our drinks. We're alone."

"I still have no idea why you asked me to have coffee. You're not even drinking coffee."

"*Elisha,*" Efraín says, pointed but blunt all at once. "Do you know why I wanted to have coffee with you today?"

Right. Roleplay. Remember the script. "You wanted to hang out. Outside of work."

"It's hard to get to know someone at work."

"You've known me since kindergarten."

He doesn't quite frown, but his eyebrows scrunch together. It's the look he gets when he's about to say something unbearably obnoxious, intentionally inscrutable—something custom made to piss me off—about how, sure, he's known me since kindergarten, but he doesn't really *know* me.

"You're right," he says, deceptively true neutral. "I've known you since kindergarten—that *you've wanted to work at NSX* since kindergarten."

"I didn't watch *Nuclear Seasons* until second grade."

Efraín rolls his eyes, utterly unimpressed with my pedantry. "Didn't you show up as Art Spector for Halloween that year, with the bow tie and the glasses, and people kept asking if you were the eleventh Doctor?"

"Matt Smith didn't wear glasses."

"Yeah, I remember you giving the same five-minute lecture to every kid, parent, and teacher who asked." He pauses. "Not Mr. Delgado, though."

"That's because Mr. Delgado recognized me. He even recognized the bow tie as the one Art wears in 'The Best Nanoseconds of Our Lives.'" I smile, remembering our elementary school janitor. "Did you know he worked on the show when he first moved here? Odd jobs around set—"

A whistle cracks through the air.

"I'd be all for this heartwarming homosocial bonding moment, but we're on the clock," Lola says. "You're both failing this active listening thing real hard."

This is what happens when you set two neurodivergent kids loose: conversational chaos, tangents galore, every detail a road worth traveling.

But we're not here to talk. We're here to work. Or talk about work.

"Sorry," I say. I know how this script goes. "I'll shut up and let you . . . agitate me."

Efraín's just *looking* again. His eyes hold none of the sadistic glee I expected given blanket permission to provoke me. Maybe that's the problem; it's not pigtail pulling without the chase.

All business, Efraín says, "You've wanted to work at NSX for years. How's it living up to your expectations?"

Despite knowing this is literally the first question in the book, it stings, right at the corners of my eyes, because that's what Ma asked after my first day. *Was it everything you dreamed it would be?* There's still only one socially acceptable response. "It's fine."

"Just fine?" Efraín asks, languorous, a glint in his eye. "This is your dream job, and 'fine' is all you have to say about it? You, who could spend an hour describing the symbolism behind Art's bow tie patterns?"

"This isn't my dream job." I used to think I wanted to be

Art Spector, until I realized *consulting sci-fi detective* wasn't a viable career path. "It's just a summer job."

"You *wanted* to work at NSX. This isn't *just* a summer job for you, so why is it that all you have to say about it now is that it's just '*fine*'?"

"For someone who doesn't believe in the American legal system, you sure know how to cross-examine a hostile witness."

"I'm just asking why you're *settling*—" Efraín stops short. "No, sorry. I'm asking: What do you like about working at NSX? What would you change?"

"Wait, so when I don't answer the way you like, you just revert to the most generic one-on-one questions imaginable?"

"I'm asking why the hell you're even *here*, Elisha. Let's cut the bullshit for ten seconds. This isn't a normal one-on-one. I didn't ask you to coffee under ambiguous pretenses. You're here because you believe something at work needs to change. So, what is it?"

"What do you want me to say? That working at NSX isn't anything like I thought it'd be? That I dread going to work every morning and spend my shift counting down until it's time to clock out?"

"That's a start."

"It's *irrelevant*."

"Why?"

"Because it doesn't matter. So what if my dream summer job

ended up being a shitty one? Everyone has a minimum-wage sob story; it's a rite of passage, the prologue to every American Dream. And that's *fine.* Because prologues, rites of passage, and shitty summer jobs all *end.* They're a means *to* an end."

"So, what? It doesn't matter how the sausage gets made?"

"Not if that's the only food on the table. Maybe *you* buy Impossible sausage patties, but the rest of us—" I bite my tongue. "Most of us can't. People buy fast food because it's cheap, and that's what this is about, right? We're all just working to survive."

"You're seventeen."

"I'm well aware."

"You live with your parents in a three-bedroom house in Northern California. Your parents own a small business. Nine months a year, your job is getting straight As. You, Elisha Goldstein, are not working to survive."

"And *you* are? You know exactly why I'm at NSX." I swallow the acidic twang of anger—and the lie—in my throat. "Why are you even *here*, Efraín?"

"You know why. I'm trying to improve working conditi—"

"No, not here, at this meeting, but—" I gesture around us. "Why are *you* working at NSX? You don't like the show, and you don't need a shitty summer job."

"What makes you think I don't need a job?"

"Because . . ." That has to be a rhetorical question. "Have you seen your house?"

"Pretty sure I live in my house ten months of the year."

"Ten?"

"What's your point, Elisha?"

"You're a bourgeois hypocrite."

"Because of the winery? Sobremesa Cellars has been in my mom's family for three generations, yeah, but it's not like I have a trust fund. If I did, I'd donate to every mutual aid fund and—"

"The fact that you can even *imagine* having a trust fund proves my point."

Efraín tenses, jaw set, uncharacteristically still. It's a dangerous thing, silent self-restraint that forecasts a storm. "Okay. Yeah. I won't deny my economic privilege there. The winery does well. You've seen my house. I have a college fund. But don't pretend you really know anything about my life, Elisha." He pauses, but I'm still processing, and he processes every silence as an invitation. "And imagining a trust fund? C'mon. You've never imagined what you'd do with a lump sum of cash?"

The ensuing tightness in my chest is apropos, because, yes, I know *exactly* what I'd do with a lump sum of cash, starting with *tightening* my chest, so to speak.

"You're the one who brought up the American Dream," he adds, "and the idea that we're just supposed to accept shitty summer jobs as a necessary part of coming of age, like getting your license or going to prom—it's a mass delusion."

"The opiate of the masses, right?" I cut in, the allusion sour in my mouth. "Because capitalism is the American religion. I think I've heard this one before."

Efraín scoffs. "You're asleep, and you don't even know it."

I laugh. I can't help it. It's either laugh or cry, and I won't let Efraín see me cry now.

"You know what, Efraín?" I push my chair back to put some space between us. "You were right. This isn't a normal one-on-one. I can wrap it up myself. We already covered *agitate.* This whole meeting has been a hands-on exercise to *educate* ourselves. You did the *inoculate* talk before, right? The National Labor Relations Act says we can't be fired for *organizing.* That brings us to 'U' for *union.* I'm here, aren't I? So there you have it; A-E-I-O-U in action." I stand up. I force a smile and turn to Lola and Naomi. "End scene."

Lola raises a thoroughly unimpressed eyebrow. "Well, kids. That was a great example of what *not* to do."

"Why are you still here?"

When I slink out of the diner twenty minutes later, my eyes red-rimmed from not-quite crying, I find Efraín fiddling with his bike.

It's a picture-perfect midsummer night, the sky still dwindling in civil twilight; none of it explains why Efraín is standing in front of me.

He mulls over my simple question, like he hasn't decided

yet if he's standing on the street corner with purpose or just misdemeanor loitering. "Waiting for you."

Nothing good can come from that pronouncement. "Dare I guess why?"

"Wanted to ask you something."

"You've already asked me a whole lot of things."

When I survey the square again, it's for escape routes. There are plenty, but I'm on foot. Efraín has his bike. "Okay," I concede, "we can talk."

En route to the gazebo, Efraín's thoroughly lost in his own thoughts. I'd offer him a road map, but I'm still traversing my own mindscape with celestial navigation.

Efraín starts pacing as soon as he's up the gazebo stairs. "Why did you *really* show up for the meeting?"

"Because I said I would."

"No, you said you'd be there *last* night, and you bailed."

"I wasn't feeling well," I say. "I came tonight because I wanted to be here. Is that really so hard to believe?"

With every passing moment, the sun dips farther below the horizon. The gazebo's dangling lantern casts long shadows over Efraín's frame.

"You say you need this job," he intones like he's reciting a crime. "You run a cost-benefit analysis before you decide whether to step into a fight." Done pulling his punches, he goes for the knockout. "You fought me on starting a union every step of the way. So forgive me if I have *questions* when you show up in the group chat in the middle of the night telling everyone to bring a damn social map."

I gulp down an incredulous laugh. "You're suspicious? Of me? Are you worried I'm a sleeper cell spy? A Manchurian union member? I think I missed that *Nuclear Seasons* episode."

Efraín shakes his head hard enough to give *me* motion sickness. "This isn't a joke. I was ready to tell you to fuck off after yesterday, but Lola asked me to give you another chance. Except I'm trying to do something *real* here, and all you care about is your stupid TV show."

"Right, the opiate of the masses. I bet you call your television 'the idiot box.' Anything with a screen—"

"*This.*" Efraín wags an accusatory finger. "This is what I'm talking about. Sometimes, you hit the leftist lingo bingo card, but you explain it like it's academic, always so fucking pedantic. There's no *blood* in it. When push comes to shove? You don't show up, or you're a day late and a dollar short, which is fucking ironic for someone who's more afraid of being late than *complicit.*

"All this time, I couldn't figure you out, but it's not that deep. Say what you want about me, but all you care about is the idiot box."

This shouldn't knock the air from my lungs. I know what Efraín thinks of me. What did I expect? That showing up well-researched to one meeting would make up for every battle I've sat out?

Efraín's given me the benefit of the doubt, time and time again, because he's a genuinely good person. He doesn't just play one on public-access TV—doesn't just play one when *talking* about a TV show.

One second I'm leaning against the railing, and the next I'm sitting on the creaky wooden bench. I hold on to my knees and focus on my breathing. My heart is making a ruckus. The world is very loud, and Efraín is watching me, and I don't know what to say to him.

That's the whole problem. I've never been able to say the right thing around him, so I stopped trying. I didn't want to hear his lectures, so I skipped the track. But if I'd kept trying—if I'd kept saying something instead of shutting down—then Efraín would know where I stand.

I look up and meet his familiar, judgmental gaze. "You're right, okay? I didn't have the purest intentions when I dyed my hair; I was just so angry at Dagny and Anya. Then, even when I said I'd come to the meeting, I still wanted to believe there was a way for me to work within the system. But then I met with Billy yesterday—"

"Who?"

"Billy from HR."

"You met with human fucking resources?" His eyes smolder with accusation. "What the hell did you tell them?"

"*Nothing*," I insist. "It was literally the opposite of concerted activity, okay? It was me, alone, trying to convince a corporate shill that wearing a button didn't threaten—" I break off. "It didn't go well. That's why I felt so sick after work. But it made me realize just how wrong I've been, since the beginning. I couldn't fully commit to the union because I was ready to give this job my whole heart, and—"

I can't say it.

"And?"

I don't want to say it.

"And the job didn't *want* me. It just wanted any warm body it could dress in a pink polo shirt. I could've been okay with anonymity. I still wanted to be there, and I've never stopped needing money. But I realized it wasn't enough to be a faceless, nameless, interchangeable part."

Tears are clawing at my eyes again, but I don't want to cry. Not about this. "I wasn't earning a paycheck selling tickets and T-shirts but by erasing myself for the sake of the brand. I'm not allowed to be a *person* on the clock. And, yes, I do love *Nuclear Seasons*, and I did love NSX, but—"

I don't know how to say it.

"But *what*?"

Maybe I've known how to say it all along but couldn't admit it.

"But 'institutional messaging' shouldn't be more important than the people who make the institution." My voice crackles, warbles, and breaks at the end. I'm breathing hard, my heart palpitating. "That includes Naomi's hair. Stanley's water flask. Everything else on our hypothetical grievance list—"

"*Oh,*" Efraín says, an entire semantic universe contained in that syllable. "So you *do* care."

At first, I think he means it as a slight, but there's no derision in his monotone delivery. Some other emotion—shock? awe? relief?—has sapped the dynamism from his speech. His whole posture transforms, a strange alchemy leeching the tension from his bones.

Another nameless emotion clogs my sinuses, phlegm I can't cough up. "Of course I *care,*" I rasp. "It . . . hurts. Did you really think I was that heartless?"

Except I do know. He called me *coldhearted* in cold blood.

But Efraín sits down next to me. "I don't know, Elisha," he murmurs. "I really don't. I can't read you at all. You're too . . . impenetrable."

"Not impenetrable," I mutter. "If it looks like I don't care, that's because caring hurts. If I can brush off misgendering, then it doesn't matter. It doesn't have to mean anything if I can stay impervious. But it's a cheap defense mechanism—the only kind I can afford. Paper armor. Not impenetrable at all."

He's looking at me with that little squiggle between his brows—it reminds me of a tilde—and I can't read *him* at all.

Now that I've started talking, I can't stop. "Despite what you may think, I'm not completely oblivious. You used to invite me to protests, rallies, and marches, but I always said no. It wasn't unreasonable for you to assume I didn't care." I have to look away because this, too, hurts. "I never told you why."

"You didn't owe me an explanation then," he says, "and you don't owe me one now."

"I didn't want you to judge me, but you've never suffered excuses. I still remember the way you tore into Amy Sharma for saying she couldn't go to that one protest because it conflicted with her cousin's baby shower. I knew the minute I tried to justify myself, you'd call bullshit. Ironic, right? I didn't want you to hate me, but that's exactly what happened."

Efraín's poised to interrupt, but I wave him off. "No, can you just let me say this? Because what you have to understand is, when I say *I'm not good at this*—I'm not just blowing smoke. I have evidence."

I can see the questions he's dying to ask, but he stops himself.

"The first time I went to a political event was when my moms took Naomi and me to the first Women's March in Santa Rosa. I don't remember much except that it was loud, and I wouldn't let go of Mom's hand. I was overwhelmed—I know that now—but that was before I got my autism diagnosis. Everyone dismissed it like the way I always cried at fireworks. But that summer, they took us to Pride. San Francisco. And I—"

I shut my eyes, as if the memory of the sun alone was bright enough to sear my retinas. Hypersaturated rainbows and screaming strangers everywhere I turned. "The whole world was *too much.* Colors too bright, sounds too loud. I was so far beyond overwhelmed. I lost Moms and Naomi, and then I was alone on the Embarcadero, having a meltdown on the sidewalk. Then—I was lucky. A very nice drag queen got me to an ever-so-slightly-quieter Starbucks, bought me a Frappuccino, called my moms, and sat with me until they showed up."

"Elisha—"

"No, just wait." I head off his pity at the pass. "I'm not blaming autism, ADHD, alexithymia, anxiety, or any other diagnosis-in-waiting, okay? I just want to explain. I can't do crowds, so protests and rallies are out. I'm a FEMA-worthy natural disaster when I talk to strangers unscripted. Canvassing and phone-banking—I mean, I couldn't even get the wrong side of a mock one-on-one right. I'm not *equipped* for activism. I don't have those skills. I make things worse. And that was all before I transitioned, before I had this added layer of shit to worry about.

"So, for the record, that's why. When you asked—when you used to ask—that's why I said no. Not because I didn't care, but because I couldn't risk it. I know that's a shitty excuse." I offer a weak, watery smile. "Impact over intent, right?"

Meanwhile, Efraín's frowning at me.

I swallow hard. "Sorry. I didn't mean to infodump my tragic social skills backstory. I—"

"You thought I'd judge you?"

"Pardon?"

"All those times—" Efraín runs a hand through his hair, cursing under his breath. "You really thought I'd hold it against you if you told me the truth. And I just proved you right by pushing so hard about work."

This is Efraín at capacity. He can't hold on to his anger at me when he's busy hurling recriminations at himself for missing ugly truths I hid on purpose. He doesn't deserve that blame. For all the times he gave me the benefit of the doubt, I never returned the favor.

"Well," I say, "it wasn't just you. I don't know if you've noticed, but I'm not much of a joiner."

Efraín huffs a laugh, and I want to say a prayer. I expected pity or a guilt spiral, but somehow, I've defused the bomb.

"Hate to break it to you," Efraín says, knocking his knee against mine, "but you just joined a union."

"Ugh, don't remind me," I joke. "Don't hold it against me."

"I won't," he says, soft and solemn like a promise.

SIXTEEN

"YOU, ELI GOLDSTEIN, ARE A HARD MAN TO FIND."

I'm halfway out of my chair in the cash room before I can wrangle my central nervous system into acknowledging that Stanley Pham is not a threat. I may not know much about him beyond his water flask, but I know he's not a threat. I also know I'm not remotely hard to find.

I go where the schedule says. Stanley was in and out of the barn all day with his tour groups, and he must've seen me working the gift shop. It's only now, fifteen minutes after closing, that I'm in the cash room under Ford's orders and paranoid eyes.

"You found me." Specifically, Stanley found me toying with stray rubber bands while Ford checks my till.

"Do you need her for something?" Ford asks, charming as usual.

"Yes, actually," Stanley replies. "Anya has a question about his time sheet."

Ford runs a bundle through the bill counter. "Anya didn't mention anything."

"She didn't want to interrupt you during cash-out."

It's a plausible explanation, credibly delivered. So why does it feel like it doesn't add up?

"So Eli's good to go upstairs? Thanks, man." Stanley pats Ford on the shoulder, a parody of the hardcore backslapping only cis men do. "Ready, Eli?"

I am more than ready to leave this room. After covertly slipping a rubber band around my wrist, I leave without performing any customary social pleasantries.

The temperature drops ten degrees in the lobby. As my sweat cools, my skin goes clammy. I swallow down my baseless, irrational fear. "Does Anya really want to talk to me, or was that a cover story?"

Stanley holds the stairwell door open for me and the door thuds shut behind us before he says, "I'd call it an escape hatch."

I should thank him, but all the words that come to mind sound either inaccurate or inadequate. I should also start climbing the stairs, but I already feel like I'm losing a war against gravity. "But you *were* looking for me."

"Lola was waiting for you in the break room. I said I'd check around on my way out."

"You're not heading out." In fact, he seems quite comfortable leaning against the stairwell wall.

Meanwhile, I'm a fire hazard.

"No," Stanley agrees, amiable. "I wanted to talk to you about something. Will your friends mind if you're late?"

If I'd nicked a penny from the cash room, I'd be able to hear it drop. But I didn't steal a penny, so I snap the rubber band again. My wrist is already red, halfway to raw. "I'd text them to meet me by the car, but we're blocking the exit path."

"You're right. This isn't the best place to talk."

I wonder, nonsensically, if this is the part where I'm supposed to invite him to coffee, except this isn't the prelude-to-union-recruitment kind of talk. I look around the stairwell, all too aware that anyone could step in from either floor at any moment—until I remember there's a third door.

Fire hazard, meet fire exit.

I push outside, blinking at the bright blue sky. This late in June, the six o'clock sun can light up a solar grid. The fire exit spits us out at the back end of the barn, near the dumpsters and the perpetually deserted picnic tables. I shoot off a quick text to the group chat.

At a shaded picnic table, I take the bench across from Stanley, grateful for my up-to-date TDAP vaccine because this thing could only charitably be described as *rustic*, all cracked paint and rusted nails. "What did you want to talk about?"

I'd guess he's wearing an inscrutable expression, but I can't bring myself to check.

Then Stanley says, "My wife is transgender."

I blink and blink, again and again. He keeps talking—it's not a secret, he's sorry for the cloak and dagger, he's been meaning to tell me for a while now—but I am processing. Stanley's wife is transgender. I don't know what I was expecting.

Then again, I don't know what I was expecting from Stanley, point blank.

I don't understand why this fiftysomething guy, who has worked here since opening day, is still rank-and-file floor staff. He knows the museum and the show. Guests are always grinning and laughing after his tours.

I know Stanley is kind. A little kooky, maybe—see: water flask—but he's the type of *kind* that can't be faked, raw sincerity that makes me cringe and compels me to look away. I've known it since he introduced Efraín and me to Dagny. I saw it ten minutes ago with Ford.

I admit, when I started at NSX, I had preconceptions about who would understand my gender. The past three years have taught me that, as a rule, the older someone is, the less likely they are to *get it.* Combining that with other cultural and socioeconomic factors, I can usually make an educated guess—or that's what I tell myself.

Maybe I looked at Stanley and thought, sure, he's kind, but he's over the hill of standard distribution for *people who understand.*

What if I'd tweaked my formula? Stanley has worked at

NSX for twenty years, interacting with people from all over the world. He lives in Sonoma County, in a congressional district that breaks reliably D+55. Why wouldn't I give him the benefit of the doubt?

Lo and behold, Stanley's wife is transgender.

"I didn't know that," I croak.

"I know. I'm telling you."

When I turn this news on its side, the surprising part isn't that Stanley has a transgender wife; it's that somewhere within commuting distance, there is a trans woman old enough to be Stanley's wife.

I don't know any trans adults in Egan's Creek. I know Lola and I aren't the only trans people; it may be a small town, but national demographic statistics dictate that there should be multiple trans kids and a handful of trans adults. They must be stealth or hermits or—

"I'd be surprised if you knew her," Stanley says. "Kim works in Santa Rosa. She's a librarian, and—"

"Egan's Creek doesn't have a county library branch, and our school librarians are part-time."

"True, but it's a little more than that. She prefers staying closer to the city. That's where her community is—where she feels safest." His tight smile stretches the definition of *smile*. "What I'm trying to say is, I know I don't know what it feels like, but I've seen the toll it takes."

I shiver, even though it's as warm as ever.

“Oh, don’t get me wrong. You put up a good front, pretending it doesn’t bother you.”

My first instinct is to insist that it *doesn’t* bother me, but that’s demonstrably false. “I’m the one having temper tantrums and emailing HR over *pronouns*—”

“Hey, no, Eli—”

“It’s just so stupid. There are so many *real* problems. It *shouldn’t* bother me. I shouldn’t feel anything if Ford misgenders me. I should just be”—I yank at the rubber band on my wrist—“*stronger.*”

The rubber band snaps.

“Hey.” Stanley pats my hand. “This isn’t a question of strong or not. It’s—” His gaze has gone distant behind his glasses. “I can’t tell Kim’s stories for her. I’m just a supporting character, but that’s the thing, okay? I’m a *supporting* character. If you asked Kim, she’d tell you that support is what gets her through the minutiae. Not just me. Her friends, siblings, and coworkers. Her queer book club and her trans support group.

“It’s a given, I think, that we’re here for the big things. It’s easy to see allyship in grand gestures, but life isn’t lived in broad strokes. We don’t exist in a still life. Life happens frame by frame, twenty-four per second, faster than we can consciously comprehend. And what happens in each frame matters as much as the supercut.

“When we talk about allyship, it’s easy to forget how important it is to support someone through the little things, too. It's nothing anyone would make a biopic about, but it's about being there when Kim comes home from a long day at work, listening to her story about the transphobic joke that no one shut down, or calling the insurance company for her when they deny her estradiol prescription, or—"

"Or offering an escape hatch when someone is stuck in a five-by-five room with a transphobic supervisor," I add, desperate to understand.

"Or that," Stanley agrees. "All I'm saying is, your strength isn't in question. How you react to a world that keeps beating you down is less telling than how *everyone else* reacts *each and every time* the world beats you down. Because every little thing matters, and every chance any of us has to do something, it's imperative that we do what we can."

"I don't know if I can believe that."

"You don't have to. Tell me, of course, if I ever overstep, but you can also tell me if you want me to do more, whether that means confronting Ford or being there if you want to talk to Anya about him, or—"

"No. Thank you, but no." I can't describe the knot of feelings in my chest. "Today's escape hatch was more than I could've asked for."

"That's the thing, Eli. I want you to know that you *can* ask. Hopefully, your life is teeming with supporting characters you can ask to help with little things and big things alike. And I'm just telling you that I'm here."

I'm not convinced *I'm* here. Because who *says* that? In real life. Who offers their friendship so freely?

Stanley's smiling, ineffably gentle. "Believe it or not, that wasn't what I wanted to talk to you about today."

"You said you'd been meaning to tell me—"

"About Kim, yes, but I wasn't planning on making a production of it. Just, after Ford—"

"I get it." I don't, not really. "But if it wasn't that . . . ?"

"You should know I overheard a lot of conversations today, between Naomi and TJ, Lola and Jaime. Sound carries in the barn, you know?"

To my absolute horror, I realize, then, that *no one* understands the importance of conducting a one-on-one in private.

"Thankfully, nobody else was paying attention, but I know what you and your friends are trying to do."

Pure, high-octane fear burns through me. "I don't—"

"Please, no pretenses. I've been a member of a few 'collective bargaining organizations' over my decades in the labor force."

"Did Efraín talk to you?"

"Was he supposed to?"

"To recruit you?" I whisper.

"Really?" Stanley chuckles. "Not yet. No need, though. I'm talking to you. And recruiting myself, I suppose. Someone needs to make sure you kids only burn down the place *metaphorically*."

Honestly, that seems like a reasonable concern, knowing Efraín.

Still, the arson talk and the fire door remind me the museum has surveillance cameras in all public areas. "We shouldn't be talking about this here."

"We're having a perfectly nice chat about my wife. If anyone asks, you can say I told you about the first time she read *Heather Has Two Mommies* during the children's reading hour."

Now I really want to hear the story.

"You already know," Stanley says, somber, "that I've worked here since the beginning. I moved here because of *Nuclear Seasons.* I was tired of being the butt of every joke in Hollywood writers' rooms, and after the subpar sitcom I'd been working on got canceled mid-season, I ran away to the setting of my favorite TV show, with Kane's own Hollywood self-exile story in mind.

"I love this museum, truly, and it has been a pleasure to meet so many like-minded people. But I've seen what this place does to true believers. The more you love the job, the more it hurts when the job doesn't love you back. I see it every season—they hire kids full of passion, ideas, naive joie de vivre, then they grind you down. And when the summer ends, I watch those same kids leave without the light in their eyes."

Stanley's eyes seek out mine, and for once, I let myself be

found. I stare back, unblinking, unsure what measure of passion he sees left in me.

"We're not going to change the system in one summer. I think you know that. But I believe in doing what I can, where and when I'm able. So if this is the summer a ragtag gang of seasonal workers wants to make a little good trouble around this place, I'm in. Put me to work."

SEVENTEEN

"BUT WHAT ARE STANLEY'S *GRIEVANCES*?" EFRAÍN ASKS ME FOR the tenth time.

It's another slow Tuesday afternoon. We're riding the beginning of a heatwave, and vacationers would rather take their chances at the state parks while it's this side of one hundred degrees and wait until later this week to take advantage of the museum's spotty AC when it's truly scorching outside.

Come to think of it, "spotty AC coverage" probably belongs on the grievance list.

"I told you. We didn't get that far." I don't want to admit that Stanley's approach was ninety percent pity and ten percent concern. "But I get the impression that Stanley has *a lot* of grievances."

"Yeah, no shit."

"He just had an interesting perspective. I bet if you asked his thoughts on how 'alienation of labor' applies here—"

Before Efraín can give me gluten-free brownie points for

the Marx reference, the barn doors screech open. I overhear the tail end of the presumptive guests' raunchy story about their escapades last night at the Brass Ass Saloon before I see them.

Three middle-aged white guys approach the ticketing counter with classic MAGA hat swagger, except only one of them is actually wearing a hat, and it's John Deere.

Dread curdles in my gut. My customer service mask is as clunky as a hazmat suit.

They're probably paying separately, so it makes sense, really, that they fan out along the counter in some display of passive-aggressive psychosocial manspreading.

I don't know how Efraín wants to play this—if he wants to tag-team the spiel or divide and conquer. I should say something. Greeting the guest is step one. Why haven't I done it yet?

I make direct visual contact with the closest man. Sunburned skin, regulation crew cut, and a frayed denim vest, embroidered patches worn as proudly as an Eagle Scout's merit badges. The snake-on-yellow "Don't Tread on Me" is trite but no more threatening than a gopher snake in the backyard. "I Plead the Second" rattles me to my bones. California isn't an open carry state, but when has that ever stopped anyone?

"Welcome to the Nuclear Seasons Experience," Efraín says. He isn't smiling—isn't effervescent or roguishly urbane in the way he usually is when he applies a soupçon of charisma. "Three tickets?"

"Hey there, hold your horses, hermano," the man in the middle drawls. He's the most clean-cut, more vintage alt-right than hillbilly elegy. He's still wearing his Oakley wraparound sunglasses indoors. "Buy a guy some dinner first. Maybe a chimichanga."

"You know I love me some nachos," Mr. Second Amendment says.

"Y'all got Taco Bell out here?" John Deere asks.

Efraín's hands are splayed flat on the counter, his veins etched in stark relief. His middle finger is twitching. Then he puts on the most shit-eating, facetious customer service grin. "There are half a dozen Taco Bells in Santa Rosa alone, but the best food is here in Egan's Creek: Lou's Deluxe Diner, right on the square."

"There's Korean BBQ–inspired nachos on special," I chime in. Here I am wondering if I should feel grateful or spiteful that Efraín's sending the intimidating, possibly-gun-toting probably-bigots my moms' way, when I should be debating the merits of drawing those same men's attention *my* way.

"Korean nachos," Oakleys marvels. "Can't believe the shit they think of."

I don't dare ask who he means by "they," but it seems ironic given that the fine people of Taco Bell gave the world Doritos Locos Tacos and KitKat Chocodillas.

I needn't have wondered. John Deere asks his buddy, using two racist, xenophobic slurs that went out of fashion before the Hays Code.

The storm drenches me in dread, chill in my bones and salt on my tongue. I take shelter inside myself, measure the distance, count the seconds between the lightning strike and the thunderclap, but—

The clapback never comes.

Efraín is a live wire, tension drawn in every line of his body, from his jaw to his biceps. He's preternaturally still and deadly silent.

This doesn't make sense. If anyone else said something half as noxious, he'd have them canceled five ways to Sunday by now. Why isn't Efraín saying anything?

Unless he's as intimidated by Mr. Second Amendment as I am, but that doesn't track. Because Efraín Juarez Reyna wears his convictions like Kevlar. On his worst day, he's braver than I'll ever be.

Oakleys' response makes John Deere's diction seem quaint, and the way he looks at Efraín when he says it . . .

The *wrongness* is a visceral thing, a shiver and a lurch and every hair on end. It isn't just the words that are wrong—though they are, vile, venom to the heart—but it's their *effect.* It doesn't make *sense* that Efraín, who fights windmills for sport, isn't fighting back. Anything that triggers a prey response in Efraín is *wrong.*

"Get out." The words come out utterly flat, as robotic as the machines that will soon automate this very job out of existence.

It doesn't register that those words came out of *my* mouth until two sets of eyes and a pair of Oakleys lock on me, heat-seeking missiles: target acquired.

"What'd you just say?" Oakleys asks.

Red-orange polarized lenses mirror my face back at me. I can't read my own expression. "You need to leave. Now."

"But we ain't bought the tickets yet," John Deere says.

"We're not going to sell them to you," I say, steady and sure but hoping Efraín backs me up sometime soon. "The museum reserves the right to refuse service. You're not welcome here. Not today, not ever."

"What kind of Cali commie coastal elite bullshit is this?" Mr. Second Amendment asks.

"This is what happens when they indoctrinate children with critical race theory in kindergarten," Oakleys observes.

"Don't we have the right to consult a manager?" John Deere asks.

Any manager would agree that other museum guests shouldn't have to listen to this, but I, personally, have no compunction about reading them the riot act if Anya, Billy, or Dagny tries to tell me that Efraín or any member of our staff should have to endure this.

I stare them down with authority I don't have, just the

strength of these few paltry convictions. "The Nuclear Seasons Experience aims to curate an experience that represents the best of the show. Hate speech ruins that *experience* for other guests."

The three big bad bigots huff, and they puff, but they don't blow the barn down. Mr. Second Amendment doesn't whip out a concealed firearm. I'm the one standing my ground. On their way out, Oakleys says to expect a letter from his lawyer, and John Deere declares he'll be leaving us a one-star review on Yelp.

When they're gone, just as the adrenaline's burning out, Efraín whirls on me, a hurricane of torrential, blustering anger. "What the fuck was that?"

I don't know what I was expecting—a five-star review and a twenty-five percent tip?—but it wasn't this. The rage I expected from Efraín five minutes ago that never quite materialized? Here it is.

"I was—" With the adrenaline gone, there's a vacuum where my false confidence was. I didn't expect him to *thank* me, but I didn't expect the riot act read to *me*. "I was trying to help."

"I didn't need your help," Efraín snaps as he pulls a grubby rubber band out of the caddy. "I didn't *ask* for your help." He wrangles his hair up, and all I can think is how much it's going to hurt when he takes it off. "I can handle garden-variety racists myself. Like any invasive species, there are other ways to kill them than brute-force weeding. Vinegar, boiling water, salt—take your pick."

"Pretty sure weeding's the fastest, but I know, okay?" After all, how many times has he pulled this savior routine with me? He knows how much I hate being the damsel. "I *know* you could've totally obliterated those guys. But you hadn't yet, and I just wanted them *gone*."

My confession sucks the wind out of his indignation. His jaw goes slack, stress sluices off his shoulders, and he slumps. His expression reverts to something I can't read. "I thought you were supposed to call a supervisor for 'problem guests.'"

"Or push the panic button, yes."

"I thought you believed in upholding the sacred handbook to the best of your ability, Mr. Goody Two-Shoes."

"No." I blink up at him. "Despite what you may think, I'm not an automaton. A strict interpretation of the handbook doesn't make sense when someone might get hurt. Those guys just now? They would've heard me radioing for a supervisor. They might've gotten angry—angrier. They could've done more violence than words alone. It made more *sense* to get rid of them immediately."

Efraín looks at me, unblinking, and I do my best not to flinch. "You're seriously telling me you *protected me* because it was the *rational* thing to do?" he huffs. "It's like you take it for granted that the rational thing is the right thing. Why do you always expect the world to make sense? It doesn't." He doesn't say it unkindly; there's no cruel intent lurking behind his eyes.

Earnest curiosity should be met with honesty, so I admit, "I *need* the world to make sense."

"Why?" His voice is calm, placid—almost as if he understands that this isn't the casual statement it might be from someone else.

"Because." I swallow, the words gummy in my throat. "Because I don't know how to live in this world. I don't understand it. Every time I think I'm close, something proves me wrong, like what happened just now."

I don't understand how three bigots walked into a museum, said what they said, and no one's the wiser. It's just Efraín looking at me, both of us trying to make sense of the ugly ethical paradoxes that define the human condition.

"It terrifies me—not understanding," I say. "Not knowing what *could* happen. I'm scared all the time. And I don't know how—" My voice cracks. "I don't know how to exist in this constant state of fear."

Efraín's still looking at me, and I don't understand this, either. Then he says, "So you admit the world doesn't make sense."

Because *that's* his takeaway. But maybe that's the best I'm going to get from him, and maybe this is how you exist in a world like ours: you admit you have no idea how to fly the plane, and you accept that most people are doing the best they can in turbulent skies.

Maybe Efraín doesn't want to argue with me any more than I want to argue with him.

"For the record. I'm sorry they said what they said." I bite my lip. "I'm just sorry."

"Are you trying to apologize for the existence of racism? Because that level of white guilt—"

"No. I'm not personally apologizing for a systemic and institutional problem, no matter how implicated in that system I may be." I offer up a wry smile. "But I am sorry that those men said that to you, here, today, and—" I consider my next words very carefully, hyperaware of my stilted cadence. "I'm sorry if you would've preferred to handle the situation yourself. Tell me if that's the case. But I can't promise I'd do anything differently if it happens again."

Efraín quirks an eyebrow. "Not much of an apology."

"Here I thought I was quoting you."

Because we've been here before, in the aftermath of an unwanted rescue, trading not-apologies for near-recriminations, suffocated by the knowledge that we will find ourselves here again, whether it's next Tuesday or next month.

The only reason we haven't been on these sides before is because I've never felt compelled on a cellular, biological, pure-instinctual level to swoop in, clapping two coconuts together in place of the white horse I can't afford.

This, I realize, makes sense.

The next time I see Efraín off the clock, he's weeding the community garden.

I just happen to look up, straight through the Jellyby's Books window as I'm sifting through fruit crates of used books, and I see Efraín perfectly framed. I watch him, distracted by the memory of him walking away yesterday afternoon, his half bun bobbing in time with his steps.

We never got another chance to debrief after the immediate aftermath of our run-in with the bigots. Business picked up, our breaks never overlapped, and by the time I met Ma in the parking lot, Efraín's bike was gone.

In retrospect, I missed him because I hung back in the cash room and mentioned the incident to Dan, who looked more serious than I've ever seen him. Dan Guzman, with his punk rock laissez-faire approach to life and management, who has ambiguously "olive" skin and a surname of Spanish origin, which could mean absolutely nothing or everything.

Dan said I did the right thing—that I should absolutely give guests the boot if I feel concerned for staff safety. He gently chided me for not calling it in afterward, but he was so nonchalant that I didn't realize I'd been chastised until three hours later.

I thought about texting Efraín then—I thought about it incessantly all night—but the subject felt too delicate to broach over text. What would I have said? *Hope you're taking care of yourself after all that bigoting those bigots did today!*

A sharp sting yanks me back to the bookstore. Paper cut. My carelessness has me bleeding over a pair of '60s New Wave sci-fi magazines—so much for my weekly mantra that I will peruse the new used book arrivals without buying anything. Of course, if that mantra worked, I wouldn't bring my Jellyby's tote each week.

When Mr. Brissenden finishes helping Mr. Xie buy enough books to start an avalanche, he grins at me and pulls out a thin volume wrapped in kraft paper. Seeing what it is, knowing he put it aside for me and understanding he's offering it to me for a fraction of its worth—I'm glad I brought the tote.

With my haul tucked under my arm, I venture back out into the sweltering heat. I look out at the modest community garden. The town council only approved a few raised beds for a pilot program three years ago—an initiative proposed by Efraín, naturally.

Despite its tiny size and California's intermittent drought conditions, the garden is well-loved. Ma helps tend it, and Mom set up the irrigation.

Today, Vanessa, the florist from Blushing Blooms, is pruning back some overzealous berry bushes. Joel the troubadour has traded his guitar for a spade—though he seems to be doing an awful lot of flirting for someone who's shoveling organic waste.

And then there's Efraín, inspecting cherry tomato vines. He's dressed in half-buttoned overalls, a muscle tank, and a straw hat that he really shouldn't be able to pull off. He's the agrarian Adonis on every agitprop poster, the hardworking everyman on an old wartime recruitment flyer.

It's ridiculous. I can't stop looking at him.

At what point does looking become leering?

He takes off his gloves and reaches for his water bottle, turning just so, and—

Yep, he definitely sees me.

I could wave and be on my way, head over to the Last Drip, and spend one of my days off reading my new finds by myself, like I planned.

But when I look past the packaging, I see the ghost of the boy I worked beside yesterday afternoon. He acted like he was fine, but how many times have I blown off microaggressions and said I was fine when I wasn't?

Stanley said it's about the little things, showing up each and every time.

I make a split-second decision—and look both ways before I jaywalk.

Efraín's waiting by the tomatoes, dangling his water bottle strap between two fingers.

As I stop a judicious six feet away from him, I belatedly slide my sunglasses back on before my mild light sensitivity kicks up a fuss. "Hi," I say, totally casual.

"Hey," he says, cocking his head. There's a question there, probably along the lines of, *What the hell are you doing here?*

I wish I knew the answer.

This shouldn't be so hard.

"Find something interesting?" he asks.

I have no idea what he's talking about until he points at

the Jellyby's tote under my arm. "Oh, um, just *People of the Fork.*"

"Julie Molina's memoir? Doesn't the museum sell that?"

"It's Judy Medina-Rhodes; you know that—" And it's quite possible from the quirk of his lips that he's messing with me. "It's signed."

He's quiet, his eyes shaded by that stupid hat, and I can already hear the earful I'm about to get about the commodification of celebrity when Efraín says, "Cool."

"Really?"

"It matters to you."

I have no idea what to say to that, so I babble. "It's mostly just essays about Hollywood, privilege—the elegies she wrote for Sam Schatz and Victor Kane are buried in there, but, um . . ." I search for literally any detail that might matter to Efraín. "The title comes from this Ladino phrase 'djente de piron,' which is an idiom about rich people. Literally, 'the people of the fork,' meaning people who owned forks in addition to spoons? Obviously that wasn't her background at all, so she was just writing about growing up in a lower-middle-class Sephardic immigrant family and trying to navigate working with these people who had silver spoons and forks and knives they used to stab people in the back and—"

"You're telling me Judy Medina-Rhodes would've been on board with eating the rich?"

I laugh, surprised. "Yeah, probably."

Efraín scratches his elbow, and God, he's probably itching to get back to his gardening while I'm tossing idioms about cutlery in cryptic word salad.

My palms are sweating, and it's nothing to do with the heat. I don't know why I'm so bad at this.

I've seen this show a thousand times, but I never learned the script. Why can't I initiate a conversation when it actually matters?

Finally, I blurt, "Are you okay?" I can't make out the tilde between his brows under the hat, but I'd bet my new prized, signed edition of *People of the Fork* that it's there. "I'm just trying to check in. About yesterday."

The moment he gets it, he tenses—it's only then that I realize just how relaxed his posture had been before. Voice tight and clipped, he answers, "It wasn't the worst thing anyone's ever said to me. They weren't even talking to me personally."

I know it's not the worst thing. I've overheard people say far worse things to him personally. Again, I remind myself what Stanley said. Little things.

"It doesn't matter that it wasn't the 'worst thing,'" I say. "It matters that it *happened*."

Efraín looks away, past this garden that only exists because he, at fourteen, stood up in a town council meeting and said it should be here.

He's shielded by the brim of his hat and the shadows under

it, but his jaw cuts as strong a line as always, and his Adam's apple bobs against the column of his neck.

Then he turns back to me with a shrug. "I'm fine."

"But are you *okay*? Because they're not always the same thing. I mean, do you want to get an alternative-milk milkshake and talk about it?"

He looks at me askance, then gestures to his dirt-stained clothes. "Not dressed for it."

"Lou's doesn't have a dress code."

He gives me a look that says he's not about to make more work for anyone by tracking dirt all over the checkerboard linoleum. His mouth does something strange that I can't begin to parse. "I'm okay, Elisha. Besides, I have to finish up here."

Then I blurt, "What are you doing tomorrow?"

EIGHTEEN

BLUE PLATE PICTURE PALACE HAS OFFERED DISCOUNT THURSDAY Mystery Double Feature longer than I've been alive. The only mystery is why "mystery" is in the title because it's almost always an eclectic sci-fi pairing curated by the theater's owner, Ms. Sinclair.

The first film starts at two o'clock, which is why I told Efraín to meet me half an hour before showtime. I have a routine: get my tickets, make two minutes of small talk with Ms. Sinclair, and claim the perfect seat. Pacing under the marquee and obsessively checking my phone are *not* part of my routine.

"Hey, Eli!"

Here I thought I'd been doing an admirable job of keeping my pacing out of view of the ticket box. Sheepishly, I face Ms. Sinclair like the kid who gets caught sneaking into an R-rated movie.

"Thought I saw you there." Ms. Sinclair has a timeless

celluloid face, but her fine wrinkles come out when she smiles. Her locs are more pepper than salt. If I didn't know the theater's history, I couldn't ballpark her age. "You want the usual?"

"Yes, but—I'm waiting for someone?"

She lets out a low whistle. "Hot date?"

I cringe like I do at some of the Paleolithic B movie special effects I see here. The concept of Efraín and me on a hot date is too much for my frontal lobe to process. "No, nothing like that. Just—" How do I classify who Efraín is to me? Classmate. Rival. Carpool buddy. Fellow worker. The constant thorn in my side whom I spontaneously panic-invited to join my sacred Thursday afternoon moviegoing ritual because I felt . . . *something*. "He's just a friend."

"Mm-hmm. That's what I used to say about Mr. Sinclair, back before he found the missing reel in the basement."

"Wh—" I almost fall for it. Even recognizing the bait for what it is, I almost let myself be pulled in because Ms. Sinclair's stories are that good. "You know what? I'll just pay for both tickets now. Both sets, I mean." I rummage through my pocket for my debit card.

I'd rather pay for Efraín than miss the opening credits. I can spare the extra $7.50 to support a local business.

Ms. Sinclair smiles, sardonic. "Sure, Eli. You and your date for the double feature comes to—"

"Two for the double feature? This should cover it." A

long arm reaches over my shoulder and slaps a credit card on the counter. Suddenly, Efraín's right behind me, leaning over me, close enough to touch. He's overwhelming, heat and the distinctive coconut-something scent of his shampoo-conditioner-aftershave-cologne-whatever.

Ms. Sinclair looks from me to Efraín and back again. "This your 'friend'?"

"Jury's still out."

Efraín doesn't laugh, not audibly, but he's close enough that I can feel his amused huff, a puff of hot air against my neck.

Ms. Sinclair doesn't hide her delight as Efraín taps his card on the reader. He does the whole thing one-handed, working around me. It doesn't occur to me to scoot over until he's already tipped twenty-five percent. I'm too busy thinking that charity is the last thing I want from Efraín. Would it be a jerk move to Venmo him $7.50 right now?

Ms. Sinclair slides over four purely symbolic Admit Ones. No one checks the tickets. "Enjoy the show, boys."

"Thank you, ma'am," Efraín says with that charming, deferential smile he only bestows upon adults once he's decided they've earned it. "I'm sure we will."

Efraín finally steps back, and I finally breathe a full-belly breath. Even for a heatwave, I swear the temperature's gone up ten degrees in the last ten minutes.

Efraín holds open the door, all mock chivalry. "What show did I just buy tickets for, anyway?"

"Oh, right." I smile, high on air-conditioning and mirth. "That's not how this works."

"How *does* it work?"

"We find out when the show starts."

Even with Efraín's tardiness, we're still early.

"I never realized this place was so huge," Efraín observes when we step into the single theater, which looks exactly how *I* would expect it to look. Red-curtained walls. Three wedges of shabby seats separated by illuminated aisles.

"It's actually small for a picture palace. Just seven hundred seats—*wait.* Are you implying you've never been here before?"

"Yep."

I stop in my tracks, my Vans snagging the art deco carpet. "This is the only theater in Egan's Creek. *How* have you never been here?"

"I've never been into movies."

"You do realize that you work at a museum dedicated to a TV show, right?"

Efraín rolls his eyes.

I stare at him, shrugging so casually, like it's nothing. Like it isn't weird that we're here, together, picking out seats for four to five hours of surprise cinema.

"This should be good, right?"

Efraín's pointing to the back row.

"Oh my God."

"What? There's no stadium seating, and you're—"

"Vertically challenged?"

"Sure. If anyone sits in front of us—"

"It's a Thursday matinee in a theater whose fire capacity is roughly seventy-five percent of the town's population. Thanks for your concern, but no one's going to obstruct my view. For your education: The sweet spot is dead center of the middle row. Best acoustics, and the screen fills your field of view without overwhelming you."

"Then by all means. Lead the way."

I get my perfect seat, the one I always seek out. Of course, it's not a *perfect* seat. It's lumpy, and the burgundy fabric scratches my skin, but I'm used to that. The absence of armrests is regrettable, but what I forget, after so many solo screenings, is how *narrow* each seat is.

Efraín fills out the seat next to mine. I scoot to the right. It's all fine.

A few people straggle in and scatter throughout the theater. Efraín's hugging his kettle corn tub. I'm checking my watch every two seconds, trying not to mistake every shadow for the dimming of the house lights.

Apropos of nothing, Efraín says, "Kind of a weird name."

"Discount Thursday Mystery Double Feature? Yeah, it's a tongue twister."

"No, *Blue Plate.* Sounds like a dinner special, not a movie theater."

"It's a reference to the Great Depression, actually."

That earns me a skeptical side-eye.

Time to sing for my supper. "Before the Depression, the film industry was booming, especially with talkies taking off. Instead of novelty nickelodeon theaters, fancy 'picture palaces' were going up all over the country. Up to two thousand seats, Greco-Roman architecture, air-conditioning—they called them 'palaces' for a reason. It was a luxury experience.

"But then the Depression hit, twenty-five percent unemployment, and no one could afford a luxury experience because you can't spell 'disposable income' without 'income.' So, these picture palaces were fighting for their lives. Instead of luxury, they offered essentials. They held weekly raffles and giveaways for things like dishes. *Blue plate specials.* Come back week after week to complete your set, except they were more popular than the theaters anticipated. Moviegoers got into fistfights over the prizes. It sounds slapstick, but it *worked.* Not all the theaters survived, but the film industry did. Because people needed movies."

"People needed food and shelter," Efraín says, that obsidian edge in his voice. "*Jobs.*"

"No, I mean, of course. But it's not just—" I'd knock my head against the seatback if it were tall enough. "Fast-forward fifteen years. This place, the original Blue Plate Picture Palace, didn't open until after the war, when movies were booming. It squeaked by when home TVs hit the market. The whole town fundraised for renovations during the Cinerama craze. But the theater couldn't keep up when color TVs became more affordable. Blue Plate closed in the early seventies, just before the advent of the summer blockbuster—*Jaws*, then *Star Wars*—unlikely salvation for a withering industry."

"So Egan's Creek had another fundraiser?"

I know he doesn't seriously want to know. But I want to tell this story—to him.

"Victor Kane happened. He went to every Discount Thursday Mystery Double Feature growing up. This is where he fell in love with film, but Blue Plate closed while he was in Vietnam. When he came back here after his stint in Hollywood, he bought and restored it. Frances Sinclair was his first disaffected teen hire. Later, he left her the place with a hefty endowment to keep it running as long as the world kept making movies."

Efraín gets that tilde between his eyes. "But Kane made TV."

"Yes?"

"Movies and TV are different."

"Sure, they're very different mediums, artistically, but in one way, they're exactly the same."

"Yeah?"

"What I said before—that the film industry survived the Great Depression because people needed movies—that was imprecise. I should've said: People need *stories.* They're comfort, yes, but also sustenance. Movies, TV, novels, comics, theater, campfire ghost stories, it's all vital, like food or water."

"You really believe that?"

"You have causes, and I have stories. Is that so hard to believe?"

He looks at me and looks at me and just when I think he's going to say something profound, he mutters, "Huh."

I want him to understand. I nudge Efraín's shoulder.

"What?"

"Look up," I whisper.

His eyes go wide at the sight of the ceiling, gaudy with baroque fixtures, but painted like the night sky. The winter constellations of the Northern Hemisphere are outlined. A mythological mural writ in stelliscript.

In the dark of the matinee, Efraín takes it all in. I watch him until the house lights dim, the projector hums, and the opening credits roll.

NINETEEN

IT WOULD BE PRESUMPTUOUS AND ENTIRELY FALLACIOUS TO attribute the calm of our second official union meeting to yesterday's trip to the movies. It's not like Efraín and I suddenly started a beautiful friendship after sitting in the dark for four hours watching *Dr. Strangelove* and *X-Men: First Class* back-to-back.

I'm so used to solo screen time that I'd forgotten I'm a talkative viewer, desperate to editorialize and fanboy over everything. I kept leaning over to whisper trivia, cinematic commentary, and sundry to Efraín. He kept shushing me, but that didn't stop him from arguing politics under his breath. During *XMFC*, I swear to God, Efraín would've been throwing popcorn at the screen if he weren't worried about making extra work for a minimum-wage employee.

We argued afterward, too, about whether peace is always an option, whether there's such a thing as "Good Germans." Okay, we didn't always disagree, but then Efraín pushed and insisted there's no such thing as good bosses.

If bosses couldn't be reasoned with, if peace wasn't an option, then why would we be sitting here working over the details of petitioning our bosses?

The thing is, we are ninety minutes in, Punch Bowl's bar is packed, and we still don't have a petition *subject.*

"Can we just go down the list again?" Lola asks, chin in her hands. "There has to be something spicier than parking spaces."

"It doesn't have to be sexy," Efraín says. "It needs to be—"

"Practical," I finish.

"—realistic."

I scan the Google Doc. We've compiled all the grievances we heard during our one-on-ones; the complaints ranged from apples to oranges to giant pumpkins. My personal, hesitant contribution—pronoun buttons—is a grape. Other people have real problems. The trouble is, the realer the problem, the less realistic it is to solve.

"Well," I say, "after we eliminate—"

"*Table,*" Efraín corrects me.

"—institutional problems and everything related to money, we're basically left with handbook line items. The two most practical options are water bottles and stools. They both have a medical component and affect every member of the staff."

"So, water bottles," Efraín decides.

Lola groans.

"Allowing floor staff to have water throughout the museum is important," Efraín says.

"As is allowing floor staff to sit down," I counter.

"I understand that, but—"

"Nah, you really don't, Ef," Lola adds.

"What am I missing?"

Lola and I exchange a glance. She shakes her head. I preemptively regret it even as I tell Efraín: "You have legs of steel."

"What?"

"You bike. *Everywhere.*"

"So? It's good exercise and good for the planet. Win-win."

"You said it. Good exercise."

Naomi explains, "Your quadriceps, hamstrings, and calf muscles are well developed."

I thank every star in the sky that my sister failed to list the gluteus maximus. "Your standing endurance is above average."

Efraín studies me with the strangest expression, not quite accusatory, but curious.

Is it weird that I have Opinions on Efraín's objectively well-developed leg muscles? It's no state secret that Efraín's objectively attractive. Under prohibited-by-the-Geneva-Conventions torture, I'd concede that I, personally, find him attractive. Admittedly, that inscrutable look he's leveling at me is its own form of torture.

Help, I mouth at Stanley, who, let the record reflect, told me not one week ago that I should ask for help when I need it. Now he just chuckles.

“Can we adjourn this meeting early?” I ask. “Or can we just stipulate that stools are important—”

“Who brought them up during the one-on-ones?” Efraín asks, suddenly serious.

“Blake,” Lola answers. “Not for herself, but—it was a recurring theme, actually?—all her complaints circled back to Jaime and how he never complains, even when he should. You’ve all seen his knee brace, yeah?”

“He tore his ACL last year,” Naomi notes.

Lola nods. “He’s mostly fine. No soccer scholarship, but medically, he’s okay. His knee just gets sore after standing all day, every day, so Blake tried to convince Jaime to talk to HR about getting a stool. He wouldn’t, so she did. The HR guy said he needed documentation, so Blake badgered Jaime to get a doctor’s note, but then the HR guy demanded an X-ray? No way was Jaime going to hand over his medical files to some HR rando, so he just wears the brace.”

“Is that normal?” Naomi asks, lips puckered like she’s just been force-fed applesauce.

“Normal for NSX,” Stanley answers. “If Billy had it his way, our personnel files would be thicker than our FBI dossiers.” One thing I’ve learned tonight is that Stanley has some conspiracy theorist tendencies; then again, most old-school *NS* fans do.

“Standing eight hours a day takes a toll on the body. Maybe not at your age, but after twenty-five years . . . Who’s to say if it's an occupational hazard or normal wear and tear?" He shrugs, shockingly cavalier. "I'm not lining up for a knee replacement anytime soon, but my knees do ache some days."

Efraín considers Stanley, a lawyer gearing up for cross. "Sounds a lot like why you never pushed HR on water bottles."

"That's right."

Efraín gets that lazy smirk he gets when he knows he's won, even when situationally inappropriate. "Are your knees aching today?"

"A little," Stanley admits. "More often than not. We're lucky senior leadership agreed to put down rubber mats last year. Luckily, the barn floor is hardwood rather than concrete, like other museums."

"Do other museums let their workers use stools?"

"Some. I've heard rumors, through the grapevine, that a few others—they've tried *this*."

"Did it work?" I ask, throat dry.

"For some of them."

"We'll make it work," Efraín says, like it's a given.

When he says it like that, with that fire in his eyes and conviction in his voice, he makes me want to believe him. I almost do. So, I suggest a vote between water bottle and stools.

Either's fine by me, but Lola's advocating for Jaime, Stanley's feeling protective of his water flask, and Efraín's presumably overcorrecting for some self-perceived unconscious ableism in his initial dismissal of stools. I don't even need to decide. "The stools have it."

"So we have our next action: petitioning management for stools at sales locations," Naomi recaps. "We've fulfilled the objective of tonight's meeting. Can we go bowl now?"

Stanley winces when he checks his watch. "I should be getting home to Kim."

"Wait, we still have to *write* a petition," I object.

"Yeah, maybe we should table that," Lola says.

"No." Efraín rebuffs her before I get the chance. "If we wait, it'll be August before we turn it in, and this will be the union's whole legacy. No, we need to move fast."

"Seconded," I agree.

"Collaborate on a Google Doc?" Stanley suggests.

"No," Efraín refuses again. "This is how activist groups fall apart."

"We need something polished, cogent, and concise. Google Docs get messy—" I can see where this is going, and maybe I should think this through, but I'm already saying, "*Fine.* I'll do it. I'll write the petition."

Surprise flashes across Efraín's face. "You're volunteering? For real?"

"Is that really so shocking?" I can feel my cheeks heating up, and I hug my arms over my chest. I feel so fucking *conspicuous* in this bowling alley bar. Not just in my body—I swapped my uniform polo and binder for an old *NS* T-shirt and a sports bra right after work—but also in this union.

The analogy is more salient than I'd like. In the same way I know I don't pass as a guy, I worry that no matter what I do, I'll never be seen as a full member of the union. Because I didn't join on day one, I expressed doubts, I tried to reason with management, and I prioritized protecting my job over protecting my sister or anyone else. Naming the sins in my head is like reciting the viddui on Yom Kippur; I can feel the rhythm in my bones as I tap my knuckles against my arm.

If Efraín still doubts my loyalty, I don't blame him. He didn't hold it against me when I admitted I joined the union out of spite, but maybe he should have.

"Not *shocking*," Efraín drawls, "but are you sure it's a good idea?"

"Why wouldn't it be?" I snipe. "Do you not trust me to write a simple persuasive essay? Do you have complaints about any of the As we've received on group projects in the past? Were there not enough pluses?"

"It's not about trust," Efraín huffs. "I'm trying to make sure you're volunteering to write the petition because you *want* to write it. Not because you don't trust anyone else to do it. I don't want you to do it if it's going to make you feel . . ." He glances up at the ceiling, as if he'll find the best-choice Mad Libs adjective written in the rafters. "You shouldn't write the petition if it's going to make you feel uncomfortable."

"I don't understand."

"I don't want you to do it just because you feel obligated, or—"

So *this* is what I get for telling Efraín before that I had my reasons for sitting out different actions in the past. He doesn't believe me when I actually volunteer of my own volition.

"If it feels like too much of a risk," Efraín insists, "then you don't have to—"

"I'm signing it," I interject. "What difference does it make if I write it, too?"

Efraín's eyes are so dark in this dimly lit bar. "It matters that *you* are the one writing it."

I don't know what that's supposed to mean. There's some subtext underneath his intonation, but I don't know what he's trying to tell me, and I can't ask him outright when he's going to so much trouble to *not* say whatever it is he isn't saying.

What I understand is this: I've preemptively pledged my signature to this petition. I want it to persuade management that we need stools. We deserve stools. We should've had stools since the beginning. They should pay for that knee replacement surgery Stanley might need sometime soon due to their negligence.

But this isn't about petition prose quality; it's about the collective nature of this action—of the union itself. There are so many things I *can't* do. I'm not the right person to conduct one-on-ones. I'm never going to inspire others to action. But this? Using words to state our grievance and make our case? This I *can* do, and I *want* to do what I can.

That want is fragile, a tender spot I'm afraid to poke. I still don't know what this means. I just know—

"I want to do it. For real."

I'd get the petition done sooner if my fellow workers weren't forcing me to go bowling.

But Punch Bowl has a late-night discount, and I'm overruled. Besides, Lola is my ride.

Well, I could've asked Stanley to drop me off on his way back to Kenwood, but something about leaving without my carpool buddies felt *wrong*.

Yes, Punch Bowl smells like feet and fake cheese. Yes, the blaring retro music and blinding strobe lights inevitably bring me to the brink of overwhelm. And yes, rental bowling shoes are a biohazard.

But there's still something in my gut telling me to stay, to forget about the petition for a couple of hours and just *be*.

So, here I am picking up the sixteen-pound marbled indigo ball that I selected solely for its galactic swirls.

Even though we could've played individually, Lola insisted we all pair up because "teamwork makes the dream work." I wasn't even surprised when Lola informed Efraín and me that we have to play together because we're too competitive to be on opposing teams.

I don't know why Lola expected Efraín would be any less competitive with a teammate who has the hand-eye coordination of a bat. Efraín broke two hundred without breaking a sweat. I gave up all hope of breaking *one* hundred after my third frame. Meanwhile, Naomi's cleared every pin with more strikes than spares, and Lola's scoring in the *respectable solid amateur* range, according to Naomi. All of which to say, Efraín's directing his competitive energy within his team.

I'm going into my final frame, tacitly ignoring the scoreboard.

"There's no shame in trying a granny shot!" Lola calls out.

"I'm *trying*." Truly, I am. In my mind, I'm stepping into the swing, releasing the ball, following through—

"For fuck's sake," Efraín stage-mutters, pure melodrama. "Hand me the ball."

Suddenly he's beside me, holding out his hand, and I don't understand. "Are you taking my turn? I'm pretty sure there's no pinch hitting in bowling."

"No, just—" Taking the ball right out of my hands, apparently. He frowns at it like it's done something to offend him—the way he usually frowns at me. "Lola, do you mind?" Efraín doesn't wait before swapping out my ball for hers.

Lola offers a genial two-finger salute.

"Pay attention," Efraín chides, and that's rich coming from him.

"I'm paying attention," I grouse. "I've been watching all of you do this frame after frame, but I clearly don't learn by observation, so—"

"Here." Efraín thrusts the ball into my hands. "Give it a feel."

I don't know what he wants from me, but I hold the ball, slick and cool to the touch. It's significantly lighter. Twelve pounds, according to the number on the side.

"Better?" Efraín asks, smug. "Good. Now show me your stance."

I move before I give myself conscious permission.

"Lower your elbow," Efraín directs. "Not like that. Like—okay, wait. Do you mind?"

"Mind what?"

"Do you mind if I move your arm?"

Is he fucking serious right now?

"I'm not going to touch you without your consent, Elisha."

Yeah, he's fucking serious right now. "Fine. Go ahead," I add because I don't want to go ten rounds about what constitutes *enthusiastic consent* for platonic touch right now.

Efraín's fingertips alight on my forearm, and I almost flinch. Not because it's rough or painful; it's not. His touch is delicate but firm, burning my goose-fleshed skin, but it's not *him.* I just spend so much time avoiding *anyone's* touch that I've forgotten—

Surprisingly gently for someone who moves through the world with the finesse of a bull in a china shop, Efraín carefully manhandles me into position. His hands rest on my shoulders.

For a single moment, he's as quiet as I am, eerily still for two boys with ADHD. Then he coughs. "I'm going to walk you through the five-step approach, but don't worry about the ball. Footwork first. Got it?"

I nod.

"Good," he murmurs.

He choreographs every step for me. When I teeter, his hands settle on my hips, and I quite literally forget how to breathe. He's saying something about keeping the body straight forward, but I don't follow because *his hands are on my hips.*

Dysphoria taunts my so-called child-bearing hips. But there's something else, sharp in my mouth and warm in my gut, that I don't know how to name. It feels different from my hips brushing against the sidewall of Lola's car or inching along the middle row at Blue Plate. It's animal and human and *Efraín*, and—

"Still paying attention?" he asks, low and perilously close.

I swallow hard. "Last month, you said you didn't remember the last time you did this. I didn't expect you to know the lingo."

"Lingo?"

"'Five-step approach'? Lingo."

"I have a good memory," he says, uncharacteristically self-deprecating. "Next, keep your right foot straight—"

"Maybe I'm just too bi for all these straight steps."

"I manage just fine." Maybe it's my imagination, but his grip feels a little tighter. "If it'll assuage your linguistic concerns, take one step gaily forward."

"Still not bi, though." If my voice sounds breathier than usual, that's my imagination, too.

"Elisha, for the love of God, will you please just proceed bisexually forward?"

I take a small step bisexually forward.

"No, no, that's all wrong. You need to lean into it—"

"But you didn't *tell* me that." I whirl around, no thought to my footwork—or the ball in my hand, let alone *his* hands.

His hands have slid up to my waist, and if it weren't for the ball, I'd be practically pressed against him. I blink at his clavicle. After work, he changed into a thin V-neck shirt. The collar dips low, revealing a tuft of dark chest hair, and I can't stop staring.

He's bracketing my body, radiating heat, and when I peek up through my wayward curls, he bites his chapped lip. I know he cares deeply about orangutan habitats, but surely there must be a lip balm that doesn't use palm oil.

"Five minutes!" Naomi calls, loud and brusque.

"Not that we're not enjoying the show," Lola chimes in, "but Mr. Xie's circling."

I haven't done anything wrong, so why do I feel like I've been caught committing another fireable offense?

Efraín doesn't let me pull back completely, though he loosens his grip. "Try the fourth step again," he instructs. "Build power." He taps my hip twice before he finally steps back.

I follow his instructions when he talks me through the final step, the slide. We walk through the approach in slow motion to add the swing. Each frame, he shifts my arm into position. I am walking into the swing, only in stop-motion animation, or those little flip-books where you flick your thumb to simulate motion.

Efraín says, "Good, just like that," and I feel strangely relaxed. Efraín's approval is such a rare, flighty thing, like a bird on the verge of extinction.

"You're ready," Efraín declares.

I want to protest. I may be able to follow the choreography with him adjusting my elbow, but I am not remotely confident in my own abilities.

I do it anyway. I don't walk myself through the steps in my head. I just hit play and let the pictures move.

The ball releases from my fingers like it came from someone else's hand. It has more speed than any other shot I've lobbed, and it only veers a little to the left as it careens down the lane, and—

Nine pins.

Lola screams, and Naomi slaps a hand over Lola's mouth.

Efraín's leaning against the ball return with another insufferable smirk, looking so pleased you'd think it was his shot. "Told you so."

"You didn't tell me anything."

"I said you were ready, didn't I?"

I don't think that counts as the great measure of faith he thinks it does.

"Go get your spare," he murmurs. Our fingers brush when I take the ball. His smirk softens out around the edges into a real smile—small, fragile, ornery as a hothouse orchid—but a smile all the same.

I don't get the spare, but I don't care. Because this—the warmth, the affirmation, and their smiles—feels better than winning ever could.

PART III

INOCULATE

TWENTY

MY NAME ISN'T ON THE SCHEDULE.

I don't notice right away. I'm on time and clocked in for Friday morning pre-shift, but I'm looking at the world through plastic packaging, thinking about yesterday's *Barbarella-Barbie* Blue Plate double feature, remembering how Efraín almost choked stifling his laughs because he didn't want to admit the Man could produce something *funny.* And how, in those narrow seats, our thighs pressed so close that I could feel his muscles tensing—

My sister, tactful as always, elbows me in the ribs and points to the note on the schedule: "Eli—see Anya."

"Fuck."

"I'm sure it's nothing," Lola says, deploying the same sweet nothings I use to reassure Sputnik en route to the vet.

Except I know better. It's been four days since Stanley and I marched on Anya's office to deliver our stool petition. That's a whole lot of something.

"It wasn't nothing when Anya asked Naomi to stay late on our first day."

"That was different." An empiricist at heart, Naomi sees every event as discrete. A single variable changes everything.

"It's probably just another department asking for an extra set of hands," Lola says. "Yesterday, I helped Eden from curatorial move top secret boxes all afternoon."

"This is Friday," I remind her. "All hands on deck."

"It's not what you think," Efraín rumbles, words seeping down the back of my neck.

I barely registered him behind me, but now I crane my neck to look up at him. "And what do I think it is, exactly?"

Efraín meets my gaze so damn calmly, but why shouldn't he be calm? It's not *his* name on the line.

"It doesn't say anything about Stanley," Efraín murmurs. I can barely hear him over the blood rushing in my head, white-water rapids of panic drowning out everything else. "If it was about the petition, Anya would talk to Stanley."

"Maybe she already did. He—"

"Would've messaged us."

"You don't know that. Maybe he couldn't. Maybe Anya—"

"Got to him? C'mon. We all signed it—and TJ, too."

"I know, but—"

"Elisha." Efraín's hand alights on my arm. I stare at the point of contact, his fingers splayed over pink cotton. None of this makes sense. "You're not alone."

Oh. The three most powerful words in the English language. Honestly, fuck him. For swearing those words like a sacred oath he'd kill to keep. For looking at me with his dark, fathomlessly deep eyes like he'd never let me drown. For touching me like he can tether me to this moment through sheer force of will.

I want to argue with him. No matter what he says, my name is alone on the page. Anya wants to talk to me alone. I have to face the consequences alone. But when I'm facing him, protests dissolve on my tongue.

Anya rattles through the morning announcements, but my attention wanders anywhere, everywhere else, her raspy voice fading into the background.

I memorize the scene around me as if I could catch it on film and live inside the frame. Stanley offering up amiable smiles to everyone. Blake slipping her hand in Jaime's back pocket, classic brat pack PDA. Dan, behind the counter, lifting something over his head in a bad John Cusack impression, but—

That's not a Toshiba boom box.

It's a metal stool. Silver. Sturdy. Utilitarian. I've seen dozens just like this in the maintenance closet.

Elbows jab my rib cage from both sides. The hand that never left my bicep squeezes.

"You'll find stools behind both sales counters. As I said, this is a trial run for a program senior leadership has been considering for a while," Anya says. "Whether it continues will depend on how *sitting* affects customer experience. Remember, this is a privilege. A bonus, for good work. Keep it up, and the stools stay."

My fellow workers—my *friends*—effuse happiness like bubbles rising to the top of a champagne flute. They are effervescent, buoyant, incandescent. They're New Year's Eve giddy, confetti and glitter, too caught up in their silent celebration to realize the twelve-thousand-pound Waterford Crystal ball has dropped straight into my stomach. They might not see it yet, but I do, in 4K UHD.

Management's taking credit for the stools. Anya framed them as a reward for services rendered. Something that was already in the works. That's what she said about the dress code changes, too, but there wasn't a paper trail.

Omitting the petition from the official explanation is a tacit response to the petition itself. Management will appease everyone on *their* terms. Dagny and Anya will write the official record. As for that paper trail? They'll shred the petition and set fire to the confetti.

Specifically, they'll fire *me*, the body of proof that refutes their story. I'm the collateral damage.

I knew this could happen. I didn't have to write the petition, let alone deliver it. I could've hidden my signature amidst the scribbled masses. I don't get to be surprised about this; I don't deserve to be upset about it.

Because there are six silver stools behind the counters.

I always knew there was no such thing as a free lunch, so if this is it—if I'm the sacrificial lamb upon which they'll feast—then that's just how the wishbone breaks. My fellow workers get their stools, and I get slaughtered.

This is what winning looks like.

Anya crooks two fingers at me.

My friends clap me on the back and reassure me I have nothing to fear. They believe the win absolves us of sin, but I know better.

I cross the slaughterhouse floor. I can't hear anything but my heartbeat echoing inside my skull. I already made my choice, but I'm not going to be all Sydney Carton about this.

Anya's waiting past the ticketing counter, casually swiping away on her phone.

In American tradition, capital punishment gives you the right to last words. Beyond fight, flight, and freeze, the fourth prey response is *fawn.* Use your last words not to atone or defend but rather . . .

"I just want to say, working here has been a privilege," I grovel. "Despite any appearance to the contrary, I love it here. Every time I walk by Kane's Smith Corona typewriter, I remember how lucky I am to be here, playing the smallest part in this legacy. I'll always be grateful for that. It doesn't change anything, but—"

"He told you, didn't he?" Anya pulls off her glasses and pinches the bridge of her nose. "I *knew* Stanley couldn't keep a secret."

"Stanley didn't—"

"You don't need to impress me, Eli. Save it for the guests."

"I don't understand."

"After Stanley's recommendation, Dan's observations, and guest stories I've overheard, I was under the impression that you wanted to do more around here." Anya's lips turn down. "Was that your way of letting me down easy?"

I have absolutely no idea what is going on, but I haven't been axed yet. "Of course not. I'll do anything."

"Only if you want it. This goes beyond your official job description, and it doesn't come with a raise. As I'm sure Stanley told you, it's hard work. Docent duties aren't for the faint of heart. So, Eli, do you want to give tours?"

Oh, fuck. "*Of course* I want to—"

"Good. This weekend, you'll shadow Stanley, all right? I'm sure you could recite the tour script backward and blindfolded, but you'll still study the docent handbook. Please stick to the script—Stanley tends to take liberties—but you'll find opportunities to personalize it, add your favorite anecdotes, highlight your favorite artifacts. Such as the typewriter, apparently."

"Apparently," I agree faintly.

"That settles it. Let's get you settled in with Stanley."

Before I've processed any of it, Anya heads to the gift shop. I can see Stanley waving at me, smiling broadly.

I don't know what I did to deserve this. Two minutes ago, I was begging to keep my job only to receive a de facto promotion?

"Here we are. Stanley." Anya nods. "She's—oh, sorry, Eli. *He's* all yours, Stanley. Eli, you're in good hands. Just keep up the good work."

TWENTY-ONE

I CAN HAVE MY APFELKUCHEN AND EAT IT, TOO.

That's the moral of the story I'm chewing on hours later.

We headed straight for the apartment above Lou's for our union meeting, and now Ma's hideous, beloved Formica table is strewn with fried pickles, onion rings, and tofu nuggets. Naomi swiped a whole aquafaba Apfelkuchen, while I asked Ma if she could whip up a batch of kettle corn.

With everyone punch-drunk, sugar-high, overcaffeinated—strung out on the rush of *winning*—tonight is more party than union meeting.

I'm the most comfortable I've ever been here. I've got one leg folded up under the other, sipping bitter diner coffee, surrounded by friends. Yes, not only fellow workers, but also *friends.*

Stanley convinced TJ to tag along. They share one side of the table, Naomi and Lola the other. Across from me, Efraín hoards the popcorn bowl, absentmindedly munching and watching the others swap work stories. He doesn't bother hiding his lazy smile.

Efraín looks up, and our eyes lock. This is the part where I'm supposed to look away, where I always look away, where I do anything and everything to evade eye contact like direct sunlight—but I don't. I don't avert my gaze or declare a public health crisis. I just look at him and let him look at me. I let him see—

Well. I suppose it's up to him what he sees.

I'm not expecting him to declare, moments later, "I know what our next action is." The chatter dies down instantaneously. Even at his most placid, Efraín oozes charismatic authority.

My early report cards indicate I've always had a minor problem with authority. "*You* know? You decided, unilaterally? That sounds a little dictatorial. I thought we were supposed to govern by consensus."

Efraín doesn't parry. "You're right. I have a *proposal* for our next action." He clears his throat. He's stalling, genuinely nervous. "I propose we make pronoun buttons—for everyone."

It's like a pin-back straight to the heart. That stab of recognition. The open wound and the prick of blood. Efraín's looking at me like he *sees* me, like he's calling a bet.

"I know we haven't discussed them," Efraín barrels on, "but pronoun buttons are on the grievance list. We had a big win today, and we need to act quickly. With another surefire win, we'll build momentum and—"

"You think pronoun buttons would be a surefire win?"

"You don't?"

I feel lightheaded. Untethered. Like I've woken up in another timeline and realized no one else remembers how the universe is supposed to be, for better or for worse. Every sci-fi show has one of those episodes. *Nuclear Seasons* did it twice. I've done *this* twice before, too. "I tried. You know I tried. I told you, Dagny and Billy shut me down."

"I know," Efraín says quietly. "I'm sorry that—"

"I don't want you to apologize for institutionalized transphobia. Tell me what you think makes this different."

"We use the same play as the hair dye. When it was just you wearing a button, it was easy for Dagny to ban it. But if it's six of us?" He gestures around the table. "Maybe more? They can't ban that."

When he says it like that, it sounds eminently reasonable. According to Efraín's logic, I could've solved this a month ago if, instead of whining to management, I'd recruited my friends.

Except they weren't my friends then. I barely have the right to call them my friends now. No matter what Efraín and Lola did for Naomi, I never would've asked them to do the same for me—especially not after I sat out the first skirmish. I may be a selfish schmuck terrified of losing my job, but I'm not self-centered enough to ask anyone else to put their jobs on the line for *buttons.*

"Well, I think it's a great idea." Stanley beams, oblivious.

"I have a button maker," Lola volunteers, and points to Efraín with a fried pickle spear. "The same one we used to make buttons to save this or stop that or vote yes-no-maybe-so. Seriously, I don't know why you don't just take it to *your* house."

"Maybe if you didn't always complain about my designs—"

"You have the graphic design sensibility of el toro bravo. Scarlet, crimson, carmine, burgundy, and blood—anything to get people *seeing red.*"

"Did you know bulls are actually colorblind?" Naomi interjects. "*Mythbusters* did an episode. Spanish fighting bulls don't 'see red' at all. They charge at the *motion* of the flag."

"Sorry, what kind of buttons are we talking about?" TJ asks. "Like clothes buttons? Because sewing on our uniforms seems—"

"Oh, no, a button as in a pin," Stanley explains.

As everyone else elaborates on the history of the pin-back button, I mash my Apfelkuchen with my fork, making a goddamn mess. I can admit that I'm not upset because I think it's too risky; I'm not really upset at all. I just don't understand.

Efraín asks, "Other questions or concerns? Because you were right, Elisha, that this isn't up to me. We won't do this if you're not okay with it. Either of you," he amends with a contrite glance at Lola. "I don't want to open anyone up to harassment. The union is about *helping* people, not—"

"Taking unnecessary risks?"

"Do you believe this is an unnecessary risk? Because I mean it. If you really think this will do more harm than good—"

"I didn't say that." How am I supposed to do a risk analysis when this very proposal upends everything I thought I knew?

I've tried so hard to do this right. To follow the rules. To work hard, earn money, and buy acceptance where I can. I've tried so fucking hard to do this alone, only to make things worse, but now when Efraín proposes the same thing on a grander scale, *somehow*, it's a surefire win.

"For what it's worth," Lola says, in her reassuring One Hundred Percent Real FDA-Certified Empathy voice, "I'll take point on this. If management missed the townwide memo that went out in preschool, I'm fine with them finding out that I'm trans now."

"You're not worried—" I break off, trying to see Lola the way a cis person might. Even if she weren't my friend, if I hadn't known her forever, I'd think she passed flawlessly. But I'm trans; I've learned to *see* gender differently.

To the average Mall of America focus group cis people, though? Where I see *flawless* and *real*, would they see cracks in her femininity? Despite early medical intervention, does her body have anomalous tells? I don't know; I can't tell. "Aren't you worried that if people see you wearing a button, they might—"

"Look twice and decide I don't pass muster? I don't care."

"Efraín's right. It could be dangerous for you."

"You know I'm not actually stealth, right? *Existing* while transfemme and Afro Latina is dangerous. I learned that before my ABCs. Trust I know what I'm doing."

Lola told me once, after I'd come out, why her parents moved here from the East Bay. Her dad's older brother was gay, and despite having lived in Oakland since infancy and wearing his biker jacket like a second skin, Lola's Tío Ignacio was the victim of a fatal hate crime, gaybashed outside his own apartment building. So Lola's dad took a hard look at his burgeoning family and, much like his parents before him, packed up and moved his wife and child to a safer place: that promised land known as small-town America.

So, yes, Lola knows risk all too well. If I were her, I would take my genetic lottery winnings, run, never look back. But this is *Lola,* who, for reasons I'll never understand, *trusts the universe.*

"I know. I just—"

"You don't trust *them,*" Efraín finishes.

Lola clucks her tongue. "The two of you should hear yourselves. No one's asking you to trust them—whoever 'them' is, anyway. We have to trust *each other.*"

I follow her gaze around the table. Naomi, stone-faced but far from indifferent. Stanley, beaming, proud. TJ, the portrait of a puzzle. Efraín, catching my gaze like a trap, just lying in wait for me to look at him, and why does he try to convey so damn much with his eyes, in a language I never learned? I don't understand any of this.

What I do know is that the six of us are here at this flea market reject table, together, with the bones of a plan to do what I tried and failed to do . . . *together.* My carpool buddies turned fellow workers turned union comrades turned *friends* are offering me a second chance.

An injury to one is an injury to all.

All this time, I've been thinking of the union as a collective security agreement, built on fear of a common adversary. But ride-or-die has never been about mutually assured destruction. It's about trust, a synonym for solidarity.

All for one and one for all.

Solidarity is a pinky promise, a blood oath, and a suicide pact all in one.

I still don't understand why *this* or why *now,* but the offer is real.

All I have to do is say *yes.*

"Okay," I say. "Let's make some buttons."

One by one, they march out of the room carefree as toy soldiers—oblivious to the dangers of the battle, let alone the perilous scope of the war—skipping off to simple midsummer evening pleasures.

I'm not jealous. Neither picnicking with strangers nor bowling in black light sounds like my idea of a good time. So I sit at the table, waiting to be left alone with my thoughts.

But Efraín doesn't leave. He stays, watching me with that insufferable tilde frown. "I thought you'd be more excited."

"I'm a very anxious person."

He snorts. "Yeah, no shit. Pretty sure you're the most anxious person I've ever met."

I don't have grounds to object, not as I'm flicking my thigh while surveying the graveyard of dinnerware on the table, calculating how long it will take before ants descend. "That's not the worst thing you've ever said about me."

This is an obsessive-compulsive germophobe's nightmare. I probably should've accepted everyone's offers to help, but I wasn't going to let them be late on my account.

"Here, let me."

I start to protest, but Efraín's already consolidating food waste. It's quick, quiet work, between the two of us. As I'm washing my hands in the kitchenette sink, Efraín asks, "Have you been keeping track?"

"I'm sorry?"

"What you said before," Efraín clarifies. "That it wasn't the worst thing I'd said about you. You keep track."

"It's not like I have some master list of the Top Ten Things Efraín Hates About Me." Just like I have definitely, absolutely never made a list of the top ten things I hate about him.

I let him take his turn at the sink. The faucet sputters on, then off again. Efraín pumps the soap dispenser, rubbing gel over his hands with minimal lathering. I watch with morbid fascination as he rinses the soapy smear.

I'm about to issue my indignant point of order—the CDC recommends at least twenty seconds because lathering creates soap bubbles, which carry away contaminants—when he turns to me. Something about the intent inked in his otherwise illegible expression glues my lips shut.

"I get that you're anxious about blowback. From the buttons. I get that you can't just turn that off, but *you don't need to be.* I meant what I said. You're not alone in this."

This might kill me. The searing heat in his gaze, the sotto voce tenor of his voice, the diminishing space between us. Every conversation with Efraín is a battle—but this? His warpath is erratic. I retreat a few steps across the kitchenette. My breath comes out ragged. "You can't say things like that."

"Like what?"

"Things you don't mean."

"What the fuck does that mean?"

"It means—" I shake my head. "It means, you say I'm not alone in this, but I don't know what 'this' means. Because pronoun buttons as the union's next action? Doesn't make sense. I know you don't think it matters, whether the right thing is the rational thing, but I don't understand why you want to do this."

"Because I *care.*"

"But you care about *everything.* Every cause under the sun—and beyond it. The environmental cost of rocket launches, the danger of space privatization, and—"

"I care about you."

"You care about everyone—"

Efraín opens his mouth to interject, but I don't give him the chance.

"—and everyone's grievances. Secure scheduling for TJ. Health insurance for Jaime. The sick leave policy for Blake. Meanwhile, Lola doesn't get misgendered, and I'm the only one who's—" I swallow the word *suffering* because what a fucking joke. "I'm the one *complaining* about the button ban. So in the great trolley problem that is late capitalism, the union should be taking on the projects that benefit the largest number of workers. We should be—"

"Your *safety* isn't a thought experiment." Efraín seethes with vitriol that sends me reeling, like I've had a near miss with a bullet train.

I lean against the refrigerator as if the cold will leach the heat from my blood, break the fever of my muddled thoughts. Every time I think I understand any of this, I uncover a new layer to this nesting puzzle box.

"I know it isn't," I mutter. "That's why I tried to handle this quietly—to take care of it alone. It was *safer* that way."

"Safer for you, or more comfortable for everybody else?"

No one bothered to flip on the light on this side of the apartment. There's just one letterbox window, the corner streetlamp casting a diffuse sodium haze over Efraín's silhouette. Half his face is aglow like wildfire, but his eyes are hooded in shadow. His hair is loose, soft black waves obscuring the line where he ends and the night begins.

Efraín has always been a rebel with a thousand causes, but I was never supposed to be one of them. He corrects light misgendering, sure, but that costs him nothing, barely worth writing off as a charitable donation. The unbearable kindness he's offering tonight is an entirely different tax bracket.

I just want this to make sense. I need *him* to make sense.

"You're right, okay?" He's two steps closer, but no nearer an explanation. "Yes, I care about everyone, but not like I care about *you*."

"I don't know what that *means*."

"Seriously, Elisha?" he asks, whisper-soft. "You don't have any idea?"

His hand alights on my face, his knuckles grazing my cheekbone before he cups my cheek. And I can't breathe, but I can feel him, in every freckle and mole, in every speck of peach fuzz I wish were stubble, in every cell of this skin that so often feels like a secondhand costume.

I feel his touch, and I feel . . . warm. Not where he's touching me, but throughout my whole body. Warm, like the thermostat's been cranked up on the hottest night of the year.

My face is hot, presumably flushed and blotchy, and sweat percolates all over my skin. My chest has gone tight, and I'm dizzy. Is this what heat stroke feels like? No, heart palpitations are just karmic retribution for overdosing on caffeine when anxious, verging on overwhelm.

Do I have any idea what this means?

Efraín's hand on my face, his gaze locked on mine, his whole body curved down toward me, so much closer than I realized, all while he's trying to convince me that he *cares* about me, not just as a string of common nouns—a friend-human-fellow-worker—but as a proper noun, Elisha Goldstein, set apart from other proper nouns. He's trying to convince me that he, Efraín Juarez Reyna, cares like—

No, absolutely not. It doesn't make sense. Somewhere, I've fallen prey to a logical fallacy, and now I'm trapped in this paradox where he says he *cares* when I *know* he doesn't.

"Coldhearted," I recite, drumming my fingers against the fridge. "Selfish. Self-absorbed. Cynical. Complicit. Oblivious. Asleep. Hyperrational. Goody Two-Shoes. Anal retentive. Brownnoser. Fuck, that's eleven, but—oh, I forgot, *so fucking pedantic*—"

"Fucking hell, Elisha." His free hand catches mine, curls his fingers around mine, and all at once, he tilts my face up until the crown of my head slams against the fridge, and he arches down and crashes his lips against mine.

Because that's what the kiss is: a head-on collision, straight from my blind spot. A burst of heat-pressure-friction, then it's gone, before I have time to process how he tastes or smells or feels. He pulls back so damn fast, I get whiplash.

I stare up at him, dazed. My cheek is bare, my hand empty. But, no, there's a cat-shaped magnet denting my skull, and my lips are tingling. That happened. It wasn't a dream sequence. I *couldn't* have imagined this.

"Fuck," Efraín whispers, wrecked, as if more passed between us than one chaste kiss. "I shouldn't have done that."

"Do you regret it?" I ask, surprising no one more than myself.

"Not—" He shakes his head, biting his lip like he's shredding evidence. "I shouldn't have done it like that."

"How should you have done it?"

He lifts his hand—the one that was on my cheek—and plants his palm flat against the fridge door, just beside my head. "I should've said—the part I regret was saying those things. Well, most of them. I stand by that last one."

I scrunch my nose, rewinding the ticker tape and coming up broke.

"*So fucking pedantic,*" he murmurs, hot against the shell of my ear. "Drives me crazy."

"In a good way?"

When he nods, his hair brushes my temple. "Should've said that first. Should've said all the quiet parts out loud. Should've asked—"

I surge up on my tiptoes and reach up to pull him down because turnabout is fair play, and I kiss him. I don't know what I'm doing, I don't know how I'm feeling, I don't know if

I'm thinking at all because this is objectively crazy. He's too fucking tall, and my fists tangle in his silky hair.

His arms immediately, instinctively move to stabilize me, one around my waist, his hand cupping my cheek again. He's burnt kettle corn and coconut lip balm. He's a lightning strike in a midsummer storm. He's the answer to a question I never thought to ask.

Gravity pulls us apart before I'm ready, but he doesn't let me go. He straightens up but holds me close.

His eyes are lovely, dark, and deep.

I am so utterly lost. Yes, he cares, he kissed me, but what does that *mean*?

"For the record," I say, winded, "I still don't understand."

"Which part? That I care about you? That I want you to be safe? That I want to make pronoun buttons to keep you safe, to make sure you feel safe, to make you feel cared for—"

"That," I admit. "The *feeling* part. I don't know what that means."

"The feeling part," Efraín echoes. "That's the whole—it's *all* feeling."

That's the problem.

I don't know what it's like to care like that. With your whole body. I care in the abstract. I intellectualize. Empathy is a conscious cognitive process, not an instinct. That was the trouble with Naomi's hair. As much as I care about my sister—because I do, of course, I care about her—I couldn't process the *care* to catalyze a reaction.

Because I only ever felt the injustice of it all *intellectually*; the care never breached the blood-brain barrier, never flooded my veins until I was *emotionally compelled* to act. I didn't feel Naomi's injury as if it were my own. "An injury to one is an injury to all" is a principle I might believe in, yes, but it comes from my head, not my heart. I can reason myself out of it when push comes to shove.

But Efraín cares viscerally. Every injury, every injustice a stigmata. He *feels* with his whole body.

I feel his heat against my chest, his arms wound around me, and I feel *this* in my whole body. I *feel* his care. Not because he said it, not because he kissed me quiet, but because he wants to make *buttons.* Because they matter to me. Because *I* matter to *him.*

He grabs my wrist and presses my hand against his chest, my palm over his heart. "Do you get it yet?"

Given the low scoop of his tank, half my hand rests against his bare skin, my thumb over his sternum, bristly curls tickling my skin. A foreign sensation, not unpleasant. Then there's his heart, the steady *thumpa-thumpa* vibrating against my palm.

I assume he's making this gesture metaphorically, to make some point based on the widespread cultural misconception of the heart as the center of emotion, rather than the limbic system, but the gesture is not without significance. Because the heart—the hub pumping blood throughout the body—is vital. Letting another access it is a dangerous display of vulnerability; it's proof of *trust* itself.

I still don't understand. I may never understand.

I don't like not knowing things. I know omniscience is a futile aspiration. I know the sum of everything I know—everything I will *ever* know—approximates the percentage of visible stars in the night sky. I know I could spend a lifetime studying data from the most powerful telescopes on earth, and even then, I would only ever see a fraction of the observable universe. There are four hundred billion stars in our galaxy alone, most I'll never see—but that doesn't mean I'll stop looking at the sky.

It doesn't mean I'll stop trying to draft a star chart in Efraín's eyes or trying to decode this feeling.

I don't know what this means, but I know I don't want to stop.

TWENTY-TWO

ON SUNDAY, BUTTON DISTRIBUTION IS IN FULL SWING—EXCEPT no one will give *me* a button. Lola insisted it would be safer to wait until everyone else has theirs.

I try to ignore the guilt lancing down my spine. No one questioned me when I said I didn't want to be the face of the pronoun button action.

Everyone took my emotional exhaustion at face value, offering the escape hatch without me asking. They're not asking for more than I have to give, even if I feel like I should be giving more.

But I know better. There's no way management won't trace this back to me. Employee zero.

Still, I humor them. I wait and watch buttons pop up on shirts and lanyards all around me.

After my late lunch, I track Stanley down to catch up with his tour group. Except, instead of Stanley, I find Efraín on the second floor of the silo.

"What are you doing here?" I ask, breathless.

"Looking for you," he replies.

"So I gathered." I cross the empty gallery. "Aren't you supposed to be in the gift shop?"

"I took a fifty-five."

The ceiling rattles above us, a few heavy footfalls, a tinny shriek, but it's eerily quiet on this floor.

"You've already been gone longer than five minutes, haven't you?"

"Not like anyone keeps track on 'emergency breaks.'"

"Everyone keeps track!"

"Guess I better be quick, then."

"Quick about wh—"

He has me crowded into the alcove by the upper stairs before I realize what's happening. He steals a kiss fast enough to evade museum security. He pulls away before my body catches up enough to kiss him back. Over his shoulder, I make eye contact with a familiar lens.

"Hey," I whisper. "Not that I don't want to live out a stock scene from every Art/Harry fic, but there's a camera *right there*, and I'm pretty sure making out on the job is a fireable offense."

"Who's in HQ right now? Do you think they'd look the other way if I Venmo'd them twenty bucks?"

"Efraín."

"No, you're right. Can't forget inflation. What's the going rate for a minor bribe these days? A hundred?"

From this angle, he eclipses the track lights, kept dim to

protect the artifacts and cool-toned to up the eerie factor. I'm face-to-face with a sight worthy of his own museum display: Efraín, happy, as close to carefree as he gets.

"I never thought I'd have to talk you out of *bribing* someone. Bribes are the epitome of capitalist corruption. I can't believe you'd—"

"I'd be exploiting a flaw in a corrupt system for the greater good."

I blush. "Why did you really come up here? Because some of the best fics take place in the compartment downstairs, but that's a photo-op logjam during open hours—"

"I have no idea what you're talking about."

"You know, episode sixteen, 'The Compartment,' which was the bottle episode filmed entirely in—" I can just barely discern his bafflement. "Okay, *this* is how I know you've never actually watched *Nuclear Seasons*."

"Ms. Hutchinson made us watch an episode during our California history unit."

"That was third grade, which, come to think of it . . . is maybe too young to expose impressionable minds to tentacle monsters and scurvy zombies?"

"What?"

"Exactly. You have no idea which episodes I'm talking about."

"Those are actual episodes?"

"Oh my God, how do you even *work* here? Wait, don't

answer that. I'm going to fix this. We're going to watch the show. I'll curate a sampler of greatest hits, and we can—" I look up at him, insecure all over again. "Unless you don't want to. Never mind. Just forget—"

He tilts my chin up. "Hey. Elisha. I can survive watching an episode or two with you."

"It doesn't have to be *with* me. I can just send you an annotated list of the best episodes—"

"Oh hell no. If I'm going to watch this, I'm *only* going to watch it with you. As long as you agree to let me take you out."

"What?"

"A date. Our next day off."

"I think that can be arranged."

"Good. Now, time for the feature presentation."

"What are you—"

He takes my hand and presses something against my palm. I know what it is—I'd be able to guess even if I didn't feel the straight, cold metal pin bisecting my lifeline. "What do you think?" he asks, soft and vulnerable, like my opinion really matters to him.

I try to study the button clinically, like he's dropped a gemstone in my palm and asked me to assess its quality, clarity, and value. I nudge him aside and hold the button up to the light.

The final design isn't that different from the mock-ups I saw yesterday. Sometime before going to print, though,

Efraín changed the background from pastel pink to lavender. Does he know purple's my favorite color?

Between my Vans, my backpack, and my phone case, it should be painfully obvious to anyone that violet is my favorite range on the spectrum of visible light. Is there some deeper meaning in the last-minute switch, or am I reading too much into this?

I'm definitely *not* misreading the text at the bottom, where he has ignored my advice *thrice* now and kept that reckless "PLEASE DON'T MISGENDER MUSEUM WORKERS!!!" line, which is *so* predictably Efraín that my face hurts from holding back my smile. Realistically, I should be grateful he used *please.*

The thing is, this isn't any gemstone he's handed to me; it's a priceless jewel. *Literally* priceless because we're taught that something's value is determined by how much someone is willing to pay for it. Efraín's offering me this gift freely. This button is worth more than every artifact in this museum combined.

"Elisha?" He's impatient, worrying his lip between his teeth.

"It's perfect."

"Honestly?"

"As perfect as it could be given that you didn't follow my instructions."

"Instructions?" His mouth quirks between a smile and a smirk. "About the—no one else complained."

"I wasn't complaining; it was a *critique.* You know as well as I do that no one was going to argue with you after you appointed yourself the button design czar—"

"Here I thought you said it was *perfect.*"

I look up at him, trying to tease out the line between bicker and banter. "It is. Subjectively. Maybe not objectively."

"So it's perfect in a 'it's the thought that counts' kind of way?"

"Yes, exactly. But also because—" I swallow down the "no one's ever done something like this for me" and shake my head. It's only then—out of the alcove, a few steps into the light—that I finally notice the button pinned to his own shirt. "I think the buttons will be effective. The *institution* might object to the *messaging*—"

"The institution was always going to object."

"—but museum guests will see them. Read them. Hopefully—"

"Listen to them."

"No one can *listen* to a button."

"Now you're just being pedantic on purpose."

"It's not a crime to want things to be correct, and even if it was? We're all abolitionists here." I fumble with the button because I'm beyond ready to put it on. My fingers slip, and the needle exacts a blood toll on my thumb. It doesn't hurt any more than Sputnik's love bites, but I don't want to get blood on my loaned-not-owned uniform shirt. Except scrunching up my shirt and angling the button one-handed requires more coordination than I possess.

"Here, let me." Efraín pries the button from my clumsy fingers. He pins it just above my name tag. I am keenly aware how close his hands are to my chest.

The button occupies collarbone territory, technically, but my heart's pounding like it doesn't know where my binder fits or whether it matters at all. Ironic, isn't it, that Efraín's close enough to cop a feel with plausible deniability while holding a button designed to remind the world that I'm a boy, in case they were misled by the size of my chest, among other lipstick-red herrings?

I want to believe Efraín doesn't need the reminder, but how am I supposed to know what any of this means when I can hear his own uneven breathing?

Then he smooths his thumb over the "he/him" like he's touching something holy. "There," he murmurs. "Now you're ready to fight the museum."

"I don't *want* to fight the museum."

Efraín's hands settle on my shoulders. "Then I'll fight it for you."

I want to fight him on it and insist that I don't want him to fight the museum, either. I don't want anyone to fight the museum. I want the museum to get with the times. Just because it's a monument to old things doesn't mean it has to be a timeless mausoleum.

The button should be a message, not a grenade. Efraín should know that. I want to explain it to him, but he's touching me. I should thank him, but he's looking at me. I don't know how to want all these things at once.

He nudges me back, and my back hits the corrugated metal wall beside the shadowbox with thirty-two of Art's bow ties. I know I'm standing in a panopticon. At least three security cameras have eyes on me. But Efraín occupies my entire field of view.

I touch his button because I can. I don't know how to thank him with words, so I just touch the button and look up at him and hope he understands these little gestures I make in place of things I can't say.

I don't know if it works, but he kisses me and kisses me and—

Downstairs, Stanley's talking about the mystery of whatever happened to Victor Kane's grandmother's crystal goblets. Heavy footfalls trudge up the staircase, and I'm still smothering my laughter against Efraín's shoulder.

"So," he whispers against my hair. "When can you start your fifty-five?"

TWENTY-THREE

"AND *THIS,* RIGHT HERE, IS MY FAVORITE ARTIFACT IN THE museum. I mean, everything about Kane's study feels magical. A little musty, but the Snoopy mug on the credenza is such a great touch. Like Kane just stepped away, but he could come back any second and—oh, right, my favorite artifact.

"That would be the script—the one under the glass on the desk. It's the first draft of the final episode, 'Who's Afraid of Wolf Spector?' If you look closely, you'll see two sets of notes in the margins. The ones in pencil? That's Kane's handwriting. But these other notes in red pen in someone else's handwriting? That mystery person crossed out 'Art' in Harry's climactic monologue and wrote 'Artie,' the first evidence of that nickname.

"Here's the thing: No one has ever claimed responsibility for those annotations. George Rhodes swears Kane showed him the draft first, with the nickname already there. In fact, no one remembers seeing this annotated draft until after Kane's death. There's a theory—well, I'll let you puzzle that out for yourselves. Take a few minutes to look around. I'll be here if you want to swap theories. Otherwise, we'll regroup in five and head outside."

I'm winded, like I was in eighth grade when we ran The Mile, and my asthmatic lungs could never keep up. But now, I've got runner's high because I'm a full-fledged docent. Yesterday, Stanley was with me all day as mentor, monitor, and moral support. Dan gave me the green light. So, this is it. Tuesday, Stanley's day off, is my first solo tour day.

No adult supervision—unless you count the adults on my tour. Which I don't, because I'm supervising *them.* You wouldn't believe how many times you have to tell fully grown adults not to touch even when there are DO NOT TOUCH placards *right there.*

"What's this theory?"

The voice in my ear startles me off balance. It's purely luck that my hand lands flat on the wall rather than the Polaroid of Victor Kane with François Truffaut on the set of *Close Encounters of the Third Kind.*

"Sorry?" I face Anya with my most professional, unfazed smile.

"The theory," Anya says, "about the red pen."

"Oh. The theory is that Kane must've shown the draft to someone else first."

"Hmm," Anya hums. "I heard it was a rogue copy editor."

"But why—" The possibilities ping-pong in my head, every what-if shattering into ten more what-ifs.

"Why indeed. That's what I like about this place. So full of mystery. The stories are so *close* here, but so many details we'll never know. That's the beauty of it, no?" Anya gestures to the gleaming open-plan gallery around us. "The Nuclear Seasons Experience is something everyone decides for themselves. We can't tell them what to think."

"No, of course not."

Two strangers from my tour are engaged in an animated debate over by the display case with Kane's three Purple Hearts about the old rumor that Kane buried his brass in a coffee can and only dug them up to use as props in Harry's PTSD allegory episode, "Apocalypse When." They're getting into it, having a grand old time. The story's more important than the truth.

"You understand, then," Anya says, "why it isn't allowed."

"Pardon?"

"The—" She lowers her voice, so the guests won't hear her scandalous words. "That *pin.* It violates the dress code."

The scandal doesn't click. Has she been watching the same debate by the medals of valor? Some of them are pins, but what does that have to do with the dress—

Pin. Pin-back. Button.

This doesn't make sense. It's been two days since the buttons made their debut, and this is the first I've heard from management. No one has said anything in the group chat. It's been all quiet on the western front.

I should've known better than to succumb to that siren call of false security. Anya approaching me alone—that should've been the first warning sign. Anya doesn't work Tuesdays; she wasn't *at* pre-shift. So why would she approach me when I'm alone, in the middle of a tour? My first tour. With guests all around us.

Is this supposed to stop me from making a scene?

"I don't understand," I admit, bald and blunt. I can't help if it comes across as blithe or blasé.

"Don't you?" Anya's eyes narrow behind her cat-eye glasses.

I'm looking at the room through a very long tunnel. It's a cheap lens effect; *NS* used it in episodes for flashbacks and premonitions. This *disconnect*, the whole world on delay, images and words out of sync, slow buffering and shitty dubbing—I'm dissociating.

I know this. I am Elisha Goldstein. I am at the Nuclear Seasons Experience in Egan's Creek. It is somewhere between eleven thirty and noon, and—

Today is a Tuesday. Lola, Naomi, and Stanley all have the day off. Efraín and TJ are in the gift shop. I'm teetering between a garden-variety panic attack and a nuclear meltdown.

None of this was supposed to happen, not today, not to *me.* Not again.

"You know you can't wear that pin," Anya says. "It's against museum policy. You need to take it off."

"I need to finish this tour."

"You need to take it off right now, Eli."

"I don't—" I blink. My vision doesn't clear, and neither does my head. Why would it make a difference if I took off the button after this tour? Everyone in this group has already seen my button. If I take it off now, I'll never be able to put it on again.

I don't move. I can't.

"Don't make a scene. There are guests here."

Of course there are guests here. She ambushed me on the museum floor.

"Be reasonable, Eli."

Anya wants me to be reasonable, but there is no *reason* here. I'm wearing a button, yes, but so are half the GSAs and three security guards. But I'm the one Anya singled out for public flagellation. The only plausible reason? I'm the one wearing a button while visibly trans. The one who already complained. The one who just doesn't know when to shut up and take it.

I'm only postponing the inevitable.

So I do the only reasonable thing and take off my button.

Anya smiles. "Thank you, Eli. That wasn't so hard, was it?"

In Jewish tradition, it's disrespectful to leave flowers at a grave site. Flowers are living things; flowers die. They are a reminder of our own impermanence, bouquets of memento mori, except no one needs that reminder in a graveyard, least of all the people buried in it. That's why Jews leave pebbles on headstones.

That's why I hate the baroque floral arrangements people leave at Victor Kane's grave.

Of course, this isn't a Jewish cemetery. Kane didn't have a proper Jewish funeral. Not because he had a tattoo or because he died by suicide—those are just myths, not reasons to deny burial—but rather because of the core commandment that a Jew should be buried among Jews.

In other words, a person should be buried with their people.

Victor Kane is buried alone. All he wanted, per the postscript on his two-line suicide note, was for his faithful German shepherd, Mondo Kane, to be buried beside him when the time came, but Victor's wife cremated Mondo, so Victor remained alone.

Alone, but for the hundreds of museum patrons who visit here, whether to pay their respects or play disaster tourist at the final resting place of the man-myth-legend.

Here, on my lunch break, am I paying my respects or playing disaster tourist?

The sun beats down on me. The world is too bright, over-exposed, and my eyes water through my letterbox squint. I should've grabbed my sunglasses. I shouldn't have come out here at all.

I don't know how I made it through the rest of the tour this morning. It wasn't muscle memory because it was *my first tour*, which will not end up in my long-term memory palace's vaunted hall of proud achievements. I thought I'd look back on that tour as a defining moment—the time I was entrusted to share my knowledge and love of all things *Nuclear Seasons* in an official capacity. I'd curated a sterling set of factoids and anecdotes for guests to wow their friends, but I don't know if I shared any of them. I remember worrying Anya would appear around every corner to ensure I didn't put my button back on.

Somehow, I made it to my morning break and locked myself in the only gender-neutral bathroom in the lobby. I sent an imprecise précis to the group chat. I don't remember what I wrote. I'm afraid to check.

I haven't read the replies, either.

When I dropped off my last morning tour group in the gift shop, I was worried Efraín might defect from the register to ask *if I'm okay,* but I made a quick escape.

Kane's grave site is outside, away from the barn, remote to all but the most die-hard fans. It's also morbid and weird, and everything I've ever learned about Victor Kane leads me to believe he never would've wanted strangers parading over his grave like it's some kind of monument.

But that's why I ended up here today, isn't it? I know Kane isn't the institution, but what is this museum if not a monument to his reconstituted memory?

I recognize those little scraps of Hebrew on Kane's tombstone because they're inscribed on Opa's tombstone, too. Key among them is Z"L, the transliterated abbreviation for *zichrono livracha*: may his memory be a blessing.

I've always believed that NSX fulfilled that promise—that it made Kane's memory something sacred by honoring his gift to the world.

But instead of *sacred*, the museum has chosen *corporate*. Instead of a gift freely given, it's a ticket purchased at a premium rate. Instead of offering community to anyone who feels alone, the institution has sealed itself shut to anyone who doesn't conform.

Does this message honor Kane's memory?

All Kane wanted was to be buried with his dog on a quiet corner of his familial ranch. Instead, I'm standing here as a cog in the cheap amusement park built over his home. Just being here is a violation of his memory.

In Jewish tradition, we honor the dead with pebbles instead of flowers, but I don't have a pebble. I have a button that isn't worth its weight in paper, let alone stone. The button is banned because it is an insult to the institution, but the institution is an insult to the man.

I wasn't trying to stick it to the man; I just want to be seen as one.

Whispering a blessing under my breath, I set my pronoun button on Kane's headstone, and I head back to work.

"I can solve that mystery for you."

I blink into the harsh afternoon sunlight. I've just dropped off my last tour outside the barn. I was planning on loitering here for a few minutes—no one can accuse me of hiding in broad daylight, right? Besides, it's not working if Eden from curatorial can track me down.

"What mystery?" I ask, straightening up.

"The screenplay draft," she answers. "I caught part of your tour. It was great, by the way."

I sincerely doubt it was great given my mental state, but Eden looks perfectly sincere. The light bounces off her gold glasses frames and the matching, glimmering cuffs interspersed through her braids as she fiddles with the strap of her messenger bag.

"I was heading downstairs when you were in the farmhouse. I wasn't planning on tagging along, but I liked hearing your take. I hope that's okay." Eden bites her lip like she really cares about whether she has my approval to join an open tour.

"Sure. Follow along whenever you want. What were you saying about the screenplay?"

She grins. "That was the reason I stopped. You were talking about the theories behind the 'Artie' annotation?"

"What about it?"

"Everything in red pen? It's Sam Schatz's handwriting. He always used the double-story 'a' but never dotted his i's."

"That's impossible." My brain's been on the fritz all day, so it shouldn't be a surprise when it short-circuits. "I've seen his signature a thousand times . . ."

"His *cursive* signature," Eden rebuts. "He usually stuck to print handwriting, especially in his letters."

"I didn't think we had any of his letters."

"The museum has hundreds, just not on display."

Strange. Sam died in 1989 and didn't leave behind much of an estate—whatever wealth he'd acquired from acting went to the hospital bills he racked up while dying young of AIDS. He didn't have family or a serious long-term partner who might've kept his belongings long enough to donate them to the museum a decade later.

What I do understand, however, is that I, a lowly guest services associate, am not privy to the inner workings of this museum. There are thousands of artifacts I'll never see, even if I manage to get the junior curatorial internship—and *fuck.* I hadn't even gotten around to considering what today means for my internship chances.

Before I succumb to the full-blown panic spiral, Eden says, "After reading hundreds of Sam's letters, trust me when I say I *know* his handwriting. He's the one who wrote 'Artie.'"

"That means Kane showed him the first draft." My brain has rebooted with surprising alacrity, firing on all cylinders. "I thought Kane didn't show anyone his scripts until he was on at least the *fifth* draft. Remember that story about how he kept reworking the script for 'Citizen Egan' until like two days before filming? Judy was begging him to let her help."

Eden's worrying her lip between her teeth again, but I have no idea what she could possibly be worried about saying now. Then she says, "Speaking of help, TJ said something to me in the break room earlier about, well, this." She angles her messenger bag to reveal a teal "she/her" button pinned to the flap.

I don't know whether to point out that that can't be good for the leather or that everyone should know better than to talk about baby socialist fight club in the break room by now.

"He said the people who made the buttons have been discussing what to do about the ban."

The official button ban came down via email early this afternoon, just one bullet point in our weekly guest services bulletin—a "friendly reminder" that the dress code prohibits "personal accessories" as well as "items containing or pertaining to political speech."

"Everyone was really worked up about it," Eden says. "Dan was asking for Blake's opinion on whether his anti-establishment punk band tees count as political speech. Blake was worried about her piercings and Jaime's tattoos, too. TJ was reassuring them and giving me a little backstory, and . . ." Self-consciously, she tucks a braid behind her ear. "I suggested an email zap."

"What?"

"It's when a bunch of people contact a target all at once to put pressure on them to do, well, whatever the objective is."

"I know what an email zap is, but how do *you* know?"

"I was a TA in grad school. I wasn't super active in the TA union, but I participated in an email zap to the dean. So, when TJ showed me the email, it got me thinking. I don't know the whole story here, but an email zap seems like a proportionate response, right? TJ said he was going to post about it in a group chat. I thought—"

"I haven't checked the group chat," I interrupt. It probably sounds rude, given that Eden is offering her help, but I just feel *exposed*. It's been hard enough being vulnerable with the union, and now everyone at the museum knows my business?

I can't meet Eden's eyes, so I pull out my phone and check the chat.

Sure enough, the union has developed a rapid strategic response based on Eden's idea: a barrage of emails expressing disappointment in management's decision and showing support for pronoun buttons.

Stanley's email template is excruciatingly polite, blame-free, and thanks the senior leadership team for *their time and consideration* like a cover letter. Anyone who's comfortable can dress it up by noting that LGBTQ people are a protected class with distinct legal protections.

The plan is to schedule the emails to send at the same time, tomorrow morning. Send to Dagny, CC Anya and Billy, and BCC everyone in the union. Hopefully by then, Lola and Stanley will have recruited more participants.

"What do you think?" Eden asks.

"It's a solid plan," I say, staring at my shoes. I don't have any constructive criticism. I also don't have any desire to write an email enumerating all the arguments I've already made.

"Do you think it would be okay if I wrote an email?"

"Sorry, what?"

When I finally look, Eden's not looking at me. She's looking over her shoulder. "I know I'm sheltered in the farmhouse," she says, her knuckles wrapped tight around her shoulder strap. "I mostly work alone, and Winston is the world's most easygoing boss. No one in admin has a dress code, not even 'business casual.' No one cares if I show up in this"—she gestures down at her cargo pants and T-shirt, which she's classed up with a blazer—"and they've never said anything about any buttons I've worn. I get that I don't have a customer-facing position like y'all do, but I hate a double standard."

"Wait, let me get this straight," I say. "You want to write an email not because the button ban affects you, but because it *doesn't* affect you?"

"Yep," Eden says.

Maybe on another day, I'd feel capable of making sense of this, but I'm so damn tired. I don't just feel frazzled but frayed at the seams. Pull a single thread, and I'll unravel completely.

"But *why*?" I ask.

Eden cocks her head. "It's not that different from a cis person wearing a pronoun button, is it?"

"Yeah, it really is. Wearing a button when someone hands

it to you—when half the staff's already wearing them—is simple. It's not a fashion statement if it's already trendy. But sending an email requires intention," I say, rubbing my palms over my corduroy shorts so I don't ball them into fists. "You sign your name, and you're putting yourself on the line."

"You wrote that petition, didn't you?"

I nod.

"Then you get it," Eden says, as if I haven't just said otherwise. "I've been here two years, and I never figured out why this place is so cutthroat. I can't say anything without feeling . . . There's a reason I eat lunch in your break room. So maybe the ban doesn't affect me personally, but what happens to all of you affects me. Because I care what happens, so, I figure, yeah, I can put my name on the line, you know?"

Oh, right. Of course. That's what that creepy-crawly anxiety itch over every inch of my skin is about. I'm afraid to sign my name to an email.

"Okay," I tell her. "The more the merrier, right?"

Eden watches me. "You know *you* don't have to send an email, right?"

I blink and reassure her, "I know," though I'm not sure I do.

What I know is that whether I write an email or not, management will hold me accountable for any and all transgender-related transgressions in this museum. But other people are going to do this with or without me. They're opening themselves up to retaliation, too.

And here I am complaining that I'm too tired to write an email for a cause that directly concerns me, for which I will be blamed no matter what I do.

If I'm going to do the time, I might as well do the crime.

Be gay, do crime. Be trans, do organized crime.

TWENTY-FOUR

"LET ME GET THIS STRAIGHT. YOU BROUGHT ME TO A MUSEUM ON our day off from our job at a museum that you don't even *like*?"

"This isn't a museum," Efraín insists. "It's a historical site."

Standing on a red-brick corner just south of downtown Santa Rosa, I can't help giving Luther Burbank Home and Gardens a skeptical side-eye. A museum dedicated to the guy who pioneered plant hybridization was not on my potential date hot spot bingo card.

Of course, *our* museum is already overshadowing Efraín's and my first date. I stayed up late drafting my email for the zap, fell asleep at my keyboard, and woke up just in time to type "thank you for your time and consideration" before Efraín was set to pick me up.

He was late, but only by two minutes, which was enough for me to see that the union came through. Efraín tried to distract me on the drive by making me read one-star NSX Yelp reviews aloud.

"Historic things happened on Kane's ranch," I argue, on principle. "What makes this a historical site instead—"

"The city of Santa Rosa," Efraín interrupts. "They declared it a historical site. It's a park, too. Does it matter?"

I squint up at him. He's a vision with his messy half bun, sun-bleached tank, denim cutoffs, and his favorite cherry Docs. "It matters to you, doesn't it?"

He looks down at me through his aviators. "What?"

I know what Efraín looks like when he cares about something just a little bit more than all the other somethings he cares about. If he won't tell me upfront, I'll figure it out myself. "Nothing. Do lead on."

He leads me into a stark white building, a converted carriage house. He confirms the tour is free with an enthusiastic girl who looks younger than Naomi and, when prompted by Efraín, tells us her entire life story, leading up to the decision to volunteer here.

Efraín keeps her talking about how the museum operates. I walk around the gift shop until a grizzled docent arrives. Thanks to Efraín, I learn that Kate is a retired biology teacher who's been volunteering here for twenty years, originally tending the gardens, then guiding tours after her knee replacement.

Kate leads us through Luther Burbank's house, the bottom story of which looks as it would've when Burbank's family lived here. Kate shows us relics such as the 1927 GE

Monitor Top refrigerator and Burbank's Wells Fargo desk with hidden compartments galore; heirlooms like his wife's glass collection and his parents' Staffordshire wedding dog statuettes. Photos of family and friends adorn the walls. This early-twentieth-century house makes for an achingly familiar museum.

Then Kate takes us to the greenhouse. Surrounded by blooming marvels, we're standing in the original structure, which was built in 1889. When the 1906 earthquake devastated downtown Santa Rosa just a few blocks away, not a single pane of glass in this greenhouse broke.

Then we're off on the "and Gardens" leg, traipsing past roses, cacti, and the sensory garden.

Efraín asks so many questions I'm afraid Kate is going to kick us out. I'm just along for the ride, thoroughly delighted by Efraín's enthusiasm. I think Kate gets a kick out of it, too, because she hangs out with us until her next tour.

I follow Efraín along the winding brick paths, each one leading to more vibrant, verdant delights. "You didn't just want to come here because it's a museum, did you?" I ask as we pass a famed Santa Rosa plum tree, bright burgundy bulbs dangling from the branches like ornaments. "This isn't a research field trip to get new ideas for the community garden or compare working conditions—"

"This place is run by volunteers," Efraín corrects me, perfectly pedantic.

“Does that make it more ethical? If they’re doing the same work—or more,” I add, glancing at a volunteer crouched in the dirt, “for free?”

“They’re here because they love it.”

“I love NSX.” I can *feel* his skeptical gaze. “I do,” I insist because, in spite of everything, it’s true.

He lets out a single, silent laugh. “I never told you why I interviewed at NSX, did I?”

I asked myself that incessantly those first few weeks, and I asked him outright during our mock one-on-one. I’m so used to the cadence of the question that I’ve forgotten to expect a response.

We round a bend back to the rose garden.

“You won’t like it,” he warns me.

“I’m not going to judge you.”

“I’d judge me. Spoiled rich kid teenage rebellion shit—the kind I’d hate hearing from anyone else.”

“Guess it’s a good thing I’m not you, then.”

“I made a deal with my mom. I thought I was going to Madera this summer, like I have every summer since the divorce. My dad manages a vineyard just north of Fresno. It’s not a formal custody thing, just routine. But after I spent Christmas there, she told me I had to get a job or an internship this summer. Something that would look good on college applications.

“I guess I thought she was bluffing? That my dad could

talk her out of—" He does that single-laugh thing again. "When she realized I hadn't applied anywhere, my mom called in a favor. She got me a gig at the Grove."

"Shit," I say, reflexive and definitely judgmental.

"Yeah," Efraín agrees.

The Bohemian Grove is the exclusive, scenic wine country retreat where former presidents, tech moguls, all breeds of one percenters, and their pet Supreme Court justices gather to get drunk and plot world domination.

"I said I'd burn it down before I worked there."

Yeah, that sounds about right.

"She told me to find something else if I didn't want to take the job. So I figured I'd get the shittiest summer job I could find, somewhere she'd be embarrassed to tell her friends. Egan's Creek doesn't have McDonald's, but maybe I should've looked into one of those dozen Taco Bells.

"I asked Lola about the body shop—it'd piss my mom off if I came home with grease stains—but Lola laughed, said someone who hates cars shouldn't work with them. Besides, even she wasn't working for her dad this summer—she told you about the breakup, right?—she couldn't work with Curtis, and she'd heard you talking about openings at NSX. And that—"

"Fit your definition of 'shitty'?"

Efraín grimaces. "I warned you."

"Believe it or not, it's not shocking that you thought

working at NSX would be shitty. I never understood why you took the job anyway."

"Now you know."

"Not quite." I hesitate. Efraín may have cracked open the door on his family drama, but that doesn't mean I should barge in. "You said it was a deal, but you didn't say what you got in return. Because if you're working here, you're not in Fresno."

"Winter vacation. Bad trade, right? Three months doing whatever she wants for two weeks with my dad."

"That doesn't seem fair."

"Fair's not part of the conversation when your mom's a successful business owner, and your dad—" He looks up at the cloudless sky. "What do you remember about my dad?"

I remember Mr. Juarez as a bear of a man with Efraín's pitch-black eyes, twin braids under a Panama hat, and a hand-carved walking stick that he used to behead a baby rattlesnake on our third-grade field trip. In retrospect, I can't believe Efraín didn't cry serpenticide, but Mr. Juarez explained that adolescent rattlesnakes are more dangerous than the adults because they haven't learned how to control their venom yet, and with six children under his care, he wouldn't take any risks.

"He was kind," I say softly.

"He is." Efraín nods. "Too kind for his own good. He met my mom the summer after her sophomore year at Princeton.

She was interning for a state senator and living with her parents, where my dad was a grape picker without a green card. Her dad came this close to disowning her."

I'm trying to follow the thread, but it takes me a minute to untangle the strands. "Your dad was an undocumented agricultural worker."

"That's the least interesting thing about him. I could tell you about how he started hybridizing grapes to breed more drought-resistant strains or how he ran a food pantry out of his truck while his church was fumigated. He lobbied the town council to start a community garden every year, and they shot him down every time. But it's not even that he's a good person who does good things. He's a good person who sees the good in everyone and trusts that people will make good choices if they're given the chance. That's *rare*; that's hard—"

A good person would know how to reassure Efraín that *he* is that kind of person, too, but I don't know what to say. I don't know what to do but listen and touch his arm in a way that hopefully feels reassuring rather than weird. "Your dad used to take you here, didn't he?"

Efraín nods. He takes my hand and guides us out of the rose garden, back toward the carriage house. "This is my favorite."

The spineless cactus doesn't look like any cactus you'd see in a Western or a succulent on a windowsill. Larger than a truck, all tangled fronds, it could stand in for the monster-of-the-week on an overbudget sci-fi show any day.

"Thank you for bringing me here," I say. "For sharing this with me."

Efraín settles his arm around my shoulders as we pay our respects.

It's a strange plant in a strange place. A garden full of mutants. A beautiful place built from hard work and bold ideas.

Then again, isn't that how all beautiful places are built?

TWENTY-FIVE

EVERYONE KNOWS CALIFORNIA IS AN EARTHQUAKE STATE. WHERE other kids grow up learning to prepare for tornadoes or hurricanes, Californians know our most imminent existential threat—short of a wildfire—is the next Big One. After growing up on the San Andreas Fault—taking field trips to the geysers and studying striations along rock faces—trust me when I say: Living with a severe anxiety disorder is like living on a fault line.

An earthquake could strike at any moment.

There are minor tremors every day, so small that you stop noticing them. But there's some part of your amygdala that's always on alert, aware that the best early alert systems won't give more than ten seconds' notice. Then, any time anything bad happens, your catastrophizing impulses are validated.

So it is equally terrifying and vindicating when Dagny's reply drops into my inbox forty-eight hours after the email zap. I'm literally on my way to work, the carpool cruising with the windows down. My shift starts in fifteen minutes, and the ground is shifting under me. This early earthquake warning hasn't bought me anything at all.

I pass my phone to Efraín, who's sitting next to me. By some unspoken agreement, Naomi took shotgun this morning, and Efraín kissed me hello like it was nothing.

"What the actual *fuck*?" Efraín curses at my phone.

"Arson, murder, or jaywalking?" Lola calls.

"Jaywalking?" Naomi mutters, vexed.

"Worse," Efraín says. "Unfair labor practice."

"It's not—" *that bad*, I don't say, because it *is* bad, just not prohibited by the National Labor Relations Board. "It's a meeting invite. Dagny, Anya, Billy, and me. Right after preshift. It's—" I swallow down my panic and pry my phone out of Efraín's death grip. "Dagny wouldn't put 'dress code' in the meeting title if the meeting were about firing me."

"That would be illegal, wouldn't it?" Naomi asks.

"If they say it's about the dress code, yeah," Lola answers as she turns down NSX's private road. "They can't fire you for a collective action. No one else got a meeting invite, right?"

"Nothing in the chat," I confirm.

"You took the button off right away," Naomi reasons. "They can't single you out."

Efraín's silence says everything. He doesn't trust bosses to follow the law.

Maybe it's naive, but I don't think I've been invited to my

execution today. There were other days when I was so sure I'd be escorted out by security, but not today. Although I agree that management doesn't care about the law, I believe they have more sense than to fire an openly trans employee two days after an email zap, which is proof of concerted activity. Dagny may be callous, but it's a calculated indifference.

Lola snags the last employee parking space. We get out of the car, but no one moves. Then Lola whispers something to Naomi, who gives me a grim nod and heads toward the barn.

Efraín's hand is on my arm. "You don't have to do this alone," he says, so damn serious. "Just say the word, and—"

"Ef," Lola cuts in, lips pursed, tangerine glitter gloss sparkling in the morning light. "I've got this. Go inside."

"I can help," Efraín insists. I don't know if he's trying to convince her or me. "I'll crash the meeting. Just let them try to fire you then—"

"I'm glad you're still on board with the ride-or-die credo here, but we're not at DEFCON Thelma and Louise yet."

Efraín's raring for a fight. I can't help but remember when Lola called him el toro bravo, ready to charge at anything and everything.

"You'd just raise the temperature in the room. Do more harm than good." Lola shakes her head. "You know I'm right."

Efraín looks like he swallowed a jumbo Lemonhead whole, but he trusts Lola's judgment, even against his own, because that's what the ride-or-die credo means. "Yeah, okay."

Then he turns to me, a flip-book of microexpressions animating his face far faster than my brain can piece together. Finally, he settles on, "Let me know if you need me. I'll be there in ten seconds." Then he presses another chaste kiss against my forehead and jogs away.

As soon as he's out of range, Lola's expression softens. "Same offer."

"But you just said—"

"Efraín isn't the right person to walk into that room with you, but he's right," Lola says. "You don't have to do any of this alone, and—" She steps closer, her corkscrew curls fluttering in the breeze. "I know how it feels, to be surrounded by friends but still not—"

"The mortifying ordeal of being known but not seen while trans?"

"Seen but not known, for me, I think."

I look at Lola and ask myself: What do I see? What do I know? I know she makes it all look so easy—living, loving, *feeling*, to say nothing of passing—but nothing is ever that easy.

I still don't know what to say to Lola's offer. Part of me—the chronically anxious kid cowering under a desk in advance of an earthquake—wants to accept. But this didn't start with union-organized button making. It started with me wearing a button on my second day of work and continuously centering myself, my pronouns, my priorities.

I've made my choices.

"Thank you for offering," I tell Lola, steady as I can, "but I'll be fine."

"Eli, it's not about being *fine*—"

"I can handle this on my own."

I *need* to do this alone.

"Let me start by saying, we're not insensitive to your struggles," Dagny Kane tells me twenty minutes later.

In the conference room next to Anya's office, I've been seated across from Dagny and Anya. Billy hasn't looked up from his yellow legal pad.

The flat-screen on the far wall is cycling through a presentation for high-roller donors. One Plutonium Tier donor could cover my top surgery down payment, and anyone in the top Polonium Tier could pay for the entire surgery outright.

I flatten out the crumpled papers I retrieved from my backpack. I'm trying to do *this* right. My original meeting-with-HR notes have headings and subheadings, points and counterpoints, and arguments for each of Aristotle's categories of rhetoric.

I'm perfectly capable of handling logos, ethos, and pathos all by myself.

"With all due respect," I begin, in a neutral tone that hopefully implies respect I don't feel, "this isn't about my 'struggles.' I'm here to express concern about this week's dress code changes."

Then I challenge management's claim that pronoun buttons constitute "political speech" by making them specify whether the pronouns or the buttons are political. I trap Billy into admitting that pronouns aren't political speech. Once Dagny says the buttons themselves are the problem, I badger them about which part of the buttons is problematic. Anya insists the "PLEASE DON'T MISGENDER MUSEUM WORKERS!!!" line is offensive to guests.

I don't disagree. "Hypothetically, if the only text was the pronouns themselves—and we've agreed that pronouns are not political speech—would the buttons still be banned?"

"It's different," Anya protests.

I watch the blood drain from Billy's face while Dagny flushes red. I *have* them. "Was the problem that everyone was wearing matching buttons?"

Dagny's sudden smile alarms me. "There's a reason we have a dress code. We need our staff to be recognizable and *uniform.* Our branding is curated as carefully as our collections."

I have altitude sickness from how close I am to convincing them, but—

Forget Aristotle. This is some Icarus shit.

How am I supposed to argue with branding?

Then I remember: When Efraín sent me his earliest button mock-ups for critique, I sent back pictures of the most effective buttons from my personal collection. He criticized my personal favorite, calling out the logo for Dr. Mburu's clinic. The *branding*.

"That's a good point." I can work with this. "The buttons would be more successful if they matched NSX branding. What if the museum made pronoun buttons?"

I don't know what I'm expecting, but it's not Anya's raspy laugh. "But who would *pay* for the buttons?"

I don't know what the correct response is, but it's not my stupid, kneejerk, "How about the Polonium Tier donors?" That response is so David-Rose-voice *incorrect* that literally anything else would be an improvement. Why wasn't Lola concerned about *me* having a meltdown?

I have to fix this. There must be something—

"Give us the room?" Dagny's abrupt not-question stops me from blurting out something catastrophically worse.

I push back my chair.

"Not you, Eli."

Oh, fuck.

Billy seems to agree because he leans over to Dagny and whispers furiously, futilely, before he follows Anya out. After all, he's an employee, too.

Dagny watches me with tented fingers. "I'm going to tell you a secret, Eli. Can I trust it won't end up as trivia on your next tour?"

I nod, dumbstruck. How did arguing about buttons turn into sharing corporate secrets?

"When my father died," Dagny says, "my mother was

preparing to file for divorce. She could never admit it and stuck to the story that she'd moved back to LA for her career. When she had a dry spell between callbacks, my mother threatened to strip the estate for parts. He'd left it all to me, but she controlled the trust. She said we needed the money, but we would've been fine if she didn't spend every paycheck on Rodeo Drive.

"I wanted to remember my father at his happiest. When he showed me around set. When he spun bedtime stories of the episodes he never got to write, a flashlight under his chin. When I called him from LA and told him I'd horrified my teacher by bringing grotesque *NS* props to show-and-tell."

Dagny's smile is faint and distant, but still the most genuine emotion I've seen her perform.

It stirs something in me, despite the wall I'm desperately trying to keep between us. How many of my teachers did I horrify with my *NS* obsession? And, God, what wouldn't I give to hear about those unwritten episodes?

Shame curdles my curiosity.

I shouldn't be lusting after her secret knowledge; I shouldn't feel any kinship with the boss who doesn't respect me as an employee, let alone as a human being.

"Why are you telling me this?"

"Because I want you to understand the price I paid for this museum a decade before I built it. I convinced my mother not to sell the estate by pursuing the acting career she'd always wanted. I hated it, but the limelight turned my father's tarnished reputation into something mysterious, something beautiful—his name got me auditions. So I took the Nickelodeon gig, my mother took my paychecks, and I didn't lose what little I had left of my father."

Dagny's watching me so intently, waiting for the socially prescribed dram of empathy her story demands.

Except I can't give it to her. It's not that I don't feel anything. I'm not that heartless; on the contrary, I know I *feel something* because my heartbeat is syncopated, unpredictable.

"What I want you to understand, Eli, is that every social interaction is transactional—but that doesn't mean we can't both get what we want. I know you want the internship. You know it's between you and Gwen. Normally, I'd schedule interviews, and I'd discuss your work performance with Anya.

"Gwen's sales numbers are better than yours, and she doesn't have a history of—shall we say—*troublemaking* on her record. On paper, she's the more attractive candidate. So what if you've given a few tours? From a hiring perspective, it doesn't matter how passionate you say you are about this museum; that's what *everyone* says."

Other people *lie* during job interviews.

"Passion does matter to me, Eli. Whether you're selling tickets or updating our collections database, I want everyone who works here to love *Nuclear Seasons* even *half* as much as . . . My father's legacy—his *memory*—should be a blessing. It must be protected. You believe that, don't you?"

"Of course," I whisper in spite of myself.

"We have to make sacrifices—*compromises*—to protect his legacy."

"What do you want from me?" I ask, too tired to maintain even a pretense of tact.

"I want to protect this museum, and I want to see the internship go to the most dedicated employee. I believe that's you, Eli."

I should feel ecstatic. Dagny's offering everything I ever wanted on a silver platter, but if this job has taught me anything, it's that if something sounds too good to be true, it definitely is. "So you're offering me the internship in exchange for . . . what, exactly?"

"Your cooperation," Dagny says.

"You want me to shut up about pronoun buttons and transphobia at the museum."

"Nothing so crass. We may be able to work something out regarding a personal pronoun button for you. As for the rest of it . . . If you see something, say something."

"I don't understand."

"Maybe you're too young to remember, but after 9/11, that slogan was a public counterterrorism initiative—"

"No, I understand the reference." I have been inside an airport, after all. "I just don't understand the relevance here."

"Let's just say, I wouldn't want you to be collateral damage in the event of any future workplace disturbances. It wouldn't just be the internship on the line. If anything else happens this summer to disturb operations, there will be *consequences,* so when the time comes, it will be in your best interest to tell us what you know. Or else . . ."

I should ask what kind of consequences, but all I can think about is my old Ken doll under the razor-blade guillotine Efraín and I made for that French Revolution diorama.

"I'd hate for you to suffer the consequences of other people's poor choices," Dagny continues. "I trust you to make better decisions."

I have a newfound sense of empathy for every bug I've ever watched Sputnik hunt.

Dagny Kane is sitting across from me, holding a carrot and a stick. Betray the union, and I'll get the internship I need to pay for top surgery. Stay loyal, and I'll be fired before I can earn enough to cover the down payment.

She can't threaten to fire me outright for concerted activity, but she's sure insinuating it.

I blink at her, struggling to make sense of everything. She looks so much like her father, a man I've idolized since I was eight years old, watching *Nuclear Seasons* for the first time, wishing I could step through the TV screen.

That first morning on the job, I said I'd bury a body if the museum asked.

Now Dagny's asking me to bury the union alive.

She has the most placid poker face, even though she knows she's holding the winning hand.

Because bosses always win.

"I'll give you some time to think it over, Eli. I'm sure you'll see we can both get what we want."

TWENTY-SIX

OUR EVER-GROWING UNION HAS NEARLY OUTGROWN THE FORMICA table above Lou's. Eden's already volunteering to take minutes. And thanks to Lola, Jaime's here—they're still working on Blake.

Everyone wants to know what happened at my meeting, and I don't know how I'm supposed to tell them. I turned down offers not to face down management by myself, insisting I could handle it, and I ended up freezing when Dagny offered me a deal that benefits me *alone.*

I didn't say yes, but I didn't say no, either.

I swear to God I meant to refuse; I wanted to object with my every moral fiber. I would've told Dagny to take her sweetheart deal and shove it—but I couldn't say anything. I couldn't claw the words out of my throat before Dagny left.

I didn't say yes, but I didn't have to. Dagny took my silence as assent.

I have no intention of betraying the union, but even I

know what it looks like. Dagny thinks I agreed, and she was actually there. What would the real story sound like to anyone who wasn't in the room?

"Delayed processing" is the cat-got-your-tongue, dog-ate-my-homework excuse. I doubt *I* would believe me.

"Management didn't change their minds," I finally choke out. "They're not going to lift the button ban."

"But you explained to them how wrong it is," Efraín states. Strange to think that just a few weeks ago I would've found that level of faith in me—that missing question mark—a shocking show of support. Turns out I don't deserve that faith after all. "You explained why it's wrong."

"They weren't concerned with ethics."

"And you talked about how it's harmful," Lola says, "and the damage it does to you. As a trans person. As a *person*."

"They definitely weren't swayed by emotion."

"You had legal arguments, too," Naomi says. "You proved that their reasons—"

"Didn't make sense?" I ask with a wry smile. "I broke it all down. I thought I was getting through to them."

And I did. For one shining moment, I thought they were coming around.

"What did they have to say for themselves?" Stanley asks. "I've known Dagny, Anya, and Billy for a long time. They're good people, at heart. I thought they'd be reasonable enough to avoid a potential lawsuit."

But who actually believes a lone seventeen-year-old is

going to *sue* anyone? Me and what army? Sure as hell not the friends I left at the door.

I can't tell them the truth. No one would believe I just froze up. They all know how badly I want the internship.

Naomi has been acting weird and avoidant for months, probably because I was willing to let her get fired for her hair color; she has good reason to think I'd sell them all out for personal gain.

Lola offered to come with me, after already sticking her neck out as the other trans employee.

Stanley . . . okay, no, Stanley would take me at my word because his tragic flaw is trusting too much.

TJ, Jaime, and Eden barely know me and have no reason to trust me.

Efraín accused me of being a sleeper cell spy after our first meeting; wouldn't it serve him right if I'd been the Manchurian union member this whole damn time? I doubt he'd even be surprised, not really.

I don't deserve the benefit of the doubt. I'm not a credible witness. I tried to warn them that I'm not equipped for any of this, but the union made buttons for me. They put their faith in me.

I can't tell them how badly I fucked it all up.

But I have to say something, so I tell them as much as I can.

"Do you think they know?" asks Naomi. "About the union?"

"I made sure Anya knew Eli didn't make the buttons," Lola says. "Everyone saw Stanley and me handing them out."

"So they know it was a collective action," Naomi concludes.

"They know more than that," I say. Here, at least, I can help. Dagny's loaded phrases and the "deal" itself only make sense if she thinks there's a game afoot. "They know it was union activity—or at least they suspect."

"And as soon as bosses suspect workers are organizing," Efraín explains, "they do everything they can to kill the union. Union busting is a whole industry. Bosses pay corporate consultants to come in and quash any signs of worker unrest."

A laugh gurgles up my throat. Dagny would never pay for a consultant when she won't pay for a batch of pronoun buttons. Besides, why pay anyone when she can bribe me to spy on my friends for the low cost of an internship?

Stanley agrees. "Even if they suspect something, Dagny would want to handle it quietly, in-house."

Bingo.

"Especially with the anniversary party coming up," Eden pipes up. When all eyes turn to her, she self-consciously tucks a few braids behind her ear. "It's a major fundraiser. The surviving cast members will be there, and media, too. Any whiff of controversy could be dangerous."

"That's bargaining power," Efraín says.

"But the party's not for three weeks," TJ protests.

"It's not about the party," Stanley muses. "It's about—"

Simultaneously, I say, "The press."

And Efraín says, "Escalation."

We exchange a look. On his end, it's . . . fond? Like he's proud of me for being on the right side of history.

I don't know about my face, but my stomach is in more knots than the garlic challah knots on the table.

Maybe that's why I can't just confess. Even though I know, objectively, I haven't betrayed anyone, I can't stand the thought of losing the way Efraín's looking at me right now.

"I know you guys think you're finishing each other's sandwiches right now," Lola says, "but from where I'm sitting, that makes as much sense as peanut butter and sardines."

"It's a *gift*," Efraín says. "If management knows about the union, we don't have to hide because they're already desperate to keep us quiet, compliant."

"Meanwhile," I continue, picking up the baton as if we've trained for this relay, "we need to decide what to do next about the pronoun buttons. *If* we want to, I mean. But if we do, we have to escalate. We had impressive participation with the email zap, but we need to ramp up the intensity."

"Hit 'em where it hurts," Efraín says. "Money and reputation."

I clarify for everyone in the cheap seats, "We escalate by going to the press—or *threatening* to go to the press."

Efraín disagrees. "We need to shame Dagny into changing museum policy."

"No, Eli's right," Stanley says. "If Dagny *thinks* we're about to go to the *Egan's Creek Citizen-Courier*, she'll compromise to prevent us from going public."

"So we write a letter to the editor?" TJ asks.

"We draft an open letter," I say, feeling more confident with every word, the plan crystallizing in my mind. "Gather signatures—"

"I can help with admin staff," Eden volunteers.

"Do we actually send it to the E-triple-C or just threaten to send it if they don't lift the button ban in twenty-four hours?" Lola asks. "Just want to know what kind of hostage-ransom situation we're getting into."

"If we do go wide for support," Stanley answers, "word will get around. Management will hear about the letter."

Relief washes over me; I can see the escape hatch now.

No one needs to know how badly I screwed up, just as long as I fix this. If the open letter is effective and thoroughly shames management, then Dagny can't come after me, either.

I won't get fired. I can make my down payment. I may not get the internship, but no one in this room will have any reason to call me a traitor or worse, a scab.

All I have to do is write one perfect letter.

TWENTY-SEVEN

THE LETTER IS AN OPEN SECRET BEFORE STANLEY AND I HAVE FIN-ished writing it. The gossip train moves faster than an Amtrak train rattling along dilapidated tracks.

Come Tuesday, I'm eking every minute out of my afternoon 51 in the conference room—a tip from Eden—drafting in the shared Google Doc with Stanley in live time. We're making good progress, but I'm keenly aware of the ticking clock on my phone, just two minutes left on my break.

Then a notification banner materializes at the top of my screen.

Anya Sobol
URGENT: GSA Interviews (Schedule Attached)

Greetings all,

Recently, the Senior Leadership team has received troubling reports of workplace disturbances. This week, we will conduct individual check-ins with all GS staff to determine h . . .

To determine what, how to survive the day?

Sweat on my skin, unsteady in my seat, I'm certain that I must've accidentally ingested polonium, and now I have twenty-four hours to live.

No, I'm overreacting, catastrophizing. Everything is fine; the museum isn't on fire. I still have time to fix this.

Because whatever rumors management has heard won't prepare them for the real thing. When they read the actual, scathing letter, signed by a critical density of the staff, they'll be forced to back down, right?

Management will back down. Dagny won't fire me. The union will keep chugging along, slowly and steadily improving working conditions for everyone.

Everything will be totally and completely fine—as long as I fix this.

Stanley Pham: Did you get that email?

Saved by my phone, vibrating on the table. Not a new email, just my break timer.

I've never been so grateful to get back to work.

When I clamber into Efraín's red Rivian two hours later, I don't ask where we're going. He fills me in on the group chat, which I haven't checked. He says there's an emergency meeting.

"Elisha?"

I read the concern in Efraín's profile. He wants to ask me if I'm okay but knows better than to ask a useless question.

"Do you remember our mock one-on-one?" I ask him instead.

"Fuck, did I ever apologize for that?"

"Did I? We both said things, but—" I look out the window, at endless rolling vineyards. "I'm thinking about what I didn't say."

"Yeah?"

"You asked me a question. *Is working at NSX everything I dreamed it would be?*"

"You don't have to—"

"I wouldn't have brought it up if I—" There's a stone in my stomach, a cherry pit I don't remember swallowing. "I never told you what I thought the job would *feel* like."

I steal a glance at him, at his index finger tapping the steering wheel.

"I thought working at NSX would bring me closer to *Nuclear Seasons.* Like standing inside these sets every day would make me part of the narrative, even if only as an uncredited, blink-and-you-miss-it background actor."

"But that's not how it feels when you clock in," Efraín says softly, no sharp, judgmental edges.

"Not even when I lead tours," I confess. "It's not just that we're interchangeable parts on the job. I know, now, that's the gig. But I still thought, doing the job, interchangeable as I may be, I'd feel something, some connection."

Efraín nods like he understands, and maybe he does. "I know I don't need to explain 'alienation of labor' to you," he starts, then proceeds to explain it anyway, which would irritate me any other day. But right now, I don't mind listening to Efraín as my personal Marxist audiobook narrator. "The working class doesn't earn enough to consume the goods it produces. That means—"

"We don't make enough selling tickets as NSX employees to buy tickets as guests, I know," I finish, without reproach. "I get it. I'm trying to be vulnerable, and you're giving me a lecture."

"It's a metaphor."

"I know. Alienation is—"

"No, shit, it's—" Efraín shakes his head. "It's meta, okay?"

"You're telling me you're using Marx as a meta-metaphor."

"I thought you'd appreciate the sentiment. Grammar nerd."

"Points for effort, but I can't give you full credit if you have to explain your meta-metaphor, which you still haven't actually explained."

"What I'm saying is, bosses are always going to exploit

any connection you feel to your workplace, but that doesn't mean it's not yours."

He shoots me a sideways glance.

I let out a shuddery breath.

"Elisha, you do have the chance to be part of the *Nuclear Seasons* narrative now. So it's not what you expected. So what? You can write yourself into the script."

"I'm not sure we should be bowling at a time like this," I say when Efraín leads me into Punch Bowl's lobby.

"Don't worry, Naomi and I just finished our game." Lola swoops in, easy breezy. "I wouldn't expect you boys to multitask like that. We're just doing happy hour."

It's strange, the four of us sitting at the same table where Efraín first announced we were a union.

Because our union isn't just the Four Musketeers; it's Stanley, TJ, Jaime, and Eden, too; it's everyone who might join once they realize there's *something to join.* Unfortunately, no one else could make this emergency meeting with zero notice.

"So, what do we know about these interviews, or whatever Anya's calling them?" Lola asks.

"I thought you would've heard something," Efraín says.

"Me? It's my day off."

"But you're the one who knows everyone," I counter. "A social leader par excellence."

"Why, thank you, but no," Lola demurs. "I only know what's in the chat."

Naomi has her laptop out, taking notes. "Our best intel is the text Stanley got from Dan. Between Thursday and Friday, Anya and Billy will pull each GSA off the floor for a 'conversation' about whether we've been approached by other coworkers about . . ."

"Rabble-rousing and troublemaking?" I suggest.

"It's all *good* trouble," Efraín protests, "like John Lewis—"

"I know." Under the table, I knock my knee against his. "But management only hears the 'trouble,' and they're going to exploit that fear of getting *in trouble*."

"Like getting called into the principal's office," Lola says.

"It's simpler than that," Efraín says. "Where's the power in a union? Solidarity. What defines a union, legally? Collective action. What makes a collective action? Two or more employees engaging in concerted activity. Together. So of course they want to split us up."

"The prisoner's dilemma," I say. "It's a classic interrogation technique. If you have a group of suspects, put them in different rooms. Tell them the first one to talk gets a deal. Imply that someone else is putting all the blame on you."

"So," Lola says, "good cop, bad cop where the cop pretends to be good by gaslighting you into believing that your friends have already betrayed you . . . so you betray them first."

"All cops are bad," Efraín mutters.

"I said the cop *pretends* to be good, didn't I? They're still the bad cop. They're all—"

"Bad cops," Naomi finishes.

"Bad bosses," Efraín adds.

"The good part—" I hesitate. "The *least bad* part is that we know their union-busting playbook. We know what they're going to ask."

"Yeah," Lola asks, "but what are *we* gonna do about it?"

"Simple," Efraín says. "We lie."

"Lying is unethical," Naomi states.

"So is illegally interrogating your employees for unionizing. If they ask questions they're not legally allowed to ask, then it's legal to lie to your boss about unionizing."

I should fact-check that, but I can't fight the anxiety crashing over me.

The longer this discussion goes on, the more I realize that our letter might not be enough to stop these interrogations from happening—especially if we can't get people to sign the letter because they're scared of what management will do to them when it's their turn in the interrogation chamber.

This is all my fault.

Management is retaliating against the union and threatening my friends. Because of pronoun buttons the union made for my sake. Because I'm the one who split myself from the group and walked into a room alone and let Dagny get in my head. Because, when it came time to fight, I froze up.

"We haven't done anything wrong," Efraín reiterates. "We have a right to organize and no obligation to declare it. We haven't manipulated or intimidated our fellow workers."

"We should reach out personally," Lola says. "Make sure everyone knows the score."

I is for inoculate, I think, too little, too late.

"Good idea," Efraín says. "We can answer questions. Do some hand-holding."

He reaches for my hand as he says it. I don't know if it's a joke or an act of reassurance. Does he think I need hand-holding? Maybe he doesn't realize he reached for me at all. Still, I look at our hands on the table, our fingers laced together.

I think about the prisoner's dilemma. It's a trust fall, isn't it? You have to trust that your ride-or-dies really would die before they'd betray you.

No one at this table knows I've already betrayed them.

Not in words. I didn't tell Dagny anything; I didn't *agree* to tell her anything; I *won't* tell her anything when my turn comes. But Dagny's going to use my meeting to demand everything I know, and when I refuse, she'll take everything away from me.

My only advantage is that she thinks she turned me. She

won't make any big moves until she talks to me. I don't work again until Friday.

That means I have time.

I trust that my fellow workers will hold steady and survive the prisoner's dilemma. But I don't need to complicate matters by making them worry about me, not again.

This is my personal Kobayashi Maru, and I have to solve it on my own.

TWENTY-EIGHT

WHEN THE LIGHTS DIM AT BLUE PLATE ON THURSDAY AFTERNOON, management has already conducted the first round of interrogations. Efraín and I sit in our usual seats, silently reading the first victims' debriefs on our phones.

Everyone has held the line. No surprises in the lines of questioning: What do they know about recent disturbances? (Nothing, unaware of any disturbances.) Have they been pressured or threatened by other employees? (Nope, good vibes all around.) What do they know about a letter circulating among the staff containing vicious accusations and lies about management? (Nothing, haven't seen any letters.)

Then, in the time-honored bad cop tradition of "Have you stopped dealing drugs to schoolchildren?" interrogation tactics, the loaded question: "How long have you been part of the union illegally operating on these premises?" Everyone successfully sidestepped the complex question fallacy by saying that they've never been part of such an organization.

I don't realize how vehemently I've been flicking my thigh until Efraín circles his fingers around my wrist.

"Elisha." He smooths his thumb over my pulse point, firm pressure that soothes me in spite of myself. "They're doing fine. We're all okay. You're safe."

I want to laugh because, God, he has *no idea* how far from safe we are and how very far from okay I am. But he doesn't know what Dagny will demand I give away tomorrow or what will happen when I—well, I haven't plotted my escape route yet. Efraín doesn't know, and I can't tell him. So I just rest my head on his shoulder, and breathe in the faint, familiar tropical aroma of his shampoo.

He drapes his arm around my shoulders, pulling me close. After the MGM lion's telltale roar, the opening sepia-to-black-and-white-to-color montage from *Soylent Green* rolls.

But Efraín keeps whispering against my curls. He doesn't tell me it's all going to be okay; he doesn't speak in future tense. In present tense, he tells me, again and again: we're fine, we're okay, we're safe.

Here, in this moment, I almost believe him.

Snowpiercer excites Efraín like no other film we've watched. At first, I assume he has a crush on bearded Chris Evans, but the more he talks about Tilda Swinton's terrifying shoe monologue, it clicks.

Everything I've ever tried to tell him about the radical

political potential of media has clicked for him. He's chattering faster than the eponymous transglobal locomotive itself as he talks about what a perfect metaphor it is for a Marxist revolution.

I could listen to him talk allegory for hours, but I also really want to kiss him. It's quite the dilemma.

We end up at Lou's, in my favorite booth in the back. Efraín slides in next to me like an absolute psychopath, and it's downright surreal. Efraín's obsessing over a movie and sitting next to me in my favorite booth. I would live in this moment forever if *Nuclear Seasons* hadn't taught me that kind of thing always has unintended consequences.

Ma comes by to take our order, and as the two of them get into a verbal volley about how the eggplants in the community garden are thriving this season, I pull out my phone and immediately wish I hadn't. I want to bury it in said garden, except the electronics would poison the plants, and then I'd be a plant murderer in addition to an assumptive collaborator.

Anya Sobol
Reminder: Check-In

Hi Eli,

Just reminding you that your "check-in" is scheduled for tomorrow morning, first thing after pre-shift. Dagny will be sitting in, and we hope this will be a mutually beneficial conv . . .

I stare at my lock screen, harsh blue light straining my eyes. It's either eyestrain or tears, but testosterone wouldn't let me cry even if I wanted to. I don't want to cry. Why am I thinking so much about crying?

I don't realize I've slapped my phone face down on the table until Efraín's hand covers mine.

His smile is so unbearably soft. "Did you get Stanley's message alert? His interrogation went fine—"

"I have to tell you something," I blurt before I can chicken out. I can't keep lying to him.

"Something you need to warn me about first?"

I can't look at him.

"You're afraid I'm going to judge you."

"Oh, you're *definitely* going to judge me."

"Hey, no, wait. You spent how many years worrying what I'd say if you told me why you couldn't do protests and shit? I don't want *this*"—he squeezes my hand in his—"to be like that."

"It's not that."

"Then what—"

"One rhubarb iced tea and a black coffee from the dregs of the pot," Ma interrupts, sliding our drinks on the table, and winks at me.

After Ma is out of eavesdropping range, I force myself to face Efraín. "There's something I didn't tell you about my meeting with management."

"You can tell me anything."

I cannot imagine *any* universe in the multiverse where I would ever feel secure enough in a relationship with any version of Efraín to tell him *anything*, but telling him that now would definitely make this worse.

"Do you remember when you thought I was a sleeper cell spy?"

"What?"

"When you asked me—never mind. Dagny asked me to spy. In exchange for the internship. And the right to wear my own pronoun button, maybe, but—"

"Wait, I don't understand," Efraín cuts in, that telltale tilde etched in place. "Dagny asked you to spy on the union?"

"Yes."

"Last Friday."

"Yes."

"Then you went to the union meeting and helped plan an action that hinges on management knowing?" He cocks his head thoughtfully. "I can't decide if that's smart tradecraft or—"

"Why aren't you mad?" I ask. "Why aren't you yelling or fuming or—"

"Why would I be mad? You didn't tell them anything."

I open my mouth to disagree, then sip my coffee instead.

It's bitter, but not bitter enough to be from the dregs of the pot, as advertised. "You aren't even going to ask if I did? You just *know*."

"If you'd told management anything, they wouldn't be interrogating everyone. Besides, Elisha, I know you."

"But I didn't tell Dagny *anything*; I *didn't* turn her down. That's the problem. She told me to think about it, and I should've said no right away, but I didn't. I couldn't. I wanted to, I swear, but everything was happening so fast, and—"

"You let her believe you'd be her mole."

"Not on purpose," I insist. "And now they're intimidating everyone with these interrogations, and when I go in there tomorrow, Dagny's *expecting* me to tell her everything."

"But you're not going to." He says it so simply, neither question nor command—just a statement of fact, said with such conviction and moral certitude. "You're not telling her anything."

I feel feverish. I want to laugh. "You don't know that. *I* don't know that."

"You wouldn't be telling me any of this if you were planning to snitch."

"Don't you get it? If I don't give Dagny something—if I don't give up the union tomorrow—all bets are off. She'll fire me, and that'll be it. No top surgery. No—fuck." I blink back tears. I don't get to be upset about this, not when I'm the one in the wrong.

"Oh," Efraín says suddenly, his grip tightening on my bicep. "Is that . . . no, sorry, don't answer that."

I've only ever heard Efraín stumble over apologies a handful of times, like that night at the gazebo. This is how he gets when his latent Catholic guilt kicks in, after he realizes he miscalculated some piece of privilege calculus he'd taken for granted.

I run back the tape on my own words.

Oh, fuck. Why does it always come back to this?

I lean back, needing that extra sliver of space between us so I don't overthink the asymmetrical geometry of our bodies. "If that was your way of asking if ninety-five percent of my summer earnings have gone straight into my personal top surgery fund, then, yes. It's not a secret, but I just . . ." I shake my head, glancing at all the familiar faces around the diner, kids from school and adults who've known me since Mom moved us here fourteen years ago. "It isn't exactly *fun* to talk about.

"Thanks to the current legal landscape, there aren't that many surgeons even in the Bay Area who will operate on an eighteen-year-old, no matter how long you've been on T, and there were never many to begin with who accept patients with *unfavorable* body types. My best-choice surgeon doesn't take insurance.

"Moms will contribute what they can, but it's still a lot. Especially because I want it done before college, and college alone is going to clean out their savings. I need basically everything I earn this summer for my portion of the down payment to reserve a date for next summer, and I was hoping to get the internship to pay for the surgery itself. It's not the end of the world without it. I can probably make it work, picking up odd jobs during the school year. But that's all academic if I can't cover the down payment. We still have a month left, and I can't afford—"

"You can't afford to get fired," Efraín breaks in when my voice cracks.

I can't look at him because whatever's happening on his face might kill me. Instead, I study the glimmering gold chain tucked under his shirt, attached to a pendant of which I've only caught glimpses. I don't know what it means. For everything I know about Efraín, for all the passion he wears on his sleeve—often literally, with anti-establishment patches on his jean jacket—there are so many secrets he keeps close to the chest.

He told me so many times that he couldn't make sense of me, but I still don't understand. I don't understand what he sees in me. I don't understand how he went from accusing me of being a spy to trusting that I'd never sell out the union.

"That's why you were holding back," he's saying softly, like he's just solved a puzzle. I don't remember him reaching for my hand again, but he's laced our fingers together without my noticing. "When you said you *needed* the job, you meant it. Because if you got fired, you wouldn't be able to pay for top surgery." He scrubs his free hand over his face. "Fucking hell, Elisha, why didn't you *say something*?"

"Um. I did say something; I said I needed the job, repeatedly."

"But you never said *why*. If I'd known, I would've—"

"Marked it as an excused absence when I declined to join the union?"

"You thought I wouldn't believe you."

"I thought you wouldn't *understand*," I reply bitterly, "but don't take it personally. I stopped expecting cis people to understand a long time ago."

He curses in quick, quiet, and thoroughly extensive Spanish that I can't translate. Now he won't look at me. I can hardly get a grip on my own emotions, so I have no idea how I'm supposed to handle it when this boy who feels so damn *loudly* curls in on himself.

I squeeze his hand. "Sorry. That wasn't fair. I told you I don't like talking about it."

He shakes his head. "You don't have to talk about anything. It just puts things in perspective. Like, fuck, you spent all week feeling like you couldn't tell anyone what really happened, so you've been carrying this by yourself. The point of the union is—"

"An injury to one is an injury to all, I know."

"No, the point of the union is that no one has to carry anything alone."

"The union can't fix this. This whole time, we've been betting that management won't illegally fire anyone, but Dagny made it clear that my luck has run out. When I don't name names, she'll give me the boot, and . . ."

The diner lights are too bright, the dinner crowd too loud.

Those tears I've been doing a pretty admirable job of repressing finally break through, percolating at the corners of my eyes.

"Elisha." Efraín cups my cheek. His hand brushes through my hair and settles at the nape of my neck. He leans down, tents his forehead against mine. "I promise you, Elisha," he whispers, sounding so much more like himself. "You're not going to get fired. I won't let them fire you."

I look up at him through my lashes, the extreme close-up distorting this face that has become so familiar and unexpectedly *dear* to me these past few weeks.

I never expected that I would *care* about him like this, or that I would believe him when he made baseless promises. But I believe him. I believe he would burn down the museum before he let them fire me.

"I know," I tell him, "but it's not up to you."

Efraín's eyes burn like an oil fire.

TWENTY-NINE

EFRAÍN IS LATE.

I should've seen this coming from the moment Lola said he was driving solo. He's lucky Anya isn't at pre-shift, either, and that Dan and Ford are running the show down here. Dan won't care if Efraín saunters in a few minutes late, as long as he's here before the doors open.

I won't be here an hour from now. I understand that is the inevitable price of my defiance. I wouldn't say I've accepted it, but I've scheduled a Lyft to pick me up. Now that top surgery is on layaway, I can afford that extravagance over the embarrassment of waiting in the parking lot for my moms.

I try to savor these last moments in the barn. On all those other mornings I was so sure I was about to get fired, I fixated on the physical space—the lights and posters and rarefied air—but today, I look at the people—these strange, funny, kind weirdos.

They're why I need to officially refuse Dagny's deal and accept my pink slip like a red badge of courage. I won't betray the people in this room who have done so much for me.

Dan wraps up and sends everyone on their way. I'm not remotely ready, but I ask Dan if I should just head up to the conference room now.

"Um." He scratches the back of his neck. "You might want to wait, dude."

"Is Dagny already here?"

"Yeah, but—"

The phone behind the ticketing counter rings. Blake answers and hands the receiver to Dan. Just before he turns away from me to create some semblance of privacy, something strange crosses his face, an expression I've never seen on him before.

Suddenly, the back-of-house doors swing open. I spot Divya first, but for someone who's always quick with jokes, she's subdued. The security manager is with her, and between them is Efraín, in a plain shirt and jeans. His Kånken is slung over one shoulder, a folder tucked under his arm. He's looking straight ahead, heading toward the barn doors, on the clock.

He's not wearing his employee badge.

This isn't the prisoner's dilemma; it's Efraín's Sydney Carton martyr moment.

I'm shaking, anger and fear muddling into something else

entirely. I want to go to him. I want to yell at him. I want to follow him as security ushers him out of the barn.

But then I feel a hand on my shoulder. Stanley's there beside me, saying, "Whatever your boyfriend did, Eli, you know he wouldn't want you putting yourself at risk, too."

Stanley's right. Because Efraín swore last night that he wouldn't let me get fired. He bet the museum would accept any scapegoat offered. So he sacrificed himself without asking anyone else's opinion. Without looking anyone in the eye on his way out.

I have never hated him as much as I hate him right now.

Because this was my mess. He's running headlong into the sword that was meant for me.

I don't know what I'm supposed to do.

But there's still Stanley's voice in my ear.

So I let Efraín leave, and I do the only thing I can do: my goddamn job.

After work, I go home. I do not pass go. I do not collect $200—unless we count my day's wages, which aren't even close.

Naomi opted to hang with Lola and our coworkers for an In-N-Out-and-kvetch session. Lola spent the entire commute trying to convince me to join, but I was too checked out. When she dropped me off, Lola not-so-subtly hinted that I should invite Efraín over. I didn't; I can't bring myself to message him at all.

I'm alone in this house but for Sputnik, who tails me like the spy I'm not. She chases me up the stairs and sprawls across my bed.

I strip off my uniform polo and remember Efraín in his civvies. It's so ironic. Efraín planned ahead to turn in his uniform after terminating his employment. If I'd been fired today, I wouldn't have had a change of clothes.

After Efraín's stunt, the rest of the staff interviews were canceled. Dagny pulled me aside, smiling, as if not a single artifact were out of place—nothing stolen, no one burned—and said she had "good news." I officially have permission to wear a personal pronoun button, and I'm a shoo-in for the internship to boot. Provided I don't find myself caught in any future workplace disturbances, that is.

There are dozens of notifications on my phone, most to the union group chat, where everyone has chimed in, and Blake has been added.

But there are plenty of messages just for me. Lola, even though I just saw her. Stanley, even though he spent half our shift talking me down. Even TJ and Eden. Those I read out of sheer curiosity because I've never texted either of them solo. TJ has sent me a barrage of hartie memes; I didn't realize he was such a fan.

Eden has attached a photo of a letter—I recognize Kane's handwriting at a cursory glance—that I'm definitely not supposed to be seeing, clearly part of some secret collection, and she's written three explanatory paragraphs.

Conspicuously absent from my notifications is Efraín, but I don't blame him. I wouldn't know what to say to me, either. Efraín knows me too well to expect me to thank him for his grand, saintly gesture.

I didn't ask for any of this.

No, that's not right. I asked for a button and a shot at the internship. I'm getting everything I wanted.

I just didn't want it *like this.*

Eventually, I open my laptop and pull up the *NS* episode list. My cursor hovers over "Who's Afraid of Wolf Spector? (Part 1)" despite the flash of the teleplay page at Kane's desk. In the finale, conspiracy theories about the Spectors come to a fever pitch as evidence of an old government contract surfaces. There's a shoot-out at the silo. Art almost dies; Harry saves him, calls him "Artie," starts to tell him something before Art passes out from blood loss.

I may be a glutton for punishment, but I'm not *that* much of a masochist. I pick an episode at random and hit play.

I'm ten minutes into my second random episode when Sputnik's ears pivot toward the door. She hears it before I do. Keys clattering, dead bolt clicking. Heavy footsteps, hearty laughter. Reluctantly, I tiptoe across the mezzanine.

"Eli—oh, hey!" Lola grins up at me as I peer over the railing. "We brought burgers."

"And fries," Naomi adds.

"C'mon down. Everyone's on their way."

Sputnik canters down the stairs toward the scent of dead cow.

"Everyone?" Dread wicks through me.

"It's Friday night," Naomi states.

"So? We don't observe Shabbat."

"No, we observe union meetings."

"So you invited 'everyone' to our house? Did you even ask Moms? What did you *tell* them?"

"The truth?"

"But they don't know about the union!"

"Of course they do," Naomi informs me.

Lola frowns, looking between the two of us, before turning back to me. "Dude. Did you think your moms would really let us keep ordering family appetizer platters for an ever-increasing number of people, no questions asked?"

I admit, "I didn't think they'd notice—"

"That your total friend count has tripled?"

"Moms never said anything to me," I say to Naomi.

"They thought you didn't want to talk about anything work-related."

"So they asked you?"

"As your sister and coworker, I'm uniquely qualified to offer insight about your mental state."

I sincerely doubt that, considering what an admirable job she's been doing of ignoring me all summer, but Naomi's clutching multiple In-N-Out bags while Lola balances two drink cartons. "Who's coming?"

"Everyone." Lola shrugs. "Jaime's bringing Blake. Stanley said he was going to pick up TJ. Eden already had plans with Divya for later, so she invited her, too."

"What about—"

"Ef?" Lola's expression sours. "Only replied to my texts when I said I was on my way to pick him up. He says it's 'inappropriate' for him to come to meetings if he doesn't work there."

"It's not *safe* for any of you to be here," I insist. "Did he tell you—"

"Dagny knows, yada yada." Lola rolls her eyes. "We're gonna figure it out."

"This isn't—not without—"

"This is happening, even without Efraín."

"I was going to say 'without plausible deniability,' but—"

"But nothing. This is DEFCON Thelma and Louise. You in or you out?"

Downstairs, the union has transformed the living room into a war room. I don't know what they're planning, just that I've heard laughter and yelling alike, and I'm trying to concentrate on this episode.

Then my door swings open, no knocking. Sputnik barrels in.

Naomi hovers near the threshold.

"*What?*" I stab my space bar with my thumb.

Naomi's face is neutral, as usual. *Decreased affect*, per the *DSM*. "Sputnik wanted to see you. Didn't you hear her scratching at the door?"

I scratch under her chin, and she purrs vociferously. "There's a lot of noise pollution in the house. Did you just come up here to play Good Samaritan for Sputnik, or did you want something?"

She drops a manila folder on my night table. "Read that."

"What is it?"

"My meeting notes, with some additional research."

"You want me to give you extra credit?"

Naomi doesn't take the bait.

"Do you remember the first thing Efraín told us about organizing?"

"I remember that he didn't tell us we were organizing until we'd already done it."

"He said that bosses lie."

"No shit."

Unperturbed, she persists, "It's illegal to intimidate or interrogate workers for organizing."

"Efraín also pointed out bosses don't give a fuck what's legal. Why would they? There's no point crying to the NLRB. We can't hold them accountable."

"What if we could?" She pauses, waiting for me to put

the pieces together, but my deductive reasoning skills are offline. "We can hold them accountable in the court of public opinion. Send the open letter to the press, just like we planned. Add something about intimidation and illegal termination—"

"It's *too late*. Efraín's gone. It's all . . . FUBAR."

This is what I get for watching too much '80s TV.

"Fine. Do what you want. I don't know why I thought—"

"What did you think?"

"I thought you'd care about your *boyfriend*, even if you didn't care about me!" Naomi explodes like a dormant volcano, finally spewing vitriol that's been churning in her for millennia, leaving scorched earth in her wake. "I should've known better. You always do this—act like your problems are so much *bigger* than everyone else's. You play the victim and act like you're so alone in everything, but you don't even see the way other people jump to help you.

"You never asked what happened with Gwen. You never liked her—good call there—but I tried to tell you, months ago, that everything with her helped me realize I'm probably aro ace. But you don't even remember because you started monologuing about how some guy at Nine Lives gave you a 'weird look' when you went thrifting for work clothes.

"When you had issues in school, Moms paid for your autism diagnosis out of pocket, but I never got an official diagnosis, just self-diagnosis-by-genetic-proxy. Or when Moms offered to buy us a used car, but you said, no, you needed that money for top surgery, so now I'm on my own for the car, which would be fine, I understand that top surgery is important for you, but . . .

"Eli, you were going to let me get *fired* over *my hair.* You knew I needed money, too, and you just told me to dye my hair back to blond. It never occurred to you that I dyed my hair for a reason—green highlights like the aro pride flag. That meant something to me, especially after the breakup, and you would've known that if you'd paid attention or asked. But you couldn't get over yourself for five minutes and just listen to anyone other than your own ego. Because I'm the common mallard in the family, and you're a—I don't know—red-breasted sapsucker."

Naomi is red-faced and winded. I've never heard her say that many words at once. My kid sister just as good as called herself an ugly duckling while excoriating me.

But now she's rubbing her arms, self-conscious. "I'll give you time to *process.* All the legal information about what to do if you're fired for organizing is in the folder. Read it, if you care."

The door slams behind her. I know I've fucked up, just like I did with her hair.

But it's too late. It doesn't matter if I *care* about Naomi or anything else.

So what if management broke the law? What *difference* does it make?

I just want to go back to watching my favorite TV show and feel a little less alone. But the stories don't feel the same in this light. I'm still alone.

I look at my laptop screen, frozen on a neo-noir shot of Harry in the interrogation room, staring at his own reflection in the one-way mirror. The screen dims; suddenly, I'm staring at my own reflection in a black mirror.

I don't like what I see.

Not for the usual reasons. It's nothing to do with my curved jawline or the missing Adam's apple. It's the image itself: me, alone on my bed but for my cat. Phone face down so I don't have to face my missed notifications. The rumble of life just below my floorboards; knowing I have an invitation but never RSVP'd.

This morning, I thought I was going to get fired because I wasn't willing to betray my friends. I was terrified to make that sacrifice.

Efraín beat me to the punch. He sacrificed himself.

But the truth is? Efraín didn't save anyone. My firing wouldn't have saved anyone, either.

Don't get me wrong, I've made mistakes. My actions put others at risk. I could've set the record straight when I saw security escorting Efraín out. My worst mistake, however, was that I never trusted the union, not unconditionally.

I always looked for escape hatches and back channels. I let the union tackle my grievances, but as soon as things went south, I took back the reins. I never truly trusted them to have my back; I never took the trust fall.

But the union isn't dead. It's alive and kicking in my living room. My fellow workers and friends took it upon themselves to keep looking for solutions because, as Efraín reminded me last night, that's the *point* of a union.

Because an injury to one is an injury to all.

Because they're all for one and one for all.

Because ride-or-die doesn't end at the parking lot, and solidarity is a two-way street.

The union *can* hold our bosses accountable—but a letter isn't enough.

I jump out of bed so abruptly that Sputnik yowls in dismay.

The living room is as crowded as I've ever seen it. Lola's sandwiched between Jaime and Blake on the love seat. Stanley has claimed the La-Z-Boy. Naomi, Eden, and Divya are arranged on the couch. TJ's camped on the floor. They have all manner of laptops, tablets, phones, and notebooks. Everyone talks over each other. No one's even noticed I'm here.

"I know what we need to do," I holler. When they look up—expressions ranging from smug smiles to mild surprise to faint exasperation—I take a deep breath. I trust these people, truly. "If everyone agrees, I mean. Rule by consensus and all—"

“Jesus, Eli.” Lola clucks her tongue. “Sure, you’re late to the party, but you’ve got an open invitation.”

“Just spit it out!” TJ calls.

Well, when they put it like that.

Sure as I’ve ever been, I say, “We’re going on strike.”

PART IV

ORGANIZE

THIRTY

ONLY AFTER I'VE RUNG THE BELL, AS I'M PACING ON THE STOOP, DO I realize that I've never been inside Efraín's house before. I sit in the driveway four days a week, but I haven't gotten out of the car since that first morning, simmering with resentment.

Today, I don't see the opulence or the hypocrisy; I just know there's a boy inside who made a stupid sacrifice for me. A boy who doesn't seem to want to talk to me. He must know I'm here. I waved at the doorbell camera like a fool.

When the door finally swings open, Efraín's scowling at me. "How did you get past the gate?"

"Lola gave me the code."

"You should be at work—"

"So should you," I quip. "I called in sick."

"You don't look sick."

"I might be at risk for heatstroke if you don't invite me in."

He steps aside. The AC is languid at best, and if Efraín's tank and short shorts weren't clue enough, I have twelve years of data from which to deduce that Efraín *obviously* sets the thermostat to 80 degrees.

He leads me up a winding staircase. His massive room lies at the end of a long hall. Rather than feeling palatial, the size only emphasizes the sparseness of the space.

It wouldn't track for Efraín to display the consumerist trappings of the average American teenager's room. Instead, he has a collection of succulents on his windowsill and sun-bleached signs from protests past tacked to his walls. A triptych of black-and-white photographs of vineyard workers hangs over his desk, and a collection of Pomo-style woven baskets sit beside his MacBook Pro. On his night table, a cluster of carved wooden animal figurines huddle next to a tangled nest of charging cables.

"What are you doing here?"

"You weren't returning my texts."

"My phone died."

"And your charger broke?"

He just shakes his head and paces like it would physically hurt him to stay still.

I look for somewhere to sit and settle for one of two wine barrel stools. Not one of those artisanal stools carved from reclaimed barrel panels but an actual wine barrel that someone sawed in half and nailed shut. It's sturdy but not terribly comfortable.

Nothing about this conversation is terribly comfortable.

"Look," I say. "I'm not going to ask why you did it."

He shoots me a piercing glance. "You think you know?"

"You thought, if you took responsibility for everything the union had done, then that would be enough to appease management into sparing me, but this was *my* fault. If we hadn't done the pronoun buttons, if I hadn't let Dagny get inside my head—fuck." I look away. "The point is, it didn't make sense for you to—"

"Fucking hell, Elisha, it makes perfect sense. I care about you. I want you to have what you need."

"But you didn't *ask me*," I protest. "I didn't want you to take the fall for me. What about the deal you made with your mom?"

"I knew what you'd say."

"You didn't think that me not wanting you to get fired for my sake was a reason not to get yourself fired?"

"That's why I didn't text you."

"So you got yourself fired for me but were just going to ghost me? For how long?"

"As long as it took you to understand."

"You're unbelievable. Truly, honestly, literally unbelievable." I stare up at him. It shouldn't surprise me that he believes his own spin—that it was noble to sacrifice himself for me, even knowing I wouldn't want it.

Efraín always leaps without looking. He turns every molehill into a mountain. After all, he started a union because of my sister's peekaboo highlights.

It follows that he would want to burn down the museum

when he realized institutionalized transphobia was putting my job at risk, but was it even about *me*?

Would he care about me if I didn't *embody* a cause? Would he kiss me if he couldn't taste the bittersweet desperation on my tongue? Would he want me at all if I wasn't someone he thought he could save?

But he didn't burn down the museum after all. He set himself on fire.

"You know," I say, my voice rough. "I've read that self-immolation is one of the most painful ways to die."

"What the hell is that supposed to mean?"

"It means you can't keep doing this."

"Doing what?"

"Helping everyone except yourself."

"Better that than help no one but myself."

I ignore the low blow for what it is: desperation. "It's not that you're going to burn out; you're burning up."

"I'm just doing my part. From each according to their ability—"

"You don't know the *limits* of your ability, let alone the scope of your needs."

"I don't need—"

"Anything?" I scoff. "You don't need to be a teenage martyr. The world needs you alive and whole more than it needs you to play Joan of Arc."

"I'm not about to let anyone burn me at the stake."

"I know. Because you'll do it for them. You'll light yourself on fire before you give anyone else the chance. You'll douse yourself in gasoline before you even consider passing the torch or letting your friends help you."

"I started a *union*."

"Joan of Arc led an army."

"She asked other people to fight her battles in the name of God. I haven't asked anyone to fight my battles. I'm fighting for the greater good."

"But you don't have to fight alone." I grab his arm, encouraging him to stay still, to stay here. "Because you've taught me what it means to show up for someone. Maybe that means it's my turn to save you."

"I'm not *asking* you—"

"To set myself on fire for your sake?" I ask. "I'm not going to, but, Efraín, I'm saying I *care*. I may not have the capacity or the *ability* to give pieces of myself to everyone who buys museum admission, but I care about you. I can take care of you, if you let me."

"What are you asking me to let you do?" He sees completely through me. "That's why you really came here, right? You have some new plan, so you're asking my permission to make a point?"

"Not exactly." I wince. "I came here to remind you—wait. You let them fire you, right? You didn't just preemptively quit?"

He nods. "Giving them the satisfaction went against my every instinct, but I figured that would sate their bloodlust."

"I don't know exactly what you said to them, but no matter how much you tried to assume the blame, everything you did was collective. We would all testify to that, but the proof is in the actions. The signatures on the petition. The number of emails. It's all there, and even if it wasn't, the interrogations were out of bounds. The evidence is ironclad."

"Elisha. In ten words or less."

I hold up my hand and count on my fingers. "You. Were. Fired. Illegally. And. We. Can. Prove. It."

"Yeah, no shit. So what? You want to add a paragraph to your letter?"

"No, I want to file an Unfair Labor Practice complaint with the NLRB and get you your job back."

Efraín sinks down on his platform bed. Shock has knocked his legs out from under him. "The NLRB takes a hundred and eighty days to process a ULP."

"I know. But you know what we can do right after we file the official complaint, right?"

He laughs, gobsmacked. "You've gotta be fucking kidding me. You—of all people—want to start a strike? Because of me? To get me back the job I didn't want in the first place and gave up *for you*?"

Efraín, ever the rebel with a thousand causes, never once thought he'd be one of them; if given the gift of foresight, he would've died before he became the boy whose face launched a thousand ships.

He levels his steeliest stare. "Now who's the one with the savior complex?"

Gingerly, I sit down beside him. "That isn't what this is."

"Then what is it, Elisha?"

I face his profile, silently urging him to look at me. "This is what we do: We save each other."

For once, I'm the one to reach out and take his hand.

He does look at me then, his eyes still dark and impenetrable, but he doesn't let go. "Even when there's no damsel in distress asking to be saved?"

"You save first, ask later, after you've done it all yourself. I never ask at all, just try and fail and try until I break—or you swoop in. Which feels condescending, yes, but that's what happens when you go it alone. That's the problem with your rogue lone wolf routine."

"I'm not a lone wolf. I started a *union*, for fuck's sake. Would someone who doesn't believe in collective power start a union?"

"Those things aren't mutually exclusive. It's not about either of us swooping in to save the other, getting on and off the white horse like some rideshare merry-go-round. It's give and take, right? You got fired for me. I'm starting a strike for you. I just need you to join me."

"But you're not asking my permission."

"I asked the rest of the union. Motion carried unanimously, but we need you to file the paperwork with the NLRB. So, I'm asking for your signature, and, well, this." I squeeze his hand. "Meet me at the picket line."

He stares at me, speechless, for approximately five seconds before he swoops in and kisses me for . . . well, more than five seconds. When he finally lets me breathe, he whispers, "That's the hottest thing you've ever said to me."

I can't repress a laugh; I don't want to. "Say you'll be there. Let me—let *us*—do this for you."

Efraín opens his mouth, then shuts it. He drops my hand. "It's not that simple."

I follow his line of sight.

The door to his walk-in closet is open. Amidst piles of clothes, an overflowing laundry basket, and a pair of Docs for every day of the week, there's a suitcase splayed open on the floor.

Suddenly, the room feels hotter than 80 degrees. I'm over-dressed in my shorts and T-shirt, sweating like a stuck pig.

"I called my dad," Efraín says. "I'm driving down to Madera today."

"But—" I swallow hard and shut down every line of thought that involves me because *this is not about me.* "What about your mom?"

"I didn't tell her. I'll call once I get to my dad's place. I'll—" He rubs the bridge of his nose. "I'll make another deal.

Let her set me up with some soul-numbing, résumé-padding part-time job. I'll take the SATs again and give her final approval of my college list. I'll swear to never even think the words 'gap year' again."

"Efraín." My heart seizes in my chest.

"Don't you dare blame yourself," he says. "I made my choices and didn't give you veto power. Besides, you're trying to get me my job back. She's never forgiven me for losing that spelling bee, but if she saw your SAT scores and college prospects, she'd probably call you a *good influence*."

"Perish the thought."

"Don't worry. I won't hold it against you."

He cracks a weak smile.

"How long will you be gone?" I ask.

He shrugs. "Don't know."

"But . . ." I blink at him. When I asked Efraín to meet me at the picket line, it was supposed to be rhetorical.

"We're starting the strike on Friday, a week before the twenty-fifth-anniversary gala," I tell him. "That gives us four full days to plan, then we'll strike in time for the week-end, as traffic ramps up for the gala. Hopefully it'll be over before then, but if not—"

"It's best for everyone," Efraín interrupts, "if I'm not there. I quit. I shouldn't be the face of the strike."

"It's literally a ULP strike. For an unfair labor practice committed against *you*."

"Only because I got there first. Otherwise, it would've been *you.* Hell, it was *already* you. Management retaliated against you, personally, for the pronoun buttons. They committed a slew of ULPs against you before—"

"Against everyone," I correct him. "The interrogations were—"

"They interrogated you first and blamed you for the buttons."

"It's all in the letter. But you . . ."

I just lectured him on taking care of himself, so I have no right to bring up what the union needs. He made a stupid sacrifice so I could get what I want, and somehow he's found a way to seize a fraction of what he wanted, too. I sure as hell can't tell him that what I need is him by my side on the picket line.

"I understand that you need to go to Fresno, and I'm glad you'll get to see your dad. But, Efraín, you'll be back in time for the strike, right?"

He presses a kiss to the crown of my head.

If that's an answer, it's the wrong one.

THIRTY-ONE

IN THE BEGINNING, SPIRITS ARE HIGH.

Participation is high, too. Lola and Naomi. Stanley. TJ. Jaime and Blake. Eden, Divya, and Miles from security. Everyone except Efraín, whom I've failed to convince to join his own ULP strike.

Friday morning, everyone assembles in the NSX parking lot, and I keep staring at the driveway, hoping to see Efraín's Rivian barreling through the dirt.

Lola stands beside me, nudging her shoulder against mine. "Sorry, babe. I thought he'd change his mind."

I tamp down my disappointment and offer Lola a shaky smile. "I'm glad you're here."

She laughs. "Wouldn't have missed it for anything."

"I know. I just . . ." Letting people know I appreciate them would be firmly in the *needs improvement* column of my workplace performance review. "I wanted you to know."

Lola smiles like she telepathically intuited everything.

"I'm glad you're here, too, Eli." She slings an arm around my shoulder, and we rejoin the group on the sidewalk that separates the parking lot from the museum grounds.

By now, it's officially pre-shift; we're officially *late* for our shifts.

Naomi does the honors of sending an email from a newly created union Gmail address to the editor of the *Egan's Creek Citizen-Courier*, with Dagny and the NSX all-staff listserv CC'd.

Our revised letter formally announces our ULP strike, then enumerates our reasons, starting with the illegal firing of an employee for protected concerted activity amidst a broader union-busting scheme and then detailing anti-LGBTQ policies, as well as discrimination and retaliation against LGBTQ employees, emphasis on the *T*. We state our demands and express our eagerness to meet our bosses at the bargaining table.

We're all in our street clothes—for half of us, that means *NS* graphic tees—wearing our union-made pronoun buttons. We have signs, too, ranging from my "Be Trans, Do Organized Crime" to Lola's "Pronouns Over Profits!" to Naomi's "On Strike."

Nothing happens.

I don't know what I expected. We'd send the email, and explosions on the horizon would tell us when to duck and cover? Instead, I'm holding my breath—literally, apparently, because Lola asks Naomi where I keep my inhaler and leads me through anxiety breathing exercises.

I'm four counts into an eight-count exhale when the barn doors burst open.

Anya power walks with her hands on her hips. Ford follows hot on her heels. Dan and Gwen trail behind.

"What is the meaning of this?" Anya yells, wagging her phone. She got our email.

No one answers, and I survey our little group. On some foolish level, I'm expecting Efraín to answer because who other than Efraín could play mouthpiece for the union?

No one outside of guest services is going to challenge Anya. Naomi, TJ, and Jaime are fundamentally soft-spoken. Blake wields silence like a lethal weapon. Stanley fears stepping on anyone's toes. Lola has frozen up like she did before she gave an emotional presentation on Las Mariposas last year.

That leaves me.

Not that I'm not terrified, but I'm not going to leave this job half-done.

"We're on strike," I announce. "It was all in the letter. If you have—"

I'm cut off by the farmhouse door. Dagny rushes out, fast, furious, and ferocious. "What the f—" She stops abruptly as she sees the museum's first guests. I can see her running the calculations, duty and damage control outweighing her desire to make a scene.

After all, the institution comes above all else. The place above its people, whether they're working inside or picketing in the parking lot.

"Anya," Dagny snaps. "Give our guests the VIP treatment. Dan, hold down the fort at ticketing. And you two"—she points at Ford and Gwen—"cover the gift shop. I'll lead our first tour group. It's not often I get to personally share my father's story with our guests. It'll be . . . fun." Her forced smile says otherwise. But she stands there, acting, while she watches the guests cross the picket line.

"*You*," Dagny sneers, zeroing in on me. "Care to explain what the hell you're doing?"

"You read the letter," I say, calmer than I feel. "You know exactly what this is about, and you know precisely what you'd need to say to end it, right now."

"Do you think this is a game?"

"Absolutely not, but we'll be here however long it takes you to realize we're not playing around. Hopefully that'll happen before fans start showing up for the anniversary. If not, we'll be right here."

"You're going to regret this," she promises. "Forget about the button or the internship. You think you're helping anyone? You're an ungrateful little child cosplaying *Newsies*."

This probably isn't a good time to tell her she's doing a good impression of a Frank Capra villain.

But I don't have to tell her anything. Because Stanley immediately beseeches her to please consider our demands. When Dagny tells Stanley that she expected better of him, Lola has a comeback wrapped in a burn. When Dagny yells at Lola, Blake shuts her down.

Everyone has each other's backs.

A strike is, mostly, waiting.

I don't notice Naomi taking pictures on her phone all morning, but just before lunch, Lola and TJ call me over. They're sitting on Hawkeye's hood, huddled over Naomi's phone while Naomi bites her nails.

"What's up?"

"Can you generate some Insta-worthy captions?" Lola asks. "Don't worry about hashtags. Just think eloquent pith."

"Pith?"

"That dry wit you hide behind those bougie billion-dollar words. But keep it short, yeah? Can you do that?"

"I make no promises."

They've selected five impressive, photojournalistic shots. I don't even know how Naomi captured my face-off with Dagny, both of us red-faced with anger. She's also photographed Stanley preaching to a throng of would-be museum guests, sharing bawdy behind-the-scenes stories that we'd never tell as docents. There's the quiet intimacy of Jaime and Blake sitting on a cooler while she adjusts his knee brace, and the sheer silliness of Divya spritzing TJ and Eden with a spray bottle.

The editing is minimal, professional. Just enhancing and clarifying the story that's already there.

I study my sister and ask myself how I missed this. I knew she'd started taking photos while birding; I knew she'd borrowed Mom's old camera. I remember, now, that the only art pieces in Efraín's bedroom were humanistic prints of vineyard workers. I only recognize the style retroactively because apparently my sister *has* a style. "How did you—when?"

Then she says, "Remember when we used to watch *Nuclear Seasons* together?" and it clicks. I used to get annoyed because she never wanted to talk about the stories the way I did, but—I never realized she cared about the medium. I missed an entire special interest.

"These are really good." It's a mealy-mouthed understatement and totally inadequate.

"I know."

I nod. It isn't enough, but I hope Naomi knows I'm listening now. Or, in the case of her photographs, I'm looking, and I'm *seeing*.

"Not to interrupt this heartwarming Hallmark moment," Lola interrupts, "but I need those captions? I want these up on the union socials before the West Coast starts doomscrolling over lunch hour."

"The union has socials?"

"Insta, Threads, Bluesky, and Tumblr; Facebook for the boomers," TJ lists without looking up from his phone.

Lola snaps her fingers. "Captions?"

Just after three, I'm sipping from a thermos of rhubarb iced tea—part of the provisions Moms surprised us with for lunch—and surveying the parking lot as new guests trickle in.

Lola, Jaime, and I spent hours trying to guess whether a guest would cross the picket line based on the brand of car they were driving. Naomi criticized our "unscientific" approach before pulling out her graph paper. Stanley reminded us that tourists often drive rental cars. Blake suggested we use state license plates instead, but Eden pointed out that no state is politically homogeneous—and labor politics don't break cleanly along party lines.

Still, I'm looking at the dirt-spackled red Rivian SUV with California plates, guessing that whoever's inside won't cross the picket line when Lola lets out an unholy squeal. She squeezes my arm, and I almost choke on my tea because *I recognize that license plate.*

Efraín parks next to the employee parking spaces, then steps out of his car.

Even from a distance, I can tell he's frazzled. His half bun is messier than usual, too many flyaways to qualify as intentionally disheveled. More damning still, he missed a button on his short-sleeved linen tunic. He stuffs his hands into his pockets and looks around until his aviators lock on me.

I'm frozen in place, torn between shock and an utterly foreign impulse to run over, hug him, and never let go.

I don't have to decide because Lola half tackles Efraín with a fierce hug of her own. Then she punches his arm. Then she laughs and drags him over to the group.

Everyone greets him with unrestrained enthusiasm and not a drop of admonition. Efraín accepts it all gamely enough, though he doesn't revel in it.

He doesn't want to be the prodigal son.

Finally, he stops in front of me. He reaches out like he wants to hug me but must read something on my face because he deliberately puts his hands back into his pockets. "Sorry I'm late. Traffic was terrible on 580, and there was a four-car pileup near Sears Point, and—"

"*Efraín,*" I cut him off, more breath than word. Something about his uncharacteristic, anxious rambling grounds me in the moment. I don't like seeing him like this. I remember how afraid I was, when I dyed my hair a day late, that it was *too late* to matter anymore.

I need him to know that it matters. It still counts. I'm not going to hold his tardiness against him. He's here, just like I asked him to be. So, I throw my arms around his neck and hug him like I should've done five minutes ago, but better late than never, right?

His arms wrap around my waist, pulling me tight. He's just tall enough to rest his chin on my head, which is cute for five seconds before I need space. I don't pull back completely, but enough to look up at him. I wrangle my heartbeat under control. "I didn't think you were coming."

He hesitates a beat too long before he says, "I forgot to give you something."

I'm immediately suspicious, not only because there's something hinky about the timeline but also because in his mind, I'm pretty sure *romance* is an alternative definition of "commodity fetishism."

He produces a little cardboard box, about the size of a Post-it pad, from his pocket and offers it to me. I don't recognize the brand, and I'm trying to make sense of the words on the box.

"Noise-filtering earplugs," Efraín explains. "They filter out ambient noise, lop off some decibels, and help you focus on conversations. They're supposed to be great for people with noise sensitivity, especially autism and ADHD. You'll probably want to try the smallest ear tips . . ."

As he rambles, I inspect the contents of the box. The earplugs are unobtrusive little rings of metallic silver plastic attached to a silicone tip, like an earbud without circuitry.

Efraín has to know that receiving gifts really isn't my love language. "I don't understand."

"After everything you told me about noise sensitivity and why you don't go to protests and rallies, I couldn't let you organize one without protection."

"You remember that?" I ask, running my thumb over the cool plastic loops.

"*Of course*," Efraín insists with a fervency that suggests I may have offended him by insinuating he'd forget. "Your comfort matters."

Under other circumstances, I'd probably feel some kind of way about how he can afford to buy assistive technology to compensate for neurodivergent deficits, but it's been a long day, spent in a small, rowdy crowd. I'm tired, and I'm glad he's here.

Still, there's something that doesn't fit, like if I tried to shove these earplugs into my ear canals with the default-size ear tips attached. "So you ordered me a pair of earplugs and drove two hundred miles because you needed to deliver them to me in person?"

He bites his chapped lip.

Everyone's been giving us a wide berth, presumably caught up in the inherent romance of gifting assistive technology, but this is no venue for an awkward private conversation. I take his arm and lead him away, toward the Sam Schatz Memorial Fountain. I sit on the limestone rim. Efraín just paces.

"Why did you really come back?" I ask gently.

"I wasn't going to," he admits, "but the E-triple-C published the letter online. My dad saw the news alert, and I finally told him everything, after however many days of him accepting at face value that I got fired 'for a good cause.'"

Efraín huffs a laugh. "My dad told me to stop being un tonto—that if I was willing to get fired for you, then I should be willing to show up for you, too. And he was right. I couldn't let you do this alone."

Not long ago, before he ever kissed me, on a morning when I was utterly convinced the museum was going to fire me, Efraín told me I wasn't alone. In that moment, his words scared the shit out of me because I didn't realize, then, that I'd built my entire identity around being alone. "Loner" was a label I chose unconsciously, yes, but I did choose it. Letting Efraín be there for me has been an adjustment, to say the least, but I'm not sure he realizes . . . "I'm not alone."

Even without seeing his eyes, I can tell Efraín looks stricken, so I catch his wrist and pull him down next to me. I touch his cheek, brushing a few flyaways back behind his ear. "I've had Lola, Naomi, Stanley, and everyone else here beside me. You know I want you here, so I'm not saying this to diminish your presence or your gesture"—because what is speeding through the Central Valley on a Friday afternoon if not a grand gesture?—"but what I realized this past week, this morning . . . I've *never* been alone in this."

I'm close enough to count his heartbeats filling the silence before he rasps, "*Good.* That's what I want for you."

It's killing me not to know if *he* knows he's not alone, either. You'd think he'd know, from the gaggle of us gathered here for a ULP strike about his firing, but I don't know. My opa would've called him a Dummkopf.

If Efraín doesn't already know, I don't know how to make him understand. Words wouldn't be enough, and I don't have a gift to offer. All I have is this strike, a communal act of service. If Efraín doesn't understand, I'll just have to show him.

I knit our hands together and rest my head on his shoulder. "Thank you."

He tenses up. "For what? The Loops? You don't have to—"

"For being here," I murmur.

Whether he sees it or not, we're in this together.

THIRTY-TWO

SATURDAY MORNING, EDEN ASKS ME TO WALK HER TO HER CAR. I assume she needs help with supplies, but when we get to her hatchback, she indicates I should get in.

"We're not going somewhere, are we?"

"No," Eden says, "but, on second thought—sorry, can you put your phone in here?" She holds up a black pouch. "Faraday bag. Sorry, I know it's overkill. I know, rationally, museum surveillance isn't tapping my phone, but tell that to my anxiety."

"I get it. Honestly."

"Also, I'm about to violate my NDA like whoa, so there's that."

"You don't have to—"

"You work for the museum, so I'd have to check with my old college roommate—she's in law school—but—"

"Am I missing something?"

"*Everyone's* missing something," she says. "NSX is

hiding—wait, did you not read the text I sent you? The day Efraín got fired?"

"A few messages fell through the cracks that day."

"Understandable. Let me just—" She fetches her messenger bag and pulls out a high-res photocopy of a handwritten letter. "This is the one I sent you."

The one addressed "Schatz."

It is, by any metric, a love letter—a lurid one. I read it twice, my heart pounding in advance of the reckoning. It doesn't make *sense*, but I check again. That's Kane's handwriting and signature. It's dated a year after *NS* was canceled.

Kane asks whether the *distance* between them is truly an *irreconcilable difference*, but—Kane was living with his family on the ranch. He refused to take any meetings in LA.

"This is—" I shake my head. "This *can't* be—"

"C'mon, Eli. You know what this is."

In context, the "Schatz" to whom the letter is addressed can only be Sam Schatz, the actor who played Art Spector.

According to this letter, Victor Kane had an affair with Sam Schatz—was, by his own account, in love with Sam Schatz—and yet, I've read everything there is to read about Victor Kane. I work in a museum dedicated to his life, in the house he lived in—where he presumably wrote this letter about loving another man.

"You know how people have tried to explain away how

Kane always called Sam by his last name in public, right?" Eden prods. "Maybe other people called him 'Schatz.' Maybe there was another 'Sam' on set. But you know better."

"Kane was born in Germany," I murmur. "It wasn't his first language, but his parents spoke it at home even after they immigrated here. 'Schatz' is one of the most common German terms of endearment. The literal translation is 'treasure,' but it's semantically equivalent to 'sweetheart' in American hypocoristic vernacular. My opa used it for my oma."

"So you understand," Eden presses, "this letter wasn't meant for Sigrid or some female lover."

"He was queer."

"Hella queer. There are hundreds of letters back and forth. After Sam died, his boyfriend found a shoebox full of these and sent it to Kane. He kept all of them in a secret compartment in his desk, but if you read all of them, he wasn't ashamed. It was Sam who left.

"Kane was willing to leave his wife and follow Sam anywhere, but Sam . . . It's a fascinating letter, but physically painful to read? In modern parlance, he'd probably ID as poly, and he believed Kane wanted this 'one-and-only soulmate' heteronormative life. Sam was convinced they'd make each other miserable outside of a showmance."

"Heilige Scheiße," I whisper. Everything I thought I knew, up in smoke. I've always been envious of Sam Schatz as who I would've liked to be in some alternate universe—or maybe it was really Art Spector, nerdy but dapper, socially inept but still repairing his corner of the world.

Sam Schatz, after all, was a party gay. He never came out in words, but it was an open secret, even before he showed up to the Emmys in a highlighter-pink blazer and a mesh tank. That, and the eventual AIDS diagnosis.

But Victor Kane—

I've always respected him, but he was unknowable. His mountain man mystique followed him in death. The closest I could get was his work—his self-proclaimed televisual opus on *alienation*. That part I understood all too well.

But this? The mere thought that, under the scraggly beard, the Carhartt flannel collection, and the miasma of gin that was his constant companion, was a man alienated by his queerness . . .

I flip through Eden's file, the sheer scope enveloping me. "Why are you telling me this?"

"I knew it would matter to you."

Tears well up—storm surge, flash flood, pick your fighter. "It does."

"And I thought you should know because—it's all connected, you know? Institutional messaging. The reason NSX won't allow pronoun buttons, and the reason none of this is on display in the museum."

"It changes the narrative," I say.

"It would change *everything*," Eden says, "if this went public. Senior management and curatorial have had major arguments.

Winston—have you met our head curator? You two would hit it off—he thinks the museum is doing a disservice by hiding this. If our mission is to honor Kane's legacy—"

"—and his memory—"

"—then this is critical information. Dagny claims she's protecting her father's legacy, and that he wouldn't want this, but—"

"But he wouldn't have wanted NSX to *exist*," I say. "Almost none of his wishes were honored. And we have so much of his correspondence on display? The letters he sent his mom from Vietnam. Birthday cards from his aunt in East Berlin. That one rude postcard from Truman Capote—"

"Dagny told Winston she couldn't possibly *out* her father without his consent."

"But he wanted to go public with Sam, right? If he was willing to out himself, then is that any different from revealing his feuds with studio execs?"

"Exactly. Remember that line in Kane's journal? He said he didn't care what happened to his things—his work could be burned—and that's how Dagny justifies the museum, right? But instead of donating his papers to UCLA or something, she founded NSX so she could *control* Victor Kane's legacy."

"And she knows the museum would lose business. From all the homophobes and—"

"Exactly."

"Scheiße," I mutter. "Institutional messaging strikes again."

"Technically, we're the ones on strike."

I look at Eden, too many thoughts, too little time. "Thank you for showing me this. Seriously." If it means this much to me, I can't imagine how much this information would mean to the world. "Is there any way I can read more of these, or—"

Eden hands me an old thumb drive with a rueful smile. "Archaic, I know. Hopefully you have access to a computer with a USB 2.0 port? Turn off your Wi-Fi first. You never know who's watching."

"We're getting interview requests," Lola announces Sunday afternoon, pulling me away from prospective guests. Engaging with them in the parking lot makes them rethink crossing the picket line.

"What do you mean?" I ask, sidling up to Efraín, who's off to one side, organizing the sandwiches Moms delivered by dietary restrictions. He should be part of this conversation. Also, I missed him. "Like the E-triple-C? Do they want a follow-up comment?"

"They want a lot more than a comment."

Turns out, TJ is D-list queer internet-famous. Between his posts, Naomi's photos, and Lola's snappy slice-of-life reels, we've gone full-on cold-and-flu-season viral. Likes, kind comments, solidarity fist emojis. Shares, retweets, and reblogs. We're making waves within the *Nuclear Seasons* fandom hot spots. Small progressive news outlets have picked up our strike as a minor human-interest story.

Or we *were* a minor story until George Rhodes, the now-septuagenarian actor who played Harry Davis on *Nuclear Seasons,* noticed us.

> **George Rhodes**
> *@georgemrhodes.bsky.social*
>
> Deeply troubled by the conditions reported by workers at NSX. I'm supposed to attend Friday's 25th anniversary party, but if NSX doesn't sit down with the union before then, I'll gladly join them on the picket line.

"Heilige Scheiße." Now that I've let the phrase into my head, I'm doomed to repeat the earworm until I reach semantic satiation.

"I know," Lola gushes. "Did we know that George was so pro-labor?"

"Sort of?" I hadn't considered how the shows' stars would react to our actions, even though I knew George Rhodes and Christine Holloway, his on-screen wife and off-screen frenemy, would be in attendance. "I think he's been involved with a lot of SAG strikes? Especially that one in the nineties, right before Judy died."

Google delivers the photo I'm envisioning: George Rhodes and Judy Medina-Rhodes in a wheelchair, oxygen tank and a cannula in her nose, in the streets, hoisting picket signs.

"Do you think we should reach out to him? Aside from

reposting and thanking him for his support?" Lola asks. "If we DM him, I bet he'd—"

"No, I don't think we're there yet. That's a big play, and—"

"And you're mortally terrified of meeting any of your heroes."

"No comment."

"About that. People want to hear our story."

I look out at our group. Spirits are still high, and we've got George Rhodes on our side.

Efraín, however, has been conspicuously silent by my side. "What do you think?" I ask. "The letter didn't go into detail about your firing because that's your story to tell, so if you want to . . ."

He frowns at the sandwich piles, already looking for his next task. This is what he's been like all weekend, brimming with anxious energy, going from one menial task to the next. He is eminently helpful, but he doesn't talk to prospective guests. He has yet to pick up the megaphone. Because I've turned down so many protest invites, I can't definitively say this is abnormal rally behavior for him, but he's the one who *brought* the megaphone. What kind of activist owns a megaphone but never uses it?

Besides, Lola's been side-eyeing him all weekend. "Yeah, Ef, have you even posted anything on your socials?"

Efraín shrugs. "My firing is the least interesting part of this story."

"But it's the most incendiary," I point out.

"And we should be careful where we're starting fires."

Lola and I exchange a glance. I've never heard Efraín express *caution* in metaphorical activist arson. I don't understand what's happening here.

But I understand caution and fire safety alike. Lola and TJ have spent more time than they admit reporting hate and playing whack-a-troll. "Efraín's right that overexposure might backfire."

"Or it'll force Dagny to the bargaining table," Lola counters.

I look to Efraín, waiting for strategic insight that never comes. He rakes a hand through his hair and looks at me.

I do not feel equipped to make this decision. Efraín has years of experience organizing, so if he thinks something is risky, I trust his judgment.

I turn to Lola. "I think it's safer if we keep doing our own thing. It's working, right? We're getting attention. Keep posting photos, reels, whatever. But keep it targeted."

Lola clucks her tongue. "So what are we supposed to say when asked for comment?"

"Direct them to our letter. That's our official statement. It should speak for itself, right?"

THIRTY-THREE

THE MUSEUM IS CL☢SED T☢DAY

MONDAY MORNING, WE'RE GREETED BY A SANDWICH BOARD IN the parking lot. Normally, security closes the gate at the turnoff. Today, however, the gate is open. It's like they want guests to see—

Oh, right.

This is the photo op Dagny wants: workers on strike, running through chants, while the museum is closed. Now picture a family of out-of-state tourists in the foreground, a kid crying like they've just dropped their ice-cream cone at the boardwalk.

"Is this online yet?" Stanley asks, scratching his head. "The museum's supposed to open in half an hour."

"Maybe they're scrounging up scabs, but the sign is a precaution?" Naomi asks, photographing the sign.

"It's Ford's day off," supplies Gwen, who joined us yesterday. "That leaves Anya, Dan, and—"

“Anyone they can conscript from upstairs,” I add. “But something seems off—”

“Found something,” Efraín grumbles, glaring at his phone. He’s sitting on Hawkeye’s bumper, so I scoot in next to him.

That something is the museum’s first official communiqué regarding our letter.

The press release on NSX’s socials is really just a statement from Dagny to the internet at large. The strike, she says, is the project of “impertinent upstarts” and “‘woke’ Zoomers” who came to the museum with a hidden agenda: to burn down her father’s legacy and call it activism.

She tries to delegitimize the strike by claiming that the fired worker only sought this job to agitate employees, and as a result, was fired for causing “significant disturbances in the workplace” that prevented others from performing their essential job functions.

Meanwhile, *I*, apparently, am bringing my “mental health issues” into work. Because gender dysphoria is in the *DSM*, Dagny’s claiming that every aspect of my identity and experience as a transgender person can be reduced to a symptom of my disorder.

I have also been responsible for grievous workplace disruptions, despite management’s numerous attempts to help me address my issues privately, and I have made dangerous, baseless allegations regarding sexual harassment against staff and guests—so you, the reader, should be concerned that I, the scary, mentally ill tranny at the ticketing counter, might decide to #MeToo you next.

Dagny doesn't refer to Efraín or me by name, which must be a concession to the fact that we're minors. However, she views the union as an "existential threat" to the museum, and on that note . . .

She's thrilled to reopen "registration" for NSX's sold-out anniversary gala. Due to strike-related disruptions, they've been forced to close today and may not be able to operate throughout the week, so they're asking fans to step up! Register to attend the party as a *volunteer*! Don't worry, they still have celebrities who will cross the picket line, so you should, too! Scabs of the internet, unite!

Fury whittles the world down to a red-hot poker.

Efraín's cursing next to me, quivering with rage.

I don't know why he's not moving because I'm standing up. Stanley's hand on my shoulder stops me from storming the farmhouse door and finding out how much of that Dagny would say to my face.

Lola's mad as hell, too, and she's back on about interviews. Eden's typing up notes for the group chat. TJ's asking about our social media response plan.

Everyone wants my opinion on something, but I'm all sold out.

Efraín's saying something about taking a walk, and I'm about to invite myself when Naomi hits my arm. Hard.

"What?" I hiss, rubbing my sore skin. I look at her, looking at the world through her phone's camera interface.

Dan's coming out of the barn.

"Well, it's about time you joined us!" Stanley yells.

"*Are* you joining us?" Lola demands. "Or are you here to deliver some message Dagny won't publish for the public record?"

"No." Dan shakes his head, bewildered. "I mean, yes, I'm joining. If that's cool with you." Dan's looking straight at me. "I just saw the thing. What Dagny's saying about you—that isn't cool. I don't want to be part of that. So, uh, if it's all the same to you, I'd rather be here."

I don't know why he's asking my permission. Dan's never misgendered me, not as far as I know, but I've also never heard him defend . . . anything, really. Given that Dan spends so much time with Ford, there's an endless supply of microaggressions to call out. That's the problem with Dan's brand of chill. He may accept the news of my gender with a single blink, but there are some things in this world that you can't just let live or let lie.

If he's finally figured that out, then all the power to him.

Wordlessly, I hand him the sign I've been using as a crutch.

In organizing, we talk about inoculating against union busting, but I could've used a booster shot against cyberbullying.

It's a universally acknowledged law of the internet that any social justice–related content will eventually reach bigots, haters, and trolls. I've been concerned since the beginning that our positive viral attention might trigger backlash.

Sucks to be right.

Everyone has put down their signs and quieted their chants to sit on the ground and doomscroll on our personal electronic devices.

It's bleak.

We're on strike, so anti-labor commenters are to be expected. Most of us are young, so it follows that many posts call us some variation of privileged, spoiled brats and indict our entire generation.

Those critiques seem downright civil compared to the rest of it.

We've attracted every person on the internet who clutches their pearls or grabs their gun when they so much as hear "DEI." We've enraged the trifecta: racists, homophobes, and TERFs.

This job has taught me that the *NS* fandom is *diverse.* For every queer who's found something meaningful in it, there are countless fans who just like scurvy zombies, grapevine-tentacle monsters, or pretty girls skinny-dipping in luminescent lakes.

Or maybe they just like guns.

They sure love the target that's been pinned to my back.

It doesn't matter that Dagny didn't use Efraín's or my names. *NS* fans speedily cross-reference the press release with the union's socials and public information and come up with our names, birthdays, sexes assigned at birth, addresses, phone numbers, and—

Yeah, no, they find my deadname minutes later.

They don't fixate on Efraín with the same ruthless ferocity, and I shred myself into pulp feeling guilty, grateful, and jealous when I see *why*: Efraín's barely in Naomi's strike photos. He's always occupied with something, never claiming center stage. At first, I wonder if he made a deal with Naomi, but when I run back the past few days, I realize that's just how he's been acting—not withdrawn, but quieter. I assume the fact that Efraín isn't prominently featured in the photos makes him a less appealing target for trolls. Meanwhile, I am *right there* in HD, imposing on the tableau of their favorite TV show while visibly trans. Low-hanging fruit for the lowest common denominator.

There is something singularly gut-crushing about reading some anon claiming he clocked me the second he joined my tour group.

Is that better or worse than the strangers who discuss Dagny's words with genuine concern? Some *for* me—how dare my parents allow me to mutilate myself?—but mostly *against* me—they couldn't imagine letting their daughter share a bathroom with me—and a lot of single-minded transphobes who are so fucking terrified by the existence of trans women that they literally can't comprehend that trans men exist?

And then there's Christine Holloway, the septugenarian actress best known for her role as Carol Davis on *NS*, and a verified X user.

> **Christine Holloway**
> *@christy_holloway*
>
> Such a tragedy, so close to home! This is what happens when the radical left preaches gender ideology and conspires to pump young girls full of dangerous hormones instead of treating their troubles. I doubt she would be lashing out like this without testosterone fueling her rage? No surprise she's raging against authority when the authority figures in her own life have clearly let her down by letting her act out these delusions.
>
> Sad.
>
> Anywho, I'll be at the NSX Anniversary Gala on Friday. Rain or shine, strike or no strike! Who's with me?

I am a queer, transgender, Jewish teenager. It was always going to end up here. God forbid they find out I'm autistic, too. I'm hitting all the boxes on someone's "today on the internet" identity bingo card.

I'm still scrolling when the first death threat rolls in.

It's a macabre party game, finding the most vile tweets to read aloud that night at Punch Bowl's happy hour.

Nearly a dozen of us are here eating cheap fried food. Or just pushing limp fries around on a plate. I don't have an appetite.

The conversation is sluggish, and I keep zoning out until people say my name.

Efraín has been by my side all day, brooding and silent. The only time I've ever seen him so quiet in the face of bigotry was the day those three bigots walked into the museum. Since the death threats started, he's been loath to leave me alone.

He's slipped into guard dog mode, and he snapped at Lola when she tried to check in with both of us about how we're coping. She muttered something about the emotional illiteracy of teenage boys before tactically retreating. I asked Efraín a variant of the same question, thinking I might get a real response because we're staring down the barrel of the same gun.

He keeps telling me he's *fine*, and even I, as emotionally illiterate as I am, can read the goddamn lie. When he flips the switch and expresses concern for me, I use the first excuse I can find to make my own tactical retreat.

It doesn't matter that some guy in the men's restroom asks me if I'm sure I'm in the right place.

What matters is when the time comes to split the check. I silently thank Mr. Xie for extending Blake's family discount to the rest of us, and then I Venmo my share to Eden. I don't think much of Blake covering Jaime or Stanley covering TJ until I catch Naomi's wince. There have been a lot of hushed sidebars around the table.

"So, uh." Divya scratches her head. "How long do we think this is gonna go on?"

"As long as it takes," I answer. "Until Dagny agrees to meet with the union."

"Yeah, but"—Divya exchanges sideways glances with Miles and TJ—"how many business days do we think that's gonna take? I thought, after they saw we were serious, we'd be back at work, getting premium pay for the party—"

"My rent's due Friday," TJ says quietly.

I feel selfish and stupid, and I instinctively glance at Efraín. He looks queasier than I feel. All those times I marveled at how obtuse Efraín was about spending money, and now I've made the same mistake.

Maybe Dagny was right to call me a privileged, spoiled brat because how did I manage to overlook something so glaringly obvious? As much as it grates, I am, technically, a child. My parents provide food, shelter, insurance, etc. Same for my sister, Efraín, Lola, and Gwen. But for the legal adults in the room? How much do I know about their financial situations?

Jaime works two jobs to finance night classes at the junior college. Blake's a college student. Eden has a boatload of student loans.

At least I know Jaime and Blake live with their parents, and Stanley has his wife, but everyone else?

TJ's rent is due. He's a part-time employee in his early twenties. Does he have a roommate? Does he have groceries in the fridge?

How many of my fellow workers are living paycheck to paycheck?

My head is pounding, and the shitty '80s music spilling from the jukebox doesn't help.

"It's just—" Jaime starts. He looks first to Blake, then to Lola, for encouragement, moral support, permission? "It sounds like Dagny isn't going to back down? Especially now that Christine Holloway's thread is getting attention."

"She's trending," TJ confirms.

"Yeah," Lola cuts in, "but is Holloway trending because people agree with her or because they know she's full of shit?"

"It feels like we're losing," Jaime says.

"I don't know about you guys"—Divya gestures around the table—"but I can't afford to lose this job. I've got *bills*, man."

And Jaime's abuela needs groceries, and Miles's toddler's childcare doesn't come cheap.

Everyone *needs*, and *I* need to say something, but I don't know what. My breaths come hard and fast, and sweat percolates on my brow.

I look at Efraín. Surely he'll know what to say. The vein in his temple is throbbing, and he's working his jaw. He must be winding up to say something that will make everything right. This is his wheelhouse. He knows how to give inspirational speeches and rally the masses; it's what he does best.

I've done my best to be the organized organizer, but it's well-established that I'll never be a social leader. I can write petitions and brainstorm creative solutions, but this isn't my role.

Efraín told me himself, didn't he? That's the point of a union. We all have different roles to play. This is his. Maybe it isn't as flashy as his old *Eat the Rich: The Musical* one-man show, but he's not a lone wolf anymore. He came back from Fresno; he met me at the picket line. He understands now. Doesn't he?

Except he hasn't said anything.

Instead, he's staring at his chipped red nail polish like he'll find answers in the cracks.

When I look up, every other set of eyes is locked on me. I've never felt so helpless, so I turn to the man who's always been there to point the way to an escape hatch.

"You know what?" Stanley says, soft and kind. "It's been a long day. We can talk about money tomorrow, okay? In the light of day, maybe everything will look different."

THIRTY-FOUR

THE COLD LIGHT OF DAY REVEALS A SWASTIKA GRAFFITIED ON THE diner's window. Red spray paint drips like blood spatter here in the beating heart of my small town.

I know the internet is a brutal, dog-eat-dog place. If someone hasn't sent you a death threat or told you to kill yourself, then you just haven't been online long enough.

But this is Egan's Creek, in idyllic Sonoma County wine country. I only know what violence in Egan's Creek looks like through *Nuclear Seasons*, but *NS* prioritized *eerie* over *violent*. A swastika in a window is *sinister*.

It's one thing for people to threaten me. I'm not going to victim-blame myself for a literal hate crime, but I acknowledge that this wouldn't have happened if I'd stayed quiet, kept my mouth shut. I made my choices. I can handle the death threats and my deadname circulating on social media. But this is my family's diner. Naomi and my moms have done *nothing* to deserve this.

Mom saw it first on her predawn run, and the four of us have been here for an hour by the time Lola parallel parks and joins us on the sidewalk. Efraín's a step behind her, immediately wrapping his arms around me.

This tableau demands a wide-angle establishing shot. Up close, viewed only in pieces, the symbol loses meaning. To fully understand it, you need to see the whole scene. This retro diner on the corner of a classic Americana town square, something out of another decade.

Maybe that's the point. Hate is timeless. It's also *senseless* because I know this isn't truly an antisemitic hate crime. I don't know who did it, so I can't know their true motives, but transphobia is the most obvious explanation. Maybe anti-labor sentiment. Maybe they're just old-school *Nuclear Seasons* purists who hate on younger fans. Perhaps most likely, all of the above.

Because that's the thing about hate: it *coheres* even as the symbols destabilize. One kind of hate can stand in for another. People looking for an excuse to hate me don't need to look far.

I wonder how many of them would call me a *pinko commie*, too.

Lola asks us how we're doing, which is a fraught question at the best of times but a nonsensical one now, for three autistic, alexithymic Jews descended from Holocaust survivors.

As our resident shiksa and most emotionally in-touch family member, Ma offers Lola a watery smile. "Oh, hon."

"This is better than if they'd thrown a brick through the window," Mom observes, and Efraín hugs me impossibly tighter.

Naomi has documented the damage with both her phone and Mom's film camera.

Ma's smile wobbles. "You're sweet for coming, kids."

Lola says, "Of course we came."

Efraín asks, "What can I—" I can feel Efraín's shaky exhalation ruffling my curls. "How can we help?"

"Do you think you kids have time to help us get started cleaning this up before you head to the picket line?" Ma checks her watch. "Do we need to make a trip to the hardware store? What is it they say you need to remove graffiti? Acetone or a razor blade?"

"Generic 'graffiti remover' followed by a razor blade," Ms. Sinclair calls, cutting across the square with two canvas totes on each shoulder. "We used to get the occasional complaint when we screened certain films." She shrugs, like it's just ancient history, long buried. "I picked up supplies from Loman & Sons."

Ma immediately thanks her while Mom asks, "How much do we owe you?"

Ms. Sinclair waves them off. "Nothing. Ben said it was on the house. Otherwise, it would've been on me."

"Thank you," I say, aware that someone should say something, but Ma's overwrought, and neither Mom nor Naomi will.

Ms. Sinclair shakes her head. "Nothing to it. Now let's get rid of that thing."

The museum is closed again, but it doesn't matter. Momentum is not on our side. *The A.V. Club, The Hollywood Reporter,* and *Variety* have picked up the story. That adage about all press being good press only applies to those already in possession of cultural capital.

Spoiler alert: that's not us.

Divya is gone, and I can't even blame her. She has bills, and what do I have? A half-empty top surgery fund.

For now, there's nothing I can do but hold the line.

Even when the hecklers arrive.

Late morning, vehicles trickle into the lot. Counter-protesters. They're exactly what you'd expect.

While a handful sign up to help on Friday night when Ford scurries out of the barn with a clipboard, most are day-trippers. Somewhere, on some sketchy corner of the internet, someone *planned* this. They planned to bring bullhorns to a picket line and yell obscenities and slurs at a union primarily composed of teenagers and young adults.

Stanley tries to reason with them. Lola excels at sassy comebacks and zingers. Blake is all silent snarls and glares.

TJ freezes up. Dan is too chill. Naomi and Gwen are just *so young* to be facing down grown men like this.

I am intermittently loud at best, and today I'm just tired.

None of us are built for this, except for Efraín, except he might as well have an out-of-office "Gone Fishing" door sign in place of his picket sign. He won't leave my side, still in guard dog mode, and it's all really fucking ironic when he's wearing his IWW tank emblazoned with the famed sabotabby, a black cat with its back arched and teeth bared, raring for a fight.

Why isn't Efraín fighting back?

The bow breaks when a man hurls a vicious yet mundane threat at my sister. After I tell him to fuck off, check in on Naomi, and subtly instruct Jaime and Dan—the burliest and most visually intimidating among us, despite their demeanors—to watch out for our more vulnerable members, I ask Efraín to take a walk with me.

He doesn't ask why; he just loosely laces our hands together and lets me lead.

As we trek across the lawn, we're technically trespassing, but the museum doesn't have the manpower to hunt us down. I cut between the farmhouse and barn, away from the silo, and all the way to the trellises cordoning off Kane's grave. I don't go inside the courtyard; I'm not going to have it out in front of a literal grave, but here on the far side, the vine-covered trellises afford us some much-needed privacy.

Efraín leans back against the trellis, deceptively nonchalant, but discreetly drumming his fingers against his thigh.

It's taking all my self-control to stop from pacing, but I'm trying to face him. So I'm tapping my foot, shaking my hands, blinking behind my sunglasses—doing everything I can to skim off my anxious energy. I've never considered myself a confrontational person; my tendency to fall into arguments is a result of my clinical inability to shut up.

This isn't that.

"Not that I don't appreciate the sentiment," Efraín says lightly, "but I'm not sure this is the time or the place for a make-out session."

"Don't do that," I snap, looking everywhere, at everything but him. "Don't pretend. Don't tell me everything's okay when we both know it's not."

"I never said that," he replies, grim.

"You didn't have to say it." I look past him, at grapevines woven between weathered slats. "But ever since you came back, you've been doing a really great impression of the not-quite-body-snatchers from 'Dell of the Dolls,' and—"

"What?"

"*Nuclear Seasons,* episode five! You'd know that if you'd ever let me show you more than three random episodes."

"Maybe I'd get it if you didn't couch everything in TV

references instead of just saying what you really mean."

Maybe it's just my imagination, but across campus, I can hear the counterprotesters jeering. I hug my arms across my chest. When I finally meet my reflection in Efraín's aviators, I look strange and small, a surreal distortion.

Finally, I say, "You said you came back because you didn't want me to do this alone. So why do I feel more alone than I did before? I understand why everyone else is pulling back—they're exhausted and losing faith—but I thought you were a true believer."

He's closer now, and he's working his jaw—that angry tic that's so familiar in the sprawl of my memory but conspicuously absent from the past few weeks. "Fucking hell, Elisha, you can't have it both ways."

"I don't understand." I blink at him through my knockoff Wayfarers. "What does that even *mean*?"

"You told me my 'lone wolf routine' was a problem, and you know what? You were right. From the very beginning. My choices put other people's jobs—their *livelihoods*—in danger. I put *you* at risk. So, I took responsibility for that. I saved your job, and I stepped back."

"You mean you ran away."

"I came *back*." He's close enough to touch me, but he doesn't close the distance. "What else do you want from me?"

"More than a pair of noise-filtering earplugs!" I hiss, then immediately regret it. If I were less raw, my filter would be stronger. "Sorry, I really like the earplugs, and it means more than you know that you thought to do that for me. More than getting yourself fired, actually."

"I thought we already had that argument."

"And I thought you realized—"

"What, Elisha? What profound lesson was I supposed to take away from your last lecture? Did you think I'd just show up at the picket line reciting strike chants into a megaphone?"

I want to argue, but . . . What *did* I expect would happen? I know Efraín. Give him a pulpit, and he can't help but preach. Maybe I thought he could turn this soap opera into his soapbox, and that's how we'd win. Efraín would seize the day and inspire the masses by telling his story.

All those silences I've been waiting for him to fill this past week. All those pictures where he's faded into the background. He wasn't minimizing his presence to protect himself from harassment; he was trying to protect the union from himself.

"I thought you knew it wasn't all on you," I say softly. "None of the bad things—the setbacks or the retaliation—none of it was ever your fault."

"The union was *my* idea," Efraín insists, "and look where it got us. You almost got fired. Someone painted a fucking swastika on the diner. That never would've happened if . . ."

"If you'd never founded the union?" I challenge him.

"Maybe not, but in that timeline? Naomi would've gotten fired. We wouldn't have stools. And I—"

"You still don't have a button, not inside the museum." He touches my contraband pronoun button, pinned over my heart. "And your top surgery fund is at risk. If I'd never taken this job, never played tourist with a time card—"

"I'd still think I was completely and totally alone," I say. "I thought you'd realized, by now, that organizing isn't about grand gestures. The union isn't all or nothing. I'm not trying to have it both ways; you're the one who doesn't know how to compromise to save your life."

"You mean, save my job?"

"I mean it's not a contradiction to say I want you here, doing your part, but that you need to let everyone else do their parts, too. That's why you believe in collective power, right? Everyone does their part. Lola's a social leader. Naomi documents everything. I write petitions. And you . . ."

Tears prickle at the corners of my eyes. I tell myself it's because I'm allergic to the flora, not because I'm allergic to *feeling* this much.

"You piss people off, and then you show them how to use that anger for good. You warn them that others will try to knock them down, and then you bring them together to storm the castle. You agitate, educate, inoculate, and organize without even trying. You're the whole damn acronym,

Efraín. The union needs you too much for you to hold back." I take his hand in mine. "I need you here with me."

"You really don't," Efraín murmurs. "You said it when I came back. You were never alone."

"No, but I'm tired and scared," I confess. "Between the cyberbullying, IRL harassment, and financial insecurity, I don't know if the union can make it until Friday. I can't keep this strike going alone."

"Everyone's still here."

"Except Divya, who can't pay her bills, and Miles, who can't afford a babysitter." I shake my head. I can't keep losing this argument. I look across the lawn, where someone from admin is leading a very small tour group from the farmhouse to the silo. "The union took on management and won, more than once. If this strike was just us against the museum, maybe we could win again. But the combined force of the museum and the dark side of the fanbase might be more than the union can handle. I learned the hard way that I couldn't go it alone. What do we do if the union can't go it alone, either?"

Efraín looks at me for so long I worry I've lost him. He doesn't let go of my hand, but there's an intensity in the way he's scrutinizing me. I stay still as he works out whatever internal battle he needs to fight before he can rejoin the war. Then he asks, "What if the union doesn't have to go it alone?"

My heart rate perks up. "What do you mean?"

"I'm not sure yet," he admits, "but I want to figure it out, together. If you still want that."

I don't need a metaphor to describe my relief, because the emotion his words evoke is a perfect match to the sensation of him pulling me closer, wrapping his arms around me, pressing a soft kiss to my forehead before pulling back. His voice is low and rough when he asks, "Is that still what you want, Elisha?"

"Of course it is."

He's vibrating at that higher frequency, the righteous indignation that accompanies his every crusade. The smolder in his eyes isn't without tenderness, but I force myself to look up at him full-on.

It's a familiar, dangerous smolder. I saw it that night at the diner when he swore he wouldn't let me get fired. He smoldered at me and then looked out the same window that was defaced this morning.

But as I look into his eyes, I'm not thinking about what that window looked like when I first got to the square. Instead, the same scene keeps replaying in my memory:

Ms. Sinclair, noticing the graffiti on the diner on her way to work and stopping by the hardware store. Mr. Loman, donating graffiti removal supplies. Lola, offering Ma emotional support. And Efraín asking how he could help.

They all gave of themselves so freely.

I blink at Efraín and break the spell. "I think I have an idea."

Efraín smiles like I just gave him the bank account numbers for every billionaire in the world for us to pillage and redistribute the wealth.

THIRTY-FIVE

AFTER ANOTHER DAY OF FIELDING HECKLERS IN THE PARKING LOT, we regroup at Lou's.

I'm punch-drunk on the revelation that Efraín with a megaphone might be one of the hottest things I've ever seen, despite my aversion to both megaphones and cheesy strike chants. But Efraín's passion is just that intoxicating. His fervent participation—refocusing himself from background to foreground—has morale on the rise, as does the new wave of positive press accompanying Naomi's fresh batch of strike photos; the internet agrees with my assessment of megaphone-equipped Efraín.

Thanks to a one-on-one with Lola, Divya's back, and Eden has brought in our most shocking recruit: Winston, the head curator.

In spite of everything, the atmosphere at the diner is buoyant. The window has been scraped clean, good as new. None of the patrons mind when we push tables together to accommodate our party.

Once the table's loaded with drinks and appetizer platters, it's time for me to share the idea Efraín and I came up with after our heart-to-heart yesterday afternoon.

"Do you guys remember that scene in *It's a Wonderful Life?*" I ask.

"Part one or part two?" asks Stanley.

"Sorry, not 'It's a Wonderful Half-Life.' The Frank Capra Christmas movie. Jimmy Stewart as George Bailey, facing down the slumlord Mr. Potter, who's basically the Monopoly monocle man?"

Everyone stares at me. Someone drops their fork. Efraín squeezes my knee under the table.

"The Monopoly man didn't wear a monocle," Naomi observes.

"Setting aside the Mandela Effect heebie-jeebies for a hot sec . . ." Lola cuts in. "Asking if we remember 'that scene' is kinda vague for a two-hour, eighty-year-old movie, dude."

"Fair. I mean when George and Mary are about to leave on their honeymoon, but there's a bank run. Everyone wants to withdraw their money at once, which is impossible because—it doesn't matter. George uses all the money he had set aside for his honeymoon to cover the withdrawals. But he asks everyone to think hard about how much money they really need to get by, and there's this one woman who calculates it down to the penny—"

"Is there a point to you butchering the one good Christmas movie?" Blake demands.

"My point," I say, "is that I have some money saved. So if anyone has an immediate cash flow problem, I can manage a strike fund—"

With equal incredulity, Naomi asks, "You're planning to do math without supervision?" while Lola protests, "*Eli*, that's your top surgery fund."

And Stanley says, "Please tell me you're not planning to turn your savings into a strike fund."

"Not exactly?" I glance at Efraín. "I mean, that was the idea, but then I was informed that my plan would 'violate the spirit of *mutual aid*,' so—"

Efraín rolls his eyes. "What kind of boyfriend would I be if I let you do something so stupidly, pointlessly self-sacrificing?"

"The hypocritical kind," I reply, "because your solution was to fund the entire thing yourself, even though your mom would freeze—" I blink, delayed processing catching up to me. "Wait, did you just call me your boyfriend? I don't remember agreeing—"

Lola snorts. "After you spend a decade bicker-bantering like an old married couple, you can skip the 'going steady' labels conversation."

"Sorry," TJ interrupts, "but what does this have to do with mutual aid?"

"Nothing," Blake says, "because they both completely missed the point of *It's a Wonderful Life*."

"What Blake means," Lola says, "is we're not letting either

of you do something so stupidly, pointlessly self-sacrificing alone. Eli, your top surgery fund is for a *medically necessary* procedure. Ef, your mom would literally kill you if you tried to cover everyone's bills after getting yourself fired. We're on strike, yeah? We're *already* in this together, so what's the point of a strike fund if it's not actually *mutual*?"

"We should make a spreadsheet," Naomi says eagerly.

The next few minutes are as chaotic as Capra's bank run scene as everyone assesses their finances. While Lola bars me from dipping into my top surgery fund and caps Efraín's pledge at half his proposed number, no one objects when Winston offers to contribute four figures. Stanley also insists on contributing a week's pay, which he argues he can afford in his two-income, zero-child household with a healthy 401(k).

And that is how the George Bailey Mutual Aid Strike Fund is born.

Then we're on to our next order of business.

Now that we're forty-eight hours from the anniversary party, it's clear Dagny isn't going to cave. Most registered attendees still plan to attend, and fans from all over the world are making the pilgrimage to volunteer as scabs.

Efraín and I bring up the other issue we discussed yesterday: The union needs help, though we haven't figured out what that means. We need *help* solving the puzzle.

"Well, we've been underutilizing one of our largest resources," Stanley muses, his hands steepled under his chin.

"The museum has done a great job mobilizing fans, but so many fans are on our side. I can't help feeling we should be reaching out to them."

"They *are* really active online," TJ says. "What else could they be doing?"

"What if we could get them here in person?" Jaime perks up. "There's nothing like the energy of a crowd to rev you up."

"But what would we *do* with them, if we could get our fans here?" Divya asks.

"They wouldn't fit in the car park," Gwen replies, clipped.

"Yeah, if the last attendance numbers I saw hold," Dan says, "the main lot and the overflow lot will both be totally full."

"What if—" Eden starts, brow furrowed. She whispers something to Winston, who nods along, excited. Eden nods to herself and proposes, "What if we offered alternative programming? If we could find a venue somewhere else while NSX is celebrating some sanitized version of history, we could have our own anniversary party celebrating the things we love about *Nuclear Seasons* and what the museum *could be*—the stories it could be telling."

Such as the treasure trove of love letters I've read and reread the past few nights instead of sleeping.

"There are certain artifacts," Winston elaborates, "that Dagny has withheld from the public, primarily out of concern that they would alienate certain elements of the fanbase."

"Victor Kane was queer," I blurt because, honestly? I have not had sufficient opportunity to celebrate this. "He had an affair with Sam Schatz and pined for him for years."

While Winston and Eden hit the highlights for the group, Efraín whispers in my ear, "You've been holding out on me."

"Since when do you care?"

"Since you care. Besides, I always thought Sam Schatz was hot."

The plan crystallizes. We'll organize our own party. I might even have a line on a venue, though I don't want to make promises until I make the call.

"Circling back to the original issue," Lola says, "about underutilized resources. Eli, remember how I brought up press requests and you said we could handle it ourselves?"

I wince. "That may have been shortsighted. Do you still have the list?"

Lola reads through the list of publications, journalists, and influencers who have reached out. The list has easily quadrupled, but one name leaves Efraín starstruck.

"Say that again?"

"Kiera Kim?"

"Are we supposed to know who that is?" Gwen asks.

"They were writing articles about labor issues for *Teen Vogue* before labor was back in vogue," Naomi supplies.

"They do impressive work," Efraín says, "talking to groups of workers who don't normally get mentioned in labor history or journalism."

"Sounds like a good fit," I reply.

"Who would best represent the union in an interview?" Stanley asks.

Stanley's worked here the longest. Lola's the most personable. TJ has the built-in social media following. Jaime has that unique combination of minor local celebrity and golden retriever energy that viewers would lap up—

"Nothing to decide," Lola says with a petite snort. "They want you, Eli."

"What? No. Why? Absolutely not," I sputter. "Why would anyone *assume* I represent the union?"

"The strike *was* your idea," Naomi points out.

"It's a ULP strike. In Efraín's name." I turn to him, hesitant after all the fears he disclosed yesterday. He may have picked up the megaphone today, but that doesn't change the fact that the boy who always rides in on the white horse admitted the horse is spooked. "The *union* was your idea, and this is your story."

"Originally, sure, but now? You're the leader of the movement. That makes you the hero of this story." He says it without any of the sour-mouthed adjectives I would've attributed to him two months ago, like he fully expects me to live up to that moniker.

"Bullshit."

I'm not a leader of men; I'm a not-so-nice Jewish trans boy conscripted to the cause by spite and misunderstanding.

Efraín lowers his voice, just for me. "You know how this

works. Magneto didn't ask to team up with a motley crew of mutants. Curtis didn't ask to be the last man alive to make it to the front of the Snowpiercer. Katniss didn't ask to be the Mockingjay. Frodo didn't ask to take the ring to Mordor."

"Actually—"

"Moses didn't *ask* to lead the Israelites out of Egypt."

"Are you telling me God chose me to lead a walkout and part the picket line? Or, okay, I guess it was the opposite of *parting*, but—"

"You know what I mean, Elisha."

"Yes, I know how stories go. The hero amasses an army to storm the castle and watches them sacrifice themselves for him all so he can go on to face the Big Bad alone. But that's not the story I'm telling. I refuse to feed that story to a reporter."

This isn't a crisis of self-confidence or a question of ego. "It shouldn't be any *one* of us because this isn't about any one of us. It's about *all* of us, together."

"Isn't the point that individual stories humanize the issues in a way collective stories can't?" Gwen asks.

"Yes," Eden answers, "but individual stories as collective testimony can be a powerful tool, too."

"We all came to the picket line for a reason," I say, looking from one face to the next, "and no one's story is more important than anyone else's." My gaze locks on Naomi, and my heart clenches when I remember the space between her story as told by me and the version she told me herself. I was so caught up in the narrative I'd written for myself—that I was completely and utterly alone—that I stopped listening to anyone else's story.

Now, with her hair up, her green peekaboo highlights are on full display, freshly re-dyed, and now that I know what they mean, they're a powerful testament to her identity. Naomi slurps her pistachio almond-milk milkshake and blinks when she realizes I've been staring. She cocks her head, wide-eyed and curious in spite of herself.

"Honestly?" I say, speaking to everyone but only looking at her. "It was just chance that it came to a head over pronoun buttons instead of something else. If we'd made different choices, we could've organized a ULP strike two months ago, the first time management threatened to fire someone without cause."

"No, we couldn't," Naomi says bluntly. "Change a single variable, and we wouldn't be sitting here right now. We're here because you were the loudest."

I assume she means Efraín because he is, both figuratively and literally, the loudest person in the room. The boy with the megaphone, calling out every injustice.

But Naomi is staring at me, making eye contact even though I know it hurts her more than me, and Efraín's hand is a reassuring weight on my thigh.

I shake my head, trying to shake loose the objections

lodged in my throat before I choke. I don't know how to explain to Naomi that I'm not loud on purpose; I'm just too stubborn to know when to shut up. If I could understand social cues, if I had any skill at masking, I'd be quiet about everything.

Then Naomi smiles at me—wispy, barely there, but positively beatific for a girl with decreased affect. I don't deserve it, but I do my best to smile back.

Meanwhile, Efraín's leaning in, murmuring, "See? You could totally be a social leader."

I playfully shove his shoulder, and then I turn back to Lola, who's watching like she doesn't know whether to laugh or cry—and might do both. I clear my throat. "Okay. Tell Kiera Kim that we'll talk to them if they talk to all of us—everyone who wants to tell their story."

Lola hesitates. "Eli, I don't think we're really in a position to make demands."

"Funny. That's what the museum thinks, too."

THIRTY-SIX

NSX Museum Workers Strike Interview Transcript

Interviewees: Divya Agarwal (security guard); TJ Egan (guest services associate); Lola Fuentes (GSA); Elisha Goldstein (GSA, docent); Naomi Goldstein (GSA); Dan Guzman (GS assistant supervisor); Jaime Jimenez (GSA); Efraín Juarez Reyna (GSA); Winston Keating (head curator); Eden Lantier (assistant curator); Miles Petri (security guard); Stanley Pham (GSA, docent); Gwen Pryce (GSA); Blake Xie (GSA, docent)

NOTE: INTERVIEWS WERE CONDUCTED INDIVIDUALLY. THIS TRANSCRIPT HAS BEEN EDITED AND ABRIDGED.

Kiera Kim: Why did you take this job? Are you a *Nuclear Seasons* fan, or is it just a job for you?

Eden Lantier: I got lucky. I felt like I won the lottery when I saw the job listing. I love the show, and do you have any idea how few curatorial jobs are out there? It's an employment desert.

Divya Agarwal: I just needed to pay my bills, man. Girl's gotta live, right?

Efraín Juarez Reyna: I applied to get back at my mom. If anyone else tries to tell you their intentions were less than noble, I promise it's nothing compared to that.

Gwen Pryce: I thought it would look good on my college applications. Not *this* job, but the paid internship. What did Eli tell you?

Jaime Jimenez: I needed a second job. I worked at Punch Bowl part-time in high school, but after, Mr. Xie couldn't afford to hire me full-time. I wanted to take classes at the junior college, too, so working here . . . worked.

Lola Fuentes: So, I'd just broken up with this guy who works at my family's body shop, and it was too awkward working together, and I couldn't ask *him* to find another job, so . . .

Stanley Pham: I think Winston and I are the only ones who can say we were *NS* fans when the show aired. I was a kid, too young to be watching it, really, but I loved it. *NS* is the reason I thought I'd try my hand at screenwriting . . . I don't normally talk about my time in LA, about the casual racism in every writers' room I ever walked into. I just . . . I wanted to write, and I wanted to like going to work every day. For a while there, I didn't think I could have both. But I realized I didn't need to see my name in credits on the screen. I just liked writing, putting on the occasional production with the theater here, and I got a job that I do love. Most days, at least.

Kiera Kim: How do you feel about working conditions at the Nuclear Seasons Experience?

Dan Guzman: It's a job. I've worked worse jobs.

TJ Egan: Some of the rules seem kinda strict?

Stanley Pham: Conditions on the floor are better than they used to be. Progress is slow, but I believe everyone is well-intentioned.

Elisha Goldstein: I don't feel like a person when I'm on the clock.

Naomi Goldstein: I don't think I'm enough of a people person to do customer service.

Gwen Pryce: I am very grateful for California's high minimum wage.

Jaime Jimenez: I used to play soccer. I was good—really good, you know? Woulda gotten a scholarship if—point is, I know something about being part of a team. And I always thought it was weird, how the managers here always talk about us as a "team" because I know what a team feels like. But they don't treat us the way you're supposed to treat your team. When your coach makes you run extra laps, you know why, but here . . . A pizza party here and there . . . This isn't how you treat your teammates. I don't know much about business, but I know this isn't how you should run one.

Kiera Kim: Have you experienced discrimination or harassment at the museum?

Jaime Jimenez: I don't know if I would call it discrimination . . .

Blake Xie: People talk, just like they do anywhere. My first summer here, I got shit because I was masking—my nai nai was doing chemo. But that's nothing compared to HR asking for confidential medical records before granting a single accommodation.

Eden Lantier: I spend most of my time in the vault, so I don't interact with guests very often. But the admin staff over in the farmhouse? If I had a penny for every time someone implied I was a DEI hire, I'd be able to pay off my student loans.

Naomi Goldstein: Did someone already tell you about the hair dye?

Lola Fuentes: You've been following social media coverage of the strike, right?

Efraín Juarez Reyna: How long do you have?

Elisha Goldstein: [laughs]

Kiera Kim: Why did you join the union?

Lola Fuentes: I wasn't gonna let anyone threaten my friends without a fight.

Elisha Goldstein: I was informed that I had already joined the union after our first action. It was unintentional. But after I saw behind the curtain . . .

Naomi Goldstein: My job was in danger. That sounds bad. I wish I had a better answer, but I don't know if I would've felt confident enough to join an underground union for other causes. But I'm glad I did.

Stanley Pham: I love these kids to death, but they're not subtle. I know a thing or two about organizing, sure, but I also know everything about this museum. I know our bosses. I knew I could help.

Kiera Kim: If you could change one thing about the museum, what would it be?

Efraín Juarez Reyna: Just one thing?

Naomi Goldstein: The union has a comprehensive grievance list.

Divya Agarwal: I could really use a raise.

Jaime Jimenez: More full-time positions, with benefits.

Blake Xie: The sick leave policy.

Miles Petri: Secure scheduling.

Winston Keating: I'd like to run my department without fear of managerial censorship.

Eden Lantier: I know sensitivity training is out of vogue, but a racial caucus sure wouldn't hurt.

Gwen Pryce: There isn't nearly enough employee parking in the car park.

Stanley Pham: I suppose it'd be nice to carry around a real water bottle . . .

Kiera Kim: Why did you join the picket line?

Dan Guzman: Because the only time I've ever been *ashamed* to work at this museum was when I read that press release.

Jaime Jimenez: Because the union got us stools on the museum floor.

Naomi Goldstein: Because the museum broke the law by union busting.

Lola Fuentes: Because the museum fired my best friend.

Efraín Juarez Reyna: Because my boyfriend asked me to.

Elisha Goldstein: Because it was the right thing to do.

Kiera Kim: What demands need to be met in order to end the strike?

Naomi Goldstein: The pertinent points are in the letter.

Lola Fuentes: All they have to do to get us to the table is give Efraín his job back and write pronoun buttons into the dress code.

Stanley Pham: Well, Efraín filed an Unfair Labor Practice with the NLRB. That's the basis for our strike, so Dagny needs to rehire Efraín. We stand by our pronoun buttons. Personally, I also believe Dagny owes the boys an apology.

Efraín Juarez Reyna: I won't be satisfied until management lets us wear our buttons.

Kiera Kim: Wait, what about your job? Don't you want your job back?

Efraín Juarez Reyna: [stares at the camera]

Elisha Goldstein: They need to rehire Efraín, with back pay.

Kiera Kim: What about the pronoun buttons?

Elisha Goldstein: Oh, right.

Kiera Kim: What message do you have for *Nuclear Seasons* fans who've been following this saga at home? What do you hope they take away from hearing your story?

Elisha Goldstein: I won't lie. This week has been rough. Anyone who needs proof, just google my name. You'll also see that a lot of that hate has come *from NS* fans—but they're the minority. They have to be. The alternative just doesn't make sense for people who love a show like *NS*.

Trusting the union to have my back has been hard. Trusting strangers is even harder, but . . .

I'm asking, if you love *Nuclear Seasons* like I do, please see the people behind the institution. Listen to our messages. See us as humans, rather than walking, talking ticketing machines and audio tours. As a fan, as a union member, and yes, as a NSX worker, I'm asking for your help. I couldn't have done any of this without the help of the union. I'm telling you now, the union can't do this without *your* help.

So if you're local, if you're willing, if you're able, please join me this Friday night at seven o'clock at Blue Plate Picture Palace here in Egan's Creek, California, for a different kind of anniversary party, where we honor not only the museum's twenty-five years but also the people who have made it possible, from Victor Kane all the way to . . . well, *you*.

THIRTY-SEVEN

IN EVERY FEEL-GOOD SMALL-TOWN FLICK, THERE'S SOME INSPIRAtional moment where *the whole town comes together.*

That's what I see on Friday night, as I stand under the Blue Plate Picture Palace marquee in my favorite Art Spector–inspired argyle bow tie and suspenders.

Ms. Sinclair gives me a double thumbs-up from the ticket box. When I asked her if she would consider letting the union borrow the theater for our alternate anniversary party, she clapped me on the back and asked why I hadn't said something sooner.

Joel, our trusty town troubadour, strums the *Nuclear Seasons* theme on his guitar.

In the lobby, my moms have done light catering to supplement Blue Plate's usual theater snacks with libations from Lou's and the Last Drip Café. Vanessa has decorated the lobby with Blushing Blooms bouquets and garlands that have me sneezing constantly. Irene has set up a selfie station with boxes of vintage accessories from Nine Lives. Mrs. Morse is running a raffle for a free weekend stay at the Plumcot Inn. Kim, Stanley's wife and an amateur ceramicist, is giving away china sets in honor of the original Blue Plate tradition. Mr. Jennings, the accountant who rents an office above the diner, is manning a donations table. In the theater itself, Mr. Loman and his sons built a wooden platform-stage in front of the screen. Then there's the fleet of vintage cars Mr. Fuentes has been restoring, which have spent the day hopscotching around the county to pick fans up from the airport, bus terminals, and SMART train stations.

Outside, fans are lined up around the block, farther than I can see.

Efraín comes up beside me in a truly devastating pleated black skirt and vest. He knocks his shoulder against mine. "Look what you did."

I shake my head. "What *we* did."

"It was a team effort," Naomi says, beaming. She looks comfortable and confident with her hair done up in an elaborate braided bun, showing off the emerald entwined with her blond curls. She's also the most dressed up I've seen her in years, in a prim corduroy overall dress.

"Ride or die," Lola agrees, squeezing in and swinging her arms up around our shoulders. The sequin fringe on her dress swishes against my arm. She's a vision of glitter and gloss. Her shiny fringe dress would be a dead ringer for the

Marienbad dress, if it were matte black instead of metallic gold.

We clean up pretty damn well for minimum-wage kids.

At seven on the dot, we open the doors to guests—no, *fans.*

Everything is free. Ms. Sinclair isn't selling tickets, just taking a head count. There are concerns about exceeding the theater's fire capacity.

We have union members scattered throughout the theater, acting as ushers and handing out programs.

The fans keep coming, and while the theater doesn't quite reach capacity, it's a near thing.

Half an hour after doors, once everyone's had a chance to grab snacks and find a seat, the program starts.

The house lights dim, and Stanley takes the stage as emcee. As a twenty-five-year NSX veteran, longtime docent, and certified superfan, he is uniquely qualified for the job, even if he did try to abdicate three times. But he's so much funnier than he gives himself credit for, and the kindness he shows his friends and museum guests shines through to everyone in the audience.

I'm observing from the back of the theater, so I can step out as needed. TJ's creating new content for our socials while Lola monitors incoming notifications as well as news of the *other* party down the road. Naomi's darting around with a DSLR loaned to her by the photo editor from the *Egan's Creek Citizen-Courier.*

After Stanley's opening monologue, there's a short film that Lola and Naomi cut together from their photos and reels, as well as clips from Kiera Kim's interviews.

Then Stanley introduces Efraín, whom the union unanimously selected as our spokesman. Efraín excels at extemporaneous speaking, and he's never more charismatic than when he's detailing injustices done to people he cares about. And the thing about Efraín?

Efraín Juarez Reyna cares about everyone.

Unfortunately, I can't focus on what he's saying because he is truly, unfairly distracting in that skirt. But whatever he's saying, it must be rousing given the crowd's hoots and hollers. I'm staring at him with cartoon hearts in my eyes when Lola hooks her arm with mine and leads me into the deserted lobby.

My eyes smart from the bright light, and the quiet is such a sharp contrast to the palpable human energy inside.

Lola and I plop down across from TJ, who seems to be logged into half a dozen social media sites on Naomi's laptop. "How's it going in there?"

"So far so good," Lola replies.

I just barely stop myself from reaching up to fidget with my bow tie. As much as I enjoy looking dapper—and I do like how I look tonight—the uncomfortable shirts are seldom worth it.

But I'm hoping tonight is worth it. We never defined what *success* looks like. It sure seems like we've succeeded in throwing together a killer party in forty-eight hours, but this is just another tool in our strike tool kit, not the end but rather the means.

I clear my throat. "How's it playing in . . . what's the internet equivalent of Peoria?"

"For us or for them?" Lola asks.

"Both."

"Our posts are getting good engagement," TJ says. "Good, not great."

"We haven't pulled out the big guns yet," Lola says. "Trust, we're fine. Unlike a certain high-ticket gala a few miles up the road."

"Yeah?" This bittersweet Schadenfreude wells up like acid reflux. I'm on tenterhooks, waiting to hear how the museum's anniversary party is floundering. "What's the word?"

Lola angles her phone toward me. "Remember, their official programming doesn't start till eight, but at this rate, it might not start at all. Craig has been texting Divya and Miles nonstop, begging for security staff to show up because Dagny's wild scheme to con fans into volunteering as scabs fell flat. Jaime has also gotten texts from a friend at the catering company the museum contracted with, and according to him, there's no one there.

"Half the guests who bought tickets are no-shows, but that's not even the worst of it. Practically everyone who had anything to do with making the show bailed. They've only got Christine Holloway and a couple minor guest stars. So I have no idea what they're going to do in five minutes when they have to put on a show unless it's just Dagny and Christine alone on the stage 'in conversation.'"

"I wouldn't put it past them to spend two hours in conversation about how we're persecuting the TERFs," I mutter.

"Sounds about right," Lola agrees absentmindedly as she scrolls. "Oh shit."

"What?" TJ asks immediately.

"Divya says Craig just panic-emailed the whole department because no one can find Dagny. Holy shit, did Dagny bail on her own party?"

Dagny has always tried to protect the sanctity of the museum as an institution. Now it looks like her messaging backfired, and she's backed into a corner.

"I don't know," I say, "but I'm ready to get back to our party. What about you guys?"

TJ just shakes his head, and Lola waves me off. "I'll catch up in a minute," she promises.

I adjust my noise-filtering earplugs as I head back into the theater. I scan the room, spotting Efraín and Jaime whispering conspiratorially in the front row, spying Naomi crouched in an aisle and snapping shots of Eden on the stage. I must have missed Ms. Sinclair's segment about the history of Blue Plate Picture Palace. Stanley and Dan are absent, which means they must be checking on our special guest.

For now, Eden's finishing up introducing the video essay that she and Winston have been secretly working on for months, in the hopes that they might someday be able to use it as an introduction for an exhibit about the lost love letters of Victor Kane.

The audience reacts viscerally, some gasping, some crying, as the story plays out on-screen, with key quotes from the letters.

I've read the letters multiple times, bawling in the privacy of my bedroom, but I can't help tearing up now, too.

Winston offers a few choice words about how concerns over "institutional messaging" and maximizing revenue have resulted in censorship of Victor Kane's legacy. He doesn't have much in the way of stage presence, so as Winston dawdles, half the audience is gossiping, the other half eagerly posting on their socials.

I'm fidgeting against the back wall, waiting for our next act, anxious at the delay. I'm wondering if I should do something when Stanley and Dan finally emerge from the wings, accompanying none other than our headliner, George Rhodes.

The noise I make is embarrassing. Then again, who wouldn't be starstruck by the sight of Emmy-winning, Oscar-nominated George Rhodes in a full tux? I didn't get a chance to meet him when he arrived earlier because I've been running point on logistics, which has been gratifying, yes, but far from glamorous.

George Rhodes, however, is all Hollywood glamour. He doesn't look like he's aged at all since the photos from the NSX opening party twenty-five years ago—except for his gracefully receded hairline.

His smile is bright and dazzling. "You know, I had a whole speech prepared, but after I saw that video, I had to rip it up. Because you've all heard the story about how I first met Victor Kane on the set of a terrible B movie, when I was trying to break out of Blaxploitation films, and he was writing his first pilot. But the story I never thought I'd get to tell? Let me tell y'all about the night I introduced Victor to Sam Schatz in a WeHo gay bar. You see, Sam and I both had bartending gigs because they sure paid better than acting."

I barely breathe as George talks about the Victor Kane he knew, who was not always a pleasant man and often a grueling director, but a brilliant artist and deeply devoted to those he loved. "It was a short list," he says, "really just the *NS* cast, his family, and that ridiculous dog, but, God, anyone lucky enough to be on that list knew. At least, Judy and I knew. Sam knew. And I hope . . . I hope Dagny knows. Victor loved his daughter more than anything in this world—so much more than he loved the show. He loved her so much."

George's voice breaks a little when he talks about Dagny, and it breaks my heart a little, too.

He goes on to talk about the show and the museum, too, and *love* remains the heart line of his speech. Finally, he thanks the union for inviting him and providing this opportunity to tell stories he feared would die with him.

After deafening applause—during which I am so grateful for my earplugs—Ms. Sinclair starts screening the *Nuclear Seasons* pilot.

The opening credits are still rolling when the doors swing open beside me. TJ's wild, panicked eyes find me. In a whisper-shout, he blurts, "Intruder alert!"

The scene that greets me in the lobby is surreal, like something out of a *Nuclear Seasons* episode—one of those nights when Rebecca and Art snuck out of the silo and into the town twenty years removed from everything they knew.

This is a little like that. Because instead of overseeing a gala in the shadow of that very silo, Dagny Kane is here, at our ramshackle, rapscallion counterprotest of an anniversary party.

She certainly doesn't look like she belongs here. We may all be dressed up, but we've got nothing on Dagny's vintage gala outfit. Her '80s royal-blue double-breasted blazer dress with military-grade brass buttons could be straight out of the *NS* casting closet. The finger waves in her bob are a nod to Old Hollywood, but she keeps raking her nails through the delicate waves.

"Oh, good," Lola says when she sees me. "Maybe you can sort out this clusterfuck, Eli. She was asking for you."

Jaime, Blake, and Divya are leaning against the wall, ranging from confused to defensive to totally pissed, respectively.

TJ's hanging back just behind me, using me as a human shield. I weigh my options, not relishing any of them, but the decision is lighter knowing I don't have to do any of this alone. Quietly, I ask TJ to go back in the theater and pull as many union members as he can.

I take a few slow, steadying breaths to quell the anxiety storm threatening my central nervous system. There's a pair of questions rattling around in my head. I pick the simpler of two evils: "Dagny, how are you *here*?"

When she looks up at me, I notice that her mascara is smudged, her sclera tinted pink. She's been crying. She hasn't answered. Maybe she doesn't trust her voice.

I never should've looked at her eyes. "I mean, I assume you left the gala and drove here. But how did you get in without anyone noticing?"

"We found her skulking *inside* the theater," Blake says.

"While George was talking," Jaime clarifies.

"I came through the side entrance," Dagny huffs.

"You mean the fire exit that's locked from the outside?" I ask.

"Frances let me in. She was my babysitter growing up here."

I follow Dagny's line of sight and gape at Ms. Sinclair, whom I hadn't noticed leaning against the concession stand counter. I can't believe she betrayed us after all this.

But she's completely unruffled. "I thought Dagny deserved to hear what people are saying about her father. Besides, the event's open to the public, isn't it? She's the public."

"She's the one percent!" I exclaim.

Lola snorts. "Dude, I think you're severely overestimating the value of the Kane estate."

"Okay, but my point still stands."

"What is your point, Eli?" Ms. Sinclair asks *pointedly.*

Time to ask the harder question. I turn back to Dagny, force myself to meet her eyes, and ask, "*Why* did you come here?"

I don't know what I'm expecting. Some supervillain monologue explaining her dastardly plan to infiltrate and sabotage our event?

But all she says is, "I wanted to see."

"See *what,* exactly?"

"I wanted to see it the way all of you see it. I needed to understand why . . ."

"What do you mean, 'it'?" Lola asks. "Are you talking about the museum?"

"The show?" Stanley asks from behind me. I never heard the doors open, but TJ has returned with almost everyone. Naomi, Eden, Gwen, and Miles are all here, backing me up.

Seeing them, I understand. "It" isn't about the museum or the show. It's always about the people.

To Dagny, I say, "You're talking about your father's legacy."

She nods sharply.

"That's what you needed to understand. You needed to see if we would still respect Victor Kane's memory even while we're on strike."

"I didn't realize you'd be showing the letters."

Eden jumps in, "You should know, Winston and I went over the ethics so many times. But Victor wrote—it was one of the later letters—he wanted to come out even if Sam didn't want to be with him because he didn't want anyone to feel as alone as he had."

"The only reason he kept putting it off was you," a new voice interjects.

It's George Rhodes. George Rhodes is standing three feet away from me, looking at Dagny with the softest expression on his face. He keeps talking to Dagny, but I don't hear him.

Because Efraín swoops in next to me, and Dan slips in beside Stanley. Efraín rests his hand on my shoulder, and I'm pretty sure I can smell George Rhodes's vetiver vanilla cologne.

Like I said, *surreal.*

But it's also painfully real.

I look at Dagny, her cheeks wet with fresh tears, and ask, "Did you see what you needed to see? Do you understand? Your father is loved. His fans still love and respect him, not in spite of his queerness, but because of it. It was why he saw the world the way he did. And that's why people like me found something to love in *Nuclear Seasons.* It's all connected—"

"Because *we're* all connected," Lola says.

Dagny looks at me. She dabs her face with George Rhodes's handkerchief and keeps looking at me. I don't know whether she's running calculations, projecting next quarter's ticket sales if she stops pandering to bigots, or just *seeing* me.

I'm still learning what it means to be seen while me.

"Okay," Dagny says.

"Pardon?"

"I'm saying yes. If you're still amenable to meeting with me to discuss certain issues, then I'm willing to meet with you, Eli. I believe we have more matters to discuss."

"Oh, right." I almost laugh. She's back to business as almost-usual right after a minor emotional meltdown. "I take it that by 'discuss' you mean 'bargain,' and by 'we' you mean 'the union,' not just me personally?" I ask, my voice unwavering despite my nerves.

Dagny frowns.

I don't know what she was expecting. I know better now than to face her one-on-one.

A long moment passes before she agrees. "Tomorrow morning, then?"

I look around the room, studying every face in turn, from Naomi's tentative smile to Lola's broad grin, from Blake's subtle up-nod to TJ's double thumbs-up, from Stanley's wink to Efraín's multifaceted smolder.

Because Dagny may be looking at me, she may have asked me, but it isn't up to me what the union does.

Solidarity is a choice we make alone to show up *together.*

Once my friends and fellow workers give their consent, I nod. "We'll meet you at the bargaining table."

THIRTY-EIGHT

WHEN THE NIGHT IS OVER, AFTER AN ARMY OF VOLUNTEERS HAS stripped and scrubbed Blue Plate Picture Palace of all evidence of festivities, Efraín and I find ourselves alone.

Ms. Sinclair entrusted the keys to me when she left after the party. Now that we've stowed the last folding tables, there's no reason I shouldn't lock up and go home.

No reason except for the way Efraín's looking at me, that is.

I don't know what I've done to deserve that smolder. I must look a mess. I undid my bow tie, loosened my collar, and rolled up my shirtsleeves hours ago. My curls are frizzy, in total disarray. This can't possibly be a good look for me.

Then again, tousled hair, sweat-slicked biceps, and that rumpled skirt make for an excellent look on Efraín.

We're loitering in the lobby, and I'm twirling the key ring between my thumb and forefinger. I look up at Efraín and admit, "I don't want to go home."

"Then let's not go home."

I'm about to object. I may not *want* to go home, but we have a bargaining meeting tomorrow morning. I need sleep if I want to have my wits about me . . .

Efraín plucks the spinning key ring right out from between my fingers and slips it into his vest pocket. I could get it back, but he's wearing that roguish smirk that shouldn't be charming, and yet, I am, against my better judgment, charmed. I am utterly defenseless when he leans down and whispers, "Meet me in the theater."

He's off before I can ask where he's going.

But I humor him. In the theater, I claim our regular seats. I sit and wait and—

The screen lights up. I blink up at the familiar image. I put two and two together and get episode fourteen, "Grapevines of Wrath." Of fucking course.

It takes longer for Efraín to figure out how to turn down the house lights than it does for him to find me once the lights dim.

He slides in beside me and kisses my cheek. "Knew you'd get the sweet spot."

"They're the best seats in the house," I state because it is an objective fact, and we've been over this.

"The best seat in the house is the one next to wherever you're sitting," he counters.

I can't stand the depth of his raw sincerity, so I squirm

in my seat and turn back to the screen. I look at Art and Harry, twenty feet tall, and shake my head. "How did you even do this?"

"I was with Ms. Sinclair in the projection booth earlier when she was programming everything. Did you know how easy it is to use a digital movie theater projector? All you have to do is push the right button." He shrugs, like it really is that easy to do something so profound for another person. "Ms. Sinclair set up a few extra episodes."

I understand why Ms. Sinclair would pick this episode, but I don't know why Efraín would pick this one out of a lineup. He just says he liked the title.

We settle in, his arm around my shoulders. He's watching the episode, and I'm watching him. He's an intent viewer, so intense in his concentration. That tilde between his brows is one of my favorite recurring characters.

After a while, Efraín says, "This is pretty good. Not exactly Steinbeck, but—"

"Can I ask you something?" I blurt.

He looks at me, the tilde asserting itself full force. "Yeah, of course."

"Now that our jobs are safe, and I'm almost certainly going to be allowed to wear a pronoun button, things are going to be different."

"That's not a question."

I lick my lips, unsure how to ask in a language he'll understand.

"Ever since the first night you kissed me, I've been trying to make it make sense. I still don't understand what changed this summer. Mutual antipathy does not a crush make, so—" I really regret having this conversation side by side in a movie theater where I have to crane my neck to look at him. "So, some part of me worries that you care about me because you care about the Cause, and one day, you'll realize I'm just me and not some symbol."

He looks at me, assessing. A tense moment of judgment—of *truth*—before fond exasperation melts his frustration. "God, you're so wrong. You gave me so many speeches about how we save each other, but you have no idea, do you?"

"Well, I know you don't like me because of the way I sling on my backpack strap."

Efraín shakes his head, thoughtful, like he's composing a persuasive argument in his head, arranging the components to make the most compelling case. "I like that you *listen* to me, even when you don't agree with me."

I agree with him more often than he thinks, but admitting that would undercut his point.

"And even when it annoys the hell out of me, I like the way you argue with me—that you're not *afraid* to argue with me, even when you know you're about to say something that's going to annoy the hell out of me."

"It's not about fear, just that I can't shut up."

"And I like that you can't help yourself. That you can't just shut up—"

"I freeze half the time when people say transphobic shit to me—"

"Not as often as you think, and when it's about other people, it's like you just can't help yourself. You say it doesn't make sense, and you don't even realize—hell, *I* didn't even realize what that means. You call out the world when it doesn't make sense because it's fundamentally *incomprehensible* to you that anyone would intentionally do the wrong thing when it's obvious what the just, fair choice would be."

"I think you're giving me too much credit."

"You're resourceful. I see now that you do want to solve problems—in unconventional ways, even—even if we disagree about means." Finally, finally, he touches me, his hand ghosting over my cheek. "I like your freckles. Especially the one on the bridge of your nose."

"That's actually a mole. Potentially precancerous. I'll probably need a dermatologist to freeze-dry it off someday."

"And I *do* like that you've been using the same backpack since seventh grade, and don't think I didn't notice that you ironed an *NS* logo patch over the hole on the front pocket or, yeah, sewed over the top seam on the strap when it started to rip."

"Oh," I whisper, but there's no "right, of course" because in no universe would I have guessed any of that. I melt against him, not with an ulterior motive, just to be here, with him. "In the spirit of reciprocity—"

"You don't have to—"

"No, I want to." I crane my neck, just so. "The whole 'we save each other' schtick? I may have given you the wrong impression. That's not what I like about you."

"Isn't it?" It's not a condemnation or a dismissal, just a statement of the World According to Efraín, and my heart breaks for this boy who thinks the only way to make the world love him is to break his own heart into a million pieces and scatter the dust over the ruins of a graveyard of lost causes.

"You're so much more than what you can *do* for the world; it's about who you *are*, how supremely *good* you are—not just your bones, but all the way through. But you're constantly trying to prove yourself, and it's never enough, is it? So, I just want you to know. I don't just like you when you're out doing the work. I like you when you're standing still."

I don't know if he believes me, and I'm still not entirely convinced I understand him. But as we stay here, sitting still, I realize we don't have to. We have all the time we need to learn each other, to learn to believe and understand each other. We have time to figure it out together.

Tonight, we're here, his arm around my shoulders, my head resting on his. We're bathed in cool blue light projected on a larger-than-life screen. We're here for forty-seven minutes, but we're not confined to this episode.

Our story won't end when the credits roll.

PART V

UNION

THIRTY-NINE

LABOR DAY IS TOURIST SEASON'S LAST HURRAH, A THREE-DAY holiday travel weekend for summer road trippers. The museum, of course, is open.

A lot has changed over the past few weeks, but NSX will capitalize on any and every holiday, no matter who's in charge.

Leadership is the most significant change since the union's fateful bargaining meeting. We had a productive conversation with Dagny, who agreed to rehire Efraín and requisition NSX-branded pronoun buttons.

Although she'd hardly given away the farm, the museum's board of directors opted to remove Dagny as CEO. Publicly, she's stepping back to focus on her family; privately, I've heard she's taking a sabbatical in LA to reconnect with George Rhodes and the remaining select few whom Victor Kane considered family.

Anya is serving as interim CEO, and Dan is reluctantly

heading up guest services. Ford quit in a huff when he heard the news.

This is my last shift in guest services, but starting next week, I'll be interning with curatorial, helping Winston and Eden put together a formal presentation for the board about their proposed special exhibit, *Lieber Schatz: The Lost Love Letters of Victor Kane.*

Today, however, I'm splitting my time, ticketing in the morning and guiding tours in the afternoon. It's the first time Lola and I have ticketed together in weeks, and it's *nice,* peaceful in spite of the hectic holiday haze.

In the sporadic gaps between guests, Lola plies me with gossip, not about our fellow workers, but about herself. Apparently, her ex, Curtis, made a brief appearance at the anniversary party, and they've been texting ever since. She's been opening up more, both to him and to her friends—letting herself be *known* in a way she was afraid to be vulnerable before her interview with Kiera Kim.

Between our deliberations on the best date locations, we also talk about the most important date on my calendar: my top surgery date with Dr. Mburu the first week of June, which I officially reserved last week.

Unbeknownst to me, the strike fund wasn't the only proverbial donations jar at our alternative anniversary party. The union—no one will tell me whose idea it was—solicited contributions for my top surgery. Partygoers—locals, out-of-town fans, and possibly a certain celebrity special guest—quickly met the target.

Three months ago, I wouldn't have believed that was possible—that anyone else would care enough to contribute. I certainly never would've asked for help. I never once thought about making a GoFundMe. I might've been too stubborn to accept donations then; I would've assumed people were only opening their wallets out of cis guilt and misplaced pity, never believing that strangers might want to help because it's *kind.*

I know better now. I'm learning to trust kindness. I'm doing my best to pay it forward, too, whether that means being a little liberal with ticket discounts or spending my entire morning break going through dozens of near-identical bird photos on Naomi's laptop to help her pick the best shot.

Not long after I come back from my break, an adult and a youth come up to my till, and I'm so comfortable giving my ticketing spiel that I don't notice anything out of the ordinary, until the tween squeaks, "Do you sell those?"

"The polo shirts? They're just uniform—"

"No, your button. Do you have them here or in the gift shop? I want one just like yours. I have my allowance. How much?"

I take a closer look at the kid, who can't be older than eleven or twelve. His Coke bottle glasses are too large for his face—but puberty, that cruel mistress, will soon rectify that.

Box braids with glittery gold beads clack together as he bobs up and down in excitement. His jean jacket displays a plethora of pins and buttons from every fandom imaginable—and a trans flag, too.

"Oh." I look down at my new, hard-won pronoun button. In magenta, yellow, and black, it isn't pretty, but it is NSX-approved, and it gets the job done.

Who am I kidding? It's terrible; I love it.

Unfortunately, management only rush-ordered a small batch of pronoun buttons for staff.

"I'm sorry, but we don't have them available for sale."

The kid's face crumples, and my heart sinks. I sell the pair tickets and watch them wander across the barn.

When there's a lull, Lola leans over. "What's up?"

"What do you mean?"

"You look like someone killed Sputnik."

"First, don't ever joke about that. Second, this trans kid asked if we were selling pronoun buttons. He was so excited, but—"

"*Eli*," Lola says with that jocular, lilting tone she puts on when I'm missing something obvious.

"What?"

"You can get another button."

"I don't have time to run upstairs and get one."

"You don't have to." Her eyes flick down to my button, and suddenly, I get it. Truly.

"Cover for me?"

Lola grins. "Go find him."

I sprint across the barn just as Stanley's about to start his tour. "Eli!" he calls out. "Wasn't expecting you until after lunch. Did you want to switch early?"

"No, I—" I glance up at him, at the easy smile on his face. "Unless you want to? Are your knees bothering you, or—"

"No, no, my knees are perfectly fine. Everything else, too." He taps the water bottle—a full bottle, not a flask—clipped to his belt. Another concession from management. "You need anything?"

I shake my head. "Just need to borrow someone from your group for a second."

"By all means."

I smile my thanks and survey his tour group. I find my mark on the far side, in gift shop territory. I cut through the crowd, grateful that I remembered to wear my noise-filtering earplugs for this shift.

"Hi," I say, trying and failing not to be awkward about this. I wave down the kid and unpin the button from my shirt. "I want you to have this."

His eyes go wide. "Are you sure?"

I nod.

"What do you say?" his parent prods.

By way of thanks, the kid flings his arms around me. Gingerly, I hug him back. "You're welcome," I whisper.

I watch the kid pin the button in a place of honor on his jacket. He's so excited, animatedly talking about all his friends back home and online who are going to be so jealous. I'm not sure if he's talking to me or his parent, but I smile all the same.

"You want a picture?" Naomi comes up from out of nowhere, scaring the shit out of me. I have absolutely no idea what she's talking about, but the kid hands Naomi his phone. I quickly check with the parent, but they just look pleased. So, I let Naomi position me, and she snaps a few shots where I try to smile normally despite the bewildered feeling in my chest. Naomi asks if she can take one for the museum's social media accounts, too, and with the parent's consent, she takes another on her own phone.

Stanley's starting his tour, so the kid hugs me one more time before dashing off.

"It would be a better picture if you were wearing a button, too," Naomi muses.

"I gave him my button. That was the point."

"I know. I saw it. But I don't think the picture tells the story . . ." Naomi sighs.

"What was all that about?" Efraín also gets the drop on me.

"What are you doing here? Wait, if you're here, who's running the gift shop?"

"Jaime's got it. Naomi's taking her fifty-two. I'm taking a quick fifty-five." He wraps his arms around my waist and rests his chin on my head to look at Naomi's phone. "Who's the kid?"

I shake my head. "He liked my button."

"So you gave him the button off your back."

"Off my shirt."

"Same difference."

"Be gross on your own time, please," Naomi interjects.

"You're the one on your lunch break. You can go upstairs any time," Efraín teases her, and I am struck by the surreal fact that none of this is actually surreal anymore. My boyfriend joking with my sister is a perfectly normal, commonplace occurrence.

Naomi rolls her eyes but promises to text me the photo before going on her way.

That leaves Efraín and me, not even remotely alone in the bustling lobby. Neither of us can afford to take 55s right now. I've left Lola alone at ticketing long enough.

"Wait," Efraín says as I'm pulling away. "You're forgetting something."

"If you're waiting for me to kiss you goodbye before I walk all of fifty feet away—"

"I wouldn't turn down a kiss"—Efraín smirks—"but I meant this." Then he's unpinning his own pronoun button and pinning it on my polo.

"Oh my God, you're so dramatic. I can go an hour without a button. I went months without—"

"I know," Efraín says softly. "I know you'd be fine without it, but you deserve better than fine. You're a good man, Elisha Goldstein."

"The Charles Schulz Museum is fifteen miles away."

"So fucking pedantic." He stifles a laugh with a kiss to my forehead.

This, too, has become commonplace.

"Are we still on for dinner with your dad later?" I ask.

Mr. Juarez is one of the holiday road trippers who drove up from Madera to spend the long weekend with his son.

Efraín nods. "He's meeting us at Lou's after work, and he'll head out from there."

"Are you sure you don't want to spend your last night with him just the two of you?"

"I'm sure," Efraín says.

I take him at his word. "Okay. Thank you for the totally unnecessary replacement button." I reach up on my tiptoes to kiss his cheek. "I'm going back to work."

"If you must."

"You must, too."

He pulls a face, but Efraín goes back to the gift shop.

I head back to ticketing, passing through throngs of starry-eyed museumgoers. Lola smiles at me as I slip behind the counter. I reclaim my till, shaking the computer awake. As the software loads, I straighten my borrowed pronoun button, still warm from Efraín's touch.

Then I get back to work.

ACKNOWLEDGMENTS

There were times when writing this book that I felt very much alone. I am profoundly grateful to the people who ensured that I wasn't and supported this book through every step of its prolonged journey. In other words, thank you to everyone who didn't give up on this book or me.

To Claire Friedman, my agent, for being my first, best champion in this industry. You've seen me at my best and worst and most neurotic, and still fought for my weirdest ideas.

To Carolina Mancheno Ortiz, my editor, for devoting such patience and care to this book. Thank you for not laughing the six-hundred-page first draft out of your inbox and then helping me wrangle this unwieldy beast of a story into a coherent thought. For the record: you were right about Fresno.

To Mabel Hsu, this book's and my first editor, for believing in me and giving "rom commie" the benefit of the doubt even when it sounded like a pitch for a *Unionizing for Dummies* handbook.

To everyone at HarperCollins who has worked on this book and contributed behind the scenes, including Danielle McClelland, Caitlin J. Lonning, Anna Ravenelle, and Jesse Feitel. David L. DeWitt, for making this book beautiful inside and out, and Rommy Torrico, for illustrating the perfect cover and fulfilling Efraín's destiny as a strapping labor poster model.

Now for the big one: to everyone I've ever worked a shitty job with, summer or otherwise. I can't name names here because there'd be too many, and I don't want to summon the ghosts of employers past. But if we've worked together, whether five years ago or fifteen: This book is for all of you.

To my fellow Wobblies in the IWW at large, and the Seattle branch in particular, for teaching me so much more about *doing good* than I've learned anywhere else.

To Jorge Alvarado, Sarah Schelde, and Alex Haupt, for being my true-blue ride or dies. Every time I write about friendship, I'm really just writing lessons I've learned from all of you.

To Miel Moreland, for listening to me ramble about this book; for saving cats, kidnapping dogs, and chasing whole warrens of plot bunnies.

To the Writer's Collective, for a decade of writerly camaraderie and solidarity.

To Ava and Charlie, for creating the boys' earliest character art.

To Kate Hume, for keeping me (mostly) sane.

To George A. Egan and his Very Good Friend, for the ninety-year-old atlas inscription that inspired "rom commie."

To my parents, for your unflagging support. Simply put, this book would not exist if not for you.

To Simon, always. Thank you for ensuring that I am, quite literally, never alone.

Finally, to queer and trans readers. Thank you for picking up this book. I hope you've found something that resonates for you in these pages, and I want you to know: you're not alone. No matter how your government and other institutions may malign or abandon you, you're not alone. Trans people have always existed, and queer communities persist in even the most adverse conditions. We find each other, and we take care of each other. And when we do—when we choose solidarity, love, and kindness—we're never alone.